SOL & LUNE

BOOK TWO

KATHRYN MOON

This is a Reverse Harem Paranormal Romance and is not suited for those under the age of 18.

❀ Created with Vellum

 Created with Vellum

Meghan,
for letting me go a little off track,
but not too much

PREVIOUSLY IN SOL & LUNE

The country of Stalor's General Dominic Westbrook and his army arrive at Lady Lumen Fenn's Manor in Oshain during the decades-long war between the two countries. A local war veteran, Oliver Spragg, encourages Lumen to leave the Manor and go north for refuge, but she refuses to abandon her home and remaining tenants. Lumen is pressured to share Dominic's bed—in exchange for protection from the other soldiers—and while the union is tense and uncomfortable, he eventually introduces her to passion. With Westbrook and his army is Lieutenant Gideon Jones, a terrifying warrior who is openly attracted to Lumen and her purity, as well as Healer Finley Brink, who she forms a tentative truce with when it comes to tending the injured soldiers. The best of all of the army's men, however, is the young boy named Colin, who acts as a spy for the army and immediately develops a close friendship with Lumen.

Lumen and Dominic find a temporary balance in their relationship, but there are constant obstacles. While he compromises and allows Lumen to keep her sanctuary to the Goddess Lune, and all the silver inside, he takes every other resource her home has to offer. When Lumen's friendship and nurturing of Colin leads the boy to make an error of judgment that costs Stalor soldiers' lives, Dominic must act again as the uncompromising general. Lumen interrupts his punishing Colin with a cat 'o nine tails, taking a strike to her own cheek. In reaction to her defiance and his own guilt, Dominic casts Lumen out of his bed, and into Finley Brink's protection.

Both Gideon and Finley are protective of Lumen, neither acting on their interest in her, even when Lumen tests the boundaries of their restraint. When Finley is injured in battle, Lumen and he grow closer, eventually developing a physical relationship, this time on Lumen's insistence. As a healer, and known for having unusual sexual habits—ones Lumen enjoys—Finley is less respected amongst the ranks and Lumen begins to feel the eyes of men on her as well as dealing with their taunts and jeers. When a few men take an opportunity to attack Lumen, Dominic catches them in time to intervene. Upon hearing the news, Finley decides Lumen would be better off in someone else's care and takes an opportunity to serve under General Meade in a different party of the army. Lumen is once again abandoned, this time to Gideon's care.

Despite her and Gideon's sincere affection for each other, Lumen realizes she has lost her home and land, as well as her own self-worth and autonomy. When she discovers that Dominic is resisting pushing his army north because he does not want to leave *her*, her emotional stability cracks. Meanwhile, Dominic knows that it won't be long until his men ransack Lumen's chapel and holy silver, and decides to hide it but doesn't tell her in the hopes it forces a confrontation. When Lumen discovers the chapel empty, she goes to Oliver Spragg and asks him to take her north at last.

With Lumen missing and Finley returned and regretful, the three men turn on each other and are forced—by Colin, best boy —to face their crimes against Lumen. Spragg takes Lumen north to the capital, where she is questioned and then imprisoned when she can give no valuable military information. Dominic and his army finally push north, and Colin learns of Lumen's imprisonment and growing sickness. Lumen, trapped in a damp cell in the middle of winter, nears death and is comforted by the dark New Moon Goddess. Dominic, Finley, and Gideon sneak into Oshain's capitol, rescue Lumen from the prison, and take her back to their army's camp. She is weak, weary, and asks to be taken to the Lunar Convent in the mountains. Finally, the men agree to listen to her wishes rather than their own wants to care for her themselves, and deliver her into the arms of the Lunar Priestess. Once there she is recognized by the priestesses as being...

V

THE NEW MOON PRIESTESS

WINTER LINGERED IN THE MOUNTAINS, DRESSING THE WINDOWS OF the Lunar Convent with thick ice, sunlight forcing itself through and tracing watery patterns on cold stone floors. Rows of women, draped in grays and blues, rested on their knees at the front of an altar glittering with silver. The wide face of Mother Lune's statue, smooth eyes cast down onto the bowed heads of her devotees, shimmered with candlelight, sunshine, and silver reflecting on itself.

In the hallways, footsteps padded in near silence, novitiates performing the necessary chores as the priestesses sat in meditation for the new moon observances. Their lips pressed together as they went about their work, eyes fixed to their hands or feet to avoid sharing glances, adding logs to fires to keep the worst of the winter chill from settling in stone rooms.

Deeper, in the heart of the convent, in a room without windows and with no candle shining and no silver gilding, Lumen Fenn crouched in front of the stone Dark Mother, shroud carved to imply the bone-thin Goddess beneath. In the hall behind the sealed door, a novitiate's steps slowed and softened from their previous quick scamper, as if they could feel the heavy and hypnotic state of the lady's devotion as they passed the door. Lumen herself felt the same weight, the stare of the shrouded Goddess like a hand on the top of her head. Her legs were numb beneath her, body hollow, thoughts empty. Information trickled in—the women traveling through the halls, the shifting fragrance of thyme in bone broth trickling in under the door and signaling that evening was near and supper would be waiting at the first appearance of a crescent moon. Just as easily as it arrived in her mind, Lumen let it pass, the steady drum of her own heartbeat serving as a ticking clock and a drowning sound to shoo away any intruding worries.

"When did he say he'd be back?"

"Shh, you know she's in there. Quarter moon."

"Will it be done by then?"

The Mallen sisters. Lumen's lips threatened to frown, and she tried to fall into the sound of her own heartbeat, waiting for the devotionless novitiates to move on.

"Only started."

"But—"

"Enough. Or the *New Moon Priestess* will hear you."

The title was given with a heavy amount of sarcasm and scorn, and the leather soles of slippers scuffed roughly in punctuation against the stone outside the door as the sisters traveled deeper into the convent.

Lumen's teeth dug into her chapped lip, trying to force the pinch of pain into a distraction from their words. She'd heard others call her by the title in whispers when no one realized she was within earshot. Or perhaps the convent thought she was deaf. Women rarely spoke to her, which meant Lumen was rarely expected to speak, and she found herself sinking into the silence and finding relief in it. Here, finally, she was permitted to exist, and the only expectation of her time and body belonged to Lune. High Priestess had never spoken to her on the subject of the New Moon Priestess position, and she didn't feel worthy of the honor, not after everything she'd done and everything done to her.

The convent was not the relief Lumen had quite expected, overfull with displaced women who no longer had homes to retreat to. The older priestesses were kind and sincere, but there was a wave of simmering anger that lingered in the halls. Lumen saw it like sunlight, pricking at her skin, trying to invade her own emptied emotions.

She released a slow sigh, turning her head gently back and forth on her neck and wincing at the noisy crack of stiff joints. Activity was picking up in the halls, stone carrying the echoes to the door of her favorite chapel room. The first sliver of the new moon must have risen. Lumen began slow stretches, shuffling to her side and holding her breath as blood rushed down to her calves and feet with hot needle pricks. On the last new moon, a novitiate had been sent in to help Lumen stretch and hobble her way down to the kitchens to eat with the others. Sure enough, again the door cracked open, spilling orange firelight from the hall torches across Lumen's dusty, blue-gray skirts.

"Ellery says I'm to bring you down to supper, so we'd better hurry before my sisters slurp it all down themselves."

In the doorway, ankles rolling to and fro as the girl twisted the skirt of her robes in her hands, was the youngest Mallen sister, Neave. Lumen studied the shadow the girl cast in the room as she raised her hands over her head and wriggled her stinging toes in her slippers, muscles protesting with an ache Lumen almost relished.

"Can't carry you myself," Neave continued, her volume a little too loud for the first rising of the new moon.

Lumen nodded and stifled a groan in her throat as she stumbled up to her feet. Despite Neave's claim, the young girl hurried forward and caught Lumen around her waist as her body failed to hold her up. Neave's shoulder dug into the side of Lumen's chest, the pair of them still a little thin after a long lean winter. Something about the girl's frame under her arm—and perhaps her direct manner of speech—reminded Lumen of Colin with a pang of memory that she struggled to force down again. She had her family's bright red-blond hair, and her skin was still brown from summer even so late in the year. There were slivers of that secret sunlight only Lumen could see clinging to the young girl too, although they didn't scratch at Lumen's eyes the way others did. It was a strange phenomenon she'd discovered since arriving. Finding those who seemed to shimmer with Sol's Fire. It usually made her stomach clench and turn, her skin hot and feverish and crawling, but looking at Neave was gentler, almost pleasant.

"You know you're allowed to move around, don't you?" Neave snarled, dragging Lumen towards the door as both their stomachs growled in harmony.

Lumen reached her free arm out, setting her fingertips just over Neave's lips without touch and receiving a scowl in return.

"It's a bunch of nonsense," Neave continued in a steady mumble. "And I'm not a novitiate. Just got dragged here with my mother and sisters." A few women were at the far end of the hall, and they glanced briefly back to Neave and her luggage of Lumen before hurrying away without a second look. Neave hissed at their backs. "There's the Mother's generosity in action for you."

Lumen shook with restrained laughter and finally found some steadiness, doing her best to hold herself up and keep up with Neave's eager pace to the kitchen.

"Anyway, moon's up," Neave said, shrugging off Lumen's arm. "You can talk again."

It took three tries to clear her throat of the dust she'd let gather there over days of quiet, but Lumen managed some words for the girl. "I like my silence."

Neave's mouth popped open, her eyes narrowed. For once, the girl was at a loss of words, either out of respect or simply stupefied by Lumen's claim. They reached the door of the dining hall, and Lumen's fingers nudged briefly against the girl's shoulder. Today, she missed touch, or maybe she missed Colin. Other days, she cringed when one of the sisters reached for her.

The tables of the dark hall were crowded with women, blue draped heads and voices murmuring like songbirds gathered around seed in summer, their hands passing plates and bowls up and down the line. Lumen's stomach growled, but the feeling of hunger was so distant now, her thoughts disconnected from the ails of her body.

"Here, sister," one of the novitiates said softly, and Lumen twitched, resisting the urge to thrash herself out of someone's hold, as she was guided to an empty seat near the head of the table. She was placed between the priestesses and refugee women, and already a priestess was filling her bowl with stew. A chunk of bread floated in the center, stale crumbs softening in hot liquid.

Why should you eat better than the novitiates? she wondered. Even in the face of the food, hunger was a background sound. She'd gone so long on nothing, to have again seemed like an error rather than a luxury.

"There's mold on my slice!"

The Mallen women were across the table from Lumen, noses wrinkled toward the bowls. Imogen Mallen's fingers were pinched around a hunk of bread, broth dripping to the table's surface as she gaped up the line of the table to the High Priestess.

"Just tear it away, Im," the middle sister said on a sigh.

"It'll have ruined the whole bowl by now," Imogen continued, voice rising in pitch.

Lumen winced, cheek turned away from the family. They shone in the dim room, flecks of light hovering around them, heat licking off their skin in her direction. They carried sunlight on them in a place that was dedicated to the moon.

"Did you escape Stalor's army so early that you have enough ego in you to complain of generosity?" one of the other novitiates hissed in the family's direction.

Imogen bristled, arching over the table. "You've no idea what lengths I've taken—"

"Enough, Imogen," Myra Mallen, the matriarch of the family, bit out. She stole the bread from her daughter's finger and dropped it into her own bowl, scooping out an overflowing bite on a spoon.

Imogen's jaw clenched as she stared down at the cooling stew, shoulders up to her ears. There was heat in Lumen's chest, her hands clenched to fists at her side as anger clogged her throat with barbed thorns that dug into her muscle and bound her from screaming. Even here in Mother Lune's house, she wasn't safe from the fire.

STARS FLOATED on the surface of the ale in Dominic's cup. They shifted and swirled as he tipped it one way and then another, the heat of the bonfire nicking at his knuckles.

"We need more supplies." Danvers stood at his back.

Dominic frowned into his cup. Was this his first or his fifth for the night?

"Again?" he grunted. "You went a week ago."

"Two weeks," Charlie corrected. "It's up to you if we starve or not."

Dominic rolled his eyes. They were already starving, or hadn't Charlie noticed? "What do we have to sell?" he asked. He'd taken strange lengths to keep the pair out of Lumen's silver after Colin and the others had refused it. He couldn't say why he didn't sell it now that she was out of his reach. Only that maybe...maybe someday she would have need of it again, and he owed it to her to be sure that it was there.

"A town just north cleared out. We found enough there," Charlie said.

It didn't seem like a proper answer in Dominic's mind, but the simple truth was he didn't *care* what Danvers and Charlie did at this point, whether it was spying or shopping.

He waved a hand at the pair. "Fine. Ask Gideon for a list."

"Jones is out cold. We've got a list."

Dominic frowned, the sound of his spies retreating growing soft and invisible under the crackle of the fire. He lifted the cup to his lips, wincing to find the ale flat and sour, but he downed it in one long drink all the same.

"Colin!"

There was nothing but quiet for a long moment and Dominic wondered what time it was. The soldiers were all missing from the fire. Had they found beds and the scarce number of women left for the night? Was it nearly dawn, and if it was, was it a dawn he was meant to see the battlefield?

"Sir?"

Dominic twisted and groaned, body stiff from cold and stagnancy, and found Colin rubbing sleep from his eyes as he approached, the door of the inn left hanging open behind him.

"Where's Jones?" Dominic asked.

"Inside," Colin said, nodding his head backward. "Healer was looking at him, but then he went off and never came back."

Shit. What was going on with Finley these days? Dominic rose slowly, swallowing the roar of ache and discomfort as he stood. He must've aged one-hundred years since they left Fenn Manor. He'd always hated sleeping out of beds once he'd finally been introduced to the comfort of them. But since they'd packed up from the Manor, he'd hated the sight of an empty bed just as much as the notion of sleeping on the ground.

"Show me," he rasped to Colin, following the boy back to the inn's bar. There were a few people left, slumped in chairs, napping through the last hours of the night.

Gideon was in a corner booth, propped up against the wall, blood caked down one side of his head all the way to his collar. The space was dim, pools of orange candlelight running into black shadows, but Dominic thought Gideon looked strangely pale. His stomach gave a dull lurch at the picture of his friend.

"Is he dead?"

"Don't think so," Colin whispered, heading for the corner. He rose on his toes, cupping his hand over Gideon's mouth. "Nah. Still breathin'. Want me to wash him up like Lady woulda done? Seen her enough times."

Dominic couldn't swallow to speak around the blade in his throat, so he nodded instead. Colin hurried to the bar, pulling an empty jug and a questionably clean rag from a hiding place. "I'll hunt down Brink," Dominic said. Although what good Brink could do, he wasn't sure. Colin was just as likely to know what remedies *she* might've used for Gideon.

The search didn't take long. Finley was up in his room, collapsed on his bed, a cold pipe sitting out on the side table, sticky black residue lining the bowl. Dominic sighed at the picture, a painful nostalgia in his chest. They were falling apart, one by one. Finley was sinking into ugly old habits, Gideon was a reckless berserker on the battlefield, and Dominic...his fight had burned away over the weeks. The puzzle of a battle lost its intrigue when all he wanted was to sleep for a lifetime. They'd been in the same town since they'd searched for Lumen, and he could see the sense of awkward ease falling over the men, the way they found themselves homes here and started to settle in.

This wasn't an army, it was a camp of refugees.

Dominic pinched Finley's earlobe between his rough fingers, applying extra pressure and a twist of his wrist. Even then, he must've left a bruise before Finley twitched and groaned, wiggling backward on the thin mattress to press himself against the wall. Dominic released him, waiting for glassy, unfocused eyes to land and widen.

"This again, Fin?" he asked, not bothering to raise his voice. He was too tired.

"My..." Finley's voice cracked like thin glass, and he cleared his throat. "My hands were shaking."

"So you thought you'd knock yourself out while Gideon bled out downstairs?"

There was no real alarm, Finley only tipped his head in faded curiosity. "Is he...?"

"Colin's looking after him." As if he could read the healer's mind, the words passed through his head, *Better Colin than him at this point.* "Where'd you even get the stuff?"

"Danvers and Charlie brought it for treatments."

"You asked them for it?"

"It's medicinal."

"Maybe, but you use it like poison," Dominic said.

Finley's eyes shut, head tipping side to side as if he were listening to music in his thoughts. Maybe he was. Maybe Dominic ought to try smoking the shit to dull the chorus of condemnation he had running in his own thoughts.

You broke her. You destroyed her home. You killed her family.

"I'm not her. I can't just heal the men with...with gentleness and- and—"

"Care," Dominic finished for Finley. Lumen *cared* for them, even as they ransacked her home and ate her food, and demanded acts of her body no woman should be made to give.

She surrendered herself until she was hollow, and only then did they see the wreckage.

"Leave me to it, Dom," Finley whispered, eyeing the pipe, even as his eyes remained black with the drug.

Dominic stared at the pipe, a glossy thing from the city that Finley had kept hold of even after he'd quit the stuff. He must've known it wouldn't last. Dominic was exhausted, hollow now too. He'd lost something in the process of stealing from Lumen and had no concept of where it would've gone. Sol knew she wasn't keeping it. Lumen had rightfully washed her hands of the lot of them. Could he do the same? Let Finley throw himself into oblivion by the end of a pipe, and Gideon the same by his sword?

"No," Dominic answered, fist wrapping around the pipe and standing before Finley's weak and clumsy form could lunge and reach for him. He turned to the window sill and found the paper and wax sealed packet of the drug, grabbing it and pocketing it away.

"You bastard," Finley hissed, stumbling to his feet, too unsteady to catch Dominic on the way to the door. "You selfish shit. You won't stop until we're all every bit as wasted and mangled as your worthless mind is. You won't let us quit while you're still determined to suffer."

Dominic shut the door in Finley's face, the words clawing out between the worn boards as he headed for the stairs. Finley could be right, he didn't know anymore. He didn't care. They would all just have to live with themselves for a little while longer until Dominic made up his mind.

A TAPESTRY HUNG IN THE HIGH NORTH HALLWAY OF THE CONVENT, between the Full Moon Chapel and the High Priestess' wing where Lumen had been summoned. Her feet stilled as she reached it, eyes catching on the eerie and familiar shape of the building it depicted. She had never been to this part of the convent in her stay. Priestess Ellery was usually the messenger for the High Priestess, and she always found Lumen in her usual dark chapel.

A small ache bloomed in Lumen's chest as she stared at the work, the bittersweet sensation of *homesickness* cracking through her steady numbness. Woven in silver glinting strands was the round stone structure of Fenn Manor, built from threads into a map. In the top right corner, a yellow and red sun shone down. In the bottom left, the silver moon dangled, crescent shape curved up to face the sun. Between them sat her home. Lumen gaped at the weaving, even as soft footsteps approached down the hall.

"Yes," High Priestess Wren said as if they'd been carrying on the conversation the whole time. "The temple of Sol & Lune. As it was, of course, before being disbanded."

Lumen's brow furrowed, and any words she might've thought of speaking—rare as they were these days—remained trapped in her throat.

"Your mother's family was, of course, descended from Lune's High Priestess there. When Sol's devotees headed south, it became a Lunar temple, dedicated to the New Moon. Eventually a residence."

"When?" Lumen whispered. There, around the corner from Sol's light, was the small hollow of her bedroom on the map, although in the small image it contained a priest holding a manuscript.

"It's been...centuries since we existed in harmony," High Priestess said, answering Lumen's vague question correctly. "Three or more generations since your family was knighted and given the temple as an estate in exchange."

Her mother had never said a thing. Which did not necessarily mean she hadn't known. Lumen swallowed. Her mother's bedroom was above the chapel, and there was a priestess on her knees in the tapestry's picture. In the courtyard, men and women stood in a circle, light from both Sol and Lune bleeding through windows and doorways to fill the space in gold and silver harmony.

"What changed?" Lumen asked, glancing at the High Priestess who studied the tapestry with equal interest.

"Nothing was recorded. It may have been a simple thing, the temple crowding, or a call from the south for more priests," Wren said, head tilting. "Our faiths weren't really at odds until the last century or so."

But we are opposites, Lumen thought, glancing between Wren and the weaving depicting perfect unity. High Priestess Wren smiled at Lumen.

"Truth be told, I prefer the idea of balance between Lord and Lady," Wren said, nearly whispering. "The best of their divinity in harmony with one another."

"He blinds her," Lumen said, without thinking.

Wren hummed and looked back to the tapestry, lips curling. "She tempers his light," she answered. "Come, I have something for you."

High Priestess Wren turned back down the hall to her chambers, but Lumen hesitated by the tapestry. It was strange to see her home this way, although it put together pieces of a puzzle she'd ignored most of her life. The Manor, in its

14

strangeness, was not a Manor at all, but a temple. Had her family been guarding it as sanctuary, or defiling it with their possession? And now she had abandoned it, left it empty and stripped in the no man's land of the war. Unless Westbrook had returned...

No. He was headed north with his army to flatten her country. If she was lucky, he and his army would leave the convent in its own peace. Unlikely. If not Westbrook, some other army would come. Stalor flew Sol's flag in battle for a reason. Her time here was only a reprieve, not a true escape.

Never safe, Lumen thought, leaving the tapestry and the hall and the memories to follow High Priestess Wren. The room she entered was bare and modest, arranged into an office with a large window that overlooked the base of the mountains down to where they fell and rolled out into hills. A fire burned bright in a large hearth to make up for the draft of the windows. There was a desk, tidily arranged with inkwell and papers, but the High Priestess was by the fire in a low seated armchair, black cloth draped over her lap. Her hand stretched to the opposite chair, and Lumen took the offered seat.

"You want a permanent place in duty to Mother Lune, yes, sister?" Wren asked, and Lumen nodded. "You've been dedicated in your work here since the very start, and sincere in your devotion, but the need for Priestesses is dwindling as chapels disappear with Oshain's grip on the country."

"I don't mind being a novitiate," Lumen said, wondering if Wren was warning her that her place here was fragile.

Wren smiled and dipped her head once. "I didn't either. I've enjoyed all my work for Mother Lune, and I see that in you. She's touched you."

The bone hand in the black dark of a freezing cell. The fight for sacred silver against men twice her size. The sharp crack of whiptails against the side of her face, leaving stars in her vision and on her skin. The impenetrable hunger of body and soul that stretched across years of loss and sharpened to a piercing needle through her heart.

"Yes," Lumen said, breath tight in her chest.

High Priestess Wren's smile was crooked with sympathetic pain. "Yes. The Gods ask for so much, don't they?"

Lumen's eyes dropped to her lap, chapped fingertips folding into her palm, nails digging into flesh. She took slow breaths, trying to wash memories out of her head, the threat of reliving those moments or emotions dangerous to the fragile control she clung to.

"It's not wrong to resent what they take from us, sister," Wren murmured, leaning forward. "You surrendered. You don't have to pretend it didn't nearly kill you."

Lumen would've said it *had* killed her, except she didn't feel reborn, only salvaged.

"It is a long road to a Priestess' robe, and a further one to my own chair," Wren said. Lumen's lips parted to say she never expected a place as High Priestess, but Wren's hand raised for her to wait. "But the road I walked, the one the other sisters here traveled and continue to march on, it pales to your travels, sister."

The old woman's eyes were pale and clear. and Lumen felt Lune's light shining on her from the gaze of High Priestess Wren, but it was an uncomfortable experience to be studied in this way, to have her troubles looked at as a blessing when they were still as tender as an open wound.

"I don't think you were made to wear white robes, Lumen," High Priestess Wren said softly, leaning back in her chair. "And it wasn't bright Lune who stroked your cheek."

Pale, wrinkled hands lifted black fabric from a lap, extending it to Lumen who sat stiffly, eyes wide on the offering.

"No," Lumen whispered.

"She cloaks you. She *claimed* you," Wren said, holding out the black Priestess robe. A New Moon Priestess' garb. "There's no training in the role, none you haven't already suffered at least. Your rank is with us and away from us."

A New Moon Priestess was as rare as the black night in the moon's bright cycle. Rarer. One had visited Fenn Manor when Lumen was barely walking, and she had the faintest memory of the woman's shadow passing through the halls. Her brothers had called the Priestess a ghost and whispered at her back. Lumen only knew she hadn't been as scared of her as her brothers were.

"I don't… I can't…"

Wren stretched, and the heavy black fabric—dark dye textured in shades of brown and purple and blue-black—pooled in Lumen's lap. "You will. You serve her already. You remind the sisters, the novitiates, even the guests, of the stillness and hush of Lune's dark hours. You remind them of the cost of devotion. Wear the robes. If nothing else, it will give you an excuse to stay away from the novitiates' chatter."

Lumen's smile was for the High Priestess' benefit. "May I consider it?"

"Of course," Wren said. "Take the robes with you. You may find them comforting."

Lumen stroked the fabric between her fingers absently. Already, the added warmth of the layer did offer relief, muting a chill she'd carried since the nights in her cell. High Priestess Wren's eyes darted to the door, and Lumen was ready to excuse herself when the wood creaked and she twisted in her seat as Priestess Ellery entered the office. Ellery's eyes landed on Lumen's lap and widened with joy, a smile blooming and digging grooves into her soft cheeks.

"Oh good, I was so hoping you'd accept," Ellery said, head tipping to Lumen who opened her mouth to explain when Ellery continued, "High Priestess, those men are at the gate again."

Lumen's blood froze, ice crunching through her pounding heart as High Priestess Wren sighed noisily and pushed herself up from the armchair. Lumen leaped up, reaching to help the woman, black robes falling to the floor unnoticed.

Wren clutched at Lumen's arm for balance and drifted to the window where Priestess Ellery was already rising onto her toes to watch the approach of riders. Lumen wanted to flee the room, the convent, the country, but instead, her feet dragged her to follow the older women to the window. She stood, pressed between them, and craned her neck to look down at the road.

The two figures were familiar, but they weren't Westbrook or Gideon or even Finley.

"Charlie and Danvers," Lumen whispered. "He's sent them to spy on me."

Wren's fingers found hers, bony knuckles cradling Lumen's shaking hand. "Perhaps, but those two have been a thorn in my side far longer than you've been with us. Sister Ellery, go and keep an eye on the Mallen women as best you can."

"Yes, High Priestess."

"The Mallens?" Lumen asked, watching the two spies descend from their horses with a wary gaze, half-afraid they might look up and spot her.

"They were the ones that brought the family here. They come back on occasion. The Mallens made no vows to us that prevent them visitors, and we offer sanctuary to any woman that asks, but…" Wren's lips pressed together.

Danvers and Charlie would disappear from Fenn Manor, but they always came back with supplies. Had they come to see the Mallen sisters every time? Even as Lumen watched, Imogen Mallen walked slowly to the spies down the road, her body sliding between theirs, within skimming touching distance. Lumen knew that closeness, knew the way it lit up nerves on her skin to be close but not pressed. She also knew that whatever Dominic had asked of Danvers and Charlie, these visits weren't included.

What does it matter? she asked herself. Maybe Danvers and Charlie cared about Imogen. Maybe this was a spark of good coming out of Dominic's ugly world. Still, when Danvers' eyes flicked up toward the window she stood at, Lumen's breath caught and she darted out of sight.

"I don't like it," High Priestess Wren murmured.

LUMEN LEFT the black robes of the New Moon Priestess folded at the end of her bed. Her nights were spent in prayers, and a warm meal, and prayers again, hoping she might be so tired there was no chance of thoughts invading and keeping her awake. It was difficult in a soft bed and a quiet room to keep her head from turning back over weeks and months and years that had passed.

Even under her best efforts, some nights she lay stiff in the bed, remembering. Dominic's growling whispers echoed in her ear, and she would turn in the bed, searching for cold. Finley's grip was like a phantom on her thighs, gently ordering her form, and she sat up in bed to take slow breaths until her heartbeat steadied. At the edge of sleep, Gideon's searing heat might rush over her skin, and the weight of his body reappeared to pin her down until she kicked the blankets off.

She wanted to forget them, but the memories didn't fade quickly enough. She wanted to flood all the hot parts of her anger with ice. The next night of the full moon, memory persisted until touches of months ago were tangibly present in the room with her.

Lumen threw back the covers and reached for the black robes, breath catching when the left corner of her eyes caught a flash of silver. There in the corner of the room, a shrouded figure sat, tucked behind the shining veil of moonlight that fell through Lumen's window. Lumen meant to speak, but no sound released and she shut her lips in relief. Lady Lune was here again with her. Lumen wondered for a moment if she'd finally come to carry her off, but this was nothing like the night in the cell. It wasn't tender companionship from her Goddess, and she was nowhere near death now.

Slowly, the shroud shifted, a slender arm beneath the dark gauze raising. When it crossed the line of moonlight, the shroud melted away to reveal a soft white hand, dressed in silver rings and delicate bracelets, pointing to the robe at the foot of the bed. Lumen's hand moved to where the Goddess pointed, fingers hesitating just over the surface.

Lune stood from the chair, and Lumen thought she might not be breathing as she waited for the Goddess to approach. The direction of the hand shifted slightly, turning to the bedroom door, and then dropped out of the light. There was no shadow figure in the dark corner now. Lune had given her orders and left. With a huff of breath, Lumen pulled the hooded robe over her simple gray-blue gown, sighing as it swallowed her in yards of fabric. She tucked it tight around herself and pulled the hood up before leaving her room to find an empty chapel where she could cast out the figures of men she'd left behind and focus on her devotion again.

The halls were quiet, but Lumen had long since mastered a silent step while sneaking through the Manor without waking the drowsy and drunk soldiers. She moved in a whisper over the stone, down to the small chapel she preferred, heart racing in her chest. Nearly out of the sleeping wing, Lumen caught the rush of voices behind a door.

"How much did you give them?"

"Enough to poison the whole army."

Lumen's steps paused at the word. Had she misheard while her thoughts roamed elsewhere?

"They'll put it in the ale?"

"The ale and directly into the town well too." That was Imogen Mallen, pride ringing in her tone as usual. Lumen thought the other voices might've been her sisters or mother.

"What about the...you know, the ones that aren't part of the army?"

"As if Westbrook's let them live this long," Imogen scoffed as Lumen's heartbeat stuttered in her chest.

"And even if he has, the reward of wiping out that branch of Stalor's army is worth the cost of a few peasants." Yes, there was Myra Mallen, cold and sharp.

Lune's guidance revealed a new direction. Lumen hadn't been sent from her room to go and pray, but to hear these words, the scheme of the Mallen family that High Priestess Wren had sensed but not known.

"Do you really think they'll go through with it? Surely they must have some friends in the ranks?" a younger voice asked. There was no sound of Neave, either she was silent in the discussion or the elder Mallen women had made sure she was asleep.

Lumen slid to the wall just outside the door, breath held in her lungs as her mind raced. At the bottom edge of the doorway, light bled over the stones. It was only the flicker of a candle, but Lumen's eyes winced away as if struck suddenly by sunlight.

"Danvers and Charlie only rely on each other. And I've made sure I matter more to them than any brother in arms."

"Two weeks for the black ore to kill them off," Myra continued.

Lumen's nails scratched against the stone at her back. Black ore was found in the mountains surrounding the holy silver. Their precious silver was mined carefully out of the pockets of black ore after it was discovered to emit poisonous dust. Putting the powder directly into a cask of ale, or a well, would lead to an over thinning of the blood and horrible intestinal problems that would only worsen until the ore was cleansed from the body.

Two weeks, two weeks until it killed Westbrook.

"And then we can go home?"

Home, Lumen thought, a sudden ache for the Manor stinging her heart. For a moment, her hopes were in unison with the Mallen family.

"We can go home when the Oshain army has turned the tide. Taking out Westbrook and his ilk is only the first strike, but it's an effective one."

Cold settled into Lumen's veins. *Let it kill him,* an icy voice offered, stillness settling in her bones and washing away the panic from the overheard conversation. She would know she was safe from him, that a price had been paid for everything he'd put her through.

"Won't someone notice that your soldiers aren't drinking too?" one of the sisters asked.

"Charlie says Westbrook and his lieutenants barely look up from their cups now. The whole lot of them will drink, and it will be done."

All at once, Lumen's hatred cleared. *Colin.* Gretchen Ramsey and her children. Inda and Jennie and the others. And with a sudden, reviving pang of her heart, *Gideon.* Could she really let

21

them all be snuffed out so quickly, and for the hunger of Imogen Mallen's revenge?

No.

Lumen pressed her lips together to stifle the moan that tried to crawl up from her chest. Tears sprang to her eyes. Danvers and Charlie had been outside the convent a little over a week ago. It might not even take the two weeks Imogen predicted to finish the small collection of soldiers and women off.

Mother Lune, let this responsibility sit on someone else's shoulders, Lumen prayed. Except that it had been Lune herself who'd guided Lumen to hearing the words. The bed behind the door creaked and Lumen's feet took automatic steps away, down the hall, a new destination calling and tugging at her heels.

Between injuries from battle and the poor eating from the winter, the black ore might do its deadly work in a timeframe closer to a week. The thought of Colin collapsed in a dusty corner somewhere behind a bar stool, skin gray with purple circles under his eyes…

Lumen's steps grew urgent as she rushed past the chapel she had planned on visiting for peace of mind. There would be none now, and it had only ever been wishful thinking. Lune wasn't done feasting on Lumen's pains.

It serves him right to be betrayed by his own spies, she thought, even as she made her way down a spiraling staircase to the front hall of the convent. *It serves him right to be poisoned by one of his wartime conquests.* Lumen ignored the way her nails pricked at her palms at the vision of Dominic Westbrook's eyes gray and sightless, unfocused in her direction. Anger stirred, and she worked to tamp it down.

This was not what she'd come here for. The Mallen women, their hunger for revenge, for a force in the war that shoved them out of their homes, was the energy Lumen had strove to avoid. It would be as much a relief to leave them behind as it would be a torture to return to Westbrook.

She was downstairs in the cool quiet hall, realizing that she was dressed in the New Moon's Priestess' robe, thinking of stealing a horse, with no supplies at hand, when a shadow crossed the floor in her direction.

"It suits you," High Priestess Wren said in a soft tone, head tipped to examine Lumen in the black robe.

"I can't keep it," Lumen said, words rushing ahead of thought. "I have to leave."

Wren's surprise barely lasted a handful of seconds as she approached Lumen. She stopped in front of the younger woman, her hands tucked into her own white sleeves.

"Who do you leave as?" Wren asked. Lumen's mouth opened in confusion, brow furrowing, and Wren continued. "Do you leave as a woman seeking personal desires? Or do you leave as a daughter of Lune?"

Lumen's lips shut and she swallowed, scrambling through the muddled shock and worry of the revelation from the Mallens, searching for a true answer to give the High Priestess. "I don't know."

"Will you go home to be Lady Fenn?" Wren asked, lines creasing in thought over her forehead.

That answer at least was simple. "No. I will never be Lady Fenn again," she said. "I need a horse. There are people whose lives are at risk and I...I am the person who can help them."

I am the person Lune chose. A year ago, such a thought would've sounded like a blessing in her mind.

"Are you the person who wants to help them?"

Lumen's jaw worked without sound, eyes drifting to the door. "In some cases, yes, I want to. In others, I think... I think I'm the only one who *would*. Would Lune want the death of her enemy?" *I don't*, Lumen realized. She didn't want Westbrook's death to sneak up at his back. He may find his own way into the grave, and maybe revenge was just a form of that, but Lumen couldn't shake the feeling that this was *wrong*.

"It sounds like you act in divine interest, and I see her shadow around you," Wren said, eyes drifting around Lumen's edges. Her chin dipped once in a nod. "Go find yourself a horse and wait for me. You'll need food, and it would be best if you had a little money."

"No, I—"

"If you act for Lune, then as your High Priestess, it's my responsibility to aid you," Wren said, pressing her hand to Lumen's shoulder.

"I am going to save a faction of the Stalor army," Lumen confessed in a whisper.

Wren rolled her eyes. "Lune doesn't belong to Oshain, just as Sol doesn't belong to Stalor. A New Moon Priestess makes her own way in faith, often in dark and muddled places. Our work on Lune's behalf is to offer sanctuary to those who need it, healing, and peace. Is that your intention?"

Lumen dipped her head. "Yes, High Priestess."

"Then go and choose a horse, Priestess Fenn. I will bring you what you need."

Lumen swallowed and listened to the retreating steps of High Priestess Wren. The madness of shock passed, the murky and ugly anger was gone too. In its wake came an aching sorrow. She was turning around, going back to the Manor, back to Westbrook. But not as Lumen Fenn, who she suspected might've died in the damp cell in the north.

Moonlight crossed the stone floor through a blue window, and Lumen stepped under its path and waited for the Goddess to return. When she did not, Lumen waited a little longer, taking deep breaths and searching for clarity. Except there was none. Returning would be painful. Facing Westbrook would be ugly, helping him would confuse her. Maybe allowing the Mallen's plan to proceed was in Lune's work too, a way to stamp out Sol's fire on their land.

Colin was innocent. The Ramsey children and Gretchen. The women Gideon hired.

Resolve cooled and rinsed away Lumen's confusion, and she pulled open the doors of the front hall, the hinges silent and missing their usual protest. Fresh mountain air rushed over Lumen's cheeks for the first time in weeks. It was still sharp and cold here, but she could smell the rich promise of spring rising up from the hills below.

The small stable was a short walk down the mountain to a

second plateau. Lumen took the rope handhold in her fist as she descended and marveled at the night. Had the full moon always made the world so bright? She felt as though she were walking in daylight, able to make out the frosted stubborn weeds that sprouted out of the mountainside, the long hare's footprints hollowed in snow.

The horses snuffled as Lumen entered the stable. There were only a handful, priestesses weren't known to make many solitary journeys away from the convent and never for lengthy distances. Lumen passed three stalls with tall, proud, moon-white geldings. One leaned over the gate of his stall, nosing at Lumen's black shoulder in invitation.

"Sorry, but I think you are too spectacular for me," Lumen whispered to the horse, stroking its cheek. With the world turning green for the new season, a white horse would stand out at a distance. It was unlikely that Danvers and Charlie would remain with Westbrook's party after poisoning them, and Lumen didn't want to offer the spies a clearer view of her from a distance.

Hay rustled in the next stall. The resident was a low brown mare with a broad back that Lumen had seen carrying the High Priestess down to the nearest village. At her feet, a shivering bundle of blanket and skirt tried to bury itself in the hay bed. One flash of that shimmering coppery hair and Lumen pushed her black hood back.

"Neave?"

The girl squirmed and peeked out from under a corner of the blankets, and Lumen was struck by the pale fear in her eye. It vanished in a beat and Neave sat up, frowning. "Lune's tit, I thought you were a ghoul. What are you doing out here?" Lumen only raised an eyebrow in answer. What was *Neave* doing in the stables? Neave huffed and answered the unspoken question. "Mother and the others are *plotting*, and I'd rather not know. Are you leaving? Can I come with you?" she added when Lumen nodded.

Lumen was surprised by the sudden urge to accept. Neave was noisy and curious and demanding, and Lumen thought she'd been enjoying her own solitude. Now she wondered if she'd only enjoyed avoiding the other residents of the convent. Still, taking Neave with her would be selfish. Removing her from the Mallen family influence might be good for the girl, but taking her in the direction of Westbrook's army, in the direction of the *war*, certainly wouldn't be.

"I'm afraid I might be doing a very stupid thing in going," Lumen admitted.

Neave stood and squeezed her way around the wide horse to meet Lumen at the gate. "Then why go?"

"It feels wrong not to."

"You're going for Lune then?" Neave asked, frown deepening harder than a child's had a right to.

"I hope so," Lumen whispered, smiling.

"You really believe in her?"

"Yes," Lumen said, remembering the peace of being alone with Lune in the cell, the acceptance of death to come, and the clear vision of her less than an hour ago.

"I hope I do one day," Neave said, eyes studying Lumen's face with uncanny interest. "You should take Sosha."

"Who?"

Neave pointed over the ledge to the last stall in the stable. "She's quiet and she doesn't kick, and I don't think she really likes it here either."

Lumen wasn't sure if Neave was referring to herself or to Lumen in the 'either' but she crossed to the last stall, meeting the speckled gray mare at the gate. Sosha was soot and charcoal gray with a pale face and dark mane and a dusting of snow and ash down her back. She huffed in Lumen's face in greeting and accepted long strokes down her cheek without complaint.

"Then she and I will be companions," Lumen agreed.

"Child, what on earth are you doing in here?"

Neave rattled the door of the stall at her surprise of being caught by the High Priestess, stirring up the occupants of the stable.

"Never mind," Wren said, holding a hand up as Lumen and Neave eyed one another. "I've been meaning to take on a new assistant. If you'd prefer the spare bed in my quarters and are willing to do some work and some learning, the position is yours."

Wren didn't wait for Neave's response, striding to Lumen with a bag over each shoulder and a pair of black gloves in one hand. They were soft, supple leather, and Lumen put them on her chilly fingers with a grateful smile.

"I suppose I could," Neave said, sneaking out from behind the gate to join them.

"There's food enough for the journey and extra layers. Coin and silver too, if you need a place to sleep for the night," Wren said, hanging the bags on a hook by Sosha's stall. "Do you know how to saddle a horse?"

"Do *you* know how to saddle a horse?" Neave asked the High Priestess with a skeptical look.

Lumen shook her head, and Wren sighed and nodded. "Well, we'll make enough time to give you a quick lesson, so pay close attention."

Lumen paused the High Priestess, her hand resting on the older woman's arm. Sometimes Lumen felt a burn on her skin at another person's touch, but there was none with Wren, she was Lune's servant through and through. They had that in common now.

"Thank you," Lumen said.

"I act on my conscience every bit as much as you, Priestess Fenn," Wren answered with a deep nod. "May Lune guide us."

Lumen echoed the words and followed Wren's lead of instruction.

THIS IS HER REVENGE, DOMINIC THOUGHT, SITTING AT A SOLDIER'S bedside and watching the man writhe in the sheets. Lune's certainly, perhaps Lumen's even by prayer. It was no less than he deserved, although he regretted that his ugly choices were now the entire company's burden.

Finley entered the sick room with stumbling steps, and Dominic didn't know if it was their shared ailment or if he'd gotten his hands on some of his drug again.

"What is it?" Dominic asked. He grit his teeth as a cramp ran through him, banding his arm around his stomach, fingers gripping his thigh to trade one pain for another.

"Nothing I can be sure of. For every familiar symptom, the usual remedy fails," Finley said, wiping sweat from his brow with a stained sleeve. "I try to heal, and they only get sicker. It's starting to feel like a curse."

Dominic scoffed as if he hadn't just thought along the same lines.

"Gideon?" he asked.

"I don't think he's conscious. Truth be told, Dom, I'm afraid to touch him," Finley said. "The most I feel confident in doing is treating pain." His eyes were glazed, and his pupils were oversized. Dominic wanted to shake him, except that he might've been equally inclined to self-medicate if he knew *how*.

Fuck. They were *dying*. The whole lot of them.

"The children?" Dominic whispered. Surely Lune would

29

spare them? Unless this curse was from Sol himself, in which case they were all doomed.

Finley shook his head. "They're better off than us. That's all I can say. And far enough out of town they might stand a chance to improve. Colin is the one I'm most concerned for. He's the strongest of us at the moment, but...not for long."

The ache in Dominic's chest didn't feel as though it were properly his pain, and he knew it really belonged to *her*. "Where is he?"

"Sleeping in my room or caring for the women," Finley said.

Dominic nodded and withheld a groan as he forced himself to stand, grimacing as his stomach threatened to snap with tension and his lungs seemed to slosh with ice inside his breath.

"I'm trying to think like her," Finley said, frowning down at the bowl of water in his hands.

"Just be glad she isn't here," Dominic said.

"We might be well if she were."

"Or she might be dead."

Dominic ignored Finley as he paled another shade to white. He took halting steps out into the hall. Finley had set the women up in the backroom of the inn on cots. There was a fireplace there to keep them warm, although when Dominic looked inside, every single form was shivering under thin blankets. Shivering was better than stillness. They were all still alive...for now.

Taking the stairs up to Finley's room left Dominic breathless and sweating, heart racing like a blur in his chest, threatening to rip and crumble entirely. He made it into the bedroom and collapsed against the door, allowing himself to slide to the floor.

Gideon overflowed the narrow bed, chest barely lifting with uneven breaths, and Colin startled from sleep at Finley's table, eyeing Dominic warily.

"You going to piss yourself?" Colin asked.

Dominic winced. He hadn't thought he would, but now that the boy mentioned it, it seemed like a distinct possibility. He shook his head all the same.

"How ill are you?" Dominic asked, studying the boy. Colin

had dark circles under his eyes and hollow cheeks, but Dominic thought those might've been there even before the illness struck them.

"Less so," Colin said. "You want me to go and get a proper healer?"

Dominic considered the idea. It was what he *should* do. Finley might not be at his best, given the state he'd been in for the past few months. It wasn't what he'd come to say though.

"I want you to go to her," Dominic said.

Colin was quiet, face blank at first until his eyes widened and his head shook slowly. "No."

"Listen—" Dominic started, shaking hand lifting between them.

"No! You can't—"

"Just, give me—"

"Let her be!" Colin barked, rising from the chair and stomping his way to Dominic who was too weak to even stir. Good, the boy was strong enough to manage the journey. "Why won't you let her be?!" Colin roared with tears sparkling in his eyes, his foot lashing out and landing squarely against Dominic's calf.

"I don't want you to bring her here!" Dominic snapped, breath gusting in his chest as the boy settled, the puzzle digging a line between his eyes.

Colin stepped back, looking over Dominic head to toe. "What do you mean?"

"I think I'm damned enough as it is," Dominic said, meaning to sound dry and terse, but only managing a weak crack in his words. "If I let you die with the lot of us… She needs you. Go to her."

"And don't come back?" Colin asked, the doubt clear on his face.

"This is my last order to you. The rest will have to come from her," Dominic said.

Colin's eyes strayed to Gideon and back to Dominic, and he was surprised the boy took so much time to even consider the words. But he wasn't surprised by his decision.

"Fine. Get out of my way," Colin said, chin raising.

Be kind, Dominic thought. *Be kind where I wasn't*. He didn't say a word. The only person who needed Colin's kindness now was Lumen, and for her Dominic wanted the boy to be equally fierce. He huffed and dragged himself away from the door enough for the boy to squeeze through. As the latch snapped shut and the sound of Colin's quick steps echoed down the stairs, Dominic's gaze found Gideon's face, and if he weren't so weak, he would've jumped to find his friend's eyes open.

"Good," Gideon rasped.

Dominic huffed a weak, wet sound, his head thunking against the thin wood wall of the inn room, eyes fixed to Gideon's. Still alive. They were all still alive, but for how much longer? Maybe Finley should be focused less on their pain and more on finding them a swift ending.

SHE'D LOST track of days in the mountains during her stay at the convent, Lumen realized. It was properly spring the lower she went into hill country. She didn't remember the route the men had brought her to the convent on, but it was easy enough to avoid towns, and there was something about returning home that came by an instinct she couldn't name.

She knew the angle of the sunset, where the moon should hang in the sky, and she knew some of the folds of land as if she could've traced her route from her mother's office window in the Manor. She picked useful herbs through the woods, and only fell off her horse by nodding off once. After that incident, Sosha was more careful with her.

Lumen suspected she had a final day's ride to reach the town, maybe less, and she could hasten the hours on the main road instead of coaxing Sosha through secret and thorny woods. With the land in flux between the two countries' forces, the road was as desolate of travelers as the woods for most of the hours. Lumen was dozing again, despite the sharp pain in her back and the stiff ache of her hips, when the sound of a cart approaching woke her.

An old man with a young girl at his side led two horses down the opposite side of the road, a cart piled high with boxed possessions. The girl leaned into his side as Lumen neared them, the same fear on her face as Neave held in the horse stall, but the man's face was open in clear awe, eyes growing wide. Lumen dipped her head to him, and he coughed and ducked his head, eyes landing on his hands.

"Priestess," he murmured, and the girl at his side mimicked his actions.

Her hood was up, Lumen realized, obscuring her face. The girl was too young to remember a New Moon Priestess, but he hadn't been, and the sight of Lumen had struck him. It was enough for a moment to make her wish she could trade the robe out for a simple cloak. And then the thought was obliterated by the sight of the young boy at the back of the cart, leaning over the edge to watch the scenery go by.

Lumen pulled the reins sharply, grateful Sosha was too good-tempered to throw her off. "Colin!" she cried, even as she wondered if she was imagining him. The mussed light brown hair, the shoes that were too thin, and the cuffs of his pants already too short.

She jumped down from Sosha's saddle, throwing back the hood of her robes as Colin sat up straight in the back of the cart. As soon as her face was revealed, his eyes went huge.

"Lady!"

He leapt from his seat, hand barely snagging the strap of his sack, and his feet thumped down the road. The cart stopped, and the old man leaned over the edge to watch as Colin and Lumen met on the dirt and stone, bodies crashing and arms circling. Lumen landed on her knees, mind numb to the jarring ache as she pressed her face into Colin's hair and took a deep breath of him. Her heart seemed to start up again for the first time in weeks, and a sob broke free where a moment ago there had been only still and sleepy calm.

Their words piled on top of one another.

"Why are you on the road?"

"Where are you going, Lady?"

"Are you well? Are you sick?" Lumen pulled away, grasping Colin's face in her hands, joy clear in his eyes even as his mouth hung open in shock. Her heart cracked and stitched itself back together in the same breath. "Oh, Colin!"

"I'm...I'm a bit better. Westbrook sent me to you," Colin said. He must've seen some flash of pain on her face, because his hands clasped around her wrists as he rushed to add, "Oh, not like that, Lady. He meant me to... to care for you. There's sickness back there. It came on quick."

The cart was moving again, its driver apparently satisfied with the idea that Lumen and Colin would see to each other. Which was true now. Lumen gathered Colin to her chest again and held him tight, waited for her pounding heart to steady, for him to not feel like a small dream wrapped up in her arms.

"Poison," she said. "In the water and ale."

"They deserved it," Colin said weakly.

Lumen frowned at the response, and then a startled laugh escaped her lips. "Not by *me*, you wicked thing," Lumen said, surprised by her own volume, her own smile. Colin only shrugged. "Come. We'll ride back. I have a few things with me that will have you well again with a bit of rest."

Colin's hand around Lumen's wrist tightened as she stood, and Lumen wished—not for the first time—that she had a remedy for a boy whose frown carved too deeply into his young face. "Lady, no. Leave them. You aren't bound to help them. You never were. Let's go somewhere better."

Gideon had offered her something like this too, Lumen remembered with bittersweet fondness. One day, she hoped to understand why it never seemed to be an offer she could accept.

"I think I am bound to help," Lumen said, covering Colin's hand with her own briefly before stroking her fingers over the lines on his face. "I tried to forget myself at the convent, but I..."

"You are too good, Lady," Colin said.

Lumen's nose wrinkled. "Or very stupid. Rosie and Inda and the others? The Ramsey family? Are they well?"

Colin's lips pressed hard together and she watched him try to force the lie to his lips, relieved when he failed and sighed, head shaking.

"Westbrook should've ordered me to keep you away, but he told me to follow you instead," Colin said, kicking his toe against the road. "Now all three of us may regret his choice."

Lumen swallowed at the mention of the man again. He'd sent Colin after her? And not to fetch her back to save them, but only because he knew she would want the boy with her. That made it a little easier to accept that she would have to try and save him along with the others.

"If it were plague and not poison, I wouldn't take you back," Colin said gruffly, reaching for Sosha's saddle and dragging himself up with a little bit of help from Lumen and a great deal of patience from the mare.

If it were the plague and not poison, I might leave them to it, Lumen thought. At least then it would be nature's will and not the Mallen's.

TWO MEN DEAD, and probably another handful by morning. Finley was too ill to work, and there was no one but Dominic left standing. If the Oshain army stormed the village now, it would be a mercy rather than a siege.

He should be inside on a cot somewhere, waiting for the last and worst bouts of sickness to take him too, but he felt...not strong, but not as weak as the rest of them. Sol or Lune or both were laughing at him, Dominic decided. He would watch the others die as punishment, perhaps.

Now, more than ever, Dominic was of the opinion that Gods had a very poor and ugly form of justice. He threw the bedclothes of the dead men onto the bonfire and coughed as the smoke hit him, but he didn't step away. Maybe this would hasten the issue.

Dominic watched the sheets smother and then pucker and smolder over the flames until black and spark-orange lace ate its way through the fabric. The pop and hiss of the fire were the only sounds in the town for many minutes, and he wavered on his feet, sleep calling. And then a pop of the fire became the steady clap of hooves on the road. Danvers and Charlie returning from their errand perhaps, to find them all half or more dead. Except it was only one set of steps.

He looked up through the flames, the vision wavering in front of him, hazy in heat. A white beast's skull bobbing through the night, like the face of a ghost. Aha! Death *had* come for him.

The head dipped, and Dominic realized it was attached to a sooty horse. The picture of its rider left him frowning, the boy asleep, drooped against a shadow figure, face slack with peace. Someone had picked Colin up and dragged him back here? Was the boy too ill to fight them off?

The shadow shifted as the rider neared the fire, and orange light snagged on a handful of shiny white marks hidden under the black hood. Dominic's heart was in his throat as he stared at the place, a constellation of scars so familiar and memorized in his mind, he knew them better than his own face.

"You came," he whispered to her, but the words were mercifully carried away by a breeze heading in the opposite direction.

The horse and its riders stopped by the fire, but Dominic couldn't force himself to meet them, and for a long stretch, no one moved. His face was numb, and he wondered what she saw on it. He prayed it wasn't the blind hope in his chest. That she'd come back to him, forgave him, come to save him.

A gloved hand reached up and revealed the face he could not manage to erase from the back of his eyelids, her skin still pale, her hair still reflecting stars and fire and the moonlight that broke through the clouds just to shine on her in admiration.

"The poison is in the well and the ale," Lumen said in lieu of a greeting. "How many are left?"

Dominic took a step toward her, and the fantasy of her return cracked at her automatic flinch. Colin woke and shifted in place before realizing where he was, finding Dominic and frowning at the sight of him.

"Only two dead so far. Soldiers," Dominic finally managed,

knowing she would want to care for the women and children first. "How did you know?"

"Danvers and Charlie have been visiting the Mallen women at the convent."

Dominic blinked, and his hand lifted to cover his mouth. Fuck. Fucking spies. He'd seen the way the Mallen daughter had hooked those two after failing with him, Gideon, and Finley, but hadn't thought anything of it when his men seemed more or less the same after moving on.

"Colin, there's a spring a bit west of here. Can you take Sosha and fetch water from there?" Dominic listened to Lumen, ached at the shifting tone of sweetness in her voice when directed to the boy.

The water. No wonder they'd all been getting worse as Finley tended them.

She slid down from the saddle, bags on her shoulders, and Colin twitched the reins and walked away with a warning glance in Dominic's direction. She pulled a canister from a bag.

"Here. The cramping will worsen at first, but if you're well enough to stand it won't kill you," Lumen said.

Dominic wanted to reply but resisted saying that he would've taken anything she offered, gladly, including poison. "There are others worse off than me. You should give them this," he said instead.

"If they're worse, it might be the last straw," Lumen said, staring somewhere beneath his chin. "If you can stand, you can drink that. Where are they?"

*I have no right to say it, no right to make you hear it, and I know you did not come for me, but just to see you...*his thought failed at that point, every sentiment too small or too tender. So Dominic kept his mouth screwed shut and led the way back to the center of the town.

"Last Finley checked, your people were better off than us. They're farther from the well, closer to the stream."

"When you're ready—" she said, slow and hesitant.

"I'll go. See who needs you," he offered.

The road crunched under the steps, words dying out.

Dominic took a slug from the canister, surprised at the bitter flavor and desperately resisting the urge to spin on his heel, see her again as if she were the ghost Gideon teased her of being, terrified that she might vanish at any second.

"Why did you come?" he asked.

She was quiet for a long time, and they'd reached the inn door, the groans from inside audible. "I don't know. Not for you."

It was said gently as if to avoid wounding him, and though he'd known as much, the confirmation carved freshly through his chest. Dominic pushed the door open, and Lumen entered, taking one sweeping look over the collapsed and moaning bodies, and then set to her work.

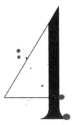

She'd forgotten the sense of purpose in the work of healing, but it came back quickly. Colin brought her fresh water, and it was gone before she'd made it through the first room of the inn. Westbrook brought more. Back and forth they went as she worked until the rhythm was enough to help distract her from the prickles of awareness every time he came near.

It wasn't that he seemed different. He looked ragged but essentially the same, frowning and glowering at everything and everyone except for that brief open moment when he'd recognized her. It was just as if he were...restraining some of his energy, shielding her from his usual heat and anger. She could stand alongside him and not want to tear away or lean closer.

The men on the floor around her watched her with glassy eyes, not in recognition but something like it, as if she reminded them of a dream they'd already forgotten. They were ill, that was all.

"Lady," one rasped, struggling to sit up as she knelt at his side.

"Just rest. Drink a little. There are rags here if you feel sick. It will take time, but you'll be all right," Lumen murmured to him. He was young and very thin from the sudden bouts of illness, but not so much that it was likely to carry him off before Lumen helped flush it out.

"Lady, please go to Inda," he hissed, and Lumen stared at him. Of course, this was Philip, Inda's sweetheart. She was surprised by the tender twinge in her chest at his concern for the girl and nodded.

"Of course. I saw her briefly. You'll both be well soon. I'll find you a room together." She looked up and found Dominic nearer than she expected, setting down another bucket of water with sweat sparkling on his brow. She caught sight of his hand shaking as he turned. "You need to rest. Eat something," she said.

"You'll need more—"

Lumen cut his breathless refusal off. "What I don't need is another patient. Sit and eat something before you go out again. And then make Colin do the same."

Illness made him pliant, and Dominic disappeared behind the bar without further argument. It was a blessing. Lumen's travels were catching up to her and pushing through seeing everyone would be enough of a challenge without wrestling Dominic's stubbornness.

The only thing to do at the moment was give everyone enough uncontaminated water and food and hope that it started a slow cleansing of the body. When they improved, Lumen would flush the poison out properly with the right herbs, but done too soon and their weak bodies wouldn't survive the purge. She didn't blame Finley for making everyone worse—he'd only done for them what she would've prescribed—and being from the south, he knew nothing of black ore.

"Who is it?"

Lumen blinked in the dark backroom, head rousing from her thoughts to find herself tending Jennie.

"It's me," she said, and then realized as Jennie frowned it was too dark for her to see, although Lumen could make out the women cuddled together on cots perfectly. "Lumen."

"Lumen?" Rosie murmured from a few feet away.

"What were you thinking of, coming back here?" Jennie asked, weak and angry.

Lumen smiled at her friend. "I heard you were being poisoned."

"Did you come to finish them off faster?" Jennie asked, and Inda gasped on her bed.

"I came to undo it." Lumen watched Jennie's brow furrow in the dark, eyes turned in her direction like she could almost make out Lumen's edges.

"You probably should've left us to it," Jennie said.

"Jennie, hush," Rosie moaned.

"That doesn't sound like me," Lumen murmured, and then tipped the cup to Jennie's lips before the woman could speak again. "If it's any consolation, I'm not sure the healing will be entirely pleasant."

Jennie's lips curved around the cup and she accepted the drink, speaking as Lumen moved on. "Ah, it is you, Lady."

"It's Priestess, now," Lumen said, although she'd barely wrapped her head around the word.

Jennie snorted and rolled with a soft groan.

Dominic was missing when Lumen made it out of the second room ready to conquer the upstairs. Colin's hair was visible behind the high top of the bar counter.

"How many more?" Lumen called to him and he popped up, eyes just visible.

"Handful upstairs. General and I told the others to avoid the well, and your people seemed to know what needed doing."

Lumen sighed and nodded. "The ale's long gone?"

"Dominic burned what was left of the casks. Found the black grime inside." Colin stretched a little farther, resting his chin atop his folded arms. "You know who's up there?" Lumen could guess. "Want me to come?"

Mother Lune, bless this boy, Lumen thought, crossing to him and bundling him against her chest again, face buried in the hair atop his head. "No. Is there somewhere decent for you to sleep?"

"No one took your old room, so I kept it," Colin mumbled against her.

"Good. Eat and then rest. I'll join you once I'm done."

"Yes, Lady," Colin said.

She trudged the buckets waiting at the bottom of the steps up to the second floor, where four deeply ill soldiers with infected wounds thrashed on their beds as she tended them, forcing them to drink and cleaning their wounds. There were only two rooms left, the one she'd stayed in during her own recovery, and the one on the right she remembered Finley using. And there were still two faces she had yet to see.

A candle was burning in Finley's room on the top of a lopsided dresser, wax spilling down one side and over the edge of the wood. Gideon overflowed the entire length and width of the narrow bed on the left, and Finley lay bundled under blankets on the floor to her right. She might've thought they were both dead if not for the pained wheezing breaths that hissed in the air.

She stoked the coals in the small iron stove in front of her, adding a small log into its belly and pouring fresh, clean water into the bowl on top. Humidity would help their breathing for the time being. She picked the candle up from the dresser, carrying it sputtering and threatening to die out every step back to the bed. Gideon looked nearly in his grave, and the sight of him bone pale and bruised, blood crusting in wounds, was the first real thing to shake Lumen out of her focus of work. She'd been resisting the thought of him, resisting the urge to come and make sure he survived, see him smiling again.

There was no room for her to sit at his side as he'd done for her, so she sank to her knees by the bed, listening to his rasps, watching the unsteady rise and fall of his chest. She took a clean cloth and soaked it in the fresh water, lifting it to his lips and squeezing it in slowly, careful not to let him choke. Her hand reached under his head, hefting it up to help him swallow, relieved when reflexes kicked in even as he remained unconscious.

"Why choose a disguise so tempting when I've already waited for you for years?"

Lumen startled and turned to find Finley curled in her direction, staring up at her with his head on the floor. Candlelight revealed the bloodshot streaks of red in his eyes, and his lips were chapped and peeling.

"Take me and leave him," Finley murmured. "He deserves to live a little longer. And I've missed the face you wear."

Lumen's breath hitched as she realized what he meant. She

left Gideon's side for Finley's, dragging him up by his broad shoulders and propping him against the wall. His eyes narrowed and flickered back and forth across her face.

"I'm not Death, Healer Brink," she said, watching his face turn slack. "Could you stand?"

"Lumen," he breathed, her name elongated with wonder.

Lumen held her breath and waited for the sting of a broken emotion's sharp edges to pass through her. "Healer—"

"Lumen, why?" he cried out. "Why would you come back here?" She huffed and rolled her eyes, sick of the question and no clearer on the answer. "Are you—? Have you…come to haunt us?"

Patience cracked like glass, and Lumen brushed loose strands of hair from her face. "Oh, honestly Finley! I haven't died, and neither have you. Now, are you well enough to stand if you had to?"

"I- yes, if I- Sol's Fire, Lumen. Yes, yes if I had to," he said, making a weak effort to prove it.

"Fine. Good. Drink this. Danvers and Charlie poisoned the well and the ale with black ore. It's deadly if you don't realize and keep drinking, but now that…now that you know, you should be able to recover with a little time," she rattled out, ignoring Finley's struck expression as she forced some of the infusion she'd given Dominic into his hands. "What are Gideon's ailments?"

"He…uh…dehydration. The last battle, he let himself get knocked around after…it's become a bit of a pattern, I suppose, so he hasn't been in decent shape in over a month…"

Lumen nodded, scanning Gideon again, pushing at his thigh to make herself room at the very edge of the bed. "You're going to feel sick when you get enough of that down, but it's just going to expel the poison," Lumen said. At her back, the warning seemed to do the trick of getting Finley off the floor and heading for the door. "Bring back safe food he can swallow and clean rags when you're done."

Finley took slow steps through the room. Lumen's back was

stiff as he moved, twisted away from him as she dribbled water between Gideon's slack lips.

"Lumen," he said, almost a whisper.

She could've turned, or answered in some way. *Isn't it enough to be here?* she thought. Perhaps it was too much or gave Finley the wrong impression. He hovered by the doorway as she pretended not to hear him.

"I'll be back," he said eventually, clearer, as he slipped out the door.

She waited until his steps creaked down the stairs before releasing her sigh. She found another pillow where Finley had been and stuffed it under Gideon's to lift his head, and then hunted through the drawers until she found some clean hand-kerchiefs. They would have to be surrendered because Lumen hated to see Gideon still covered in blood this way.

She was cleaning a wound on his jaw, one stitched carelessly shut with a clumsier hand than her own, when he stirred and grunted. One large, bruised hand rose and wrapped around her wrist. Lumen watched, not aware of the way her lips curled upwards, as Gideon dragged her wrist to his nose, taking a deep and ragged breath.

"Swee' spirit, that you?" he said, volume cracking and vanish-ing, so she read the words on his lips.

"What did I say about stitches?" Lumen asked, the havoc of her heart settling as Gideon's grin struggled to stretch. His eyes blinked but resisted opening, so she continued. "You seem to have a second nasty habit now too."

"Hmm?"

"Getting poisoned," she answered.

He was quiet, almost sleeping, when the words finally sank in. "Poison? 'M dying?"

"Nearly," she said softly.

His eyes stirred behind his lids, and he drank more greedily from the cloth on her next attempt. "Better get another look at you before I go," he growled, and finally his eyes opened. "You come to say goodbye?"

Lumen's next breath was uneven, a soft laugh mixing with

rising tears. "Not yet," she said, and she let her fingers run along the uninjured side of his jaw.

"You look different," he said. His eyelids were drooping again, struggling to stay open, gaze fighting to focus on her.

"You look terrible," she teased, studying his grin again. "I'd like you to drink more water."

"Makes my throat dry."

"That was the poison. This will help."

He grunted and made to sit up, although it was only a twitch of his shoulders until Lumen reached to help him. She was stronger than she would've expected, able to help pull him up against the headboard with her arms around her chest. There was a broad hand on her back and an arm loose around her waist, a careful embrace, or one barely managed by a man too weak to grasp her to him.

"Thank you," he said. "I hope it doesn't hurt you to be here."

His arms dropped and she was free, but Lumen rested there against Gideon's chest, where no one but they would know about the crack in her resolve. She *did* come back for his sake, pretending otherwise would be a useless lie. It hurt to return but Gideon was worth the pain, even if the last thing she ever did for him was keep him from Death's doorstep.

I've survived worse, she thought, but saying so out loud would only make them both melancholy.

45

Finley had never been much more than a decent healer, better since he'd learned Lumen's family tricks and methods. Since her return to the village, he was the worst he'd ever been. Not that Lumen required much help. Within three days, she had the whole regiment on its feet again, even if their steps were wobbly and made them breathless. Everywhere he turned she was marching by in those eerie black robes of hers, her face and hair twice as pale set against the dark color.

Colin stayed close at her heels. Like a guard dog, Finley thought.

"Quit gawking at her," Dominic muttered.

"Oh, have you managed to avoid staring?" Finley snapped back.

Lumen was descending the stairs, crushed against the wall as she and Colin guided Gideon down between them. There was color on the great warrior's cheek again, although Finley wondered if it wasn't a blush from being near Lumen.

"I at least make an effort," Dominic said.

Finley would've argued except when he glanced at Westbrook, he realized the man had his back deliberately turned from the stairs. Finley tried to mimic him and found his neck *ached* with the desire to turn his head and set his eyes on her again.

"How long until we can take the men out on the field again?" Dominic asked him.

Finley stared as the question spun through his head. "You can't be serious."

"I've been stalling this entire time. Either we meet Oshain in a skirmish, or they will come and test us here."

"Dominic, the entire company's been *poisoned*," Finley said.

"Yes. Something I was very careful to keep from being public knowledge. Otherwise, we'd all have had our heads chopped off a week ago, or been dragged into an Oshain prison."

"Shut your fucking mouths, would you?" Gideon growled.

Finley spun and found Gideon trying to wrestle himself in front of Lumen like a shield. He glanced at Dominic and saw that irritation had bled out, leaving shame behind. They all had first-hand knowledge of that prison, Lumen more than any of them.

"Enough," she said, mild as ever. "You made it down the stairs, now sit before you fall over and cut yourself on something less impressive than your enemy's sword."

Finley's heart swelled at her chiding, and it wasn't even directed at him. Gideon beamed at the woman and shuffled his way into a bar chair. Desperate to pull her attention to him for a moment—she'd barely looked at him since he'd mistaken her for the specter of Death—Finley spoke without thinking, tattling like a child. "Dominic's trying to take the army out to battle."

"I heard," Lumen said, fussing with her sleeve. The black of the cloth seemed to shimmer with darkness, even in sunlight, and it made Finley's eyes trail away. "Two days. Three if you can spare it. And you'd better not be very ambitious in the fighting."

"Wha—?" Finley gasped.

"You're sure?" Dominic asked.

Sol's Fire, he wanted to scream. He wanted to stand in the middle of the room, waving his arms and just *scream* at the lot of them. Lumen was here, *in front of them*, and she'd saved their useless and damned lives for probably the fiftieth time, and she was *here*. And yet Dominic was able to think of war, and Gideon managed to sit there as docile as a well-fed bear in summer, and not grasp and paw at the woman as if they hadn't all been trying to kill themselves slowly for the weeks she'd been gone. As if they weren't half-insane with want and relief at the sight of her.

"I don't like it, but yes, I'm sure," Lumen said. "There could be a cost, but I think it would be higher if you let them come and find you here."

"You don't…you don't have to *plot* for Stalor just because Oshain failed you," Finley spat out.

"Brink, shut your fool mouth," Dominic snarled.

"She's not!" Colin barked.

"Don't mind him," Gideon said to Lumen.

Finley couldn't face any of them, not as he watched Lumen's spine straighten and her chin lift. He knew that look perfectly, had dreamt of it after leaving her in his worst moment of judgment.

"I am the New Moon Priestess now, and I have no allegiance but to Lune and those who have need or want of my help," she said softly, eyes slashing against his chest. "I went to the trouble of making sure no one died after my arrival, and I'll give my opinion on keeping it that way. War and all."

"P-Priestess?" Finley stuttered.

It wasn't a surprise, exactly, and made sense of the robe and her return, but it seemed to make Lumen into something more foreign than before. More untouchable.

"Do you need an escort back to the convent?" Dominic asked, taking her announcement in stride, staring at his own hands on the bar top.

"No, and I'm going to the Manor first."

That had all three of their heads whipping in her direction. She was staying? Not with them exactly, but near?

"Colin is coming with me," she added, face fixed and hard in a challenge that Dominic only responded to with a limp nod.

"I'll tell him where to find the silver we hid," Dominic said.

Lumen frowned. "You didn't give it out to him and the girls like I asked?"

"We didn't accept it, Lady," Colin said, leaning into her side.

"Priestess," Finley corrected, and then flinched when the boy glared at him.

49

She sighed and shook her head, reaching back to pull her hood up, hiding her face from the room. "Fine. What's the nearest encampment to the Manor after yours?"

"Nothing closer than us," Gideon said, hand twitching in her direction and then falling to his side again. "Anything comes up from the south, we'll get you word."

Dominic grunted his agreement, and Lumen headed for the door. "We are in your service, Priestess," Dominic said, sudden and sharp.

"No," she said from the door.

"You've saved our skin plenty by now, Lumen, so let me say this," Dominic said, and now finally, his eyes took their fill of her back, shrouded as it was. "If you have any need of our help, send word and we will come. Then and only then, I promise you."

Finley dug his nails into the wood of the bar, splinters distracting from the urge to run to her, to whisper an order in her ear that might make her stay. Her shoulders slipped lower, and the hood of the robe jerked up before she left the inn, Colin hot on her heels.

He waited until the door swung shut. "I hope for her sake she never sees us again," Finley lied.

IT WAS strange to see the Manor from this direction, the view of coming home. With her father and brothers fighting through the war, Lumen's mother refused to travel. She could see now where the temple had been altered to disguise itself as a home. The front hall was an addition, its window brighter and oddly shaped compared to the ones that circled the old structure.

"Does it hurt to return, Lady?" Colin asked.

She folded Sosha's reins in one hand and lifted the other to comb through his hair where he rested his head against her chest. "I'm not sure yet. I...lived there alone for a very long time, and that was painful too although I told myself it wasn't."

"You won't be alone again," Colin said, cuddling in closer.

Lumen smiled and squeezed her arm around him briefly. The

convent was crowded, full of voices and movement to disturb Lumen's meditation. The prospect of the empty Manor, together with Colin, was a more welcome thought, even after all she'd suffered there.

"We have a great deal of work ahead of us, I'm afraid. The winter wheat will be up soon, but we're far behind on spring crops."

And Oliver was gone, although she couldn't find it in herself to care.

"We'll catch up," Colin said, simple and optimistic, and Sosha seemed to nicker in agreement.

Lumen had a sneaking suspicion that High Priestess Wren had allowed her to steal their best horse, because Sosha hadn't made a peep of complaint even after they'd rescued the silver out of the bottom of the stream where Dominic had sunk two bagfuls of the stuff, weighed in place by rocks.

"You mean to stay then?" Colin asked. "You didn't say to them."

Lumen's jaw clenched at the mention of the three men, and she forced herself to loosen and relax. "Do you remember when you showed me the morning the sun and the moon were at opposite ends of the house, facing one another?" Colin nodded. "I learned at the convent that my home used to be a temple where those of Solar and Lunar faith would share and practice together. I'd like...I'd like for it to be that again, I think."

Colin didn't scoff or question her plan, ludicrous as it sounded to her own ears. Who would come? Who was even left in this no-man's-land?

"Am I good enough to be a part of such a place?" Colin asked.

Lumen's voice cracked, sob and laughter combining in surprise. "Oh, Colin. I think you are the very best of us."

"I would help you no matter what," he said.

Lumen slouched in her seat and buried her teary eyes on the top of his head.

"They found them."

Dominic jerked in his seat, rousing from sleep he hadn't even realized he'd fallen into. Gideon was leaning in the doorway of his restored office at the back of the inn.

"You're joking," Dominic said, clearing the grit from his throat.

They'd survived a battle the day before. Survived the poison set out for them. He was beginning to wonder if his life was tied to Lumen's, not that he would ever burden her with the thought. When she was near death, they'd brought her back. Now she'd repaid that. How many more times would they trade the favor, and was it selfish to wish for it?

"I'm not. Lumen was right. They were hiding out in an abandoned farm not far from the convent." Gideon's arms crossed over his chest. "What are you going to do with them?"

Dominic groaned as he stood. Sleeping in a chair was shit, but he'd tried to sleep in the bed Lumen used the night before, and that was so much worse for sweeter reasons.

"Let me see," he said, and followed Gideon out the door into the bar.

"Our guests have arrived, lads," Gideon called to the thin assembly of soldiers lingering in the bar and playing cards.

With a rustle of chatter, the men stood from their chairs—including the man Finley had been busy wrapping with a bandage. He tied the cloth off as they walked toward the door and then waited until he could step to Dominic's side.

"I saved some of the black ore we pulled from the well," Finley offered.

Dominic only answered with a nod. The well was still out of commission according to Widow Ramsey's advice, but she said it ought to be safe by late summer. As if she expected them to still be here in another three months time.

It wasn't just the army who left the houses and shops of the village to convene in the street. It hadn't been just the army to drink the poison. Widow Ramsey was there, her children held in the arms of two soldiers who flanked her at either side. The women who'd become lovers rather than whores to his men, there between their sweethearts. Sol, what were they now? They looked more like a town than an army.

They formed a circle around the two men on their knees in the street. It took three men to hold Charlie down, and still he twisted and arched toward Danvers who faced the opposite direction. Danvers glared up at Dominic in his slow approach, chin raised high in defiance. All the buried anger and resentment that Dominic had sensed, but assumed was held in check, now blazed like a fire on his former spy's face.

"Surprised to see me so well?" Dominic asked. He hadn't meant to taunt, to make a game of this moment, but the habit of playing the bully was hard to unlearn.

"You are a plague on the men who serve you," Danvers hissed. "The whole world is just flesh and fodder to you, but at least you knew how to do *one* thing right. One thing, for years and years. We won. We conquered. We moved north. Until suddenly, you had a taste of pussy you seemed to prefer."

Gideon snarled at Dominic's left but remained still.

"You think I didn't want to keep some of those women you tossed off your back?" Danvers asked. Dominic's brow twitched. This was about Lumen? "She made you weak and worthless."

"She saved your life, you fool. Charlie's too," Finley scoffed.

"Soldiers die all the time," Danvers said with a shrug. "We don't get sick in the head over women."

"Noted," Dominic said, and Danvers wasn't the only one in the road who looked shocked by his mild delivery. "And who was it, Danvers, who gave you the instructions to wipe out the lot of us? If I'm the disappointment, why kill the entire army? You're right. I've been a worthless general for Stalor. You knew where I slept. You know how to kill a man without so much as waking him."

Danvers' eyes twitched and his jaw clenched as the words landed. Had he not realized he was being played by the Mallen girl, or not cared? Dominic stepped forward and crouched, body loose and relaxed as he met Danvers' hateful gaze.

"Must be something about Oshain women, hmm?" he asked,

the joke a worse poison on his tongue. Gideon might punch him for that one, but so be it.

"Just kill us, Westbrook. Send us back to Stalor to have my back stripped and my wrists chained."

There was some cunning in the man's eyes as he bargained. A year ago, the two possibilities were equally likely. Dominic could make an example of betrayal to his men, or he could hand Danvers off to the higher-ups in the South to punish and recycle. If Dominic's guess was correct, Danvers was betting on the latter, on Dominic being too soft under Lumen's influence to do the act himself. And if Danvers and Charlie were given over to Stalor they would be made to suffer, but they'd also likely be risked back in service. Dominic had written plenty to his superiors on their talents and successes in the shadow work of war.

Danvers' breath was uneven as he waited for his fate. There was fear there, but the flavor wasn't as exciting to Dominic now.

"I wash my hands of you," Dominic said, rising, ignoring the way his body creaked and groaned. Shit, was he getting old, or just tired?

"Wha—?" Danvers gaped up at him.

"Men, they're yours to do as you please with, just make sure I don't have to look at them again," Dominic called out to the hungry crowd, voices rising like a low growl.

On the far right, Widow Ramsey murmured to her soldiers, accepting her children back from their arms and taking them from the center of the town with a low nod to Dominic. Gideon was at his back as he stepped away, Danvers calling out to him, eyes growing wide and white.

"Wait! Wait!"

"Do you want me to stay and see it finished?" Gideon asked him.

Dominic shrugged. "Do you think they won't?"

"Jennie has a knife in her hand," Finley said, head tipped. "I think they haven't got a chance of surviving."

"It's up to you. I have no further argument with them," Dominic said, and headed back to the bar for another hour's sleep.

"Can't we plant chickens or something?" Colin grumbled.

He and Lumen were on their knees in the garden, putting in the lettuce and snap-pea sprouts they'd been tending in the kitchen for the last two weeks. Her nails were now caked with dirt, and she'd left the black robe upstairs in her new bedroom—it was easier and more familiar to fall back asleep in her old bed than she expected, or maybe she was too tired from all the work.

Lumen snorted and glanced at him. There was dirt up to his elbows and spotted all over his face. "The soldiers ate all the chickens. But I bet we can scrounge up enough to buy one or two. You'll have to resist eating them for a while. Will the eggs do?"

"Better than vegetables," Colin said with a huff and a shrug.

Lumen sat back on her heels, wiggling her numb legs out and letting her skirt get damp in the earth as she sat. "Would you like a break?" she asked, gentle and without any intonation. Colin pushed himself to work at her pace, but he was still young and easily bored, and it would be a long time until he was able to enjoy the fruits of their effort.

"I could go into the woods and set a snare or two," he said, eyes widening hopefully.

Oliver had taught him the snares and while the efforts had been fruitless so far, it couldn't hurt to try, especially if Colin needed a change of pace.

"Rabbit would be nice," Lumen answered with a nod. "Back by sundown."

"Yes, Lady," he said, leaping up and running for the rowboat.

Lumen ignored the ache in her back and the hunger in her belly, setting back to her work of planting. The air was wet, and there was a thin blanket of gray clouds heading in their direction that would be good for introducing the seedlings to the garden plot. She and Colin would have to make do on a thin dinner, but they'd been doing as much since their return to the Manor.

Someone had sent them back with flour and small bags of sugar and salt, and Lumen had foraged enough mushrooms to make meals that curbed the worst of the hunger. The Manor was sparse and empty still, but it needed less care than the land, and the beds were still there to fall into at night. Sometimes she turned a corner and the memory of a kiss or a touch passed over her skin. Sometimes she stared at a bloodstain still coating a stone like rust and the walls didn't feel hers, as if Dominic might return to claim the place again at any moment. For the most part though, the days were good. Monotonous, exhausting, bare, and beautiful days.

"I thought maybe you would've moved on by now."

Lumen jerked and looked up, jaw dropped as she stared at the woman with soft copper hair who stood at the edge of the land, frowning at her.

"Jennie!"

Jennie fidgeted, scanned the horizon, and wrapped her arms and shawl tight around herself. Behind her, a squat mare panted and nibbled on the grass, bags hanging over a makeshift saddle.

"Did you mean what you said, 'bout me having a place here if I wanted it?"

"Yes, of course!" Lumen's groan was strangled as she stood, legs still a little too stiff to hold her straight, but she made her way to her friend. "You left the village?"

"I'm sick of all the men and...and I figured you could use an extra body here. You really want to stay?"

Lumen's answer came easier to her now, as if she hadn't

understood the pull back to the Manor until she was there to do the work. "It's different for me now. I'm not here to preserve my home, honestly. And I have no people left to protect. But I...I would rather be working this land and praying in this place and...healing those that need me here. There's hardly any foraging to do at the convent and—"

Jennie held up her hand. "I understand, Lumen, I do." Her eyes trailed over the ground. "I was a farmer's daughter, so I can help with the land. Not sure what kind of Priestess I'd make. I like sex too much, not that I plan on...you know, setting up shop here."

"Lune doesn't take a vow of chastity," Lumen said, and then glanced out to the Manor. "Just...treat yourself with respect and make your own choices in that regard. Not for Lune's sake. Your own. You have a place here, no matter what."

Jennie smiled, eyes studying Lumen with care. "Is that what you will do, La- Priestess?"

Lumen swallowed. The thought of sex was maybe not the *furthest* thing from her mind, with too many reminders of the act left in the Manor, but it was not a painless thing to think of. She thought over her words to Jennie in regard to herself and then nodded slowly.

"Yes."

Jennie nodded and sighed, rolling her shoulders. "Well. Jones packed my horse with so much supplies, I think it may go bad before the three of us are able to finish it. I'll put it away and come back to help you manage the rest of this."

Lumen stayed standing in place as Jennie dragged the reluctant horse toward the kitchen door. Gideon had sent Jennie with food for them? She grimaced at the warmth in her cheeks and the twist in her belly, and tried to bury the wish that he had brought Jennie himself. Not to stay, but just...

No. Back to work.

No one seemed to know when or why the fighting on the battlefield ended, only that it came to a slow and confused stop, men still armed but backing away from each other slowly with wary gazes.

"What do we do with these ones, General?" one of the younger soldiers asked, dragging along a wounded Oshain soldier by the arm. Gideon frowned at the wound in the young man's side. That was a painful wait for death if they left him to it, and Gideon doubted even Finley could fix him, although he guessed who might succeed. There were others too, in varying states of injury.

"Bring them with us," Dominic said.

Gideon's eyebrows shot up. "We don't take prisoners," he hissed.

"We haven't," Dominic answered under his breath. "But we also used to gain fifty miles in a month."

Gideon didn't comment on that. They hadn't gained fifty miles since the early fall.

"They won't trade land for us," one of the Oshain men rasped, his arm hanging limply from his shoulder. Shit, if Gideon had that injury, Oshain never would've got their hands on *him*, he'd still be fighting.

"Fine," Dominic said. "Take them to Finley."

Gideon waited until the majority of their ranks were taking the short trip back to the village before finding his horse and urging it to Dominic's side.

"What are you doing?" Gideon asked.

"What would you say if I said I didn't want to push north?" Dominic asked.

"I'd say that's seemed obvious since winter. Is it because of her?"

"No." Dominic's grip around the reins tightened and then relaxed slowly. "Not...exactly."

"We can't—"

"I know. I know, Gideon, honestly. I have no intention of forcing her into any further association with me. But what happens if we push north?"

"More will come from the south," Gideon said. He'd worried about the same plenty during the last few weeks. "It's a wonder they haven't already."

Sooner or later, Stalor would send ranks to refresh the old, and the presence of Lumen in her home would raise curiosity and worse for the woman.

"I've been putting them off, saying we're holding a line that allows the others to forge ahead," Dominic muttered. "Eventually, my reputation won't be enough and they will come. And I..."

"Don't want to leave her defenseless," Gideon said.

"It's a piss strategy, completely illogical, and almost certainly impossible," Dominic said, the snap and snarl returning to his tired voice.

Gideon frowned and continued the ride in quiet, trying to think like his friend. Dominic acted with purpose, always, but Gideon wasn't quite as quick as the general and now Dominic wasn't even being predictable.

"Are we taking prisoners, or are you trying to..." he let the words wander off, the idea at the back of his head so ludicrous.

"I haven't decided," Dominic said. "Oshain's grabbed a couple of our men in their time."

"Shit, Dom, where are we going to put them? We don't have a jail."

"Just keep weapons out of their hands and information out of their ears. If they run, they run."

Gideon gaped at the scenery of Oshain as he processed this bizarre twist. Dominic was taking prisoners, and he wanted them left *comfortable*. It wasn't mercy, he knew that much. It was potential for something so strange and far-reaching, Gideon wondered if the poison hadn't gone to Dominic's brain.

"I'll go tell Fin," Gideon said, nudging his horse forward. If he was having trouble wrapping his head around this new turn of events, Sol knew Fin would need it explained backward and forward three times at least.

He rode ahead of the men on the road and right to the inn, tying the reins to a post and hurrying inside.

There was no hot water ready, no bandages or needles clean and waiting, and a sinking weight sat in Gideon's belly as he headed for the stairs.

"Fin!" Silence answered Gideon's thundering steps up to the room where he'd left Fin at dawn. "Brink, get up! Men are coming back." Gideon shouldered open the door and gagged at the dense smokey and sweet smell hanging in the air. "Damnit."

Finley was collapsed in the bed, eyes half-lidded and gaze unfocused, arm hanging limp over the side. Gideon grabbed at his thin cheeks, shaking his head slightly and pinching the skin.

"Wake up, asshole," he growled.

"Fuck'ff."

"You can't do this, Fin," Gideon said, dragging him up by the collar, Finley sagging inside his own shirt, head rolling backward without the strength to hold it up himself. "What do you want, huh? You want to go back to the city and wait for the orders from that bastard missing father of yours, hmm?"

"'M done, Gid. Done with it all," Finley murmured, eyes shutting and trying to wiggle his way out of his own shirt so he could fall back into the bed.

The pipe on the bedside was burnt down, all the resin turned to ash, and given the strength of the smell in the room, it hadn't been nearly long enough since Finley took the drug for him to come downstairs and stitch a man's stomach shut or reset a shoulder.

"Let me go, Gid," Finley muttered.

"That shit won't kill you fast enough," Gideon growled at Finley. He reached down, dragging the tall man out of the bed and up over his shoulder. Finley either didn't care about the treatment or the blood rushing to his head left him unconscious because he didn't make more than a brief kick of complaint. Downstairs, outside the inn, the men were just starting to arrive.

"Put everyone that needs mending in a cart and someone fetch me Rosie," Gideon barked at Philip. He needed to get the patients loaded up and on their way out of town before Dominic realized what he was planning.

"Lumen."

It was the gentle, cautious tone coming from Jennie's usually brash lips that offered the first hint of trouble. Lumen was upstairs in the office, stringing fresh herbs from the ceiling, restocking her mother's coffers of medicines.

"It's...Jones has brought injured men," Jennie said, frowning from the doorway.

Lumen held her breath for a long moment, suddenly dizzy on the chair she was balanced on. "I see. Get water boiling. I'll... I'll see them in the same place as before."

"Yes. I just...it's...they're wearing Oshain colors, just so you know," Jennie said.

Lumen sank quickly to the seat as Jennie disappeared from the doorway. War prisoners? War prisoners and Dominic sent them to *her*? Why? Because he couldn't bother wasting Finley's time on anyone other than his own men?

Fire burned through her, and Lumen scrambled off the chair, snatching up her black robe and dropping it over her head as she made her way out of the office and around the balcony to the stairs. She was working up a good tirade in her head with every step. That she would tend the men, but by no means turn them back over to Dominic or his men. That she should've let him fester with black ore poisoning while she cured everyone else.

Except when she made it out to the front steps, Dominic was nowhere in sight. It was only Gideon and Rosie with a cartful of men in various poor states, including Finley collapsed and unconscious in the midst.

"I'm so sorry," Gideon said immediately as she took a steadying inhale, the heat rushing out from under her skin. "We can turn back."

And there was no fooling sincerity when it came to Gideon, those dark eyes full of apology, wincing slightly with the expectation of refusal.

"No, come in," Lumen said, tossing the speech she'd prepared onto the vanishing fire of her anger and taking a visual inventory of the injuries.

It wasn't until one of the Oshain soldiers, a slightly older man with gray streaks in his beard and skin gray from blood loss, reached for her that she remembered the role High Priestess Wren had bestowed on her with this robe.

"Priestess," he whispered, bending and stiffening with the effort. "Is it my time?"

A New Moon Priestess would visit the bedsides of the dying and sit with them until they passed.

"Not yet, brother," Lumen said, turning and offering her arm for him to lean on.

Jennie was hefting a bucket of steaming water, Colin close at her heels with the rest of the supplies, as Lumen reached the infirmary—no use calling it a dining room now, really, those days were long since gone. Lumen helped the soldier into a chair, found the deep gash on his arm, and gestured for Colin to start cleaning it for her.

"I'll be right back," she told the man. She passed the others on her way back out to the drive, their heads bowing low as they passed, even the one Stalor soldier she recognized. She found Gideon at the cart, frowning down at a prone Finley. "What's his injury?"

"Stupidity," Gideon said. Lumen let out a surprised snort of amusement, and Gideon's gaze turned to her, warm and sweet and teasing. "He doesn't need healing, he needs to sober up."

Lumen hummed and stepped down to join Gideon, tugging Finley's arm up from the cart and sniffing at the sleeve. "That's not tobacco."

"No, sweet spirit. I...I didn't mean to bring him here to be your problem to solve. I just...should he be solved?" Gideon asked.

Lumen watched Gideon's throat bob as he stared down at his friend. Was he asking her to lay judgment on Finley's life and whether or not it was worth saving?

"That's going to be up to him." Gideon sighed and nodded, and Lumen found herself surrendering before she even realized.

"Take him to a room upstairs to sleep it off. I can flush the drug out, but getting through the withdrawals will be messy work."

Gideon's hand rested on her back for a second before he tucked it behind his back and stepped away, throat clearing. "Thank you, Lum- Priestess."

She fought the urge to correct him and forced her steps back to the Manor where the injured were waiting.

THE ARMY HAD TAKEN its cots with them after decamping from the Manor, but there were few enough visiting this time that Lumen simply offered them the remaining beds in the house.

"What do they mean to do with us, Priestess?" one Oshain soldier asked.

"I'll find out. You're under my protection now," she said, fingernails biting her palms as she watched the promise ease the worry on the man's face. He nodded and relaxed, and she left the room, shutting the door behind her.

She paused against the wall, taking a deep breath. Gideon wouldn't bring her these men to help, just so that he and Dominic could torture them, would he? And if that was their intention, could she really live up to the protection she'd just offered? Maybe. She held *some* power over Westbrook, and she would use it if she had to.

Was Dominic trying to put her in an impossible situation? Dangle the safety of innocent men in front of her nose in order to draw her back under his boot heel? He'd be sorely surprised if that was the case.

She found Gideon and Finley in his old room, Gideon stretched out asleep in an armchair with his head propped against the wall. Finley was out too, her own medicines at work, which was good. He would sleep through the night and the ugliness could start in the morning.

Lumen crossed to Gideon and set her fingers down on his arm, the touch flaring old memories to life. She stroked over the muscle and dark hair there, and then held still as Gideon stirred, his eyes opening and searching out her face. The automatic growth of a fond smile made sunlight flicker over his skin, and Lumen pulled away, retreating into her cold.

"What do you have planned for those men?" she asked.

Gideon hummed with thought, the sound like a rocky rattle, and Lumen backed away another step to cool herself against the wall. "I know what it looks like, and I wish I knew for certain the answer. But believe me, sweet spirit, I don't think Dominic has any cruel or violent intentions for those men. My only orders were to make sure they didn't have access to weapons or information."

"Were those your instructions for me too?" Lumen asked, frowning and thinking of how her silver knife had gone missing, how she had never really known anything about Westbrook and his plans for the army.

You could have, she reminded herself. *If you'd cared to.*

"Lumen," Gideon sighed out, and shook his head. "I have no excuses for that, just regrets."

"Why didn't I find something to use against you?" Lumen asked, watching Gideon frown, stare at her. "That's all they wanted from me in Oshain, just some piece of information to use against you. And I never...I never even went looking."

Gideon's hand stretched to her, but waited halfway, inviting her touch without demanding. "Sweet spirit, that's not who you are. Sol and Lune know, if I'd realized what was coming, I would've armed you with the secrets myself. I swear it." The words were choked in his throat, and Lumen's retreat failed, her feet carrying her back to his side, wrapping her arms around his shoulders. His own circled her waist, face tucked to the skin of her neck, breathing her in. "Fuck, I'm so sorry."

"Shh," she murmured. Gideon was all warmth around her, and it was strange and uncomfortable to be embraced again, but a part of her welcomed him. His size and strength, his honest care. It all tangled together like thorns in her chest, painful and sweet and dangerous.

"No, listen," he whispered, pulling away and turning up his face, eyes wet. "I was so greedy to have you, I pretended my pleasure was your own. I put your pain as other's responsibility when I had the power to do something for you. We were wrong from the very start. I wanted to possess you the second I set eyes on you, and I should've protected you instead."

Lumen whined, squeezing her eyes shut against tears and shaking her head as Gideon continued to list his offenses.

"We pushed and demanded and took away your choices."

"Stop," she moaned, as the thorns seemed to twine tighter. "Please stop."

"Lumen," he croaked.

"I know, Gid, believe me. I…I *lived* it and I remember and…" She sighed, and the tension holding her upright crumbled, leaving her sinking over the arm of the chair and into Gideon's lap. It was familiar and safe, but it reminded her of all the other times she'd taken comfort in the same place, and all the horrible reasons why.

"I'm sorry I took too long to do what was right, made you doubt that I would be the man to keep you safe."

She sighed. Her head fell to his shoulder, and that stale and sweet ale scent of him filled her nose. Her skin prickled to be near his again, and it was awful and complicated and lovely.

"I'm not asking to be forgiven," he said.

"You are forgiven, Gideon. And I have my share of blame—"

"No."

"Yes," she said firmly. "I did what I could to hide from you how…how desperate I was to be out of the situation I was in. I should've told you, I knew you were sincere in how you felt. When the silver went missing I just…felt like I'd failed in the single purpose I'd given myself since you all arrived at my door. And so I did something that I knew would anger Westbrook, make him feel like a possession had been stolen out from under him too."

"I don't like to hear you take this on yourself," Gideon said.

Lumen leaned back against the side of the armchair, giving them room to stare at one another. Gideon had collected more scars while she was away, and her fingers itched to map them. He was handsome and ugly all at once, without Finley's refinement and with too much of Dominic's raw power. He was dangerous, not because he would ever let harm come to her again, but because he was capable of thawing at the ice she used to hold her anger and heartbreak at bay.

"Gideon, I..." Her brow furrowed, wondering if anything needed to be said.

"You are a vessel for Lune," Gideon finished for her, echoing the words she'd used in refusal when he'd offered to take her away to somewhere new to begin again. "I know, sweet spirit." He reached up with one hand, stroking warm fingers over her cheek and nodding slowly. "I'm only here to be what you need from me. Nothing more."

Lumen's head sagged on her shoulders, and Gideon leaned in, grazing a kiss over the scars on her cheek. Then he lifted her from the chair and set her on her feet. "Get your rest. He'll sleep through the night."

She nodded, stumbling for the door, aware of every inch of space she put between them. "Call if you need anything." He was only next door to her, and she knew all too well how easily she might hear him.

Lumen stretched in the hall, bones cracking and cold air rinsing over her. There'd be a frost in the morning, but the crops they'd started would withstand a little bout of cold weather. Her fingers dug into her shoulders as she shouldered open the door to her bedroom. She pulled the black robes off, draping them carefully over a chair, and paused, turning her hands over in front of her. Sunlight shimmered on her skin, up her arms. If she had a mirror, she wondered if she would see a bright mark on her cheek where Gideon had kissed her.

The strange shift in her sight and her senses since her night with Lune was something Lumen avoided examining too closely. Lune's touch didn't alter her faith, she'd always believed the Goddess watched over her. It also didn't make her feel worthy, the way High Priestess Wren and the others at the convent seemed to think it should. Lumen had sunk so low to find herself in Lune's embrace, it could hardly be called a blessing.

She rubbed her wrist against her skirt but the smudge of light didn't alter. Fine. She huffed and pulled back the covers of the bed, sliding under and squeezing her eyes shut. At her back, the shadow of heat embraced her, rough, chapped fingers stroking the back of her neck. She rolled to her back and a mirror of Gideon's weight covered her, a throb of interest and pleasure and aching in her core.

"Fuck," Lumen muttered, rolling onto her belly and whimpering.

She could survive craving Gideon. She knew better than to think she could survive surrendering herself again.

Finley arched over the edge of the bedframe, heaving bile into a bucket, and Lumen pretended to examine the sleeve of her robes as she covered her nose.

"You'll stay until you're recovered," she said, the words muffled but not enough to keep Finley from hearing them and glaring at her with bloodshot eyes.

"I'd be recovered if I just had a little—"

"That's not recovered, Healer Brink. That's submission."

He paled, either from her use of the word he'd teased her with or because he was going to be sick again. His back heaved and he sagged. Maybe it was both.

"I'll have a word with Gideon and then bring you some broth." She didn't wait for Finley to answer, he was occupied. She shut the door firmly behind her and then, with a concerning and wicked pleasure, slid a bolt through the handle from the outside to lock him in. That would give him something to get worked up about when he dragged himself out of bed.

Outside on the drive, Gideon was waiting at the cart with the mended Stalor soldiers and a few of the simpler fixes from the Oshain army. Rosie had Lumen's instructions for their care and enough supplies to manage the work as long as no one took a turn for the worse.

"They'll need somewhere dry and warm to sleep," Lumen said.

"And good food to eat," Gideon added, nodding. "I remember your instructions, swee- Priestess."

Lumen swallowed. It didn't feel right for him to use the title when he spoke of her, but she was grateful he didn't use his pet name in front of the soldiers.

"What will you do now that Danvers and Charlie are missing?" Lumen asked.

Rosie twitched on the bench of the cart and stared at Gideon, who scuffed his hand over his mouth and shrugged. "We'll find someone to take their place. Dominic won't call Colin back if that's what you're worried about."

Lumen shook her head. "No, it's only that we've been going through the Manor, and now that it's not a house…I have some more things to sell. I don't know what, if anything, they'll be worth, but it's only to get us to the harvest. Some new chickens and goats."

"Load it," Gideon said, brightening and stepping to her. "I'll take care of it myself."

Lumen smiled and cocked her head. "And if you had to cross the border?"

Gideon grinned. "I'd manage."

Damn him and that mangled grin of his, she thought. If she could've put her heart in a corset she would've, if only to stop it swelling in size every time this man said something foolish and sweet. "I've put too many stitches into you, Gideon Jones, to see you caught. Send someone better at stealth."

"Yes, Priestess," he murmured, bowing briefly. Except Gideon's murmur was a growl of a voice. It was a cloudy, cold day, and still Lumen winced at the glance of sunlight that slashed between them. Gideon fell back at her reaction, clearing his throat and turning back to the cart. "I can take some now, the rest when you're done with Brink?"

She nodded, staring at his back. This was better, it was right for them to feel uncomfortable around one another, wasn't it? "I'll go…get it."

Jennie's lips were twisted on her face, amusement glittering in her eyes as Lumen turned to the door. "We went ahead and brought the best of it out," Jennie said, hefting the two crates of odds and ends under her arms. "Won't get much, but enough to help some."

"I'll make sure you see the most for it," Gideon said, brushing past Lumen and taking the two boxes Jennie held with ease.

"Here's some silver to cover any difference. Thank you, Gideon," Lumen said, handing over a few of High Priestess Wren's coins. "We'll do what we can for Healer Brink."

Jennie retreated back into the Manor, and the cart was full of the soldiers ready to be moved. She and Gideon weren't alone as he approached her on the stairs, but they might as well have been.

"It's not your responsibility to save him, sweet spirit," Gideon said, soft enough to keep the words between them. "I know that. And if you don't want him here, I'll gladly drag him back."

"He'll decide for himself if he wants to recover," Lumen said. "I'll do what I can to convince him that's worth the trouble."

"If he becomes a burden or he…makes things difficult for you, send him packing," Gideon said, eyes sliding over her shoulder with wary concern creasing the corners.

Her hand skimmed his shoulder before she'd given herself permission to touch, and her fingertips came back infused with heat. "I'll manage, Gideon."

His throat worked as he swallowed, gaze drinking her in, face uncommonly serious. "I'll see you in a few days."

Lumen nodded, lips pressed together. Gideon was too easy to adore. It made him horribly dangerous.

"You *what*?" Dominic hissed, eyes wide.

"I left Finley with her," Gideon said, rolling his shoulders.

He'd expected this response, wondered at his own decision to take Finley to Lumen. He'd meant what he said to her. It wasn't Lumen's responsibility to fix the idiot, not even as a Priestess. It was just that if anyone could judge whether or not Finley could heal, or should heal, it would be Lumen. She was stunning in strength, even if it wasn't a breed he'd ever known before.

"Are you...Sol's Fire, Gideon, why on earth would you drop him in her lap like that? After everything- after all- we *cannot* keep throwing our weight and problems at her, man!" Dominic roared, arms exploding at his sides, palms slamming to the top of his desk.

"I agree," Gideon said, helping himself to a chair he was never offered.

Dominic panted down at the tabletop. "You agree. You *agree,* and yet you did it anyway?"

"Is there any of the shit left here he can get his hands on when he gets back?" Gideon asked, ignoring Dominic's temper for the moment.

Dominic sighed and sagged into his chair. "Not that I can find. Danvers and Charlie are buried, so I'll make sure no one gets Fin any more."

"Good."

Dominic grunted and glared at him from across the table. A candle sat on the surface, and even though it was cold in the room, Dominic hadn't bothered with a fire. "I want us to be out of her life," he said.

"Then push north," Gideon answered, watching as Dominic flinched. "You want that for her, but not for yourself. For yourself, you want to give back what you took from her. What *we* took from her as if it might take back her anger and sorrow. But we're poor as shit. We can't buy all the books and furniture and art back, and she's making the place a temple, so she doesn't want it anyway."

"What do I do?" Dominic asked, thumbnail scratching at the scar on his cheek.

"She wants chickens and goats. She wants to farm her land. She doesn't want you to hurt those men from Oshain. And I think she wants... wants to be left as is," Gideon said slowly. He'd held her, touched her, even had a brief taste of her cheek left on his lips after she'd left the room the night before. But he hadn't missed the little glimmers of fear on her face, and the twinges of pain in her eyes when he moved in her direction. Seeing those felt like turning his sword on himself, but worse because it had been her to suffer.

"I have no expectation," Dominic said, barely audible, eyes on the flicker of the candle.

"Good," Gideon said. He had no expectation, but he was ashamed to admit that he had a *wish*, however foolish and unfair it was to Lumen.

"If Finley causes her a single moment of trouble..." Dominic growled, knuckles white around the arm of the chair.

Gideon nodded. "I know."

"OH, just give up won't you!" Lumen snarled at the man.

She was at her wits end on tending Finley, and if she wasn't sure the worst would be over by the next day, she'd gladly toss him out into the night.

"Let me out, Lumen!" Finley hissed, lunging in her direction. He always stopped before reaching her, even in the height of the mania of craving. Desperation was clear on his face, sweat forming on his brow as his body shivered and ached for a lungful of the numbing smoke.

"Priestess," she spat back, just because it made him flinch.

"They'll have thrown out all I had by now, just let me go back to the village," Finley moaned, teetering in the center of the room. If he fell to the floor she *would not* catch him. Let him whine over the bruises.

"They'll have thrown out everything they could find," Lumen agreed, trying to resist the urge to press herself to the door. He could pin her there. He hadn't turned on her yet, but it might only be a matter of time. "I'm sure you had stashes."

Finley rolled his eyes and shook his head, body sagging. *Here we go*, she thought. Finley in a temper was one trial. It was when he became maudlin she really lost her patience.

"You of all people should leave me to my own destruction,"

Finley whispered, stumbling back to the bed, landing with a wheeze of breath. "After everything I put you through."

"Fuck you," Lumen said, and Finley's head shot up. "Oh, you should see your face right now. *Offended*. You're offended that I'd call you out on this horseshit? Don't you dare take my emotions and use them as your excuse to poison yourself, to waste a perfectly adequate mind that might be used to *help* others and instead apply it to the best way of doing nothing with your life!"

"Adequate?" Finley scoffed.

"The only thing wrong with you is your absolute self-involvement," Lumen continued, shoulders squaring and chin lifting. "You aren't cruel, you aren't sick, and you aren't even really a coward, you're just more concerned with how things turn out for *you* than others."

"I left for you!"

"Liar!" Lumen cried. Thank Lune they'd put the Oshain soldiers on the other side of the Manor although even that might not be enough to mute this argument. "You left because staying meant you might have to face me being angry at you, or possibly revealing yourself as being a complete and utter shit if Dominic told you to quit me—"

Finley rose to his feet, voice rising and red flushing through his cheeks. "I wouldn't have done it!"

"But you did do it! You walked out without a word or an excuse! I even know why you came with the others to pull me out of the cell."

"Lumen," he pleaded, head shaking and tears filling the edges of his eyes.

No. There was no stopping her now. She'd put up with Finley's moans, his bitterness, his childlike whining. As bad as she'd known the withdrawals would be, they were infinitely worse when fueled by his self-pity.

"You decided you preferred how things were. Better to have me in your bed than out of it, best to go and fetch me out of that prison I'd landed myself in before I wasn't any good for the pleasure!"

There was satisfaction in watching him freeze, the horror plain on his face, the knowledge that he was wondering if these horrible accusations were true about himself. Unfortunately, it also happened to leave Lumen's throat raw and swollen, her heart pounding too fast in her veins, and her stomach clenching as though it was turning to stone. There was an impulse to apologize, retract the words. They were designed to cut him, and that had never been a role she relished.

"You have your demons, Finley," she said, the fire she hated finally cooling on her skin. "I see them. I've met a fair share of my own, believe me. But the only thing you're doing with that drug you're smoking is giving them a meal to feed on."

"Lumen...you—" His voice cracked and faltered. He stepped back, turning aimlessly in the room. "I can't face myself. I thought it would be better if...now that you're back, if I just wasn't here anymore."

"Why? So your army can send me more men to manage and heal?" Lumen asked, folding her arms over her chest.

Finley frowned and stumbled over to the bed. "Fuck."

Lumen pressed her lips tight and waited to see what direction his mood turned next. Angry, and she would leave him as she found him, yelling and pounding at the door. Sorry for himself, and she...would probably leave then too as well.

Instead, he seemed to settle, head tipping up to stare across the bedroom at her. "What do I do?"

They watched each other for a long stretch of quiet.

"Stay well," Lumen said. "Do the work you know. Quit trying to destroy yourself for every mistake you make, and endeavor to make fewer."

Finley huffed and fell forward, palms catching his face at the last moment. He groaned, the sound strangled behind his hands.

"You might always want to vanish," Lumen said. "That's not a symptom we can treat."

"It comes in waves," he said.

Lumen swallowed, her arms sliding down to her stomach to hold herself back from crossing to Finley. He would have to live with himself, she was not a cure to what plagued him.

"Try to learn to swim," she said, and he huffed although it sounded more like a laugh than a scoff. "I'm sorry, Finley."

"No, don't say that. Whatever was said…" He sighed, heavy and weary. The fight was gone from the room, and Lumen wanted to escape more badly now than she had when they were screaming. "You're right. Enough. I'll…tomorrow, can I help you with the men?"

There wasn't much left to do for the remaining patients, aside from keep wounds clean and wrapped, but she knew how well occupation kept her head out of painful thinking. "Of course," she said. At the very least, giving him the work would give her some of her time to get back to the garden and the fields. "Try to sleep for now."

He huffed and shook his head.

"I can make some tea," she offered. *Just leave*, she thought.

His smile was half-hearted, and he shook his head again. "Nothing ever worked better than…" His eyes landed on her hands at her sides, and Lumen remembered his head in her lap and the fine and silky texture of his hair running through her fingers. She tucked them behind her back, and he twisted away from her on the bed. "I'll feign sleep at the very least," he said.

She nodded and backed her way out of the room, holding the door shut in front of her as she caught her breath in the hall. For a moment, she debated locking it from the outside. Did she hesitate over showing a lack of faith in Finley or was she considering leaving it open so he might leave in the night? She slid the bolt in place as quietly as she could and hovered in the hall. If he started howling again, she didn't want to be in the room next door, forced to listen.

Lumen snuck back downstairs, heading for the kitchen where she could work or fall asleep at the table. Nearly there, the sound of soft weeping bounced against the stone and reached her ears. She tiptoed the rest of the way, eyes growing wide as she found Jennie hunched over the table, shoulders shaking with muffled crying. Lumen's foot scuffed against the floor in her approach, and Jennie flinched but didn't look up.

"What is it?" Lumen asked, reaching the woman, hand

hovering over her back before committing to the touch, stroking down Jennie's spine and back up again. She knelt at her side.

"It's nothing, Lady," Jennie whispered. "Nothing new, just the aches of life rising up."

It comes in waves.

"You know what hurt men can give," Jennie said, exhaling in a shaky sigh. "I can never decide if it is a comfort to think that is simply how things are, or if I have just been very unlucky. Men want girls like you."

Lumen stiffened in place, the accusation stinging in her ears, but when Jennie glanced at her, it wasn't with anger.

"Fine ladies," Jennie murmured. "They think you are different than farmer's daughters, and that by having you, they'll make themselves greater than the men they were born as."

"You are every bit as fine as me," Lumen said, relieved when Jennie nodded.

"I would've made a very bad wife," she admitted with a snort. "But I am worth loving."

Lumen lurched up, and Jennie caught her, their arms knotting tightly around one another, breaths bound in their chests.

"I hate to cry over worthless men like Danvers and Charlie, but sometimes it can't be helped," Jennie said, half-shrugging in Lumen's embrace. "Tell me something, Lady, do you wear this because of them?" She tugged on the sleeve of Lumen's robe and leaned back.

Lumen frowned. "No! I… I suppose they were a part of the path that brought me here. But my life has been in a phase of waning ever since I was a girl. My family dying, my country withering. Westbrook…Brink, and—" She couldn't say Gideon's name. He had contributed, but not knowingly, and she'd meant it when she told him he was forgiven. "I don't excuse them, but I see the cycle my life has been laid out in. I *am* the New Moon Priestess." Every day it was a little easier to say, an identity more familiar to wear. She knew darkness, and she could do her part to shelter others. Lune had chosen her for her ability to continue giving even when she had nothing, and while Lumen didn't always relish the role, she didn't wish it on another either.

"What makes you her, milady?" Jennie asked, frowning, eyeing Lumen with her sharp stare. "The New Moon is a dark and fearful night we all wish to end. I may not know much about Sol or Lune, but hours of terror just don't sound like you."

"The point of the new moon isn't to be afraid or to fear that dark will last forever. It's knowing that it can't, and waiting together for light to return," Lumen said, certain and simple. "It's faith."

Jennie hummed, and her smile was sly. "Ah. I see. That sounds right then." She leaned forward and dropped a kiss against Lumen's forehead. "Goodnight, Priestess."

Lumen remained kneeling, wondering how Jennie had tricked her into optimism, for long minutes after Jennie left the kitchen.

8

LUMEN WOKE WITH A SMILE ON HER LIPS AND A SMALL FINGER tapping down the length of her nose.

"Pest," she mumbled.

"Gideon is coming up the road with another cart and men, Lady," Colin answered.

Lumen groaned and sat up in bed. She was still in her dress from the day before and overdue for a change of clothes. She'd kept her black robes on while the soldiers and Finley were in residence, but it was starting to turn warm during the days, and the added layer left her itchy and hot by evening.

"More injured?" she asked.

"Couldn't tell. Definitely goats though," Colin said. "Here, I made these."

He placed a warm soft roll in her open palm, and Lumen beamed at the boy. "You remembered?"

"Jennie helped," he admitted. "She's up in the garden."

"All right. I'm up too. Go and tell Finley to check on the men in their rooms, and I'll change and go down to meet Gideon."

"We're letting the ass out of the stall today?" Colin asked.

He leaped from the bed as Lumen lunged to tweak his nose. "Don't talk like that!" she said, but she was laughing, and he left the room proud of himself.

She gritted her teeth as she undressed, avoiding the sight of herself in the mirror and splashing cold water from the basin over her skin. By a strange and forgotten habit, Lumen opened her dresser and paused. There were her things, shifts and jumpers and gowns. Dominic had sold off her mother's clothing at the very start but not...

She swallowed hard and grabbed a clean shift and a simple dress from when she was younger. It was a little short, but it fit closer around her lean frame now than her old things. She'd round out when the harvest came, but until then this would suit and no one would see the awkwardly high hem from under her Priestess robes.

By the time she made it downstairs, the activity had moved to the back gardens and fields. She reached the yard, marveling at the men who were surveying the field before finding Gideon wrestling a goat who had its teeth caught in his sleeve. A bright laugh burst from her lips and Gideon looked up, eyes on her immediately. He grinned, and the goat yanked a patch of muslin free and ran toward the water with it.

"You brought the men back?" she asked, and he glanced over his shoulder at the men by the fields.

"Most of them. Ones who wanted to come."

"And the others?" she asked, wary of the answer.

"They're at camp. Not being harmed or nothing, it's just... after what happened to you when you crossed the border, none of us are sure what those soldiers will see. These men here lost their homes during the war. No families amongst them now, so..."

Lumen stared at Gideon, and then past him to the soldiers. "What, are you...giving them to me?" she asked, horror lifting her voice an octave.

Gideon snorted. "No, sweet spirit. Well, we gave them the option to come and help, and they accepted. If the estate can use men..."

She covered her face with her hand and tried to breathe through the dizzy spell. There were houses, although she wasn't sure what kind of state they were in now. Having someone other than Jennie and Colin to farm with her...did she really think she could manage all those acres herself?

"Yes, all right. The Ramsey's cottage, and Sarah Blythe's, those must remain open for now," Lumen said.

Gideon hummed and nodded, moving to her side and looking out over the fields with her. "Ramsey's got herself a couple sweethearts from our ranks. She could probably move back, bring their help with her." At Lumen's startled look, Gideon ducked his head. "We kept an ear on it, she wasn't pushed. The men helped her with the little ones through the end of winter is all. They're good folk, or I would've stepped in on her behalf for you."

"I'm not a Lady now, Gideon. These men won't be my tenants," Lumen murmured.

"But you will be their Priestess," Gideon said, turning to face her. Lumen's cheeks grew hot where his eyes fastened to her skin.

"I have no power to refuse them if they want the land," she said. The choice wasn't hers now that her only claim on the land was as Priestess in the temple.

"Yes you do," Gideon whispered, head dipping. "They would listen. *I* will listen. This isn't a bribe, Lumen."

She sighed and nodded. "Then yes, it would help to have them here. What happens if Stalor sends more men?"

"Let Dominic and I worry about that for now," Gideon answered. "Where are the tools? What needs doing?"

⁂

"How many ways are there to eat eggs?" Colin asked, lifting a forkful to his mouth, still steaming.

Jennie and Lumen smiled at one another over the table.

"Enough for you to get sick of having them," Jennie said, grinning at Colin's scoff.

Gideon had brought them back four laying hens. Lumen was considering spending the silver on a rooster too, now that some of the Oshain soldiers and the last of her former tenants had returned. They could give chicks away when they hatched, eventually even have enough chickens for meat. For now, there were eggs at breakfast, and soon there'd be goat's cheese to spread on toast.

Was this the slow brightening from the dark place of her life, Lumen wondered? Was her path in life now waxing? She'd turned Jennie's teasing tone over in her head and picked at its possible meanings, too afraid to ask.

"We can pick wild onions in the woods today, cut them up and bake them in a pie with eggs and mushrooms," Lumen said.

"Could we get a cow, you think?" Jennie murmured, eyes drifting out the back kitchen door to watch the goats graze. "Is it unholy to wish for butter?"

Lumen groaned softly at the mere thought. "Perhaps, but we'll have to risk it."

"Never had it," Colin said.

Lumen draped her arm around his shoulders and rested her cheek briefly on the top of his head. "It will take us a while, I think, but we'll make a goal of it."

"Is gardening and healing all a Priestess really does, Lady?" Colin asked.

"Hmm...well, today a Priestess will wash the linens and spend some time in prayer," Lumen said. "And gardening. We're all out of patients, I'm afraid. Jennie, would you go and check on Gretchen Ramsey?"

The woman had moved back with her children and two soldiers in tow just a couple days after Gideon mentioned the idea. Lumen believed Gideon when he said he trusted the men who'd worked their way into Widow Ramsey's life, but she trusted Jennie to see to the truth of any relationship, just to be sure.

"Can I go with her and visit the enemy soldiers?" Colin asked.

Lumen choked on a bite of egg, and Colin beat her back until she could speak. "You may, but please don't call them that."

"Make yourself useful, don't just gawk," Jennie added.

Colin finished his plate, lifting it to his mouth to shovel the last bites in as Lumen stared and Jennie howled and swatted across the table at him.

"Little beast," Jennie murmured as Colin jumped up and ran from the table.

"I'll go check on the goats!" he called.

"You are a goat!" Jennie answered.

"Baaaah!"

Lumen laughed, dropping her fork to the table and clutching over her heart as the belly heaving bright cries of laughter burst free.

Jennie grinned and waited for Lumen's last giggles to dissolve. "I can do the laundry if you'd prefer."

Lumen shook her head and returned to her plate. "You're not the maid, Jennie. It's a bright day out, you and Colin should soak up the sun."

"And you shouldn't?"

Lumen's nose wrinkled. "Sunlight and I don't get along as we used to. It hurts my eyes now." She didn't notice the silence until she looked up to find Jennie frowning and studying her.

"She really changed you, didn't she?" Jennie asked.

Lumen swallowed and nodded briefly.

"Colin and I will visit the others then. And we can manage to care for the plants. Take some time for yourself, in prayer if that's how you like it."

"Thank you, Jennie."

FINLEY PICKED at the ends of his fingers and paced the length of the bar. He stopped as Dominic emerged from his office room at the back of the inn.

"Well?" Finley asked.

Dominic frowned at him. "We've been idle too long if all you can do is pace."

"Of course we've been idle too long!" Finley snapped. "You know we have. And if I can't smother the boredom in smoke, and there's nothing for me to do with my hands—"

"Stalor has decided we need more men to push ahead," Dominic said. "They're sending a battalion to be absorbed into our company. One with a proper lieutenant to replace Gideon."

Gideon—sitting peacefully in the corner, sipping a pint of ale —looked up from his cup with an arched eyebrow, the recent scar on his jaw shining in the sunlight.

"S'pose I expected that," Gideon said with a shrug, but his eyes narrowed. "And Lumen's Manor?"

"They want to camp there. They assume we left it empty."

Finley sucked in a sharp breath. There, this was what he'd been afraid of. "We should have urged her back to the convent. We still could!"

"And all the men who've just made their homes on the land?" Gideon asked.

"I don't give a fuck about those men!" Finley shouted, gaze glaring at his friend.

"But she will," Dominic said, sitting down across from Gideon, leaning back in the chair. He combed his hair back with his fingers and let his head fall, eyes shutting.

Finley's steps finally paused. They were right. It would matter to Lumen what might happen to those soldiers. "We've burdened her again," he said.

Gideon frowned, thumb wiping up a drip of ale from the rim of his cup. At least neither he nor Dominic attempted to disagree.

"You asked me what I thought I was doing by keeping those men," Dominic said, looking to Gideon, his voice low even though they were alone in the bar. Finley crossed and fell into the open chair at the table.

"You wanted her to have soldiers," Gideon said, shrugging. "Men who would fight for her. *Could* fight for her."

Finley startled and glanced to Dominic, who was nodding slowly. "Lumen is hardly a general," Finley said.

"And that number of men is hardly an army," Dominic agreed. He groaned and straightened, rolling his shoulders. "Fine. I will say this to the two of you, and you can tell me I'm mad and we'll sort ourselves from there." He met Finley's eyes first, who had no idea how to respond without knowing what was coming, and then to Gideon who nodded, and had a look of understanding as if he somehow knew *exactly* what was coming. How much had Finley missed with his head in a cloud of smoke?

"I don't want to fight this war any longer," Dominic said. "Not for Stalor."

Finley braced himself against the back of the chair, hands pressed to the surface for the table. "Oshain?" he asked, even though the very thought was ludicrous.

Dominic scoffed and rolled his eyes. "No. Of course not. Tell me what she wants, Gideon."

Finley looked back and forth between the two men, lost in the thread of the conversation, the strange and impossible direction of their thoughts.

"She wants the war to end," Gideon said simply.

"Dominic," Finley whispered, disbelief on his tongue.

Dominic ignored him. "Gideon, ask the men if any would be willing to fight their own people. Tell them they can leave our ranks if they'd rather not. Or wait to see if we are insane. But if they're willing, you'll ride with them *south* of the Manor, temple, whatever she wants it to be. Take the men who've settled there with you, if they'll go. I don't care if you kill the soldiers or send them back to report to the Commanders, my orders are to keep Stalor from rising to Lumen's door again."

"Dominic this is insane," Finley said. "Stalor has already crossed that line. *We* saw to that."

Dominic nodded and scratched at the short crop of his beard. "East and West of here, I know."

"We'll have them beating at our door," Gideon said, not in warning but as if he were mulling it over. "Oshain too, eventually."

"But not all at once," Dominic said.

Finley gaped at them. "You're likely to land yourself in a bloodbath."

"Who is Stalor sending?" Gideon asked, head tipping.

"Victor Cantalion," Dominic said, flipping on the letter and reading from the page.

Finley's gaping shock stuttered to a stop at the familiar name.

Frost cold rushed through him, freezing all the nervous panic and worrying and replacing it with horror. "What? Let me see that."

Dominic passed him the letter, and Finley read through the carefully worded expressions of doubt and mistrust laid out. They were sending a new lieutenant to keep Dominic in line and on task. But...there it was. Victor Cantalion.

"He trained me for the army in battlefield medicine," Finley said brow furrowing.

"You know him," Dominic said, leaning forward.

"He introduced me to opium," Finley mused. Professor Cantalion had been the first person to pass Finley a pipe, after finding him experimenting with some of the medicines that made hearts race back to life. When Finley collapsed in the haze of the drug, Cantalion helped himself to a lazy and thorough violation of Finley's limp form.

"He's the one?" Gideon asked, the question loaded with Finley's full experience, not just the drug use. He growled softly at Finley's nod.

Finley wasn't certain if he was relieved or not to hear the man had been removed from his position over students or concerned he was now placed in a position of power over soldiers. "Why on earth would he be a general?"

"He's not," Dominic said. "See? No title. Army is scraping the bottom of the barrel these days. They send us out, but not enough men return home. I'm sure they promised him better pay and a role off the front lines if he managed me back into usefulness."

Finley swallowed and folded the pages, fingers spread over their surface, eyes still seeing the words written there. "What happens to the soldiers if you take their leader?"

"They'll fight," Gideon said with a shrug. "Or, I suppose, if they're confused about what side we're on, they might surrender."

Finley looked up and met Dominic's calculating gaze, a strategy deeper than 'Protect Lumen' finally turning gears in his head.

"How many extra uniforms do we have?" Dominic asked.

"A few," Finley said. "Formerly belonging to dead men."

"Give them to the Oshain men," Dominic said, and Gideon nodded. "Fight who you have to. Absorb the rest." Dominic pushed back from the table and stood straight. He didn't look hopeful to Finley's eyes, but there was determination there, and enough intelligence to tie his tongue of any further accusations of insanity. "I am the best Stalor general in three generations. Gideon, you are the most terrifying force of any army on the continent. If that doesn't inspire enough boys and broken men serving under a drug-addled abuser to surrender, we were never going to survive this war."

Gideon waited until Dominic left the bar, heading out into the street, a warm breeze snaking in through the door. "Not his *best* speech," Gideon said, eyebrows waggling.

It was never his intention to see her before the battle, but Finley kept grousing that they ought to at least *warn* Lumen for once. Dominic had no intention of another Stalor soldier setting foot on her doorstep—not any that hadn't already, at least—not to his last breath, but he supposed it was a possibility they would fail. It had happened, if only a handful of times, and this was one of their stranger missions.

"What do you mean, you're taking the men to fight, south of here?" Lumen asked, eyes widening. "When? Why? Who on earth would you be fighting in the south?"

They were alone together although Dominic thought he could see Jennie and Colin's face peeking out of windows every so often. The sun was setting behind the building, out beyond the woods, and Lumen was bundled in her black robes, face just visible beneath the hood. He was trying not to stare. She was not traditionally beautiful, or he had not realized her appeal the first time he'd seen her, but now she was *precious* to him and his gaze coveted the sight of her.

"Stalor."

Lumen drew her breath in as if she thought it might be her last, slow and deep, her lips parted in shock. "I don't understand. You're not fighting for Oshain," she said, a statement of fact rather than a question.

"No," he said, fighting the urge to scuff his boots against the ground and shy from her fierce stare.

"Dominic, if you do this…" Her eyes narrowed and her head tilted, silken blonde strands of hair falling loose from beneath her hood. "What kind of army will you be?"

Yours, he thought. He grunted and shrugged in answer, trying not to smirk as he imagined Lumen's response to his unspoken thought. Would she scoff and berate him, or simply bury that silver dagger of hers in his gut at last?

"You may see the men passing, nothing more," Dominic said. Finley would have to make do tending the sick.

Lumen's eyes narrowed. "And if they're slaughtered?"

His teeth gritted. One of these days he was going to break them completely. "Gideon will send someone to warn you. You should leave, back to the convent."

She raised her hand to cover her eyes, white fingertips peeking out from the heavy sleeve of her robes. His worst fear was that she would refuse, try to stand her ground again. If what Finley said about Cantalion was true—he knew it was, Finley only lied to himself—Dominic would make himself sick thinking of the man reaching her. But Gideon had his orders. Cantalion was to die first, and hopefully tidily without many more casualties.

"You keep saying 'them,'" Lumen said, lowering her hand.

"There's a chance Oshain has eyes on the village and might try to seize an opportunity. Gideon and I agreed I would stay with the rest of the men, in case."

Lumen stroked her fingers over her bottom lip, and Dominic fought every muscle in his body that demanded he stride to her, replace her touch with his own, with a kiss, some distraction from the worry now plaguing her. Damn Finley for talking him into coming. He should've sent Gideon instead.

"This is because I came back," she said.

"This is because I haven't moved my army in nearly a year," he said. They were both right, but he'd rather the blame rested on him.

Her chin turned away, eyes slanting to him, and desire punched him in the gut better than Lumen could land a knife any day. He missed that look, suspicious and wary, trying to make out his intentions.

"Tell Gideon to bring the wounded to me when they are done," Lumen said. Dominic started to shake his head, and she glared at him. "Don't argue. You can't ask them to ride forty miles or more back to the village before Finley can tend to anyone, and if he does it in a field they'll all die anyway. They come here."

His lips formed a smile, and she huffed and turned away.

"You've lost your mind, General," she bit over her shoulder.

You've got your spirit back, he thought. He turned back to his horse. It was late, and she hadn't offered *him* a place to stay for the night, but it was warm enough. He could camp in a field on the way back and send Gideon down to meet Cantalion's men by tomorrow evening.

LUMEN NEVER SAW Gideon and the men leaving, but she stood in the orchard listening to their calls to one another, the horse hooves beating against the road. She kept her back pressed to a tree, resisting the urge to turn and seek them out, stare at the faces of the men who walked willingly towards treason or something worse.

And if they failed?

If they failed, that would mean Gideon was dead. Lumen could not imagine a world where he would surrender, and she knew with a strange clarity that he wouldn't let another army from Oshain or Stalor reach her.

"Speed it up, lads!"

Lumen squeezed her eyes shut, pressing her head hard against the trunk of the tree at her back, nails biting her palms at the sound of Gideon's voice.

"Oh! I beg your pardon La- Priestess."

"Gretchen," Lumen said, catching her breath and opening her eyes to discover Widow Ramsey, arms and hands full with her children.

"Are you going to see them off?" Gretchen asked, eyes flicking over their shoulders.

Lumen swallowed and shook her head. The desire was there, but she was afraid if she got one good look of Gideon, or worse, a smile from him, she would do her best to drag him back to the temple.

"Are you afraid for them?" Lumen asked.

Gretchen glanced at her children, but the older of the two was hunting for treasures in the grass. "Yes," she said.

"It's madness," Lumen breathed, shaking her head.

"Is it? To go to battle for peace?" Gretchen was watching her as Lumen looked back.

"Is that what it's for?"

"It is for my men," Gretchen said with a shrug. "And I think others go to protect each other, the men who've been at their sides since conscription. Oshain doesn't care about us. Stalor doesn't care about the men they've sent, either. Did anyone ever send your mother any comfort for all the sons she surrendered? Her own husband?"

Lumen sighed, heard Gideon's laugh growing fainter, and shook her head.

"I'm afraid, but for the first time, I've heard of a battle that doesn't sound entirely useless. I would go and watch it if I could. I would carry a sword too, if I knew how." Gretchen Ramsey was strong, even in her expression, and Lumen took a deep breath and used the other woman as a mirror, squaring her shoulders and standing straight from the tree.

"I can take the children back with me," Lumen offered. "Colin will play with them while we wait for your return."

Gretchen hesitated, staring toward the road, before sighing. "I promised Zeb I would pack to run, in case they didn't succeed. Thank you though, Priestess."

All the comfort Lumen had drawn from the conversation vanished at the reminder that there was a chance this fatal plan might fail. She would return to the temple and ready the infirmary until she was too exhausted to stand. And then all that would be left to do was wait.

"WHY DON'T you go to the temple and wait for us there?" Gideon asked, eyes laughing.

Finley ignored him, rolling his head on his shoulders, wincing at the crack of his neck. It did that every time now, and every time the sound surprised him.

"May not even be any fighting," Gideon said, shrugging. "Might just see me and surrender."

Some of the men they sat around the fire with laughed and cheered at the idea. Finley knew better. There would be fighting. Strangely, for once, he looked forward to it. Gideon watched him as Finley stood again, pacing around the ring of men.

"Though…" Gideon continued, watching with understanding, "I have a mind to let our healer get his blade wet."

Men cheered again and laughed, but Finley paused in his pacing, staring through the flames at the challenge of Gideon's arched eyebrow.

"I wouldn't mind," Finley said, and the laughter hushed.

"Who do you want?" Gideon asked, even though he knew perfectly well what the answer would be.

"Their leader," Finley said, and one man choked on his beer. Finley grinned at Gideon, eyes narrowed, and admitted, "But I might need your help."

"Gladly," Gideon said, dipping his head.

"Don't know as a Priestess is likely to be too wooed by killing, Healer Brink," said Philip, smile nervous and shaking, as if he expected retribution for the teasing.

It came, but not from Finley. "She's not a prize," Gideon barked, and the young man's eyes dropped to his hands.

"You're right though," Finley offered the man. "She wouldn't. This one's for my own pleasure."

Or his peace of mind at least. Finley wasn't interested in the revenge of the act, but he wanted to be damn sure Victor Cantalion never made it within five miles of Lumen. He was moving again, without realizing, circling the group. Gideon's hand flashed out, nearly tripping him, but Finley stumbled and steadied himself, taking Gideon's hand and pulling the heavy man up.

"You'll make them anxious," Gideon murmured. "Come, let's train a bit. Burn your energy."

"Won't I need it for the fighting?" Finley asked.

"In my experience, terror keeps you moving well enough," Gideon said gravely.

Finley wondered what Gideon even remembered of terror, he'd been fearless in battle for almost as long as they'd known one another, an animal of strength and rage. But that wasn't even half the time he and Dominic had been together in the wars, so maybe Gideon did have a history with fear.

"It won't be noble fighting if I help you kill him," Gideon warned. "We'll have to be sly."

"I don't care," Finley said.

Gideon nodded. "Good, then neither do I."

They worked together, Finley gradually improving, blocking with more success, until exhaustion turned the tables. It was enough activity to help him sleep, even as his chest heaved, still catching his breath. The sleep was fitful, thoughts of Cantalion drawing up the memories that smoke would've buried. Hands on his skin, under his clothes, unwelcome arousal and the betrayal of his own body under someone else's mastery.

Gideon shook him awake at dawn, dodging Finley's flailing arm. The sky overhead was pink and smeared with purple, and the men were smothering the coals of the fire.

"They're a mile away now. Stretch and be ready for fighting," Gideon murmured.

Finley scrambled off the ground. "Do we eat?"

"Not unless you want to throw it up, Healer," one of the men from Oshain said.

True. As Finley stared across the field at the small shadow of approaching men, his stomach gave its first jerk. Cantalion was in that crowd, and Finley had declared he wanted to be the one to kill him. It was still true, but he wished it was already over.

"Do we march to meet them, sir?" Philip asked.

Gideon jerked and stared at the young man, amusement quirking his lips at the deference. "No. Let them wonder why we're here and save ourselves the breath for fighting." To Finley, he leaned in and added, "Reserve your energy if you can resist pacing."

Finley held his breath. They only had two dozen men, and it looked as though twice that many were on their way. *Gideon's good for at least ten of them*, he reminded himself. As long as Finley didn't make himself into a distraction, they would win. Maybe it would be due to confusion, or acceptance, but they would be the victors in some way. Gideon would dispatch Cantalion himself if Finley couldn't manage it.

Manage it, Finley commanded himself. *Take this back. Keep Lumen out of his reach.* Her vulnerability brought Finley to his knees. To a man like Cantalion, it would be something to manipulate.

The wait was agonizing, watching the shadows of soldiers grow as their own small company shifted restlessly in unit. Finley had never stood at the front lines before, always waiting at the back for those who needed immediate mending or a merciful end. The sun was rising at his back, sending mist up from the grass. How long would they fight? Would it be quick and simple or would they have to take every life before them?

"Breathe," Gideon whispered, nudging his shoulder.

Cantalion was at the back. Finley didn't see him until a man stumbled at the front, exhaustion gray on his face. Good. They were weak with travel, and it would make the task easier one way or another.

Cantalion was old. That was the first thing Finley noticed. He was old and stooped on the back of his horse, the only horse of the whole party. His black hair was thin on top of his head, skin red from days of marching up from the south. He smirked as he found Finley, who wondered if it felt worse to be remembered.

"Ah. Familiar faces, finally," Cantalion croaked. He looked around the empty field. "Not the village you wrote to our leaders about."

"That'd be another sixty miles north," Gideon lied. "But you won't see it."

Cantalion continued forward, his men breaking to the sides to let him through. His watery amber eyes flickered over Finley for every handful of men he glanced at. "Did you think we needed an escort for sixty miles?"

Finley's fingers were stiff and frozen around the hilt of his sword at his waist. Gideon's body was loose and easy, stance almost friendly if it weren't for the fact that he blocked a third of the road behind them with his size alone.

"You'll surrender here," Gideon said. "This is where Stalor ends. You step beyond it under *my* instruction, but it won't be for Stalor. Not Oshain either. The leaders of these lands have stolen enough from the men and women who feed their coffers. How many of you even have homes left to return to, if Stalor would ever let you rest? Today won't be our last battle, but it can be your last march if you turn your back on the country that turned its back on you decades ago."

Cantalion barked a laugh, eyes widening, looking over the line of men who faced him. He glanced at his own troops whose brows folded. Some looked worried, others baffled.

"You're an army without country?" Cantalion asked. He frowned, and his eyes narrowed. "Where's your general? Has Westbrook let his men run mad?"

"Westbrook watches the north," Gideon said. He stepped forward, and a few of Cantalion's men stumbled back. His voice lowered to a growl, carrying around the small party of men standing still in a field on a quiet, mild morning. "My speech was for your men. You won't be granted the luxury of surrender. My orders are to see you dead."

"Is this a joke?" Cantalion asked. Finley wondered why he didn't look scared yet. If Gideon came growling and asking for his head, he'd at least break a sweat.

"It's no joke, Cantalion."

"General Cantalion," the old man snapped, eyes flashing in Finley's direction.

Well, now he certainly wanted to be sick. "You're not a

general. Not even a lieutenant. You might've been if you delivered these men to Westbrook, but that will never happen now," Finley said. "You weren't even a proper healer, you only trained us. Poorly."

"Brink," Cantalion said in greeting, lips curling. "So it is madness then. You've all been diddling your whores and losing your minds up here in the north, haven't you?"

Finley drew his sword free of the long sheath, satisfaction ugly and crawling in his numb chest as Cantalion finally revealed a flicker of worry. They might be mad, but he'd still have to fight his way out of here, and he'd probably never seen a minute of battle. Probably wasn't planning to as Westbrook's jailer either.

"Men!" Gideon barked, and Cantalion's horse skipped back from sound. Behind Finley, their ranks whooped. "Who do you fight for?"

They whooped again, a strange cacophony of answers that didn't match. Their mothers. The names of fallen soldiers.

"Lumen," Finley breathed softly.

Cantalion's men reached for weapons, eyeing each other, waiting for an answer to the confusion.

"Will you fight until the end?" The men roared, and Cantalion had to jump from his horse, unable to control its response. Gideon hunched, arms wide, sword in hand. "Join us!" he screamed, the words turned to an unlikely threat with his blade pitched to the air.

He launched forward, Cantalion and his men barely managing to draw their own weapons. Finley was jostled by the men rising up behind him before he too ran into the cluttered fray. Gideon was after Cantalion, and Finley realized he had to be quick or risk getting stabbed before reaching his quarry.

"I don't- I don't understand," one man said as Finley passed

Philip grabbed the man's arm that held his sword and pulled him close. "If you want to die for Stalor, fight me for the privilege. If you want an end to war, be my brother."

Finley skirted a swinging blade and grabbed the reins of the horse, dodging its kicks and clucking his tongue to reassure it, herding it back out of the mess of men. "Come, settle, there now. Wait aside here," Finley whispered to it, turning to look back through the crowd.

Gideon was there at the border, blade pounding against Cantalion's raised sword, a feral grin on his wild face. Finley knew his friend could have the man crumpled and broken with another strike if he wanted, but Gideon held him in the fight, bullied and pushed with his strikes and yet never finishing the work. For a moment, Finley couldn't breathe. Let Gideon end it. Let him wait here with the horse and never look Cantalion in the eye again.

The horse had its own opinion, apparently, because it butted against Finley's back, nudging him back to the fight, to Cantalion and Gideon locked in their uneven battle. His sword hung from his side, and Finley ignored the trembling of his hand as he charged forward.

Gideon beamed at him as he saw him, foot kicking out to trip Cantalion and spin him in Finley's direction. Cantalion was already panting, eyes watering and widening as he spotted Finley.

"Please," he gasped. "Spare me. I'll- I'll fight for you. I can heal- Please—"

Cantalion had found him in a little attic room of a brothel, inhaling pungent fumes from a bottle he'd mixed himself, just to see what it did to his mind.

"You'll kill yourself like that," Cantalion said, smiling and crouching in front of the bed where Finley sat cross-legged and bare-chested. "Here, try this."

"No!" Finley roared, swinging the sword down. It was a wild swing, more energy than aim, and it landed against the shoulder of Cantalion's armor, making Finley's hand ring with the impact until it was numb.

"It's like dreaming," Finley murmured, weighed down by the drowsy effects of the smoke. A hand stroked down his back and back up again.

"Yes. Do you like it?"

Finley hummed.

"Did you enjoy the whores? Did you get off? Let me feel, eh?"

"No! No! No!"

The sword beat down for every exclamation, clumsy and heavy, landing on metal and metal and metal. Finley switched hands when his right throbbed too hard.

"Watch, Fin," Gideon warned. "Watch him!"

"Does this feel good? Sol, look at that. You like that."

"Fuck you! No! Monster! Fucking bastard!" Finley's spit landed on Cantalion's face, skin red, eyes angry and bloodshot.

"Fin! He's got you!" Gideon's shoulder rammed against Finley's, pushing out of the way, the big man taking the brunt of a slashing blade in his own thigh.

At the sight of his friend's blood on Cantalion's sword, Finley swung again, higher and truer this time, although the sword still shook in the air, even as it landed on the back of Cantalion's neck. Bone crunched, and a strange and ugly angle was forced against the old man's throat, head tossed back. It wasn't a clean cut. There was very little blood in fact, as Finley stared at where it connected. More came up, bubbling from Cantalion's lips as he dropped to the ground.

Gideon stumbled against him, and Finley didn't catch him so much as stopped the momentum that nearly sent them both falling.

"Enough, Fin. Good work," Gideon grunted.

"You're cut," Finley said, looking down at Gideon's thigh which was bleeding steadily.

"Been cut before. Get my belt. Fighting's done."

Finley startled and looked back behind him. There were very few bodies on the ground and none with faces that Finley recognized, although everyone looked a bit blurry to him now. The fighting was done. Cantalion was dead. They had more men.

"Belt," Gideon grunted.

Finley nodded, then scrambled to start his work with numb and bloody fingers.

10

"Here they come, Lady," Colin said, toes perched on the window ledge in a perilous pose that made Lumen want to snatch him down to safety, if it weren't for the fact that he had a view of the road. "It's a big group, so I think it must be good news."

They'd won, or they'd lost to a large party of men. It wasn't even evening yet, and Lumen wondered if that was a promising fact.

"Yep, there's Jones on a horse."

Lumen sagged against the front door, her forehead resting there, palms splayed and clammy from a day of nerves.

"Are you relieved that we're safe, or he is?" Jennie whispered.

"Hush and let me have this," Lumen muttered back.

"I'll go and take the water in for you," Jennie said, touching Lumen's back briefly. Jennie would tease to her endless amusement but never judge, and Lumen was constantly grateful for her company if not always her humor.

Lumen hesitated at the door, torn between fussing in the infirmary or waiting to greet the men. At the prospect of facing Gideon with the worry she was sure still lingered on her face, Lumen was ready to retreat.

"You'll send them in?" she asked Colin.

"Yes, Lady," Colin said with a nod before frowning out the window. "Fool's gone an' injured 'imself again."

Lumen yanked the door open. There could only be one fool

Colin meant, and he was the only man Lumen had a selfish interest in the fate of. She forced her steps to slow down the stairs as the army marched up the drive, but even from the short distance the vivid reds and browns of blood were clear on the outsideo Gideon's thigh. He was a little pale, cheeks a little too red, but he grinned at the sight of her, and Lumen knew she was failing to hide the anxiety burrowing through her chest.

"What've you done now?" she snapped.

"Saved my life," Finley murmured, helping to lead Gideon's horse, his head dropped. Finley looked...dazed, maybe? Had he lost his will to the drugs again so soon? "None of our own casualties, and I can manage the work we do have. Gideon's the worst off of the lot."

"As usual," one of the soldiers chimed in from the crowd, receiving scattered laughter.

"It's not as bad as it looks," Gideon said with a shrug.

There were so many new men, and while they looked wary and confused at their own presence in the pack, Lumen couldn't see evidence of very serious fighting. "You did it," she breathed.

Finley sighed and glanced over his shoulder. He *was* clear, but there were speckles of blood Lumen could make out now that he was closer. He'd been in the midst of the battle this time.

"Don't know to what end yet," he said, more to himself, before looking back to Lumen. "I'll make a mess of the stitching."

Lumen waved her hand, head shaking. "I'll do it." She paced to the other side of Gideon's horse, holding out her arms to help him dismount.

"I can manage, sweet spirit," Gideon murmured. His eyes were glassy.

"Not a chance," Lumen said. "Can you manage stairs?" It would be better if she could give him his room back, let him sleep in peace and comfort for the night.

Gideon slid down from the saddle, and Lumen pretended she offered some support, although the truth was more likely that Gideon was holding himself up to keep from crushing her. "'Course I can," Gideon grunted, his steps stiff.

Lumen leaned back to glance at Finley, locking her knees as Gideon gave her a little of his weight.

Finley nodded and shrugged. "Should be all right."

Gideon's arm was heavy and hot over her shoulder. He smelled like sweat and blood, pungent and tart, and his breathing was heavier than it ought to have been.

"Colin, get me plenty of hot water up to the bedroom west of mine?" Lumen asked. "And my tools for stitching?"

Colin nodded and ran ahead. At Gideon's pace, the boy would make it up to the room with everything before they did.

"How long have you had the belt on?" Lumen asked as the strap brushed against her side in their slow travel.

"Few hours," Gideon muttered.

She glanced up at his face and found him growing paler. "Pain?"

"Not so bad," he lied, and then grinned as she scoffed at him.

"Well if not now, you'll be in plenty later when that has to be loosened."

The stairs were a slow process of Gideon using his good leg while he balanced against Lumen, and even she was breathless and sweaty by the time they reached the room. There were two large bowls of steaming water waiting for them, a chair pulled up to the fireplace where a small fire burned off the chill of the room.

"Those pants will be ruined," Lumen mentioned. "Go stand by the chair."

Gideon limped his way over as she pulled the black robe off over her head under his watchful gaze. "You don't wear it as you work?"

"Around the others, I would," she said, her eyes hesitating and focusing on his wound before admitting, "With you, it feels like a pretense."

She crossed to him, kneeling at his side, and tried to ignore the heat of his gaze on her face. The stitching kit waited on the seat and she pulled the scissors free, cutting around his leg and letting the fabric fall around his boot. There were new wounds, barely healed over, and Lumen blinked back tears. His skin was dirty, covered in bruises, and he was a little thinner as if he'd lost muscle while he was sick or during the idle time in the village.

"If I pull the fabric out from under the belt, will it be too loose?" she asked.

"Shouldn't be," Gideon said, and then grunted and buried the pained sound as she tugged the pants free.

"Drop them," she said.

"What?" Gideon squawked, wavering in step and gawking down at her.

"Drop your trousers, Gideon. I need to be able to clean you up, and I need to be able to see to work."

Lumen refused the blush that tried to flood her cheeks, looking up at Gideon's startled expression. She lifted an eyebrow, and he chuckled, loosening the ties and lowering the waist down. He was naked underneath, because of course he was, and his cock twitched at the slightest graze of her eyes. The hem of his shirt covered the base of his length but not much else, and Lumen was surprised by the sudden spark of heat in her belly at the sight of his girth, red and soft. Or it was soft, it was coming to life the longer she looked at him.

Gideon cleared his throat. "Sorry, I—"

"Don't," she said, her own voice rasping.

She reached for a clean cloth, dipping it into the hot water and then applying it to the new gash without warning Gideon. He hissed and flinched before holding still as she cleaned his thigh. The skin around the belt was puckered and dark, and she wanted to work quickly on patching the wound so she could help ease the spot before the constraint did any damage.

Gideon made very little noise or movement as she treated and stitched the wound, he never had, too used to the feeling of a needle in his skin or letting his head go somewhere else. The pain at least seemed to distract his arousal, cock softening again.

"They gave up easy," Gideon said, a little strain in his words.

"Who did this?"

"Their leader," he answered, continuing as Lumen frowned. "Don't mourn him, sweet spirit. I know enough of the man's work to say those men are better off without him."

"Finley said you saved his life."

"Finley needed to fight this battle. I was only his shield."

Lumen sighed, finishing off the stitches. Gideon's hand moved from his back to cover the side of her head, and Lumen leaned into the touch, eyes falling shut.

"Tell me your worry?" Gideon asked.

"That fighting these battles is just another way for you to keep me bound to you," Lumen said.

Gideon hummed, and Lumen relaxed further into his gentle touch, relieved he didn't react poorly to her confession. "I worried it might be that too," he said, and his gaze was heavy as she looked up, his thumb resting on her cheek. Thinner he might be, but Gideon was still a bear of a man, broad and huge above her, and instead of feeling him as a threat, he was a wall between her and the rest of the world. A shield.

"You're nothing to be claimed or won in a battle, sweet spirit. We know that now, with every breath in our lungs. I think…" He swallowed and bent so that his face was nearer to hers. "I think, if you asked us to leave, we would do it. I don't seem to see colors in the world when you aren't near, and I don't have the mind of a man when I feel you in danger, but I will go where you direct me, even if it's to the other end of the world away from you."

Lumen's breath came out in a watery puff, and Gideon's thumb captured a tear, wiping it away. He stood straight and winced. "Better get that belt now," he said.

Lumen nodded, blinking rapidly, fingers fumbling at the tight buckle of the belt. Gideon grunted as she loosened it free from the tooth, and she ignored the spark of sunlight scorching her fingertips as she gently massaged his skin, gradually releasing the belt from around his thigh. Gideon's hand left her face, curling into a fist, and out of the corner of her eye Lumen could see the slow rise and richening of his cock, lifting the hem of his shirt. His breathing was heavy and uneven, but this time Lumen knew it wasn't the pain, or not the pain alone. Her touching was skimming near his ass and between his legs, working the blood slowly back into the muscle.

Controlling a man's arousal was powerful. Her fingers itched to flick up, brush against the heavy sac hanging under his engorged length.

"Take your shirt off," Lumen instructed, eyes fixed to the wound now lightly dewing with blood. Gideon grunted above her again, and she wasn't sure if it was a question or not. "You're filthy, and you're going to get an infection if you aren't more careful. Undress and I'll wash you. Then you can rest while I find you some food and a solution to those pants."

Gideon muttered as he scooped his shirt over his head, and Lumen thought she caught the words 'killing me.' Was she trying to torture him? She knew what it would mean to Gideon, or at least the physical agony it would be for him, to be naked and touched by her. It was pleasure without satisfaction. She *wanted* to offer him the first, it was the latter she was terrified of granting.

"There's no tub," he said, eyes on the fire, body bare and dusted with grime and blood, painted in bruises.

"I don't want you soaking with that wound out," Lumen said, standing and clearing away the bloody needle and used rags. She found a clean sheet in a drawer that she could use as a towel and switched to the fresh basin of water.

"I could do it myself, sweet spirit," he whispered, like he didn't want her to hear the offer but felt he should make it anyway.

Lumen stopped in front of him, warm wet cloth in one hand and her makeshift towel in the other. His brow was furrowed, eyes fixed and studying her.

"I want to," she said, watching for his reaction. He sagged with a sigh and nodded, head drooping.

Lumen took a long, greedy, examination of him and moved to his back, starting at his shoulders. She dug into the muscles there and he melted cooperatively, knots giving way under her touch. The warmth of him soaked into her hands and up her arms as she worked, and for once, Lumen let the heat build. Neither of them spoke, and there was more in the quiet than could've been said between them in the moment. It was a hypnotic touch, and she realized how much she had missed the feel of his skin against hers. She stepped as close as she dared, Gideon radiating warmth against her front.

Gideon groaned as she tugged on his hair, washing the back of his neck and beard, his head tipping back in offering to her. There was a mirror over the fireplace, small but enough for Lumen to see the picture of his face slack with pleasure, lips parted and chest panting. She washed one arm and then the other, savoring the flex of muscle in response to her touch. The sour smell he'd walked in with relented to a natural, sweetened scent.

When she moved to step in front of him, Gideon stopped her with an outstretched arm. "If I take a pleasure from this you don't mean to offer, I think it would be better if we stopped, sweet spirit," he said, voice broken and gravelly as it had been while he moaned and rasped praise in her ear in the bed they shared.

Lumen coaxed his arm down, moving in front of him. His cock was stiff and bobbing, the head glossy with leaking arousal, and she recalled the bitter salt on her tongue from taking him in her mouth. Gideon swallowed hard as she stared at him and moaned briefly as she continued her work over his throat and chest.

"This might be all," she said, thinking aloud, and his stomach twitched under her washcloth. "This might be all I can do. Is that cruel?"

"No," Gideon said, guttural and rough. "It's more'n I deserve."

His legs were shaking, and Lumen didn't know if it was because he was resisting desire, or was tired and weak. The head of his cock was red and weeping, begging for her tongue or her hand. Lumen knelt and Gideon shuddered, chest heaving as she continued to wash him, from his feet up to the crease of his thigh, mapping and remembering the shape of him. Some of her favorite memories were still missing, his weight atop her, the texture of his tongue between her legs, his hands cupped around her face to hold her in place for his kisses.

You're just glad he isn't dead, a cooler voice warned in the back of her head. *Do you really want to be possessed again?*

Lumen paused at Gideon's feet, one hand wrapped around his calf, the other high on the inside of his injured thigh. The mental warning had a strange effect on her, a longing and a comfort and a nervous turning of her heart in her chest. Did she want to belong to Gideon? Could she separate the man in front of her from the pain she'd gone through the last time they were together?

Lumen rinsed the cloth again and then looked up, meeting Gideon's stare as she washed his stiffened length. A long groan escaped him, his eyes narrowing as he fought to keep them open and on her face. Lumen reached up to his arm with her other hand and pulled herself up from the floor. She released the cloth from her fingers, and it landed on the stone with a wet smack. Her hand wrapped around his base, squeezing, and Lumen leaned into Gideon's chest to savor the shudder of his body in answer to her small touch. She stroked him, pumping loosely, and rose to her toes to press her forehead against his, feel the wet puff of his breath on her lips. He was scorching against her palm, pulse thrumming with energy she craved having unleashed on her.

She stroked her thumb over the head of him, gathering the wetness, and Gideon's hand snapped around her wrist, holding her in place. Lumen's heart stopped, eyes widening, finding his latched to hers.

Caught, she thought in a brief panic.

No, Gideon hadn't captured her, she reminded herself. It was *her* who'd lured him into a gentle trap.

"Not if you're going to regret me," he breathed, loosening his hold. His voice ached, dark eyes full of pleading. "You know, you *know* how badly I want— but not if you'll wish it undone, Lumen."

A whine crept up her throat, and Lumen pulled her hand from his skin, arms sliding between them against his chest. Gideon wrapped himself around her as she buried her face in his chest, taking deep lungfuls of him and trying to stave off tears. Desire was madness and she'd *wanted* to succumb to the melee.

He made soft sounds, hands stroking her back. "I won't let anything hurt you, sweet spirit." Not him, not Stalor, not Dominic, not even her.

"I'm sorry," she gasped.

"Hush," he said, scuffing a kiss to the top of her head. "Was only sweetness."

Gideon *would* think so, that she was only trying to be sweet. Lumen knew better. She wanted to *conquer* him, or at least their attraction to one another. He made no move to release her, and Lumen soaked up the moment for longer than she deserved until she felt him shake a little against her.

"Go lay down," she said, pulling away slowly. His hands stopped at the curve of her waist, and Lumen smiled up at him, certain he wasn't even aware of how he held her. "I'll send someone up with food and look into something clean for you to wear."

Gideon reached up, tipped her chin and took a long look at her. "You're well, though?"

She was a disaster. "I'm well," she said.

Gideon nodded and released her, hobbling to the bed, groaning as he sank down. Lumen tossed the used water out the window and gathered up her supplies. She glanced once more at him before reaching the door, reclined on the bed with the sheet slung over his hips, arousal only half-eased. With sudden clarity, Lumen realized Gideon would probably manage the deed himself after she left the room, and her feet almost stuck in place, the idea somehow an injustice in her head. Which was sick and unfair of her.

"Sweetest touch that ever killed a man," he said, winking at her.

Lumen swallowed her gasp and escaped the room, tears springing again. He'd said that before, after Dominic had dropped her and before Finley had worked up the courage to bed her. She should've grabbed him in that hall and held onto him then. Finley would never have had the chance to break her heart, and she would never have started a game of war with Dominic, exchanging her body in order to hurt him and try to force him out of her life.

Or maybe things would've gone worse, she thought.

Jennie was in the kitchen, some kind of stew brewing on the stove, and she looked twice at Lumen, the first cursory and the second concerned. Lumen dumped the bowls and medical supplies aside.

"What happened? Did he touch you?" Jennie growled, dropping the spoon into the stew pot and grabbing Lumen by the shoulders.

Shame ran over Lumen like a heavy rain shower, and she let her eyes drift shut under the rush. "I touched him," she said shaking her head. "Where's Colin?"

"Bossing Finley about, don't worry about the lad. Here, sit down. Did he coax you?"

"No, no, it wasn't like that," Lumen whispered, falling into the chair Jennie pulled for her. She dropped her face into her hands, elbows propped up on her knees. "I wanted him."

Jennie's knees cracked as she knelt in front of Lumen. "Wanted or want? Lune knows, past and present can get muddled when it comes to sex and lovers."

"I was so...empty after they brought me back to Oshain. It was awful, but I think I preferred it," Lumen said.

"Preferred to what?" Jennie asked.

Lumen lifted her chin to face her friend's frown. "The wanting."

Jennie laughed, face fractured with sympathy. "Oh, lady." She pulled Lumen into her arms. "You were left alone for far too long. You're not wrong, the wanting is awful. Sometimes the men are cruel. Or you know you'll be no good for them. Sometimes they're just fools."

Lumen sucked in a deep breath, and Jennie released her, settling forward, her arms crossed on Lumen's lap, chin perched to gaze up.

"That numbness was your heart shutting out the hurt. I can't tell you it will come back," Jennie said, blue eyes wide.

"No, you're right. And I don't want it, not really. I've been… I've been happier. Having you and Colin. It just…"

"Happiness makes room for wanting more happiness," Jennie said knowingly. "Which is it? Is he cruel?"

"No!" Lumen cried, appalled at the thought. Gideon had never been cruel. Maybe a fool, but he wasn't now. "I… I'm a priestess."

Jennie lifted an eyebrow. "You told me a priestess could have a man if she wanted one."

"But I am the New Moon Priestess. Can I be Lune's vessel if I…share myself?" Lumen asked.

Jennie's lips pursed, quirking to the side. "I suppose that's between you and her." She laughed as Lumen huffed and leaned back in the chair. Jennie stood with a grumble and patted Lumen's thigh. "Go and speak to her."

Lumen sat, staring into space, thinking over Jennie's words. Lune had guided her back here, Lumen was more certain of that, even without Lune's touch directly guiding her. Was she really afraid of the Goddess' disapproval over what she did with her body for pleasure?

"Is it possible to have sex without surrendering a part of yourself?" Lumen asked.

Jennie paused her stirring at the stove. "Yes, of course. But it's not possible to *love* in that way, Lady."

Lumen nodded and left the kitchen. It was love she was afraid of.

THE SKY WAS DARK WHEN LUMEN ROUSED HERSELF, ALONE IN THE small chapel. She'd gone to empty her head of swirling thoughts, and instead, spent hours organizing them into something she could face.

Lune had brought her back to the Manor for a task more complicated than cleaning the rooms and restoring it to a temple. Gideon, Finley, Dominic, and the others were tied into her fate—or she to theirs—and she suspected this strange and dangerous turn of their forces in the war had a part to play. Those were the easier things to accept. The difficult ones Lumen couldn't blame on Lune. Her feelings for Gideon were her own, and the Goddess could take no credit or blame there. Lumen craved the friendship and protection and devotion Gideon offered, but she couldn't accept them and hold herself separate from him at the same time. She had a choice to make, and one without divine involvement.

Lumen stretched from her place on the floor, the world quiet around the small room. Silver glinted in the windows, restored by her and Colin on that first night of their return. It looked silly and decorative to her now, especially compared to the rest of the stripped temple, and if it hadn't been holy silver, Lumen might've considered selling it for animals and grain. Which was an unsettling change in feelings. She tried to appreciate it now for the nostalgia of her childhood.

There was a bowl of cold stew waiting for her by the door,

and Lumen carried it with her out of the chapel, steps slow down the hall as her body eased out of the stiff discomfort from her place on the floor.

Would Finley be in bed with Gideon, watching over him? Or would they be in an embrace after Lumen's selfish advances?

Not if you're going to regret me.

Lumen stopped in the hall, staring out at the open courtyard, the light dim as the new moon neared.

She did not regret Gideon. She *would not* regret him. If he must have something from her in order for her to hold onto the parts of him she needed so badly, she would learn to live without whatever he took.

She finished only as much stew as she managed to eat on her way to the stairs, leaving the rest under an arch for some stray critter to find. Jennie and Colin could chew her ear for it tomorrow.

Lumen ran up the stairs and past her own door, waiting outside Gideon's listening for voices. She pushed her way in slowly, afraid to wake him if Finley was there too, but with the coals of the fire still glowing, it was clear there was only one shadow in the bed. She slipped inside, barring the door behind her, waiting for Gideon to wake and catch her.

He was wounded in battle, and now he's sound asleep. Lumen smiled at the picture of his back facing her, mottled with bruises she wanted to tend and old scars she would covet. Her black robe was still on the chair where she'd left it, and Lumen fussed with the ties of her dress, eyes fixed on Gideon's slow breathing. She considered leaving her shift on, and then remembered how jealous her own skin had been of her hands while she'd bathed him.

Naked, her skin prickled with awareness, nipples pebbling in cool air, her sex dewing with every step closer to the bed. She would slide in behind him and remain like that for the rest of the night if he stayed sleeping, or only wanted to rest, as long as they could be close.

A hushed laugh escaped at the thought of Gideon waking to

find her naked in bed with him and deciding to simply hold her. *Unlikely*.

She sat on the edge at his side, and Gideon stirred and rolled, eyes squinting and face gruff and stern with a frown. He froze, eyes widening, as he found her breasts in his face.

"Am I in a fever?" he asked.

Lumen grinned, reaching out and pressing her hand to his forehead, sighing as he leaned in. "No, you feel fine. But you're right that I should have checked."

Gideon cleared his throat and scooted back on the bed, grimacing at the reminder of his injury. "Sweet spirit, what are you—"

Lumen shifted, knees resting on the edge of the bed, and Gideon's hand came up to cup her bare hip and help her balance. She slid one hand into his hair, tugging his head back to bring his eyes up from her sex to her face, a smile curling on her lips. The other hand stroked his jaw, thumb brushing over his bottom lip. Gideon licked her fingertip, not in any wicked attempt but in a clear desire to taste her again, and Lumen's lips parted on a sigh.

"I'm claiming you," she said, watching the words soak into his expression, shock and longing writing over his eyes and cheeks and lips. She bent forward until her face hovered over his, and said, "And I won't regret you, Gideon Jones."

There was a moment of silence and then Gideon's soft growl rumbled between them, the sound shooting straight to Lumen's belly and down between her thighs which she pressed together. He surged up, lips catching hers, teeth snagging, and Lumen leaned into the kiss, holding his face to hers and moaning against his tongue as it sought entrance. He grabbed her hips, lifting her easily, pulling her over his chest and rolling them down into the bed.

Her heart hammered in her chest as Lumen arched into the kiss, Gideon's arms wrapped around her back and hips, his body falling between her legs in open offering.

He tugged away, nipping at her jaw, nuzzling down against

her neck and pausing the frenzy, even as his cock began to swell and nudge between them. "You're certain?"

"Yes," she said, releasing his jaw and trying to reach between them to fit the head of him against her as she'd done months ago.

Gideon chuckled and rose up to his knees, cool air rushing between them as he grinned down. "No, sweet spirit. It's been too long, I'll hurt you." He bent his head, sucking on the curve of her neck, and Lumen's eyes widened. She'd forgotten how that felt. Her legs spread wider and she rocked, sheets and blankets kissing at skin Gideon wasn't touching.

"I used to be 'little spirit,'" she said.

"I remember," he said. His voice was lovely and low when he was in bed with her, already she could hear the smile in his voice, the joy of sex thrumming through him. "I missed you too much, it left a great hole in me. Nothing 'little' could've made a pain so vast."

Lumen gasped, and Gideon pulled away, easing down onto his side. There was a white bandage around his leg, and she realized she'd left the room without finishing her work earlier. Had he done that or had Finley?

"We'll hurt your leg," Lumen said, frowning, skimming her hand over his hip, eyes distracted from the bandage by the bounce of his cock.

"My leg doesn't feel a thing, all my blood is elsewhere," Gideon said, although he was in no rush to slide back between her legs.

She laughed, and he dragged her closer, mouths landing clumsy but close. Gideon's hands and arms were greedy as her own had been earlier, but his fingers never neared her sex.

"Won't you touch me?" she whispered, clutching at his back.

Gideon grinned, hand on her back sliding over her ass and pulling her thigh up over his hip to open her. He groaned, brow furrowing as he touched her center, finding her slippery and soaked.

"I've missed you too," she said, breathless, leaning into the touch.

"I can be sex for you," Gideon rasped. "If that's what you want from me."

He started to scoot down the bed, and Lumen startled, grabbing his shoulders. "Gid, wait!" She tugged, and he shifted up, welcoming her closer with an expression open and waiting. "I'm sorry—"

He kissed her before she could finish. "Don't be, Lumen. I would offer you anything."

"Gideon, I *know*," Lumen said, taking his face in her hands again. "This isn't just sex. This doesn't need to be sex at all if that's…if it makes it clearer. I want *you*."

"I'm only a warrior, sweet spirit," Gideon said, searching her eyes.

Lumen tried to smile, wavering and nervous as it was. "Then fight for me. Not on the battlefield. Here, between us."

"I don't want to force—"

"Gideon Jones, what about me coming to you naked and aching for your touch says *force*?" she snapped. He laughed, that bright barking noise, and Lumen's smile widened in earnest. She leaned in, pecking at his lips, his cheeks, the bridge of his crooked nose. "I won't lie. I am scared. But not of you, Gideon. Be strong when I want to waver and I *promise*, I won't run again."

Gideon sighed, and she realized someone—probably Colin— had brought him the mint leaves to chew on. "Doesn't seem right I should get what I want after you were so hurt."

Lumen kissed him again, and then again until he was answering, deeper and slower caresses than they'd been sharing just a few minutes ago. "I thought I should not be happy after everything that happened, too," she said, feeling him stiffen and holding him tight so he couldn't pull away. "Please, tell me I'm wrong."

He hummed, nose nudging her ear. He sucked on the lobe, and Lumen shuddered, another wave of arousal heating inside her. The ice she'd been holding onto was rushing away, and she realized it was not Lune that made the cold shield, but her own anger.

"I hate to call you wrong, but you've certainly never been less right," he said.

He kissed beneath her ear and turned her into the bed again as she laughed. He crawled down, hands taking her thighs in full grip and spreading them open. He licked his lips, staring openly at her sex on display, and Lumen bit her smile. *Beast*, she thought fondly.

"You know I love your cock, Gideon. You were afraid to hurt me before, and you never did," Lumen said.

Gideon grinned at her, feral and happy, and started to shift down onto his belly, hard cock trapped against the bed. "True. But I miss feasting on you." His head bent low, but high enough for Lumen to see his tongue stretched. She held her breath in her chest, body tense on the bed, as the very tip skimmed up the lips of her pussy. An agonized note of pleasure fought its way up from her chest and Gideon groaned, the bed shaking briefly as he fucked into the sheets.

"Fuck, your taste," he growled. "I might come before you do."

"Gideon," Lumen whined, trying and failing to roll her hips up for more. She was trapped by his hands, their grip gentle but unrelenting in holding her in place.

"Don't worry, sweet. If I do, I'll suck on your pretty pussy until I'm hard for you again. Shouldn't take long."

"If you don't start—" Lumen's impatience died as Gideon laughed and dropped his mouth between her thighs without further preamble.

He kissed her deeper than he'd taken her mouth and with twice the exclamation of satisfaction. Lumen cried out, fingers diving into his hair to hold him to her. The bed creaked, and Lumen realized Gideon might not have been teasing in his threat. He would come against his belly and the sheets, and torment her with pleasure until he was desperate to fuck her again. And it would be *divine*, but already she knew it wouldn't be enough.

"Oh gods, Gideon! Please! Please, I want you close. I want you against me," she pleaded until his tongue circled her clit, and she thrashed with the sudden threat of ecstasy.

He sucked and licked, mouthing and moaning against her, fucking her with his tongue and then using it as a perfect lash of pleasure against her clit.

"Touch!" she cried. "Your fingers, Gideon. Please. Fuck—"

He granted her wish, the first finger a sudden reminder of what *sex* was, her recollection of the stretch an exquisite shock and reality.

"Yes!" She yanked on the strands as if Gideon would let her steer him back to his focus on her clit.

He granted her plea, a second finger joining the first. Lumen's voice left her. It wasn't pain, but it was pressure, driving to a fine point on where Gideon teased her with his tongue. She stared at him with a mouth parted on a silent shout. He was sitting up on his knees now, and she wondered if he came or was trying not to and then she didn't care. Gideon's lips wrapped around the spot and he sucked hard, two fingers pumping rough and deep, and Lumen lost control of her own body as it twisted, a hazy shattering of light rushing through her from her center outwards. Her hands flapped against the bed, and wetness rushed over Gideon's fingers, pressed back against her own skin. His mouth vanished from her center but his thumb replaced the pressure, softer and swirling, coaxing her back down to the bed with a gradual easing.

Lumen's eyes opened to find Gideon hovering over her, his hand at rest on her sex, something both soft and dark in his expression.

"The picture of you right now," he said, lips curled.

Lumen smiled, satisfaction erasing days and weeks of nerves and confusion. Here was the most dangerous bit of the act, the lovely welcoming feeling at the end of pleasure. Except now with Gideon, there was no uncertainty of what brought her to the moment.

"Come closer," she said.

Gideon settled over her, and Lumen sighed with the press of his chest against hers. She raised her legs up to wrap them around his hips, careful to avoid his bandage. He reached between them, hand wet with her release cupping at her breast, plucking at her nipple. Their cheeks pressed together, Gideon kissing at her jaw. Her breath came thinner beneath him, Gideon knowing her love of the crush of him.

"You are the most beautiful sight," he said against her ear. "Every time I get to watch you come apart like that for me, I forget to breathe."

"You will have to acclimate," Lumen said, rocking against him, the pinch of his fingers around her nipple drawing out aftershocks in her weeping cunt. "I need you breathing, Jones."

"Yes, Priestess," he growled out, rolling over her, the head of his cock—still hard, thank the gods—nudging at her entrance. Lumen shivered and gasped at the word in that tone. The dark rasp continuing as he spoke, "I breathe to worship you."

He arched, licking and biting down her throat over her shoulder, on a path to the breast he'd been playing with. He sucked at the pointed tip, growling and leaving her trembling, while his left hand started the treatment with her other breast. Lumen's hands scrabbled at his back, trying to pull him up against her, her hips lifting to find his cock. He suckled hard, and Lumen made a noisy broken sound.

"Gideon, please! You know I'm ready. Please, my love!"

Gideon froze, bit lightly on Lumen's breast, and then collapsed against her. His mouth took hers with a sudden and urgent command, rough and thorough. Lumen clutched to him, distracted with the force of the kiss until she felt the slow and stretching invasion of his cock fitting itself at her opening. She moaned into the kiss, dragged her nails over his old scars, and tightened beneath him, forgetting the act.

"Settle, sweet," he said against her lips, and Lumen huffed and remembered to relax.

They both held their breath as Gideon began to sink in, and his head lifted for them to hold gazes, Lumen's mouth hanging open as she relearned the stretch of her lover inside of her.

"Too much?" he asked, panting, sweat pricked on his brow.

"Never." She kissed his jaw, and together they groaned as he rocked, sliding deeper. There was a point where the intrusion became tense, and Gideon must've seen the strain in her eyes because his head dipped and he licked into her mouth, body patient as he distracted her, sucking softly on her bottom lip until she was sighing, shifting beneath him and drawing him deeper.

They caught their breath as Gideon's hips kissed hers. His hands swept beneath her, covering her shoulders, and Lumen brushed his hair back from his face, sipping on his mouth. He moved slowly, drawing out in a gradual drag that left her feeling every inch, shivery and panting against his lips, and the returning press stole her breath completely. There was no animal in the bed with her now, but a man expressing devotion in the most agonizingly thorough way he could.

"You're mine," Lumen whispered, and he groaned, his thrust rushing and striking deeper. "Mine," she repeated.

"I've been yours this whole time," he said.

His hands around her shoulders gripped tighter, and Gideon reared back, shifting inside of her, making sure to strike an angle that left Lumen wordless. She became wild beneath him, trying to urge him faster, deeper, and Gideon continued his slow and thorough assault of her senses. His tongue licked over her pulse, lapped away the sweat on her skin. He shifted one hand to the back of her neck, fingers holding tight, and the other down to the base of her spine, lifting him against her.

Lumen forgot herself, clawing at Gideon's skin, trying to pull him into her with every thrust. Every time he filled her, she sang for him and every time he reared back, she whimpered at the loss. Her skin was hot, pulse pounding in her ears with the sound of their breaths. Gideon was whispering praise in her ears, broken for low groans as she squeezed around his length.

"Fuck," he muttered, the slow pace faltering.

"Yes," she urged, trying to ride him from below.

"I don't want it to end, Lumen," Gideon groaned, face torn with worry and rapture.

Lumen swallowed around the moan in her throat and caught her breath, nuzzling Gideon's cheek. "It's not ending, my love. I promise."

Gideon shuddered again, back tensing under her hands, and

then he was unleashed. Lumen shouted as his weight nailed her to the mattress, body rutting. His hand on the back of her neck held her to him, his tongue as voracious against her mouth as his cock was inside of her. The constant simmering heat that circled her hips began to flare in a sudden burst, and Lumen fought to join Gideon in his rhythm, his body a repetitive pressure against her swollen clit, cock pounding a beat that rang through her veins.

"Gods, Lumen!" he gasped, and then he snarled, pulling his face from hers, teeth latching onto her throat.

His hands flew to her arms, tying their fingers together and pinning their hands down in the bed. Lumen had been suspended on the edge of a second orgasm somewhere in the mix of Gideon's slow and patient lovemaking, but it was his frantic need that finally set her off, bowing into him, shuddering with scorching euphoria lighting up her skin. Gideon held her in his grip as he flooded inside her, fucking her through both of their finishes and then through her aftershocks with stuttering nudges of his cock, as if he didn't quite know how to stop.

Lumen was limp beneath him, muscles exhausted and strength burned away. She squeezed his hand and stroked her cheek against his as he softened the hold of his teeth on her neck. His hips stretched hers open, and he made no move to pull out.

"Are we healed?" Gideon asked, soft and rasping.

Lumen pulled her hands free of his, but only so she could wrap her arms around him again as her legs lost their strength and fell to the bed. "I think we've made the bargain to heal together," she said.

Gideon hummed, and she felt his smile against her neck. "My leg might need a new stitch or two," he said after another moment.

Lumen squeaked, jerking beneath him, and Gideon laughed. "You forgot, didn't you?"

"I think I...I might not have cared. Here, let me." Lumen wiggled beneath him, and Gideon smacked a kiss on her neck.

He rolled them with a groan until he was on his back with

her draped over him like a blanket. "Not tonight, sweet spirit. It will wait until morning with the rest of the worries."

She should've insisted. Or at least reached for a blanket. Instead, Lumen sighed and sank against Gideon, his fingers undoing the bed-made tangles of her hair and soothing a path over her spine until she was fast asleep.

VI
THE FROZEN
WAR

F<small>INLEY WOKE EARLY IN THE ATTIC ROOM OF THE</small> M<small>ANOR TURNED</small> temple, and pretended for a moment that it was months ago. He would turn in the bed and collide with Lumen, drawing her against him, savoring a moment in a rare and sweet morning. The lie was broken by a draft crawling up his unguarded spine. Lumen was somewhere nearby but not with him, never with him again.

He rolled out of the bed and made half an attempt at straightening his clothes before giving up altogether. No one would care. He stretched, back cracking, and went to check on Gideon's leg so Lumen might sleep the morning away without dealing with their lot.

Downstairs, he pushed the door open to the soft snores of Gideon at rest, and the sun falling through parted curtains onto the bed. Immediately Finley felt...peaceful, tempted to go and join Gideon and press to his side, just for the sake of touch. There was a sweet and airy scent in the room alongside Gideon's heavier male aroma, and the combination melted tension in Finley's shoulders.

He took a step closer, and the tension snapped back into place.

Lumen was in the bed, held to Gideon's chest by his thick arms, dwarfed in his company. Her face was slack with sleep, slight shadows under her eyes but no other sign of weariness or stress. Her hand was high on Gideon's chest, clutching to him, and Finley froze as she shifted, one leg sliding under the blankets to cover Gideon's. He could make out the soft swell of her breast just above the sheet, pressed against Gideon.

The entire picture made Finley's heart seize, the perfect contrast and harmony of the pair of them—all of Gideon's rough and crooked edges, Lumen's ghostly and delicate coloring. There was no familiar word for the strange combination of feelings in his head. Jealousy, anger, sorrow, relief mingling together. He stayed longer than he should have, longer than a part of him really wanted to, waiting and watching to see if the clear comfort and ease between the two sleepers might fracture, some sign that Lumen needed to be *rescued* from a fate she'd already fallen into before. There was none, and the urge to flee and escape the sight of a morning he'd just fantasized over finally won out.

Finley retreated the way he'd come, head pounding with questions. He wanted the drugs back now more than ever.

LUMEN WOKE SLOWLY, aware from the start of where she was and whose face was pressed into her hair, whose hand cupped and held her hip. It was impossible to mistake Gideon's warmth or the way he occupied a bed and seemed to frame himself around her. She didn't rush herself, and Gideon didn't attempt to rouse her with his usual impatient appetite for sex. Neither of them spoke or did more than shift in their embrace until voices began to echo softly outside the door.

Gideon leaned back, and Lumen opened her eyes to find him gazing at her, a laugh in his look and twitching on his lips.

"Is it your intention to keep me here? Pantless?" he asked.

Her lips parted, surprised squeak rising and Gideon growled a laugh, rolling and pinning her slightly so she couldn't scramble from the bed.

"Oh, Gideon! I forgot," she said, trying to sit up and failing under Gideon's weight. It *was* a tempting idea.

"I let you," Gideon said, grinning. His head bent, but only just enough to put himself in reach, leaving it to Lumen to fill the space. She arched her neck and did so, smiling as he kissed her with slow licking draws on her lips.

"There's nothing left that would fit you," she said, falling into pillows and catching her breath. "I meant to mend what I cut."

"Fin and the others will send something back from the village," he agreed, scooting down the bed until his feet hung over the edge and his cheek rested on her breast.

Lumen stilled briefly, and then let her hands travel through his hair. It was getting long, hanging in his eyes occasionally, and she would offer to cut it if he had to go back into battle.

"Can you...can you really stay?" she asked.

Gideon sighed, breath hot on her skin. "I will stay if you ask. Or I will go back, even pantsless—"

"I meant what I said last night," she said. It was a little easier to talk of the heavy things like this, without meeting his gaze head-on.

"I know you did. I'll put my sword down if you want me to, but I would rather fight for you," he said, turning his head to kiss between her breasts before settling again. She locked her fingers in his hair, and Gideon hummed in pleasure. "That would take me back to Dominic and the others sometimes."

Lumen nodded slowly, staring unseeing up at the top of the bed, imagining all the wounds he might return to her with, or even the day he might not return at all.

"Stalor will send their armies here," Lumen said, her fingers trembling as she combed them through his hair. "If Oshain senses the weakness, they'll push back harder. There are no allies to call on here, Gideon. Do you really believe this can lead anywhere but death?"

His arms slid out from under her back and he rose up on his palms, studying her. "You're afraid?"

She frowned, nose wrinkling. "I've been afraid my entire life in one degree or another. How could I not be now?"

Gideon sat up, resting on his heels. He lifted her from the bed, without much apparent effort, seating her on his lap.

Lumen shivered and reached for the blanket, wrapping it around their shoulders.

"No country can win a war if its people won't take up arms," Gideon said.

"They are already armed."

"Then we will convince them to set them down."

Had she done wrong in drawing Gideon back to her? He might survive the war if he'd carried on as he was, pushing north and winning battles. But what Dominic and he proposed now? They would be hammered at all sides by every possible foe.

"Sweet spirit," Gideon murmured, kissing her lips and all around, down to her jaw while he waited for her anxious thoughts to pass. Lumen took a deep breath and nodded, waiting for him to continue. "I'll go where you direct me. What do you really want?"

It was a strange combination of fantasy and memory that came to Lumen's mind. Her brothers and mother and Gideon and Colin and Jennie and Gretchen Ramsey all at a harvest feast together. The Manor stripped and washed in white and blue and gold, with Priestesses turning the halls. Many hands in the fields until the fallow ground was made useful again in order to feed more mouths. Mostly though, Lumen imagined how it might feel to know that war was ended and would not come knocking on her door again. She came up empty at the thought.

"This is treason, Gideon," she whispered.

"Yes," Gideon agreed. He frowned, and his stare strayed across the room. "There should be a word for when a country fails its people."

Lumen exhaled slowly. "If I could imagine any outcome... even the most impossible one, I would want to be here at the end of the war, knowing that the people I cared about were safe. But Gid—"

He cut her off with a kiss and leaned back smiling. "Then that is what we'll strive for. And if you've a mind to change where we end up, you'll tell me?"

"All right," she said slowly. Gideon made it sound so simple, but it wasn't like before when he thought their being together meant she would follow him into war. She might tell herself that they could leave before it was too late, but 'too late' was sure to come without warning them first.

"You keep your eye on the destination, sweet spirit. I'll manage the obstacles."

"You are one man, Gideon Jones," she cautioned.

"I am your man, Priestess."

Lumen shivered and blushed at the claim, and Gideon grinned, leaning forward and taking them back down into the blankets, his beard scratching against her throat as his tongue stroked over her pulse. Sunlight warmed her hands as she stroked them over his skin, and it filled her veins, rushing down to her core as Gideon sucked and nibbled and kissed every inch of her.

DOMINIC WATCHED THE ARMY RETURN, its numbers more than doubled by the new men. Finley was in the lead, the men on foot behind him answering the curious stares of those in town with equally interested expressions.

It worked. Dominic couldn't really believe it, even as he stared at their new forces. They'd taken a mass of Stalor's last men right out from under their noses. How long could he stall with this advantage before Stalor realized what they'd done?

"Philip," Dominic snapped to the young man whose arm was wrapped around one of the dark-haired woman—he'd never really learned their names, too occupied by another. "Grab some of the men and find rooms for our new numbers."

"Yes, sir," Philip said, straightening, although his hand slid into the girl's rather than dropping away as it might've done months ago.

Was Dominic's new reputation the kind that allowed for sweethearts and hand-holding? He swallowed the lump in his throat and strode to meet Finley on the road, frowning at the second count of men.

"Where's Gideon? Is he..."

"He's...with Lumen," Finley said slowly.

Dominic frowned. "Injured? What happened?"

"He was wounded, not badly," Finley said, staring down at the reins in his hand. "Let's go in, I'll tell you how it went."

Dominic knew a stalling tactic when he heard one, but if Finley thought the conversation needed privacy, that was fine with him. They may have absorbed dozens of fresh soldiers, but those were men who had the expectation they'd be fighting for their country. More than one might take the opportunity to inform Stalor of Dominic's new position in the war, and it was still a fragile one.

Dominic headed for the inn as Finley slid down from the horse, leading it to the trough by the stables before joining him. They walked in silence back to Dominic's office. Upstairs, the ceiling creaked and thumped rhythmically, a low groan released. With new men, they might need new women too. There were too many established romances, and Dominic was fairly sure the ladies in the village couldn't rightly be considered whores since no one was paying them recently. He didn't want fights breaking out over lovers.

"What's going on with Gideon?" Dominic asked, shutting the door behind Finley and crossing his arms while he stared across the space.

Finley helped himself to a chair and braced his elbows on his knees. "He's fine. Leg wound, and it's stitched shut now. His pants were ruined, and Gideon's a beast so..."

Dominic's brow furrowed, shoulders relaxing cautiously. That couldn't be all. That was hardly worthy of a private conversation. "So someone needs to go back and fetch him."

"I- well, yes. Day after tomorrow."

"Day after? I could ride the night, and he'd be out of her hair by the morning." Dominic watched Finley's lips press thin with a growing sense of dread. "Spit it out."

Finley's gaze flicked to him briefly before going distant across the room again. "I walked in on them this morning in bed together." Dominic choked and Finley sat up, hands raised. "Not like that. Well, I mean, clearly it *had* happened. They were sleeping."

Rage boiled sudden and hot, the room flashing red and yellow in his eyes, a brief imagined glimpse of the two entwined. Dominic's fist landed against the wooden door with a sudden bang, the frame rattling in answer. "He should've known better!" he yelled. "Enough! We've done enough!"

"Dominic, stop," Finley said, jumping up and drawing Dominic back from the door before he could go storming out, south to Gideon where he might be able to beat some sense into the man. "Dominic, can you really prevent her from forgiving him if it makes her happy?"

"Happy?" Dominic spat, rounding on him.

Finley grabbed him by the shoulders, fingers digging in tight and those glass green eyes finally meeting his. "Gideon was beaming of course, but I saw her as we were leaving. She was smiling. Not at us. Just, to herself, walking through the Manor smiling. He would never hurt her, Dom, you know that."

Dominic snarled and tried to pull away. Where had this new strength of Finley's come from? "Let me go."

"Not if you're going to grab a horse and ride there to storm in on her peace," Finley said, hard and loud, cracking through the tempest in Dominic's head.

He took a breath, and Finley raised an eyebrow. Lumen had really taken Gideon back into her bed? Or he had dragged her into his? If Finley was right and this wasn't just…just their usual way of cornering a woman, if Lumen had chosen this and willingly and *happily*…

And not him. Dominic wasn't surprised not to be back in her bed, but more surprised that she would willingly take any of them on.

"I talked to Gideon, and he said the day after tomorrow, before the new moon," Finley said, sighing and slowly releasing his grip on Dominic.

Two days with Lumen alone, only Jennie and Colin there to protect or step in if she needed…

If she needs what? he thought. This was Gideon, not a stranger.

Dominic knew exactly what his friend's intentions were. The only thing Lumen was in danger of was being exhausted or sore from too much pleasure, and even that seemed unlikely with how gentle Gideon tried to be with her.

"Fine. I'll go myself." Finley frowned, eyes narrowed, and Dominic answered his glare. "I'm not going to do anything to upset her. I just want to see for myself."

Finley sucked in a deep breath and turned on his heel, combing his fingers through graying brown hair. "I can't stop you."

Dominic wondered if he should tell Finley that he *could* stop him if he was really determined to, Dominic wouldn't fight him physically, not over this, and Finley was stronger than he thought.

"Cantalion?" he asked.

"Dead," Finley said, a hollow note in the word. "By my hand, although Gideon took his sword to the leg in the process."

Dominic sighed and clapped his hand on Finley's shoulder briefly. "Gideon's taken plenty of swords to plenty of places. Good. One success for us."

"With more trouble to come from it, no doubt," Finley muttered, but he stood straighter all the same.

A fist knocked lightly against the office door and Dominic stepped back, leaning against the table and crossing his arms over his chest. "Come in."

Philip walked in, a dirty letter in his hand. "This came by way of a runner who's asking to stay."

Dominic lifted an eyebrow and nodded to Finley to take the letter and read it. "How are the newcomers?"

Philip shrugged. "Fine. Curious. Mostly, think they're relieved to be here. Girls are doing what they can to scrounge up some food, and they've brought enough supplies to do us good."

"It's from Meade," Finley said, frowning at the letter before looking up to Dominic. "Oshain's beat them in a battle and has their territory under siege. Most of his party is dead."

"They'd made it to just east of us," Dominic said. He turned to his desk and rifled for the map. Meade was the general Finley had run to when he left Lumen in the winter. He was a bit of a careless leader, who mostly made his strides by following Dominic's.

"What's the likelihood of Oshain keeping Meade alive?" Finley asked to Dominic's back.

"They will if they want to interrogate him. The rest of the men won't stand a chance. If Oshain has gained that ground, they have us at two sides and could easily force their way west of us as well."

"You want to fight for the territory?" Philip asked, brow furrowed and tone doubtful.

"No. But I want to get those men out if we can. No use wasting lives if we can help it," Dominic said.

Finley's head tilted slightly, eyes keen on Dominic's face, reading what was unspoken. Rescuing those men from Oshain would add to their own numbers and with a stronger bond of loyalty.

"Do we wait for Gideon?" Finley asked, and Philip paled.

"We probably better," Dominic said, trying not to smirk at the younger man.

Philip was a good soldier and a good fighter, as were the rest of the men from their core. Even better than their strength, the men of this army knew how to survive. But Dominic knew how the younger men looked up to Gideon, like something between a shield and a good luck charm when they went to fight. Going after Oshain for the sake of a rescue mission rather than a simple skirmish was higher risk, and the men deserved to go into it optimistic. Philip left the room with a nod, and Finley huffed a laugh behind his hand.

"What?"

Finley stared at him for a long pause and asked, "Are you hoping if we delay it might get Meade out of the way first so you don't have to rescue him and deal with Stalor?"

Dominic growled and pointed to the door. "Get out."

Finley's smile flickered as he left the room. Dominic wasn't sure if he should be flattered that the healer thought his strategy was that involved, or ashamed that he was partially right.

"WHERE'D YOU LEARN THIS?" GIDEON ASKED, WATCHING THE BOY untangle his snare from around the rabbit's neck.

"Spragg taught me," Colin said, frowning slightly. "Guess he was good for that."

Gideon grunted, not sure he was in agreement. Although Colin was at least putting meat on Lumen's plate, so he couldn't rightfully argue. Lumen was in prayer when Colin had arrived in the bedroom with a borrowed pair of pants from Widow Ramsey. They were comically short and a little tight around the waistband, but Gideon wasn't generally choosey about clothes. He'd left with the boy, heading east around the lake into the woods. As much as Gideon might've liked to spend the day drawing Lumen back to bed with him, he wasn't used to being laid up. He also didn't want to be in her hair if she didn't want him there. She was a Priestess now, trying to make a proper temple out of the Manor, and he wanted to prove that he wasn't a conquering soldier making demands of her time to please himself.

"Lady says we can try and catch fish in the lake, but I'm never fast enough with the net," Colin said.

"Bet we could make a trap to put out and draw up," Gideon said, and the boy looked up with bright, pleased eyes. "I used to watch the women make 'em in the markets. We just need some good straight branches and twine."

"I don't think Lady likes rabbit very much, but she never says

137

so," Colin mused. "It'd be nice not to eat the same thing every night."

Gideon followed Colin through the woods, new saplings tugging and scratching at the threadbare borrowed pants. His thigh was a little sore and slow still, but his stride was longer and Colin moved more carefully. Gideon watched the boy, thoughts turning. Colin had been caring for Lumen the right way since the beginning, he knew more about her tastes and likes and wishes than any of them.

"What else does she want for?" Gideon asked.

Colin threw a glance over his shoulder, a slight smirk, but he didn't hold back. "She and Jennie want a milking cow. She wants to take down the bookshelves in her father's study because she said it used to be a chapel too with a good view for the full moon and sunshine. Think she'd like it if there were proper observances and people who came for the holidays and the like. She wants a good full kitchen with plenty cured for winter so she can take care of folks when they're sick. She thinks she's not the Lady of the estate now, but she still is a bit. Wants people to watch over, and wants to be able to do right by them."

Gideon's heart ached at hearing it all. Lumen's goodness burned at him, as did the understanding that he'd played a part in getting in the way of her happiness.

"You think some folks will come for the new moon?" Colin asked, checking on a snare and finding it empty.

Gideon cleared his throat. "Don't know. Maybe. There's some Oshain soldiers in the area now." A dark and crooked shadow sat farther up ahead. "What's that?"

"Used to be a house," Colin said. "Think it looks haunted now."

Gideon walked forward until he could see it more clearly through the trees. It was large, or once was large, with some of the bones of the structure burned away, but the stone frame of the first floor still standing, as well as a grand looking fireplace. "Don't think even ghosts would make a home out of that," Gideon mused. "Come and have a look with me?"

Colin shuffled at his back, and Gideon saw with a glance that the boy was genuinely spooked by the site of the decrepit structure.

"You're more likely to find a rabbit's den than any ghosts," Gideon said, sparking interest. "Maybe a fox or two."

Colin huffed and shrugged, but he ran close to Gideon's side as they approached. The old house had been burnt in a fire, but the left side still remained, although barely. The remainder of the roof and the second story had collapsed in on the floor. The wooden frames were all coated in thick layers of moss. The whole thing was rightfully abandoned and left to decompose here in the woods by the look of it.

"Do you think this was the old house before Oshain gave Lumen's family the estate?" Colin asked, looking at shattered rafters.

"Could be," Gideon said. He stepped through the open break in the stone wall where a door would've been. The floor was laid stone so it was safe enough for them to walk on, if somewhat overcome and carpeted by moss as well. Gideon leaned on a wall, holding Colin back, and the structure groaned and threatened further collapse.

"What are you thinking?" Colin asked.

"Thinking I wish I knew how to build a house," Gideon said, grinning at the boy.

"Why?"

"So our Lady could have her temple without me mucking it up. I would be close but not in her way."

"You would make a very bad Priestess," Colin agreed, drawing a barking laugh from the man.

"That I would!" Gideon straightened as he realized Colin was studying him closely, with a stern twist of his small lips. "Go on, lad. Someone ought to give me hell on her behalf."

Colin sucked his teeth and spun slowly in a circle, ignoring Gideon's words in favor of examining the house while he thought. His frown was fixed when he faced Gideon again. "I don't mind that she can forgive you. An' I don't mind that she'll have you back again even, but you just can't mess up, you understand? No, listen. I'm not saying what's your fault and what's not, or anything like that. An' Lady can make her own choices," Colin said, lifting his chin high and fisting his hands at his sides. "I'm just saying she's had enough hardship and from now on... from now on, she shouldn't have to anymore. So you can't mess up."

Gideon crouched low, ignoring the strain in his injury. He was face to face with Colin, and if the boy did want to throw a punch or two Gideon would gladly take it. "I can't promise that, but I can promise you I intend to do my best to be a shield for her. And I think I can do my part not to cause any hurt, yes."

Colin sighed and relaxed, arms flapping. "All right, I suppose." His eyes lifted over Gideon's shoulder, head shaking slightly. "I think you'd be better off starting from scratch properly, but Mitchell will know if you ask him."

"Rodney Mitchell?" Gideon asked, standing again and easing his weight off his bad leg. Mitchell was one of Widow Ramsey's new beaus.

"He was a master builder before the war," Colin said with a shrug. He took another thorough look around and frowned. "But he weren't a magician, so I don't see as how he'll be much help with this."

Gideon laughed and turned to start their way back to Lumen. "If I start over, I start over. Do you think she'd like it?"

"Having you out of the way? Probably," Colin said dryly.

Gideon caught the boy around the waist and tossed him over his shoulder, rabbit and all. Colin let out a peal of noisy laughter, and Gideon grinned at the sound in his ear. He would try and keep it up all the way back, just to make Lumen smile at the sound.

LUMEN STRETCHED her legs under the kitchen table, smiling as Gideon's eyes flicked up from his plate, narrowing slowly on her. He licked his fingers, slow and thorough, and Lumen swallowed hard. His own legs stretched, trapping theirs together, and he grinned behind his cup.

"What's that smell?" Colin asked, nose twitching, turning in his seat towards the oven.

"Smells sweet," Gideon agreed, winking at Lumen when the boy's back was turned.

Jennie snorted, and she and Lumen exchanged a sly glance. "Jennie and I came up with a surprise for tonight."

"Bet you never had a strawberry before," Gideon said leaning forward on his elbows to nudge Colin's attention.

"A *straw*berry?" Colin asked, nose wrinkled.

"Are they not common in the south?" Lumen asked, surprised.

"Not in the city, and especially not for the poor," Gideon said. "I've only ever had one, and it was 'cause some rich gent was spoiling one of the girls where I grew up."

"Is it good?" Colin asked. "Sounds like something that belongs in a barn."

"Well, finish your meal and you'll find out," Lumen laughed.

Colin was nearly done anyway, just a few scraps of vegetables he'd been moving around like it might disguise that he was avoiding them. He skewered three of them on his fork at once and shoved them into his mouth.

"Beast," Jennie scoffed.

Lumen cleared her own plate, ready to take the others on her way to the stove when Gideon stood. He grabbed her's and Jennie's and then Colin's, taking them over to the sink. He bent as he passed her, dropping a kiss to the top of her head, and Lumen blushed.

This was different, even when she hadn't imagined it could be. Her home was still empty, although the addition of three was a welcome fullness compared to being alone. The war was still surrounding her, but even if she thought it was insane and likely to fail, Gideon and the others did feel like a barricade up between her and the danger. Colin's laughter made her smile, Jennie's sarcasm made her laugh, and Gideon...

She stood, touching his back on her way to stove, savoring the warmth against her palm and the swell of his cheeks at his own smile. Gideon was some combination of playful and protective, overwhelming and tender. She slept soundly next to him, instead of tossing and turning in her own sheets, although they'd done plenty of that together *before* retiring for the night.

Something will change, a cold voice warned. Rather than worry at the warning, Lumen accepted the fact. This peace and companionship might be temporary, but at least she'd known it, for however long it would last.

Lumen grabbed towels in her hands and pulled the tray of tarts from the oven, red sticky juices overflowing the pastry. Colin was on his knees, facing wrong-ways in his chair with his neck craned to watch her deliver them to the table. He leaned forward and took a deep breath, and Lumen grinned as he licked his lips unconsciously.

He looked up at her with wide eyes. "It's like the jam you'd put in the buns?"

Lumen nodded. "A lot like that, although strawberries are sweeter. I'll show you where to find them, and if you pick enough without eating them, I'll make jam. I need to see if there's honey to be had in some of the hives too."

Colin reached for a steaming tart, and Jennie slapped his hand lightly. "Wait a moment, beast. If you burn your tongue, it won't taste half as good."

"Come here, sweet spirit," Gideon whispered in her ear, drawing her to sit in his lap on her own chair.

She stiffened, waiting for him burrow against her neck, or his hands to go wandering over her, but he only locked his arms around her waist and set his chin on her shoulder. Lumen set her own hands over his, tracing the pucker and wrinkle of the scars on his knuckles with her touch.

"I have some silver left the High Priestess gave me. Do you think we might be able to get—?"

"Yes," Gideon said before she could finish. He shrugged as she leaned back in his hold. "Whatever you need."

Then they would get a rooster, Lumen decided. And maybe a cow too.

Gideon's hand reached out, fingers pinching the shell of a tart and dragging it closer. He hissed and gasped at the heat but ignored the pain, making Lumen laugh and Colin brave his chances.

DOMINIC LEFT to fetch Gideon at an ungodly hour before the sun dared show its face. It wasn't that he wanted to tear Gideon away from Lumen sooner exactly, or at least not entirely. He rarely slept and never for long. The impatience to see for himself what Finley claimed to see, some certainty that they hadn't destroyed Lumen's chance of happiness forever, was too strong to resist.

He realized as he stood back on the eastern edge of the property, staring at the gazebo, that he hadn't really believed Finley. Lumen sat on the steps down to the dock, pressed against the archway of the gazebo, with her head thrown back in laughter. The sound was clear in his ears, even from where he stood partially hidden from a good distance. It was loud, bright, and stuttering with giggles. At her side stood a naked Gideon, hands on his hips.

Dominic didn't know what they were saying, but Gideon's own bark of laughter was loud as Lumen swatted his leg. All at once, Gideon went charging down the dock to the water. Lumen jumped up as Gideon leaped in, arms and legs flailing. A great splash came up, a softer bubble of laughter.

"Argh!" Gideon bellowed as he burst up from the water. "Fuck! It's cold!"

Lumen was melting against the beam, holding herself up for support as she gasped for air through her humor, a hand reaching up to wipe tears from her eyes. Gideon threw his hair from his face, swam in a small circle, and called to her, making her shake her head.

Dominic closed his eyes. High hiccuping notes and softer sighing gasps of her voice in his ear continued, and he gave himself a moment to imagine her smile, her eyes on him. Somehow that was more painful, and he let it go.

"Gideon Jones, don't you dare!"

Dominic found himself staring again, watching Gideon prowl up the dock to the gazebo where Lumen backed away slowly, her hands raised. She stopped when he was near, their heads close to one another. Dominic couldn't read their expressions or hear their words, but he could imagine. Imagine Gideon coaxing her closer with some combination of filth or sweetness until she was disarmed enough to be caught in his grip. Except it was Lumen who leaped, Gideon catching her as she held his face in her hands and kissed him until Gideon was stumbling back to brace them against a beam in the shadow of the gazebo.

Enough, Dominic thought to himself. He turned his back on the scene and took a deep breath, waiting for the anger and the jealousy to rise up. It was there, simmering gently in his gut, but it didn't worsen. He was angry, he was jealous, mostly though he was relieved. Lumen was happy. Somehow, after everything, she was laughing and smiling and loving a man.

Gideon will be good to her, Dominic decided. He left them to their moment, searching for somewhere closer to the temple to wait for Gideon. He heard a clatter coming out of one of the upper windows, the sound of wood splintering and being tossed about. Frowning, Dominic headed in to find the sound.

It was the study he'd used while they occupied the Manor, now stripped to its bones. And even those were being dismantled.

"I can't reach those high ones!" Colin said, pointing up to the top shelves of the bookcases that surrounded the room. "Who built the damn things?"

"Men," Jennie said, wiping her forehead with her sleeve, staring up at the shelves. She wasn't much taller than Colin.

"What's this about?"

The two spun to find him rolling up his sleeves and stepping carefully over piles of discarded wood. The shelves must've cost a fortune, measured and fit to the room, carved in decorations. Lumen would get nothing for them broken up like this.

"What are you doing here?"

"Waiting for Gideon," Dominic answered Colin's snarl. "He's busy, and I thought I'd come to see what the commotion was."

Jennie's arms crossed over her chest. "Lumen's trying to restore the room to a larger chapel. There's even some art left on the walls under these shelves."

Dominic moved to where they stood and saw the crack in the back of the shelf, a swirl of silver flake and indigo paint revealed behind the structure. He held his hand out for the iron pry in Colin's grip.

"I can reach," he said when Colin pulled away from him.

At least it was something to do.

By the time Gideon and Lumen arrived to see their progress —Gideon dressed and Lumen looking more rumpled than she had by the lake, her hair now loose down her back—Dominic had caught up with Jennie and Colin's progress on the shelves.

"Wasn't expecting *you* to come," Gideon said. He was wearing a pair of pants at least two sizes two small, and Dominic nodded to the sack he'd dropped by the door.

"There's a change of clothes for you in that. Tomorrow we go west to Meade's camp. It's been taken by Oshain, and there are soldiers held prisoner there," Dominic announced.

He'd only meant to make it clear to Gideon that there was good reason to draw him away from Lumen, but he realized his error as the peaceful and pleased expression she wore faltered with worry.

"I only want to get the men out," Dominic said to the lovers.

Gideon was standing slightly in front of Lumen, acting as a shield, and there was something in his expression that Dominic thought might be him working up the nerve to refuse an order. Lumen tugged on Gideon's hand where it was wrapped around hers, drawing his gaze to her.

"Go change," she said. She looked to Dominic and added, "I'll observe the new moon here and meet you in the village? I can bring remedies."

"Sweet spirit, no," Gideon said, low but careful to temper his tone. "It'd be better for you to stay here."

Lumen pursed her lips at Gideon and lowered her chin. "I've seen Finley's stores. The best he can do is set bones and get someone like Rosie to stitch wounds. Someone will get an infection, and I've been gathering plenty. I'll come up and help mend."

"Take men on the road with you," Dominic said, risking her ire. "Just in case."

She glanced at him without expression and dipped her head in a nod. "Come," she said, tugging on Gideon's hand and leading him from the room. Gideon followed her gentle direction, grabbing the bag by the door on his way out with a fierce glance over his shoulder at Dominic.

"You sure bring cheer with you, don't you, General Westbrook?" Jennie mused.

Dominic's head whipped to stare at her, a biting answer on his tongue, but he swallowed it down and went back to the work.

GIDEON RODE in silence at Dominic's side, night cool around them but only enough to be refreshing after the sweat he'd worked up helping Jennie and Colin. Gideon was stiff, and it wasn't the injury on his thigh, which was no worse than any other he'd managed to gain himself in the past decade. No, this was to do with Dominic directly, he simply hadn't sorted out how or why.

"I wish you would just speak whatever it is that has you in a temper," Dominic said. "Finley said you were *planning* to come to the village before the new moon."

"And I am," Gideon growled.

"Gideon, I can't force you to return with me if you'd rather not—"

"Of course I'd rather not!"

"Well then turn around and quit being an ass!"

They glared at each other, their horses leaning away as if they expected their riders to suddenly jump and pummel one another. Which *might* happen. Gideon settled and then grunted.

"I'm going back to her," Gideon said, stubborn and hard.

Dominic sighed. Ah. That's what this was. "Good, someone

should be there to keep on eye on the south."

"I'm going back for *her* not you!"

"Oh for fuck's sake, Gid, *fine*."

"*Fine?!*"

"Yes, fine!" Dominic roared.

Gideon was baring his teeth, deep lines between his eyebrows, back tense. And then suddenly, he wasn't. He leaned back, stared at Dominic, and then laughed, grin replacing all the feral anger of a moment ago.

"What the fuck, Gideon?" Dominic asked, releasing a breath slowly. Sol's Fire, he'd thought Gideon was going to attack him, and he hadn't known whether or not he'd defend himself.

"I thought you were going to try and keep me from her," Gideon said simply, shrugging and snorting. "Or leverage yourself between us."

Dominic flinched and sucked a breath. He deserved that. It still stung.

"I have no intention of interfering," Dominic said, crisp and rough. He huffed and shook his head. "Fuck, Gideon, I've learned that lesson plenty, don't you think?"

"I should hope so," Gideon said, and then he sighed. "I doubt my own intentions too if it makes you feel better."

It did a bit. "Don't. I saw her. She's…" The Lumen he'd seen in the gazebo was a woman he'd never met before and doubted he would ever be privy to in the future. Not unless he took to spying on Gideon and her together, which was a form of masochism he wasn't prepared for.

"We have to hold them back, Stalor and Oshain," Gideon said, low and grave. "For her."

"Yes," Dominic agreed.

He hoped the other men would find their own reasons for the cause, but he knew his own. Without the hope of forgiveness or reconciliation, Dominic would fight for Lumen. He had stolen from her, and now he would give his life to restoring what he could and protecting what she had left. He glanced at Gideon, who sat straight-backed and steady on his horse as they rode together. That would have to include his friend now.

ON THE DAY OF THE NEW MOON, LUMEN ENTERED THE CHAPEL before dawn, taking her place on the floor in front of Lune's altar. It was easier than she expected to fall into the quiet meditation of pure silence. The room was familiar, even the floor in front of her nose had patterns she'd memorized growing up. The incense she'd prepared was fresh and the product of her own woods. When Jennie and Colin joined her after sunrise, they were quiet and comfortable presences to share the space with.

By midday, the chapel had more visitors. The Ramsey children were as quiet as children could be and when they tired, Colin took them out to the courtyard to play. Lumen stretched her aching back and took one brief glance around the room. The space was full of soldiers, familiar faces and the new Oshain men too.

They were gone again by evening, and Jennie and Colin returned after dark to help her stretch and ease her way out of her stillness. Together, the three of them ate a silent dinner in the kitchen. Lumen kissed both of their cheeks before heading up to bed.

It was the most peaceful day she'd had since last summer, and the sweetest new moon she could remember for years. She was not alone now, the thought regularly striking her with surprising comfort.

Jennie woke her the next morning with a cup of tea on the

bedside table, and by sliding in next to Lumen, resting her cheek on Lumen's shoulder for a brief companionable quiet. Then they rose, gathered the supplies Lumen had packed, borrowed a spare horse from a local soldier, and rode with Colin to Westbrook's town, as Lumen thought of it in her head.

They arrived just as Westbrook and the others were returning, and the prickling anxiety and worry Lumen had ridden the day with vanished as she caught a grin from Gideon, who led a cart of injured men.

"No stitches for me," he greeted when they met at the inn door.

Lumen reached up, gripping his jaw in her hand and squinted at the bruising around his temple. She pressed her thumb to the spot, and Gideon grimaced around his smile, but didn't howl. Nothing fractured then.

"I suppose I'll have to be satisfied," Lumen said, and released him.

In a snap, Gideon's hands cupped around her waist and he crowded her briefly, head dipping down to growl softly, "You'll be satisfied later, but for now, how about a kiss?"

Lumen rose to her toes when Gideon didn't force the claim, held his mouth softly with her own until that flutter of tension passed. He was alive and in good humor, which was all she could hope for.

"Don't overwork," Gideon murmured against her lips, and then he released her and opened the inn door for her.

"I'll go and grab extra hands," Jennie said.

"Send someone for water from the spring," Lumen added.

"I already have." Finley was inside, helping a man down into a chair as Inda hurried about the room, restocking candles in lanterns until it was bright enough for them to see their work properly. He met Lumen's gaze briefly, a nod of acknowledgment, before returning to the door to help other patients inside. Lumen crossed to the counter where she lined up her collection of treatments, reaching around her to lift a jar and examine the contents when Finley joined her.

"Echinacea tincture," she said. "For infection."

Finley nodded. "How much?"

"Just a few drops a day. How serious are the injuries?"

Finley turned to the room, surveying the men. "Mostly minor. One man though…there's nothing to be done, I think. A sword wound through the stomach and damage internally to more than one organ. It's a long and painful death."

Lumen pressed her lips together and looked down the length of the counter. "I have some seeds that can cloud the pain. They're dangerous in high doses but…"

"But it hardly matters in his case," Finley finished for her. His eyes were clear now, and she noticed that his hands were steady again. She was glad for him that he seemed to have control of himself once more. And glad for the men who needed his help. He met her gaze and nodded his head. "I think you should go ahead with it. I'll manage the tincture since most of these men are still worn down from illness anyway. Do you have any of your cider potion?"

Lumen smiled at the description and shook her head. "Not yet. I'll pick apples soon and start it fermenting."

"You're overworked," Finley said, studying her face, probably seeing dark circles under her eyes.

"No, only busy. I enjoy the work in the warmer seasons," she said. She just had trouble sleeping, knowing Gideon was in battle.

She realized they were standing together, speaking almost like friends, and wondered if some of the ugliness had broken between them during their argument. She'd shown him the truth of her anger, and it had taken a weight from her shoulders. Either way, it was good to be peaceful in Finley's presence.

"I'd say you should've stayed at the temple, but I don't have the resources you do," he said, eyeing her supplies.

"I know," Lumen said, and smirked when he flashed her an irritated glance. He huffed and rolled his eyes, starting to move away. "Come to the temple some day when you don't have fighting to think of. I'll show you where to find the ingredients you'll use most."

Finley swallowed, head turned in her direction for a pause

before he continued away without an answer. Perhaps not completely peaceful then, Lumen realized. There was still plenty of awkwardness to share.

She found the dying man without much trouble, taking him a small cordial of belladonna and brandy, and sitting with him while she waited for it to take effect. When he was drowsy and the tension was carried away by the effect of the herb, she did what she could to clean around the wound so he might suffer a little less. When his breathing was faint and shallow and he was fast asleep, she moved on.

There were small wounds to be stitched, plenty to treat with a honey salve, and gallons of tea to be brewed for lungs full of cold and wet. She and Finley exchanged brief words in passing, mostly keeping track of who they'd seen and who still needed their attention. Westbrook entered long after the army's return, slightly bloody and exhausted looking. He passed her, heading directly back to his office, and she wondered briefly if she should go and check on him until Finley headed in directly after him.

Good. That was for the best.

When the soldiers were slowly cleared out of the inn and taken to find beds, Gideon appeared, taking a seat with a cup of ale in hand, and watching her work with a fond and mischievous smile on his face.

"I can manage the rest," Finley said when he returned.

Before Lumen could offer her help, Gideon stood from his seat and came to stand with her, his hands claiming her waist. "You'll make our healer feel useless at this rate, sweet spirit. Come sleep, and I'll take you back to the temple in the morning."

"Go," Finley said, lips quirking as his eyes slid away from them. "I'll sit with him." He nodded to the soldier Lumen had cared for first, whose chest was barely moving. Lumen suspected the man would be gone by morning, could almost sense the cold hovering around him. She knew that sensation, had lain on the floor of the cell with it surrounding her.

She touched Gideon's hands at her waist lightly, and he released her so she could go to the dying man. She wasn't sure what to do, exactly, only that Death was in the New Moon's domain and empathy called her to his side. She rested her hands on the man's shoulders, felt the gentle rattle as he tried to breathe while his body failed him, and the weight of the Goddess settling into her shoulders.

"Sweet spirit?"

Lumen hushed him, and the room fell silent behind her. She closed her eyes, and for a moment there was only quiet, the smell of chamomile and honey and echinacea heavy in the air. Up between the bite of fresh herbs came a fragrance that was sweet and earthy and sour, cloying but faint. Death, hanging over the man under her hands like a cloak, one she'd worn herself months ago. There was no hot bite of life clinging to him, a vicious set of teeth Lumen hadn't even realized she'd possessed in that cell until she sensed the absence of them with this man.

Soft hands, bony and fragile, rested on her shoulders, the cloak of the Goddess cool and light on her skin. Lune was with her, wolf's muzzle soft against her ear. Together, they tucked the edges of death around the man in the corner, bundling him safely and kindly, to be carried over.

Someone sucked in their breath behind her, and Lumen knew that some small part of this moment was visible to the men behind her. In front of her, the soldier gave a last, wavering sigh and then he was still. Lumen's eyes opened and she straightened, Lune's touch evaporating around her. She waited, afraid to turn and see the faces of her witnesses. She'd acted on instinct, hoping to ease the last hours of suffering, but when the spell of certainty was over she wondered how others would react. Would Gideon fear her?

No. His hand settled on her shoulder, guiding her around to face him, eyes worried but not frightened.

"Tired?" he asked.

She was now when she hadn't been minutes ago. She nodded, and Gideon guided her to his side, arm draped around her shoulder. Finley was closer, gaping openly at the now dead soldier.

"How?"

Lumen didn't really have an answer for him and anyway, her gaze was fixed to Westbrook. He must've reappeared from his office while she was standing over the soldier. He stared at her, face unreadable, arms crossed over his chest.

"I don't know," Lumen said, her stare locked with Dominic's. "It just seemed right."

She wanted to say that it wouldn't have happened if the man hadn't already been dying. She couldn't simply *take* life, she'd only helped death come on a little faster. Except she didn't really *know* that. She hadn't known what she could do at all until it had happened.

"We'll take him to be buried," Dominic said, his eyes sliding away from her to Finley. Whatever he was thinking, he kept it hidden.

Lumen followed Gideon's nudges to the stairs, leaning into him as he led her up. She recognized the route they took, and the door he headed towards, and they both slowed to a stop before arriving. He had taken the room she'd used while resting here in the village. She could hardly call it living there since she was barely managing the act at the time.

He frowned at the door and then tipped his head to hers. "I forgot. We can take another."

"No, it's all right," she said, stepping forward and pushing it open. The bed was unmade, and the room was messier with Gideon's things strewn about, but that made it more welcoming for her. "Did I do wrong downstairs?"

Gideon shut the door behind them and then lifted the hem of Lumen's black robes. She shed them and sighed as they lifted from her shoulders. "Do you think you did?" he asked. Lumen shot him a worried look, swallowing hard. He sighed, and sat on the bed, spreading his legs and pulling her to stand between them. "No, sweet spirit. I don't think you did wrong. I think I am just glad it was only the four of us in the room at the time."

Lumen hummed and then sighed as he dug his fingers up her back, working at tired muscles. She turned, and Gideon threaded his fingers through her laces, loosening her dress until she could wiggle out of it.

"I don't rightly know what I saw downstairs," Gideon said. "It was like there were two of you, but one wasn't you at all."

Lumen stepped out of her dress and tipped Gideon's face up to hers, relieved by his usual openness. She dipped her head and Gideon accepted her kiss gladly, lifting her from the floor and drawing her onto his lap.

"That was your Lady Lune?" he asked. Lumen nodded, and Gideon hummed. "Does it frighten you to do as she asks?"

Lumen took a deep breath, turning the question over and over in her head. "Yes and no. It's like knowing something with absolute certainty, but still being full of the question *why*?"

"Bigger questions than I try to answer," Gideon agreed. He scanned her face, the candle on the side table flickering and twisting the shadows on his face to the left and right. "Is she done with you for the night, then?"

"Yes," Lumen said, leaning in. "I'm all yours."

Gideon beamed at the declaration and turned, falling back to the bed and taking Lumen down with him. He tucked her into his side, arms wrapped firmly around her, and pressed a long kiss to the top of her head.

"You gave that man a mercy. I don't mind you acting on Lune's behalf, as long as she doesn't mind me caring for you afterward. Even if I did march under Sol's flag."

Lumen untied the collar of Gideon's tunic and kissed his throat. Privately, she wondered if Gideon was hers for just such a reason, their differences balancing in their union.

Finley flushed at Lumen's light scoff. "Oh, Fin, really? What good is a leech when none of these men have enough blood as it is? Look at them."

He grimaced and scratched lines out in his old notebooks, embarrassment mingling with a mild pleasure at her chastisement. It was good to see Lumen sharpening her wit against them again. "The army doesn't send your leafy greens in their supply cases, Lumen."

"There should've been a garden here in the village," Lumen mused, looking out the inn window, no doubt waiting for Gideon to return, ready to escort her back to her temple.

"I'm a healer, not a farmer," Finley muttered.

"If you treat a man who hasn't any strength with leeches, you're neither," Lumen answered crisply. Pink flashed on the top of her cheeks, but she didn't back down when Finley stared across the table at her in shock.

He coughed a laugh and looked away before she could see how delighted he was to have her snapping at him. His worst mistake was forgetting what a strong spine Lumen had when she felt strongly about something.

"There's spearmint and parsley growing wild by the ditches," Lumen said. "I can point it out to you."

Finley hummed and nodded, looking down at his notebook. He scribbled the words he refused to speak. *Time spent with you is equal parts blessing and curse if I cannot touch and taste and breathe you in.*

They were interrupted before he could bring himself to look up again. "Lady. Priestess, I mean."

"Lumen is fine, Inda," Lumen answered, and Finley was able to enjoy her open smile unobserved as she turned to smile at the young woman.

Behind the pretty dark-haired Inda, stood Philip, bouncing on the balls of his feet, cheeks full of smile. He was twice as broad as his sweetheart and shone golden where she was dark and pale, but his eyes never strayed from Inda for more than a moment. Finley could relate to the feeling.

"Lumen," Inda said, giggling as she took Lumen's offered hands. "Philip and I were wondering if you would, or if you could...that is..."

"Would you marry us, Priestess?" Philip blurted, blue eyes wide. His light hair was mussed on top of his head, and Finley wondered if he'd been carving his fingers through it, or if Inda had.

"*Marry* you?" Lumen said, loud enough to attract eyes from around the room of the inn. Dominic himself swiveled on his seat with a glower.

"It doesn't have to be fancy, or the right words or nothing," Inda said, her smile threatening to split her face right in two for how big and joyful it was. "It's just if anyone were right to tie us together, it'd be you to do the ceremony."

Lumen gaped. "I-I couldn't. I mean, I'm not even...I'm not trained for such a thing, and really it should be—"

"But you're a Priestess," Philip pressed.

"A *New Moon* Priestess," Lumen said, and she glanced at Finley with wide eyes as if he might offer some support. Maybe they were both thinking of the night before when she'd escorted a man into his death. Could such a woman, such a *force* be applied to a wedding?

"You're the only option that wouldn't just be...us for ourselves," Inda said softly, squeezing Lumen's hands. "Which is alright, if you'd rather not. But I'd...I'd like it to be you, Lady."

Lumen's mouth hung open, eyes sparkling with possible tears, and the whole room seemed to hold its breath. Dominic was up off his seat, glower in place and arms crossed, but Finley thought he caught the slightest curl of his lips at the corner.

"All right. Yes," Lumen said, nodding slightly, dipping her chin as if she were shy.

The room went up in a great cheer, and Inda pulled Lumen from her chair with a squeal and a tight hug. "Oh, Lady, *thank you*. Could we come to the Manor? The temple?"

"Yes, I think it would be right there," Lumen said, laughing and nodding, hugging Inda back. Philip was clapping and grinning with the rest of the room. "The full moon?" Lumen asked. "To give me a little time to prepare."

"Whenever it suits you, Priestess. Thank you! Thank you!" Philip said. He leaped forward as if he might try to take a hug for himself, and Finley shot him a brief warning look.

Lumen was smiling and blushing and Inda had her tight in an embrace, but Finley knew the signs of anxiety on her face, the shying away and the deep swallows. She was reaching the threshold in a situation that made her nervous, and Finley was relieved for her when Gideon burst in and Inda drew back.

"What'd I miss?"

The company laughed, and Lumen slipped free from between Philip and Inda to go and tuck herself against the shelter of Gideon. Finley fisted his hands behind his back and then looked down at the table to see the words he'd written there. He snapped his notes shut and listened to the happy chatter of the room saying their goodbyes to their Priestess.

A wedding in a little less than two weeks. A wedding during a war. What a strangely sweet and gentle notion to celebrate, and yet Finley couldn't help but look forward to the event. He found Dominic across the room after Gideon had taken Lumen out to the horses. Sympathy and understanding were shared across the crowded room full of laughter and congratulations. She wasn't theirs, she never would be, and yet she was tied to their world and they to hers.

Finley hoped he could make peace with that.

"WHAT'S THIS?" Lumen paused in the doorway of the bedroom she and Gideon shared—her own bed was too small to reasonably accommodate Gideon regularly, and she drifted back into his without complaint.

In the center of the open floor, the large basin used for bathing in the kitchen was sitting, full of steaming water. The room was hot and humid, a fire going with a kettle hanging over it to refresh the tub.

"You bathed me," Gideon said, nudging her into the room. "I thought I might return the favor."

Lumen blushed, and Gideon kissed the color on her cheek. "How did you manage this?"

"Many trips," Gideon said, grinning.

"I never know where you are all day," Lumen mused, brow furrowing as Gideon closed the door behind them and returned to her. He lifted her robes up over her head—she'd worn them to visit the new men who'd moved into homes around the estate, and to check on the Ramsey children. She spun before Gideon could reach her laces and teased him, "I didn't realize you could be so sneaky."

Gideon hummed and drew her to his chest. "I work in the fields, I help repair houses, and I keep myself out of your way so you can do your work. That way, I can have you to myself at night," he added, low and heavy, head dipping as she rose to her toes to meet him halfway.

Gideon's kiss lingered, his tongue slipping out to wet her lips, but he pulled away as she opened to him. "Turn, let me undress you, sweet spirit."

Lumen obeyed, listening to the rustle of the ties, shimmying out as Gideon rucked the fabric over her head. "Sometimes I don't feel the title is rightfully mine," Lumen said.

"Hmm? Priestess?" She nodded, and Gideon wrapped himself around her. "Because of me?"

She covered his arms with hers and turned her head to nuzzle against his jaw. "No, well, not in the way you mean. At the convent and even when I returned, it was like I was trying to stay...hollow. Like the new moon. Now I have family again in Jennie and Colin. There are people living and working the land again. You and I are..."

Gideon's hands traveled to Lumen's hips, lifting up the fabric of her shift and taking it over her head so she stood naked in front of him. "Lovers," he supplied when she could not, head lowering to her shoulder to kiss wetly over her skin. "I can't guess your Goddess' intentions, sweet spirit. But when I see you in your black robes, tending the ill or working on your potions—"

"They're only medicine," she huffed.

"Or easing a man past his pain and into a peaceful death," Gideon continued, guiding Lumen gently to the bath, taking her hand to steady her as she stepped in. "You are not the woman I sleep next to at night, or the one wiping jam off Colin's cheeks. Just as I don't come to your bed as the bloody warrior from the battlefield now."

He settled down on the stone at the side of the tub, scooping in handfuls of water to rush them over her skin. Lumen mulled over his words with a small private smile. The tub was small, but Lumen did her best to sink in and stretch, exposing her form to Gideon's greedy gaze. Her life was gaining fullness again, and she was old enough now to appreciate its return. But Gideon was right, she could fulfill her role as the New Moon Priestess, as a Priestess for Lune in general, and still savor these new moments of sweetness.

"I don't mind a little of the warrior taking me to bed," Lumen admitted, watching Gideon still, his eyes darkening on her breasts before rising to her face. Lumen grinned and lifted her legs to dangle over the far edge of the tub, spreading them open in invitation.

Gideon chuckled, rising up on his knees to loom over her. His hand stirred the water to lap and lick at her skin, and his body blocked out the glow of the fireplace.

"You weren't ever hollow, sweet spirit," Gideon said in a whisper as he leaned over her. "You were healing."

LUMEN PANTED as she wrestled the wild grapevine around the pillar in the courtyard. To her right, Jennie cursed in the same task.

"Couldn't we have used the little chapel? Or the new one?" Jennie asked.

"I like the small one for prayer," Lumen said. A wedding should be a celebration, not a solemn and quiet event. "And the other isn't ready yet either unless you feel like scrubbing walls for the next four days."

"I might. Might be better than this damned stuff," Jennie hissed as a branch scratched her cheek.

Lumen snorted, resting her arms for a moment and leaning her head against the warm stone. The sun was beating down on their backs, midday hungry and hot as summer rose over the country. "Inda and Philip deserve to have the sun shining down on them as they marry," Lumen said.

Jennie sighed. "That I cannot argue."

"Besides, doing this keeps me from thinking about the fact that I will have to perform a ceremony I have only ever seen once," Lumen said. And even then it was the Ramsey wedding, and she had been closer to the back and not entirely paying attention.

"The hand-fasting? I remember pieces of it," Jennie said. "I can help. Let's finish wrapping these last two pillars, and then I'll bully you into planning your words."

"And the cake," Lumen reminded her.

A wedding was a great deal of work for a single day, Lumen thought. But it wasn't just a celebration for Inda and Philip. Lumen had chosen the full moon and midsummer for the day, and Gideon told her that most of Westbrook's army was attending. This was a fete for the season and everyone who'd survived the year.

"Do you regret agreeing?" Jennie asked.

"No! No. I only wish it were already over," Lumen laughed.

THE BLACK ROBES didn't seem right for such a merry occasion, so Lumen washed her old cream dress and left it out in the sun to brighten. She would play the part of a normal Lunar priestess for Inda and Philip. She and Jennie and Rosie and the other women tucked fresh wildflowers into the grapevine they'd wrapped around the pillars and made a crown for Inda to wear with her best bright blue dress. The army brought good ale, and Lumen made a cake full of fresh fruit and decorated with violets pressed to the surface.

Lumen's heart was in her throat as Inda and Philip made vows to one another, surrounded by a circle of witnesses, their friends really. She wondered if either of them *had* family or if, like her, they were finding new members in this strange patch-worked community.

"Join hands, crossed over the chalice," Lumen said, trying to speak clearly but finding volume hard to muster. She knew the eyes in their direction were for the couple and not her, but it made her nervous all the same.

She lifted the braid she and Jennie had crafted from a clean sheet and slid it beneath their crossed wrists. "By the tying of this knot, your lives unite together," Lumen said, twisting the long braid around their clasped hands. "By the fashion of the cord, you are bound to your vows to one another."

Inda and Philip had eyes only for another, no longer 'whore' or 'soldier' or even simply 'lovers', but husband and wife. Lumen wondered when they'd felt one form of connection transform into another, and her eyes flicked up to where she knew Gideon was standing in an archway, smiling at her.

"May the knot remain tied as long as love lasts, may your hands remain joined in love and never broken in anger." Lumen tied it twice more before finishing with a third as she said, "May what is bound before the Gods be not undone by man. Hold to one another, and strength will grow between you."

Lumen stepped back, and the courtyard was full of happy cheering as she took the chalice beneath their tied hands—full of water and honey and just a bit of brandy—and lifted it to each of their lips in turn.

Someone would help them free of her knots later, but for now, everyone would enjoy sweeping the new couple in their arms, tied together. When it was time to eat and dance, the knotted braid would be wrapped up for them to keep somewhere safe.

Jennie was the first to pull Inda into her arms, taking Philip with her, and Lumen backed away from the small altar they'd fashioned at the center of the courtyard, retreating to the cool shadow.

"Well done."

Finley stopped her with a brief touch to her elbow, and she turned to face him. Of course, he was also hiding beyond the height of the celebration. Neither of them had ever been as fond of the crowds as Gideon.

"I managed it, I don't know if I'd call it 'well done,'" Lumen said with a shrug. "How are the men from the eastern camp?"

"Better. Keeping an eye on the village for us with some of the new party."

"You trust them?" Lumen asked.

Finley frowned, his gaze directed over her head in thought. "I don't know. I don't think Dom *trusts* them. I don't think they trust us. But I think any soldier in this war is badly in need of respite after all this time, and they're willing to accept that much."

"I think the peace will break," Lumen admitted. She'd said as much to Gideon, and he'd frowned and tried to ease her away from the thought. Gideon wanted her to feel safe, and she suspected he also was so determined to see her so, he refused to imagine the obstacles.

"It will," Finley agreed, cool eyes sliding down to meet hers. "That doesn't mean we won't have warning to give you though."

Lumen nodded. It was whether or not she would follow the warning that concerned her.

"There you are," Gideon said at her back.

Finley backed away a step, eyes dropping to the floor, and

Lumen turned to find Gideon smiling, easy and joyful like the rest of the party.

"I have something I want to show you before it gets dark," Gideon said. "Come with me?"

She accepted his hand, and by the time she'd turned back, Finley had melted away into some shadow. Gideon led her out of the crush and through the kitchen to the back of the temple, heading for the lake.

"You have some of the look of a bride today yourself, sweet spirit," Gideon said, arm slung over her shoulder.

She wrapped her own arm around his waist and didn't comment. She suspected she had some of the thoughts too, as she'd performed the ceremony, wondering if she would want to stand on the other side of the altar. There was a great deal between her and Gideon, but it still seemed fragile, or at least at risk from the war.

"What do you have hiding in the woods?" she asked as they started on a faint path beaten through underbrush she didn't remember. There were recent boot prints in the mud, so it must've been a trail Gideon had been using plenty in recent days.

"A project I've been keeping secret," he said, squeezing her shoulders. "I was going to wait to show you, but you looked as though you need a minute of escape from the festivity."

Lumen reached up with her free hand to tangle her fingers with Gideon's in thanks. "I suspect those festivities will only grow in enthusiasm before we get back."

"It's a good night for camping, and you know I won't mind tossing folks out of your temple if you want me to." Lumen laughed, aware that it was an honest offer and not just Gideon's humor. "I liked the words you said on their behalf, sweet spirit. About strength growing." Gideon was quiet, their feet crunching through the woods, birds overhead letting out brief cries and then escaping through the rustle of the trees. "Do you think we will reach that place?"

Lumen's steps paused, and Gideon's with her. She grasped his sides and turned him to face her, surprised by his shy reluctance. Her hands slid up his chest, and Lumen's skin tingled as Gideon's worried frown melted into a smile. It was so easy to please him, to make him happy, and he put so much effort into returning the gesture.

"I think a great deal grows between us," Lumen said, stamping down nerves to gaze back at him directly. "Strength and love included."

Gideon beamed and scooped her up off her feet with a low rumble of happiness, and Lumen was ready when his mouth clasped to hers, tongue sweeping in. One arm was banded around her hips to hold her up, and his other hand reached up to cup the back of her head. Lumen surrendered, offering herself up to his affection and desire, and it was painless finally, easier than breathing.

"I don't deserve you," he rasped, nose nudging against hers.

"I disagree. Would you like to argue the topic?"

"No," he laughed. "I have something more important to show you."

Lumen expected to be set back on her feet, but instead she was carried deeper into the woods, held firmly in Gideon's arms.

16

HE WAS NEAR ECSTATIC AND WOULD'VE BEEN COMPLETELY, IF NOT for the anxiety of watching Lumen stare open-mouthed at the house. She was finding it in herself to love him. He'd seen her strength for himself—as she'd stood on the top step of her Manor and stared Dominic in the eye, declaring herself Lady of the Manor—and knew it was here between them. She was a different woman today—still a Lady as far as Gideon was concerned, but even more powerful than a title.

"You're rebuilding it?" Lumen asked, eyes wide on the new shell of the old house in the woods. "Gods, Gideon, the sheer amount of work this must've taken."

"Had lots of help," he said with a shrug. Which was true, but he'd done the demolition on his own and his body had suffered under the effort. He was used to aching, and with no battles to fight, tearing down an old house was as good a way as any to use the fire that burned through him every day.

He glanced at the house. It was only really two rooms so far, with the start of a second story and roof. He'd torn away what was left of the old place and scrubbed the stone clean before working on the left half with the fireplace still intact. Mitchell said they'd have the second story done before fall, which meant Gideon could live here properly.

"A temple doesn't seem like the right place for me," Gideon said, watching Lumen for her reactions. "But I wanted to be close—"

"It's yours?" Lumen gasped, spinning to him.

He couldn't read if she was happy, or angry, or anything at all, so he rattled on, "As long as you don't mind. Thought this way, you could have your temple as it really ought to be and privacy at the New Moon. And I'd be here if you needed me." Lumen's brow furrowed, and Gideon cursed himself. "It can be for someone else if you don't like the idea."

"I do like it! I do, really. I think I am just…" Lumen swallowed, and Gideon rubbed her back until her lips started to curve. "Do I come to visit you here, or do you come to the temple, or…" she trailed off and then laughed softly. "Is this *our* home, or yours?"

Gideon pulled Lumen through the door at her question, grinning and chest pounding. "Ours if you want it, sweet spirit." He gave her a brief moment to look around the open room and the stairs that would eventually lead up to a bedroom, and then he crowded her to the wall, reaching up to tilt her head back to look at him. "There will always be a place for you wherever I go, Lumen."

He bent his head to kiss her, sating himself on the subtle flavor of her, the plush of her mouth. A thought occurred to him. and he pulled back, smiling as she chased him for more.

"There'll have to be a room for Colin too then. I'll talk to Mitchell about extending the bottom floo—"

Lumen surged up, hands dragging him back to her, a happy sigh falling against his mouth as she sucked and nibbled on his lips, wiggling closer. His hands made greedy passes up and down her back, settling on her ass and holding her against him as he stepped forward, pinning her to the new walls. The house still smelled of fresh-cut cedar, and the windows had yet to be scavenged so bird calls came ringing through, mingling with Lumen's pretty whimpers.

She'd gained some of her health and weight back since the winter, and it gave her new softness that Gideon relished sinking against. She was regaining her strength and her hunger. The passion she once let him lead her into, she now took for herself.

Her hands dug between them, tugging his tunic loose from his pants and pulling free the ties. Gideon pulled away from the kiss, traveling over her jaw with soft bites and licks, down to her neck, sucking on her flesh like summer fruit. He'd made a study of what left her breathless, and what made her wet between the thighs, and if she wanted to hurry then he would be sure she was ready.

Lumen's head thunked against the wall as he hunched and kissed over her collarbone, making light marks with scrapes of his teeth. They'd fade before they made it back to the party, and Lumen could keep her Priestess' dignity in front of the other soldiers. She arched, thrusting against him, and Gideon mouthed the skin above the collar of her dress, squeezing her ass through her skirt. When he made to lower to his knees, Lumen held tight to his arms to hold him.

"No playing," she gasped. "I want my beast."

She said the words gently, some old subjects still tender between them, and Gideon lifted his head to meet her gaze. Her cheeks were pink, lips wet, and her eyes were dark with desire and ringed with shining silver. He grinned and released a soft growl, and Lumen's face lit up with easy pleasure.

You lucky fucker, he thought, Dominic and Finley's voice mingling in his head with his own. She'd taken him back with a heart twice as open, and he wasn't entirely sure how it all had happened.

Gideon stood, looming over her, making that low purring sound that turned her eyelids heavy and her breath panting. He would've liked to lay her bare on their bed, watch her hair tangle against the sheets as he thrust into her, but that would have to wait for later. He pressed his chest to hers so he could feel her breathing, rapid and needy.

"Skirts up, sweet spirit," he said, watching Lumen's tongue wet her bottom lip.

He helped, hands sliding to ruck up fabric, and then opened his own pants, lowering them just enough. When he caught the first glimpse of Lumen's sex, slightly shining and sweetly rosy,

Gideon scooped her up by the back of her thighs and pinned her to the wall.

"Oh!" she gasped, smile stretching and a soft giggle escaping.

"You like that?" he asked, lining up their hips so he could tease her pretty pussy with his cock, stroking the outside and readying his length with her arousal.

Lumen's hands clutched at his shoulders, and she whined as she realized he held her still, hips in his grip and back pressed to the wall. "I do," she breathed, breasts swelling against the line of her collar.

He leaned in, and sucked over her pulse, continuing the slow roll against her. She was scorching hot and making him slippery with her own desire, and he was quickly becoming hard to the point of painful. But he liked this moment, the desperation before the union, the wondering and knowing how it would feel to sink into her again, feel her clutching him head to toe, base to tip.

"Gideon, please," she breathed.

He liked that too, her begging. No, he *loved* that. Every bit as much as when she arched her eyebrow at him when she thought he was full of shit, or the way she pushed herself to see to everyone's care, even when it left her feet blistered and her body sore. She could see to others if she would let him see to her.

Gideon nuzzled her jaw, and he stopped his teasing, the head of his cock nudging and dipping into her entrance. "I love you, sweet spirit."

Lumen gasped, either at his sudden thrust forward or his words. "Gods, Gideon, yes! Love you!"

He groaned as molten velvet sucked at his length, Lumen's high breathy notes were music drowning out the worries in his head, her little nails digging into his back to drive him on. Her mouth was open in silent shock as if she'd forgotten how good it felt when they were joined like this. He hadn't. Hadn't forgotten the impossible grip she took on his length and thought whimsically that it matched her grip on his heart, although he knew it'd make her laugh if he said so.

"Don't stop now," Lumen said, gasping and smiling.

Gideon huffed and started to fuck her in earnest, not too rough at first although he knew she'd demand it of him by body and words before they were done. Lumen raced to her endings, but Gideon loved the act itself too much to rush to the finish. Her eyes fell shut, lips parted, the wet slaps of flesh filling the room along with her soft sighs and whimpers. Gideon leaned in to take those with his mouth, swallowing her cries as her legs wrapped around his hips. Their tongues twisted together, and Gideon moaned as she squeezed on his length.

Someday, he'd have this every night. Every morning. He'd fight the war back from their door every day too if he had to. He felt almost bad for the others, Dominic and Finley. But not enough to stop.

"Oh fuck, Gideon, more," Lumen moaned, tearing away and offering her throat again. He latched on with his lips over the long muscle, giving up his slow, long strokes in favor of fast, shallow ruts, not drawing out but staying deep inside her, grinding against her little button until she was shaking all around him.

Mine, he thought. *Hers.* She was scorching on his length, the fire barreling forward, swirling in the pit of his gut and licking down to his sac as it drew up. Fuck, they would be done soon and he never wanted it to end.

Gideon drew out, and Lumen cried at the loss, eyes wide with the shock. "Windowsill," he growled, stepping back on wobbling feet. He could make this last a little longer, he was sure of it. He spun her to the sill, now every bit the beast she'd requested. Lumen laughed, and Gideon grinned, pushing her down to her elbows and then flipping her skirts up to expose her pretty ass to his view and the sunlight.

"Gideon yes!"

He drove back in, watching his length sink into her this time, her glistening red flesh swallowing every inch of him. He glanced up, and Lumen's smile was tucked against her shoulder, pale eyes watching him coyly. Her fingers were wrapped around the edge of the window, a breeze falling through to caress them both and stir her hair.

"Touch yourself," he growled.

Lumen bit her lip, and one hand vanished beneath her skirts. He knew the exact moment she obeyed his order, her eyes fluttering shut and her cunt squeezing him tightly. Lumen moaned, head dropping as he started up again, full drives of his hips, fast and just hard enough to make her knees shake. He wrapped his hand around her hips to keep her from falling and then let himself fall into the hypnotic rhythm of fucking, every deep thrust drawing out a grunt and a bubbling threat of pleasure that it might be his last.

Lumen's back shuddered, her breaths fast and high, fingers making her skirts shake over the floor, and Gideon grit his teeth as she came with a soft wet rush and flutter all over his cock. He fucked her through it until she sounded desperate and anxious, and then let himself go to pieces, falling over her back. His hands slapped the stone, and he rose up on his toes as he came with three quick, uneven snaps of his hips, heat exploding in his gut and shooting forward to fill her.

They moaned together, and Gideon gathered Lumen up against him as he sank to his knees. Her head dropped back to his shoulder, breasts heaving as she caught her breath. Gideon reached a shaking hand up to soothe the hair away from her face as he slipped out from inside her, the pair of them whimpering.

"Good?" he asked.

Lumen snorted, and her head rolled until her temple rested against his cheek. "More than good, Gid," she said.

His chest swelled with pride. He'd strive for even better that evening when she'd had enough of the party.

GIDEON'S CHEST was warm against her back as they sat at the fringe of the party circled around the bonfire. Revelers spun in circles around the edge of the blaze, arms raised, shrieks of happiness like wild cries of animals at night. The ale was running low, the food had all been devoured, and soon happy exhaustion or rowdy desire would take everyone to their beds.

It had been a rich day, between the wedding and Gideon taking Lumen to see the house he'd been building in secret. Hope seemed to cluster in the air around them like the sparks leaping off burning logs, and Lumen wondered if the feeling was every bit as fragile, liable to burn out on its path to the heavens.

Lumen was ready to turn to Gideon and coax him up to bed, when Colin broke out of the circle of dancers, running and stumbling on his way to where she sat in the frame of Gideon's body. His hand stretched out, fingers wiggling as he stood before her, gasping for his breath.

"Come and dance, Lady," Colin said.

Gideon vibrated at her back with a soft laugh, and Lumen shook her head, waving her hand. "Go on, go back to the others," she said.

"Not without you!" Colin's cheeks were bright with exertion, his smile spread wide. There was no sign of his deep frowns or the little line of worry between his brow tonight, and his grin was infectious.

"One song," Gideon said in her ear. "I'd like to watch."

Lumen blushed, although she couldn't say for sure why. Colin took his chance, catching her hand, and Gideon's wrapped around her ribs, lifting her from the ground with little effort. She glared over her shoulder at her lover, but her lips were already twisting in a smile. Gideon rose from the ground as Colin tugged Lumen to the frenzied circle, falling in place between grinning Jennie and an incandescently tipsy Inda.

Her first steps were only stumbling as the frenzy of the circle tugged her along. She wasn't buzzed and dizzy from alcohol like the last time she'd danced by a fire, and she didn't have the same giddy high of movement the rest of the dancers had worked themselves into. But she promised Colin a dance, and his smile was so bright as he glanced over his shoulder at her. Lumen picked her feet up faster to meet the tempo of clapping hands and shouting song from the men outside the circle.

Through the flames, she caught a glimpse of Gideon circling the fire, moving from where he'd sat with her to join Dominic and Finley under the shadow of an old oak. It struck her to see them all together. Those were the three men who'd known her, at least physically. Even though they were friends, they seemed impossibly different to her. Gideon was a strange combination of innocent and warrior, as happy to treat her like a delicate object to be treasured as he was to rut her like an animal at her command. Finley projected cold control in an attempt to disguise a fragile craving to be cared for, and Lumen suspected that she and he had more in common in their temperaments than she was ready to admit. Dominic, however, she understood less now than she had months ago while hating him.

Was he changing or had they refused to know one another? He'd been the fearsome general from the start, predictably demanding. Lumen remembered those first nights in his bed with detachment, remembering that she was unaware of how to proceed and confused at her own shifting reactions to his touch. There was affection later, a dreamy kind of hesitant kindness and attention to one another, but Lumen didn't think of that man as the same one who stood glowering under the oak. This was a new stranger. Not the cruel general who ruled over others with merciless law. And not the teasing seducer who held her pleasure under his touch as a victory that could be used to bargain emotions from her.

As if her thoughts had traveled to him, Dominic looked up from the ground, locking eyes with her as she ran her third ring around the fire. She was flushed and breathless, and her cheeks were still full of the smile she'd shared with Colin. He didn't look away and his expression didn't shift. There had been a point where she'd read the faintest twitch of his face and understood its meaning. Now she was sure they were two people who knew both intimate details and yet nothing of one another.

The circle turned, and Lumen gasped as the connection broke. Dominic was only a piece of her history, fragmented and painful. In another nine months, he might vanish from her life completely. Or they might all be dead if the army's mission failed.

The clapping teetered off, and clammy hands released their grips, dancers falling out of the ring. Lumen remained standing in place, facing the fire and the rising sparks, her chest heaving as she caught her breath.

"Are you troubled, sweet spirit?" Gideon's hands clasped her hips, drawing her back from the bonfire's hot glare.

"Only because I let myself be," Lumen admitted with a wry smile. She turned in his grip and sagged against his chest.

Gideon frowned, and Lumen lifted her head, resting her chin against him so he could see she was mostly joking. "I think the young ones are going for a swim," Gideon said, as a whooping crowd took off at a run toward the lake.

"The young ones?" Lumen asked, nose scrunching as she smiled. "Am I an ancient one, then?"

Gideon's somber worry cracked, and he grunted a laugh. "Diving into lakes during the full moon is no past time for a Priestess." His hands slid from her waist to her ass, and Lumen squeaked as he lifted her, arm banding beneath her bottom to hold her to his chest. "Would be much more seemly for her to be escorted back to her chambers."

"And once she reaches her chambers?" Lumen asked, holding her laugh in her lungs until it tickled.

"Then she'll need to be attended," Gideon said, voice lowering. He took long strides away from the bonfire with her in his arms. Over his shoulder Lumen spied Finley and Dominic turning away, heading for the wedding camp at the edge of the field.

"Attended how?" she asked, to play along with his teasing.

"She must be undressed, washed," Gideon said, pausing briefly to nose against her ear, nibbling the lobe until she shivered. "Kissed, and worshipped...fucked until she cannot think of worries to trouble her."

Lumen sighed and toyed with the ties at Gideon's collars. "She will leave her worries on the fire for tonight."

"That's all I ask, sweet spirit."

"YOU'RE ABOUT TO TRAMPLE THE WILD GINGER," LUMEN WARNED.

Finley froze in place, foot lifted in the air, and grimaced at the floor of the forest. Was it the spiky leafed cluster with the white flowers? Or the fat heart-shaped leaves laying low against the ground?

Lumen joined him, crouching and pulling up a tangled system of roots, fat round leaves rustling as she showed him the thick base. Her fingers smudged away the dirt and she broke a piece off, passing it to him. He took a small bite, eyebrows raising at the peppery and sweet flavor.

"It can be used to soothe stomach cramps and also as a contraceptive, although not as reliably." She pointed to the other plant he'd been at risk of mowing down. "That's ground elder."

"The one used for cordials?" he asked.

"No that's regular elder," she said, smiling and ducking her head. "Ground elder will help with arthritic symptoms."

Finley huffed and shook his head, glancing around the lush woods. "You have an entire vocabulary of sight where all I see is green."

Lumen shrugged and stood, passing him the bundle of wild ginger. "I have a lifetime of searching through the woods with my mother, and on my own. When she was still alive, I would simply follow her and help gather. After she died, I realized she understood the patterns of growth and I had to learn them too. Wild ginger likes shade and open space. If the ground is dense

177

with trees it won't grow, but in an open spot like this it will cover the floor."

He nodded and gathered it up. He would memorize the information she gave, even if he had to do it one herb at a time.

"You know, I don't mind gathering more than I need. Gideon can always bring you supplies with my notes," she said, gently to avoid his temper.

Finley swallowed down the offended bite of ill humor that threatened to snap and shook his head. "You shouldn't be responsible for us."

"Like you and the army shouldn't be responsible for me?" Lumen murmured.

She turned away from him, stopping near the path to pull up more ground elder. Finley's heart beat with a heavier tempo in the following silence, unsure how to answer her. Unsure if he *should* answer her.

"We're only trying to undo the damage."

She shook her head, silver eyes glancing over her shoulder. "You know it's too late for that. It's done. I'm hardly the first woman, and your army was hardly the first to commit those kinds of crime."

"That doesn't make it right."

"No. But it can't be undone."

Finley was breathing too heavily, as if they'd been running through the woods. He followed her to a tree, and this time he recognized it and its purpose. Ash, with its leafy seed pods hanging in vast clusters. He grabbed a handful, and Lumen's lips twitched with approval.

"We might stop it from happening again," Finley said slowly.

Lumen looked at him again finally. She was a force of nature in her stillness, somehow able to act as a whirlwind that threatened to drag him closer, without so much as blinking her eyes. She nodded, and her grip loosened around his soul.

"Let's go down to the water. We'll find nettle on the shady banks," Lumen said.

Nettle by the water in the shade, Finley thought with one

side of his mind. With the other, he wondered what Lumen really thought of their new mission in the war.

"Gideon goes north with you and the others tonight?"

He nodded before remembering she had her back to him. "Oshain wants a battle. Dominic thinks they'll try their luck from two directions, just to test us." He watched her closely, her hands appearing from within her deep black sleeves to fuss and fidget together. "But he's Gideon, so you'll see him back here as soon as the fighting is done."

"You'll send word if he's hurt?" Lumen asked softly.

Finley's fists tightened. She cared for Gideon, worried for him, and he assumed he must be jealous. Except, with the jealousy mingled a kind of gratitude. She gave Gideon a reason to fight in battle, yes, but also one to survive. And if Gideon ever needed a miracle to save him from his own blind bravery, Lumen would be just that.

"Of course," he said. "He's more careful with himself when he has you to return to."

She only frowned deeper in response, and Finley considered kicking himself, except he'd have no way to explain the odd action to her. Lumen pulled gloves from the pockets of her robes and passed them to him, nodding to the weeds on the bank of the lake as they approached.

"You'll remember nettles," she said, sharp and confident.

He was less certain of the fact, but he'd make the effort.

SIX DAYS LATER, Lumen paced the drive in front of the temple, the sky deepening to violet on the horizon. Three days before, when she expected Gideon back from the battle with Oshain at any moment, one of the new soldiers had arrived with word. Gideon was well, he had an errand, he would return by nightfall in three days more time.

Lumen had gone directly toward the stables to saddle Sosha and follow the soldier back to the village, certain Gideon must've been too injured to ride back to her. Jennie and Colin had coaxed her back inside with reassurances. Finley was not too proud to refuse to call for her if she was needed. Either Gideon needed to heal for a few days or he was on a mission for Dominic. A brief urge to throttle the general passed through her, but it was half-hearted. Dominic was trying to stay out of her life as best he could, and if he'd made a demand on Gideon it was unlikely that he'd done it only to torment her.

Her patience was thin at best. The soldiers who'd gone to the battle in the north had already returned. She needed to see Gideon and know that he was safe. Her body was restless and aching, wondering and worrying over him.

A blue shadow appeared over the swell of the road, the broad shoulders on the front of a low wagon unmistakably familiar to her. An animal's low bleat echoed up from the road, rising in pitch and volume. Lumen's laugh was sudden and breathless, relief stealing the air from her lungs as she realized the reason for Gideon's absence.

She shook her head as he reached her on the road, and the cow in the cart let out a second agitated cry.

"What have you done?" she asked.

"Colin said your birthday was coming," Gideon said, grinning. "Thought I'd better find us a cow for that butter and cream you've been craving."

Tears sprung to Lumen's eyes, and she raised her hand to cover them quickly. "Where on earth did you find a cow?"

"Oshain left the east unguarded, so I went with one of the young lads to a farm that's been supplying all the armies. They had four dairy cows, but we talked them out of one."

Lune's light, she was crying over the thought of butter. Or more likely, the lengths Gideon would go to see her happy.

"Come up here and let me drive us home, sweet spirit."

Lumen swallowed and flicked the wetness off her cheeks, reaching out to Gideon's waiting hand and letting him pull her up into the cart. He flicked the reins, and then Lumen's arms were around his neck as she peppered kissed up his jaw to the corner where it met his ear. His beard was growing thick since he'd been away, and while it was coarse, Lumen didn't mind the tickle and scratch against her skin.

"Come closer," he huffed, arm circling her waist, holding her to his side so tight she could only just breathe. "I've hungered for you while away."

"And you've made me sick with worry," Lumen growled, although now the worry was transformed to delight at having him back and happy surprise with what he'd brought for her.

Gideon clucked to the horses and tilted his head to offer Lumen his throat. She leaned away and snorted. "You're filthy," she noted.

"I've been on the road for days," he said.

"Then you'll have to hunger until I have you dusted off. The beard may stay at least," she said. Gideon's eyebrow raised in surprise, and Lumen offered him a wicked grin. "Until I decide if I like how it feels against my sex."

"Wicked spirit," Gideon growled. "Call for Colin when we get to the doors and have him settle the cow in."

Lumen hummed and feigned thought. "I don't know. I should like to name her and see her settled before I retire for the night."

"Call for the boy or I'll fuck you in the haystacks and then we'll both be filthy," Gideon growled.

The cart stopped by the doors, and Lumen pulled herself free, jumping down just as Jennie and Colin threw the doors open. "We have a new guest!" Lumen cried. She glanced back at Gideon and winked as Colin and Jennie both shouted and cheered, and the cow bellowed in answer.

THE STARS WERE thick in the sky the night of Lumen's birthday. Jennie had fashioned a quilt out of old curtains, and the four residents of the temple had spread it over the grass for a picnic. There was goat's cheese and tart apples and mushrooms in an egg filling pie, sweet biscuits, and the last of the season's strawberries with cream poured over the top, and their first glasses of fermented cider.

Lumen was drowsy on the blanket, her head resting on Gideon's stomach, his fingers in her hair and her own in Colin's. Jennie returned from the kitchen, a fond and soft smile on her lips.

"Let me take the boy up to bed," Jennie whispered.

Lumen almost refused, it was lovely to hold him like this, sleeping and safe. Then she caught the sly smile Jennie shared with Gideon over her head, and realized they would be left alone like this under the stars together.

"Five more minutes," Lumen bargained. Gideon didn't twitch, just continued brushing his fingers through her strands, and Jennie nodded and relaxed on the blanket.

Peace won't last, the warning voice whispered in her head. Lumen brushed it away. She knew as much, but she deserved this moment. She was falling asleep, eyes blinking at the stars, fingers stilling in Colin's hair when Jennie deemed their time up.

"Thank you," Lumen murmured as the woman scooped the boy up.

"Thank you, Lady," Jennie whispered, nodding and retreating to the Manor.

Lumen expected Gideon to ravage her the moment they were alone, but Gideon excelled at surprising her, and they remained still for several moments until her curiosity won out. Lumen rolled to her stomach, resting her chin over her hands on his chest.

"When is your birthday?" she asked.

"Don't know," Gideon said with a shrug. When she sat up, he smiled and tilted to his side, tugging her to face him, their hips nestled close. "I think it's in the spring. No one at the brothel got to celebrate their birthday, and we didn't have the money anyway. My mother said she didn't remember, but I think it was in the spring. Every spring, she'd find something small to give me. A toy or a treat she could share with me."

"We'll pick a date," Lumen said. "Or celebrate when you're in the mood to."

Gideon grinned. His hand settled on her hip, pressing gently, guiding her to her back. The grass cushioned her body. They'd found a smooth stretch of land to gather on, and while it wasn't as soft as their bed, Lumen had no complaints as Gideon nudged her legs apart with his knees, balancing above her on his palms.

"And if I've a mind to celebrate now?" he asked.

Lumen laughed, trying to turn away from his persistent stare. He steadied himself on one hand and used the other to turn her head back.

"I'll have to think of a gift to give you," Lumen said.

Gideon hummed, eyes narrowing. He lowered over her, and Lumen held her breath as he pressed his lips to her forehead. She exhaled, shaky and sighing, and Gideon shifted his lips, trailing them like a feather down the length of her nose and making her laugh. He hovered over her lips, eyes on hers, and smiled slowly.

"What?" she asked.

"I can see the stars in your eyes," he said.

Then he was grazing his mouth over hers, gradually deepening the kiss. Lumen's hands traveled up his back, rucking up his shirt so she could warm her fingers against his skin. She arched and tried to rub herself against him, but he held his body just out of reach. When her lungs burned with the need for air, Gideon drew away, sucking briefly at her jaw, and down her neck. He settled on his knees, and then his hands were on her breasts, massaging and gripping.

"Gideon, please," she sighed, although she liked this slow pace of his tonight, tender and careful and patient. They were pretending there was no war, she thought. Pretending to be lovers without a painful story of finding one another.

She tugged his shirt up over his head and immediately regretted it as he pulled away laughing. The new moon was only a few more nights away so the light was dim, but it stood out on the scars on his chest, casting them in deep silver. He was a giant sitting over her like this, and beautiful, a god of war whose flame was smothered in the dark of night.

Gideon's eyes trailed down from hers, over her throat marked with his kisses, to where his hands covered her breasts through her dress. His thumb swiped across the top, feeling the tip of her nipple pebbled through fabric. He crouched, and Lumen held her breath as his lips wrapped around the spot, thumb and forefinger pinching her flesh. At first, it was only muffled friction, him mouthing over the dress, and Lumen laughed at the awkwardness. And then it grew wet from his tongue—hot and sticky and scraping at her sensitive flesh.

"Oh gods," she breathed, and Gideon growled in approval.

He soaked the fabric and sucked the spot until she thought she was tight and sharp enough to cut the threads. Satisfied, he retreated, moving to the other to repeat the process. Every breath dragged her taut nipple against wet and cooling cloth, and soon she was panting, enjoying the scratch and the foreign sensation of being touched while Gideon was focused elsewhere. What would it be like if there were two of him? The stray thought ran through her head and brought with it a shocking fantasy of an entirely different set of hands and lips joining Gideon's. She pushed it away, arching into Gideon's mouth, focusing on the pressure of his teeth and tongue manipulating her flesh until she was grounded in the moment and gasping out pleas for more.

Gideon sat back on his heels, fingernails scratching over the wet material of her dress. Lumen moaned and reached for him, but he wiggled away, scooting down the blanket until she realized what he was after. Her hands joined his in pulling her skirts up over her hips, and she finished the work as he braced her knees apart to make room for his shoulders.

Sitting up on her elbows, Lumen looked down and caught Gideon's feral grin as he eyed her center under the faint light of the crescent moon and stars hanging above them.

"Here is my present, sweet spirit," Gideon growled.

Lumen laughed, landing on her back as Gideon pressed an open-mouthed kiss to the top of one knee, and then the other. Back and forth, he worked his way up the inside of her thighs. Cool air on wet fabric teased at her breasts, and Gideon's hot breath stung against her swollen and expectant sex.

"I could spin to you, and we could enjoy each other at the

same time," Lumen offered, hips riding the air and trying to draw Gideon to his goal faster.

"And deny me my chance to sink into your sweet cunt with my full length while you're swollen and slick from riding my beard through your pleasure three times?" Gideon asked. Lumen giggled at the threat, and Gideon's tongue flicked out, licking a stripe up her lips. She moaned and fisted her fingers into the blanket as she realized he was serious.

"Gideon, wait—"

He didn't wait, diving in with lips and tongue and teeth against her, his beard teasing at her ticklish skin while he focused his attentions on her core, tongue thrusting in and upper lip caressing her clit. Lumen cried out and tilted her hips, opening herself for more.

Fine, they would celebrate their birthdays together if this was how he liked to do it. She could have her revenge by morning, no doubt.

"Fingers in my hair, sweet spirit. I want you to steer me," he hissed.

Lumen sucked in a deep breath, wrapping her legs over his shoulder and taking a firm grip of his curls. She tugged him closer against her and cried out as he growled and renewed his touch with twice the hunger. Three orgasms before he would fuck her properly? Lumen rocked her hips with all the demand that made Gideon wild with lust. Three wouldn't take long.

DOMINIC CLOSED HIS EYES, FACE TIPPED UP TO THE SUN, AND LET his horse lead him over the shallow hills.

The northern winter may have been brutal and desolate, but as summer deepened, Dominic began to appreciate sitting in one place for so long. The scenery grew lush and fragrant around the village. He accompanied a group of men down to the Fenn estate to help with the farming more than once and found the task a calming kind of exertion. He indulged briefly in a fantasy of growing up in the north as a farmer's son, until he remembered that all the farmers' sons had been conscripted and died in the war by the command of generals like him.

More surprising, he began to find inactivity peaceful instead of irritating, and took the opportunity to leave the village and wander the land on horseback. It was probably foolish, they were still at war although it appeared to have cooled and lost even more of its pace since midsummer.

Hooves beat like a soft drum, nearing him in a valley near the stream—the horse was more than happy to wander to the water —and Dominic frowned and released a brief sigh before straightening. He tightened his grip on the reins and turned to face the rider. It was Rodney Mitchell, and all of the lazy day's peace evaporated. Mitchell had his cottage with the Ramsey woman and children near Lumen, and would've been riding since dawn to find him.

Dominic met him halfway, already prepared for the news.

"Stalor's on its way. We put a man in the quiet parts south of us and he sent word last night. I've been to the village already," Mitchell said.

Dominic nodded. "Good. I'll ride to meet them. Race back, ready whoever is willing to fight."

"We're all ready, sir," Mitchell said, dark face hard with determination. "It feels good to fight for a home I can actually see at the end of the day. We're not giving it up."

Not unless Stalor snatched their lives from them. That was Dominic's job, ensuring that wouldn't happen.

He rode fast back to the village and found the men already grabbing what was left of their armor and weapons. There was a cart loaded with Finley at the helm, and Dominic pushed through the crowd.

"Nicholson, Richards, Lawerence, Yardley," Dominic rattled off three more names of soldiers, directing them to the back of the cart before he turned to Finley. "They're our best next to Gideon. Take them down ahead of us, as fast you can, and I'll meet them on the field. I want you to go to the temple."

Finley balked, eyes wide, and Dominic raised his hand to hush him. "Tell Lumen you're waiting on us to arrive after the fighting, but if you get word that we've failed, you take her and the boy and whoever else you can reasonably grab, and you run them out of reach. Back to the convent, over the line, I don't care. I'll make sure you hear it before it's too late."

"And if she won't go?" Finley asked, brow furrowing.

Dominic huffed. "Do what you have to."

Finley might like to think he was too gentle to throw Lumen in the back of the cart, but Dominic knew they were all too desperate to see her live to fail in the task at this point.

"Hold them back, Dominic," Finley said, gathering up the reins as the last man loaded himself into the wagon. "That's the only way this ends well."

Dominic sucked in a breath, but couldn't find the words to answer before Finley was wheeling the men down the road as fast as he could.

FINLEY WANDERED through the temple the next morning, struck by how much it had changed. The army had turned the Manor into wreckage, but Lumen had turned that wreckage into something holy, and now the place felt ancient and sacred unlike anywhere he'd ever been before. The walls of rooms were barren of art, and the stone had been washed to reveal its age, carpets rolled away to show the paths feet had traveled for decades, centuries probably. He was more than usually aware of his own presence in the space, listening to the echo of his steps on the stone, the rooms empty of the clutter of others that he'd grown used to.

Jennie and Colin must've been out of doors because he never crossed paths with either, but he found Lumen in the workshop they'd shared briefly. Aside from bedrooms, it was the only room he entered that still looked inhabited, and it was full and fragrant with the clutter of drying herbs and labeled bottles and scraps of paper.

Lumen sat hunched over a table, pestle in her fist, grinding a mixture slowly in the mortar. There was a slump to her shoulders and an unevenness in her pace that came from exhaustion.

"You should rest," he said, and immediately regretted speaking as she flinched at his voice.

"I can't," she said, grinding faster.

He opened his mouth to reassure her. Gideon would come back. Stalor wouldn't reach her again. Everything would be fine. But he wasn't Gideon who had faith in his own luck, and he wasn't Dominic who was so determined to be the victor he couldn't imagine any other outcome.

"Will you give me a task to distract me?" he asked.

Lumen sighed but straightened. He was glad she wore her usual clothes, rather than the black Priestess robe, it made her more familiar. She stood away from the table and went to stretch toward the rafters. Finley crossed the room to her, reaching with ease and bringing down a bundle of herbs.

"Those too," Lumen said, pointing to another. "And over

there in the far corner. There's muslin on the counter. Wrap a little of each up inside them, I think they will work well as compresses to fight infection."

Finley set to the work, trying to focus to resist watching her, but the task was too easy to do with half his attention elsewhere. Lumen had started mixing a new blend, something for fever if Finley guessed the ingredients right, when her hand began to shake. He paused, pushing aside the wrapped herbs, and her sudden gasping breath rang clear in the room. He froze, watching like an idiot as Lumen's sobs fell in stuttering breaths from her lips. The pestle was dropped and her palms braced against the table, back heaving as she fought herself, trying to bind up the sounds and her own tears.

Move, you bastard, Finley thought, although it was Gideon's voice. He left the counter and crossed to stand at her side, expecting her to flinch again. Her cheek turned away, but she didn't leave or rush away from him. This isn't about you, he reminded himself.

"They'll win this battle," he said, wishing he could touch her, could draw her to him.

Lumen's head tossed on her neck, something between a nod and a shake. She hiccuped for breath, nails digging into the wood. "And the next?" she asked, voice tight and cracking. "The one after?"

"Maybe," Finley said, wincing at his weak answer.

"Was I meant to leave you all for dead?" Her elbows hit the table, face falling into her hands, and she only sobbed harder as he rested his hand on her back. "If I've come back for this, and Gideon—" a high pitched whine sounded against her hands, and she gasped for several breaths before she could speak again, "— just to end up dead, or running, or in a cage. I can't, Finley, I can't!"

It was his name that broke his resolve, or set it in stone. Finley pulled her up from the table, his hands around her shoulders, and spun her to face him. He drew her tight against his chest, one arm across her back and his other hand in her hair, gripping her braid and tucking her face against his neck. Her sobs hitched and then strengthened, and she tugged at the sides of his sweater, fingers digging into the knitted stitches and clinging to him.

He didn't say a word, he shared her fears for every mark and he wouldn't lie and tell her they were unfounded. When she reached a peak and struggled to breathe, Finley stroked a rhythm up and down her spine, exaggerating his own slow breaths until she began to match them. He tightened his hold on the base of her braid, and Lumen's lips parted against the base of his throat with a soft gasp before she softened against him.

This he knew how to do at least. He failed with the right words, but he was familiar with her responses, knew she relaxed in another's control. After many, many minutes, when the sobs had faded and her breathing was slow and even and she was practically limp against him, he released his hold on her hair. Lumen's head tipped back automatically, eyes swollen and cheeks shining. Her lips were a little red and wet as if she'd been biting on them, and he wanted to suck and soothe on the spot. A moment passed, and Finley's head dipped.

There was salt on her lips, and wetness against his nose from where tears had coated her skin, but she was still familiar to him. He knew the exact swell of her mouth as he took it in his, knew that clean and crisp scent of her. She didn't kiss him back and dread seemed to float upwards through him, like a weight in reverse. First, he was queasy, and then his heart thumped in panic. His throat tightened with regret, and finally, his head caught up and he pulled away.

Lumen's eyes were wide on his, baffled.

Fuck. *Fuck*.

He needed to apologize, but instead, he said, "I know what to do here. Go to your bed and sleep. There's plenty of time before we should expect them back."

Lumen swallowed, stared at him in silence while he held his breath, and then nodded once. Finley's arms seemed heavier as he drew them away from her, forcing himself to step back, give her room to maneuver to the door. She balanced herself briefly with a touch against the table, and Finley swallowed as she looked him over once, head to toe, and then drifted to the door and out to the hall. Either she was following his orders in a daze or taking the opportunity to escape his unwanted advances. He resisted the urge to follow her, he'd done enough damage.

Sol's fire, Gideon might actually strangle him.

DOMINIC REMAINED ON HIS HORSE, watching the injured men trail through the entrance to the temple. Lumen had her arms around Gideon's neck, her cheek pressed to his jaw with her eyes squeezed shut, the pair of them embracing to the side of the steps. Dominic's jealousy had softened in the past month. He was jealous that Gideon could be forgiven where he could not, and jealous of his friend's ability to care directly for Lumen's happiness where he could only fight the forces that surrounded her. Mostly though, he found himself jealous of scenes like this, to be outside of an embrace that was shared with sincere and mutual relief to be together again.

Gideon murmured in Lumen's ear, and she nodded, releasing him and going to a man who struggled to limp up the steps. Gideon, bloodied but uninjured, turned and strode to where Dominic sat high on his horse, his hand cupped against his torn side.

"Can you get down like that?" Gideon asked.

Dominic frowned and tried to slide off the side of the horse, relieved as Gideon caught him and steadied him on the way down.

"You'll need that looked at quick," Gideon said, glancing over his shoulder at Lumen's back retreating through the doorway.

"Not her," Dominic said. "Tell Finley."

"She can mend your wound, Dom," Gideon said, amusement in his eyes contradicting the obnoxiously sympathetic smile he wore.

"Tell Finley," he said, harder. "It's a good scratch, but it's not getting any worse and it can wait till the others are seen. I'll be in..."

He swallowed the rock in his throat as he realized he'd been about to say 'my room,' which was in fact Lumen's room and...

"Use your old one. She and I share mine," Gideon said.

Gods, could the conversation get any more unbearable?

"I'll take Danvers and Charlie's in the attic," Dominic grumbled, not thinking of the extra effort of getting himself up there.

Twenty minutes later, facing an empty room without any bed at all, Dominic shuffled himself to Finley's own room and landed on the mattress. He shucked his armor off to the floor and laid down, hand still on his wound as if he could keep himself from getting blood on the sheets, and fell asleep with less effort than the act had taken in weeks.

A moment later, or maybe hours if the grit in his eyes was an indication, Dominic woke to Finley fussing with his clothes.

"Why didn't you just wait in the infirmary with everyone else?" Finley groused.

"Wanted a rest," Dominic lied. He hadn't wanted to be Lumen's problem.

"So you come up here to make me work on you in the dark? Take your shirt off and use this to clean yourself up so I can see the damage. By candlelight," Finley spat under his breath, moving around the room and lighting candles until there was enough light to see each other.

Dominic took the clean wet cloth in one hand, shrugging out of his shirt. "Can you manage the stitches?" he asked.

Finley's fingers sometimes pained him and grew stiff, and managing a small needle was possible but uncomfortable for the healer. He crouched in front of Dominic, grabbing his thigh and twisting him about without mercy.

"You don't need stitches. It's cut some of the skin back and the healing will be a bit messy, but I can clean it up and bandage you well enough. You'll have to drink Lumen's teas and use her salves to limit the risk of infection."

"Fine...argh!!" Dominic tried to pull away as Finley scratched at the wound.

"Hold still."

"Warn a man, Brink!"

"Did you come up here so none of your men would see you whimpering as I poked the wound?" Finley asked.

Dominic growled and glared down at Finley's head. The healer was washing the area, drawing up fresh blood and scraping away barely healed redness, but Dominic held back his hissing complaints this time.

"What has you so vicious, Healer?"

"Nothing," Finley snapped.

Dominic's eyebrows shot up. He'd been joking mostly, but now he knew for certain that he wasn't the only one with an open wound to be poked at. He'd waited in quiet, looking away as Finley finished dressing the area, bandaging and wrapping his ribs. His touch only grew more brusque with every passing second.

"Did the men make comments again?" Dominic asked. Maybe sending Finley to watch over Lumen had stirred up some of the old mocking about Finley's strength.

"What? No. It's...it's nothing like that," Finley said, shaking his head and sitting back on the floor. He stared down at his own fingers, flexing them over his bent knees and then tightening them into fists.

"Did the work leave your hands in pain?" Dominic tried.

"I kissed her."

There was no mistaking the 'her' in the situation, and for a long stretch of silence, Dominic accepted the idea that Lumen had forgiven Finley for his crimes too. That soft jealousy returned, bitter and aching, but also acceptance with it. Then Finley looked up, and Dominic realized that this idea was impossible, no one would look so tormented after such a reconciliation.

"She was upset, and I calmed her. And then she looked up at me and..." Finley groaned, and his head rolled back. "Fuck. How stupid can I be?"

Dominic resisted the impulse to answer. "What did she do?"

"Nothing. Didn't speak. Didn't move. Just stared at me. I told her to go get rest and she went. Won't you punch me or something?"

"That's Gideon's domain now, I think," Dominic mused, head tipping.

Finley huffed and lifted his head again, nodding. "I expect that any moment now too."

If someone had told Dominic to spend the day alone with Lumen, could he expect to fare much better? Maybe. Lumen would never let herself cry in front of him again, he suspected. She certainly wouldn't hold still while he kissed her.

"Can I taste?" Dominic asked, leaning forward.

Finley stiffened, crumpled on the floor in front of him, eyes narrowed and brow furrowed in confusion. Dominic waited. The request had come unbidden but he wondered, was there still a little of Lumen on Finley's lips? Could he pretend?

"Are we going mad without her?" Finley whispered.

Probably.

Dominic leaned forward, and Finley shifted to his knees, their mouths meeting in a clumsy crash between them. They froze together, lips parted, tongues sneaking out to flick over flesh. Dominic had been naked in a bed with Finley plenty, had shared a woman between them, but they had never kissed. Strangely, it was usually Gideon who took their affection. Dominic and Finley were too similar in their need for control.

He tested this new compromise with a slow, wet, pull of Finley's thin bottom lip. For a moment, there was a whisper of a flavor he'd been missing for months. It might only be his imagination, but even that was better than nothing. Dominic waited for Finley to pull away, but they hovered there, breath mingling and mouths brushing. Finley leaned in, and Dominic swiped his tongue across the other man's mouth, sliding in.

It had been months without any kind of touch, any heat from another person's mouth, any hand on his skin not landing in battle or patching him up from an injury. They moved in hesitating caresses, silent aside from the slick sound of the kiss and the soft rustle of fabric. Finley rose on his knees, Dominic's head arched over his, and sucked briefly on Dominic's tongue. Dominic groaned at the back of his throat, cock stirring in his pants, and they both froze.

Finley retreated, eyes narrowed in suspicion, lips shining from Dominic's kiss.

"Fuck it," Dominic breathed, grabbing Finley by his collar and dragging him up.

He stood, throwing Finley to the bed, one hand holding him there by his chest, the other diving into short strands of hair to fix him in place for another, more demanding kiss. Months ago, Dominic had considered paying one of the women on hand to fuck thoughts of Lumen out of him, but he'd known—reluctantly—that sex wasn't really what had fastened Lumen so deeply in his thoughts. At least with Finley, there was no mistaking who was with him, and no pretending he was not wishing for someone else. They both were.

Finley was stiff on the bed beneath him, accepting the assault but without response. Dominic forced his knee between Finley's thighs, nudging it against Finley's covered length. Finally, the healer broke, groaning into Dominic's mouth as their tongues fucked together. Finley ground himself against Dominic's thigh, hands reaching between them to rub over Dominic's cock. Dominic rutted against the touch and moaned as Finley began to undo the laces of his pants. He pulled away from the kiss, tearing Finley's shirt up his stomach and over his head. They grappled at skin and clothes, breaths panting and fingers scratching in their urgency. Dominic tripped out of his boots and pants, falling forward and barely catching himself above Finley.

Finley wrapped his hand around Dominic's length, the first unfamiliar hand to touch him in months, and Dominic groaned, throat arching. Finley's hand was dry and calloused, rough on his sensitive cock, but even the scratch was better than months of loneliness, not that he'd admit as much. He bucked into Finley's grip, shamefully aware he might finish over the other man's stomach in a startlingly quick display of desperation. He kicked off the last leg of his pants, and then suddenly the room turned around him, Finley's hands on his hips throwing him to the bed.

Finley's pants were sagging down his thighs as he fit himself between Dominic's spread knees. His hair stuck up at the odd angle where Dominic had held it in his fist, and his cheeks were bright. Was it anger or arousal? His impressively long length was half-hard, and Dominic's temporary relief began to mingle with wary awareness.

"You forgot what kind of man I am, General," Finley hissed above him. He leaned forward, one hand going around Dominic's throat. Not tight, but not loose enough for Dominic to sit up and throw him off without real effort. His other raised hand above Dominic's tightly pressed lips, fisted except for two outstretched fingers. "Suck."

Dominic's eyes narrowed, and Finley looked down his nose at him, patient and watchful. *You could refuse*, Dominic thought. Finley's cock was twitching and growing in the quiet, just the control of having Dominic trapped beneath him enough to arouse the man's interest. Dominic had fucked men, Gideon mainly, and mostly when they were young and didn't have the coin to spend on the army's whores while traveling. But he'd always been the one in charge of the situation, or at least the one to do the fucking, even with Gideon who most would've assumed demanded the lead. Finley would probably turn it over if Dominic pressed the issue, but he was curious about Finley's tastes and what it might feel like to be on the other end of a cock for once.

He parted his lips, and Finley's eyebrows lifted briefly with surprise before his fingers slid into Dominic's mouth, fucking against his tongue. He tasted herbal and sweet like honey, some of Lumen's mixtures no doubt. Just thinking of her had Dominic's eyes falling shut, and he sucked in earnest, forcing his tongue between Finley's fingers and enjoying an unexpected burst of pride at the other man's hiss. Finley crawled closer to him, cock bobbing against Dominic's, a dull and temporary kind of pleasure.

Finley pulled his fingers free of Dominic's lips, one hand still cupping his throat, and Dominic tensed when the wet digits skipped his cock, kissing briefly against his sac with a tap, before diving between his cheeks and burrowing against his tight hole.

"Relax." Finley's voice was flat, the opposite of persuasive, and Dominic huffed in answer. His throat was released, and Finley grabbed onto his cock with a sudden efficiency that made him arch and moan, fisting and pumping him like he was driving him directly to orgasm. He squeezed at Dominic's head, pre-cum slipping out onto his thumb, quickly spread down his staff. Dominic squeezed his eyes shut and fucked up into Finley's hand wildly, resenting that he was being finished so early, but also desperate to feel that release. It came with a sudden spike up his groin, unsatisfying and fast but effective all the same. He groaned and arched, hot sticky liquid spilling down the length of his cock. Finley stroked him until he twitched away, and then watched as Dominic sagged and panted on the bed, limp and used up.

A moment later, a finger wiggled up into his ass, the tension bled away by his orgasm.

A rough laugh escaped Dominic's lips. "You bastard."

"You were never going to relax," Finley said mildly. "Besides, there's more to enjoy, you'll see." His finger drew free and then stroked up Dominic's messy cock before returning. This time, Dominic sighed and softened into the intrusion, amused by Finley's manipulation of his pleasure. The long finger worked him loose, a second quickly added. There was a slight burn of the stretch, but Dominic was reasonably used to pain and the harsh orgasm had loosened his head, at least to being used by Finley. Finley's fingers stroked and rubbed inside of Dominic's channel, stretching and then pressing and swirling, massaging him open.

"Go on then," Dominic hissed, annoyed with the slow treatment.

"Shut up," Finley said, lips twitching, continuing in his almost searching touch.

His thumb pressed outside, close to Dominic's sac, and the search landed. An unbidden groan rolled up out of Dominic's chest as warmth flooded his veins and pressure built in his groin.

"Good isn't it?" Finley asked.

Dominic swallowed instead of answering, testing his own response by rocking onto Finley's fingers and gasping as the heat flared. Finley pulled out, and Dominic refused to believe that the sound he made was a whimper—it was annoyance in his throat, not need. Finley twisted and rummaged on the floor.

"What are you doing?" Dominic ground out, wanting to drag Finley's hips to his and force the man inside.

"Hang on, here this will do." Finley poured oil out of a jar and into his hands, and Dominic frowned. "Don't worry, there's nothing special in it." He slicked it up his own length and then bent forward as his cock nestled against Dominic's hole.

Dominic hissed and stiffened as Finley pressed in, lungs gasping for air. Finley didn't stop, or even remind him to relax, only released a long, low moan, hands bracing against Dominic's shoulders and squeezing hard enough to bruise. Dominic lifted his head, taking Finley's face in his hands and drew him in for a thick kiss to distract from the terrifying pressure and pain of being filled. Finley shifted slowly and in small measurements until Dominic's tension eased. His hand loosened on Dominic's shoulder and then reached down, pushing his knees back, some of the tight pressure opening for faster, rougher movements. There were brief instances of the heat and shocking pleasure from Finley's fingers, but they were more distant, and Dominic tried to turn and twist and rock his hips for more.

His tongue swept and plundered in Finley's mouth as if a kiss could measure the same as the intrusion of Finley's cock in his ass. Finley grunted and moaned into the kiss as he fucked Dominic, perfectly aware that no matter what control Dominic had on his mouth, he had the entirety of Dominic's body at his mercy. It scratched at Dominic's pride just as much as it made his adrenaline rush with exciting danger. He hated to be mastered every bit as much as Finley did, but the exploration of new sensation was a minor consolation if only he could get a little more of that heat in his veins, that brief glimpse that there was something bigger than the burst of ecstasy as he came.

Finley pulled away from the kiss, moans louder, hips harsher, cock driving deeper, and Dominic bit at his throat in retaliation for the deep slams inside of him and the sharp snap of hipbones against his ass. He squeezed around Finley's long cock, and Finley's rhythm stuttered so he did it again.

"Yes!" Finley hissed. "Fuck, yes!"

Very well, then. Dominic rocked and dragged on Finley's cock, surprised and pleased by a return of his cock to life, jumping and growing with stiff arousal. Finley's hands wrapped around his hips, holding Dominic still for one rough thrust, and then another, and a third until hot release spread up inside of him. Dominic's nose wrinkled at the thought. He should've demanded the other man pull out first.

Finley did pull out, and it was a messy and unsatisfying feeling for a moment, Dominic aware that he was leaking on the bedsheets like a woman. Finley looked down at him with a drowsy kind of satisfaction, and then his smile grew at the sight of Dominic's half-hard cock. He pulled away, and Dominic nearly got up to clean himself, when suddenly Finley's fingers were refilling him, immediately hunting down that forward and strange place that made even Dominic's hands and feet throb like they were an extension of his cocks.

"Sol's Fire," he groaned. Wasn't Finley done with him by now? Except he was suddenly grateful that wasn't the case.

"It is a little like that," Finley murmured. He seemed to hold a knot of muscle between the fingers up Dominic's ass, and his thumb behind his sac, and he rolled it in his touch.

"Fuck, gods," Dominic growled, half tempted to tear himself away, terrified of how much stronger this was than a good tight pussy or his own practiced fist.

Then Finley lowered his head, sucking Dominic's length into his mouth, and Dominic wouldn't have escaped even if the Oshain army was tearing down the door. He writhed and rock and begged as he never had before, thrilled and embarrassed to be undone by his friend. Finley sucked until his cheeks were hollow, able to take Dominic's entire length between his hand and mouth.

Fire burned behind Dominic's eyes, and he gave himself over to the drum's pulse of bliss in his veins. It was not one orgasm, but a thunderstorm of them, making him shudder uncontrollably until he was squirming backward out of Finley's touch. The candlelight in the room seemed to dim as he escaped, the temperature of the air cooling on his skin, sweat dewed across his temple and upper lip and on his chest.

"Enough, enough," he muttered.

Finley laughed and released him for a moment, standing and shedding his pants finally before crawling back into the bed, sitting against the wall and watching Dominic catch his breath along the foot of the bed.

"Do you want company here or to be left alone?" Finley asked, although Dominic suspected the man had already made the decision for him, given he'd finally finished undressing.

He was tempted to kick Finley out, overwhelmed by what Finley had known about his body that he never had.

"Stay," Dominic said. He pushed himself up on wobbling elbows and reached a hand out to Finley, who dragged him up the bed. They stared briefly at one another, and then Dominic settled for sitting at his side, close enough to touch but without curling into the other man. "Where'd you learn that?"

Finley laughed and scrubbed his fingers through his hair, sinking down into the bed and shoving a pillow beneath his head. He was wiry, but more muscular than he looked while dressed, Dominic realized. And now Dominic understood why the women had screamed under Finley's touch. It wasn't pain, or not pain alone. Finley understood a body's limits and secrets in a way most didn't.

"It was one of Cantalion's tricks," Finley said softly. Dominic frowned at that, and Finley shrugged, glancing up at him. "I know. It's complicated."

Dominic hummed in agreement, and left the bed, blowing out the candles around the room. He returned and slid in next to Finley, their backs touching as they faced opposite sides of the room.

"I didn't think of her," Finley said.

Dominic huffed and blinked at the dark. "Yes you did," he said, and Finley sighed. "So did I."

I<small>F</small> S<small>TALOR</small> <small>AND</small> O<small>SHAIN</small> <small>WERE</small> <small>TO</small> <small>COMMUNICATE</small> <small>DIRECTLY,</small> Lumen suspected her newfound community would not have survived the summer. The army drifted back and forth between the temple and the village, scouts constantly on the lookout to see who was attacking from what side. She waited for the day when the south and north rose up against them at the same time and the army divided, but it didn't come. *Only a matter of time,* her dark voice warned her.

If the soldiers were exhausted from the constant juggle of battles, Lumen carried her own weariness from traveling to and fro to see to their injuries. She widened her usual territory for foraging to keep up with the demands of minor injuries and preventing infections. The small chapel filled up for new moon prayer with the added new residents in the area, and small cabins and cottages were springing up on open land. Gideon did his best to keep her out of the fields so she could focus on her more spiritual works, and he would've kept her out of the post-battle infirmary if he could have. Lumen had learned stubborn-ness and relished putting her foot down.

She never lost her desperate need to see Gideon safe when the swords were done clashing, no matter how many skirmishes passed. Although Finley had been right that Gideon took more care with himself on the battlefield now.

"You haven't corrected any of my wrappings," Finley said,

moving to her side where she was reorganizing her stock after the bustle of nursing.

His voice was smooth in her ear as he stood like a tall shadow out of the corner of her eye, but one she was finding comforting the more hours they spent working together like this. The tension between them from her arrival was gone, or it had grown into a friendship built from their work and their worries. His intensity had retreated, and in its wake there was new room for her to grow more open and bold. As for the kiss... Finley never mentioned it, and she decided it might be wiser to let it go. He still had feelings perhaps, and she still had...Gideon.

"That's because you've finally started using my technique," she said, glancing across the room to a soldier with his wrist recently wrapped. She passed Finley a cup of white willow bark tea to give to the man for his pain and swelling

"For someone with no formal training, you are awfully sure of your methods," Finley said, lips twitching with a smirk.

"For someone with formal training, you had an awful lot to learn from me," Lumen answered.

Finley huffed and shook his head, fingertips grazing against the back of her hand and leaving a trail of glittering warmth as he took the cup and crossed the room. Lumen watched him walk, eyes snagging on the breadth of his shoulders leading down to the nip of his waist, heat tickling her cheeks, before she caught sight of Gideon waiting in the doorway to the courtyard. Gideon's eyes were warm with amusement, arms crossed over his broad chest, and Lumen found herself flushing and turning away in embarrassment. With friendship finding a balance between her and Finley again, there was one unfortunate side effect, she was reminded of their ease and attraction before he'd abandoned her.

Heavy arms circled her waist and Lumen paused in her work as Gideon swept her back against his chest, body bowing over hers to press his lips to the side of her ear. "Saw that, Priestess."

Lumen squirmed out of his hold, and Gideon laughed, grin crooked and genuine. She turned and looked him over head to toe.

"You didn't miss anything the first eight times you checked me for injury," Gideon said, chucking his fingers against her chin. "Done here?"

"Just about," Lumen said, nodding and relaxing as he dropped his teasing.

She leaned her face into his hand, and Gideon's smile softened. "You've got circles under your eyes. Finish up, and I'll bring some food up to the room. Put you to bed before you can find another task for the day."

Lumen was about to object, she wanted to check on Colin and make sure he wasn't overwhelmed with all of his new chores —he'd volunteered to take on the chickens and goats and their cow Henke—when she saw the color of the sky outside. The sun set late this time of year, but it was already well into night, sky inky and speckled with starlight.

"Everyone's retired for the night, sweet spirit," Gideon murmured. "Get up to bed, and I'll meet you there."

She sighed and nodded, accepting the grazing kiss on her cheek. Finley had finished escorting the men out of the infirmary and joined her in tidying up the supplies. They worked quietly, and maybe even comfortably, although Lumen found herself self-conscious with the healer after Gideon caught her staring.

"Goodnight, Lumen. Get your rest. Lune knows we'll probably be heading back to the village to stand against Oshain tomorrow," Finley said. His hand touched against her shoulder and he paused, head tipping to stare at her.

"Will it ever end, do you think?" Lumen asked, meeting his eyes. Gideon was so confident and optimistic, and Finley's pessimism was almost a reassurance. At least his worry matched hers.

"I don't know," Finley said, and the nervy scratching anxiety in the back of Lumen's chest settled, comforted not to be the only one who saw this as a new but similar version of the war they'd already been immersed in. He stepped closer, frown turning down his thin lips. "Is it worse for you than…?"

Than before?

"No," Lumen said, head shaking and shoulders sagging. "No, I would rather be doing this."

Finley sucked in a deep breath and nodded, rolling back on his heels. "Good, so would I. I don't know if it can last, or if it will turn out the way we hope. But I hate myself less these days." He shrugged and turned away from her, wandering to the door. "Go sleep, my lady."

He was out of the room as his voice tugged at her heart, twisting it in an odd, bittersweet direction. Rather than dwell on the feeling, Lumen hurried out and across the courtyard so she could join Gideon. He was waiting for her in their room, the window open to let in a breeze, and a mix of foods crowding a plate on his lap.

Lumen groaned as she stretched and took off her black robes, and then went ahead and wiggled out of her dress, opting to eat in her shift and finally cool off for the day.

"Did you not bring Brink with you?" Gideon asked as Lumen climbed onto the mattress.

She stilled and gaped at him as his feral grin grew, and a barely restrained chuckle shook his chest. "Oh, Gideon, don't," Lumen huffed, trying and failing to steal the plate from his hands as he raised it over his head. She sat up on her knees, but he caught her by her hips and tugged her down to his lap, pecking his lips across her face as she growled and tried to wiggle away.

"Tell me the truth, sweet spirit," Gideon said. "I know you are mine again, and I'll never belong to anyone but you. That's not a question."

"I thought I was meant to be fed and cared for and resting," Lumen snapped. But her light temper just made Gideon joyful with playing, and it was difficult to glare at his brilliant smile and maintain her annoyance.

"I'll feed you if you answer my questions," Gideon coaxed, nuzzling her cheek and nipping at her jaw.

"I'll go to bed hungry," she said.

Gideon growled softly, arms lowering down the plate to fit between them. "Won't have that," he said.

Lumen took a slice of warm toast with goat cheese spread over it and topped with tomato, Gideon's free hand stroking her thigh aimlessly over her shift. The cheese was tart and creamy, and the toast was perfectly crunchy and chewy. She took one bite of the tomato and realized Gideon was winning her over with some secret art of patience and good food. Or maybe she'd only been hungry and easily irritated before.

"Alright, ask," she said.

He flashed her one triumphant look, fighting his own smile, and squeezed his hand around her thigh. "Do you miss him?" She shook her head. "Do you forgive him?"

She swallowed and thought harder, and then finally shook her head again. "Not for leaving. Maybe for not knowing his own mind, but not for leaving without saying anything. I'm not angry at him now. I just don't forgive his actions *then*."

Gideon's eyes wandered up over her head as he processed the thought, and finally he shrugged. "But you like to look at him. Ah, see, you're blushing again. I'm not trying to embarrass you."

"You are a bit, admit it," Lumen said, arching her eyebrows and smiling.

Gideon remained unrepentant. "You could have him if you wanted. Just for sex. I could leave you two alone, or I'd be in the room if you wanted."

Lumen sat perched on Gideon's lap with a smear of goat cheese at the corner of her mouth and a slice of toast raised in front of her open mouth. It wasn't what she'd expected, although maybe she should have. If this were Finley in front of her, he'd be offering to leave and let her fall in with Gideon instead. Gideon's solution was somehow simpler and infinitely more complicated. Not to mention how it seemed to raise the temperature of the room into a blaze.

"Gideon, I..." Lumen set the food back on the plate and kissed Gideon's thumb as he wiped at her mouth. "I'm not sure that I could."

Gideon frowned. "He wouldn't say no."

Lumen laughed, recalling the brief, soft kiss Finley had pressed to her lips weeks ago. No, he probably wouldn't. He no longer looked at her with that recently kicked expression, waiting for her to take him back in, but his gaze wasn't entirely light.

"I don't think it would just be sex," Lumen said, applying the words delicately, holding Gideon's gaze. "And if it wasn't, I'm not sure I'm in a place to...trust him with anything more."

That was all it took, Gideon hummed and nodded, setting the plate down to the side and drawing her close for a slow, shifting kiss until she was wrapped all around him, his hands bracing her back.

Gideon leaned back, laughing as Lumen chased him for another kiss, and waggled his eyebrows. "I could fuck him for you if you wanted to watch."

The sound she made was more like a goose's honk than a lady-like laugh, and Gideon snorted in answer, falling back to the bed and balancing the plate on his chest. "Feast, sweet spirit," he said with a wink.

Lumen licked her lips, Gideon's mint fresh on her skin, and planned to do exactly that as she drank in the deliciously wicked man below her.

DOMINIC SAT in the corner of the bar, watching stares flick in his direction before heads turned away with a snap. Ale was running low now that small battalions were closing in around them, and bad moods were surfacing in the ranks. The men were starting to grumble behind Dominic's back as if he wasn't perfectly aware of the problem, as if he didn't feel the same ache in his feet which seemed to threaten with every step to walk directly off his legs for a few hours respite. They were holding almost fifty miles of territory between Stalor and Oshain, and the strain was growing too great. Any day, Stalor and Oshain would call for battle at the same time, and splitting their ranks would be the end of Dominic's effort to hold the land.

A note lay on the table. Oshain declaring they would 'see him on the field in four days' time.' Their generals were growing cocky, even as Dominic plucked men from their numbers and absorbed them into his own.

Finley entered the bar, a large bag stuffed with his efforts at foraging without Lumen's guidance. Thorns pricked out from the loose weave, snagging on Finley's wool coat. Dominic sat forward and caught the healer's glance with a subtle wave of his hand, pointing to the seat next to him. Finley glanced down at his sack and shrugged, sliding into the seat. Dominic passed him the paper, aware of how the rest of the room watched them. The men would know what was in the note, they'd seen him holding plenty before.

Finley scanned it, jaw working and brow folding. "So be it."

"What if we didn't meet them?" Dominic asked.

"And let them march directly here?" Finley returned.

Dominic licked his lips before answering. "We can't hold this town *and* Lumen's temple."

"Try speaking plainly, Dominic. It is your strategy that counts here, not mine."

"I want to move us south. My priority is there. Let Oshain take back this town, find it empty as they march in."

Finley planted his hands on the surface of the table, leaning far back in his seat. His stare wandered across the bar, meeting the eyes watching them until they turned back to their own company. "And if the men would rather abandon the south?" Finley murmured.

Dominic swallowed hard and nodded. He'd wondered the same thing. "I dragged them all into this twisted position, I wouldn't abandon them."

"Would you abandon her?"

"I would warn her, and Gideon, and..." Dominic huffed. He wanted to throw his head down onto the table, but that was a private kind of hopelessness he didn't need to share with a quarter of their ranks.

"Put it to a vote," Finley said.

"I'm afraid to hear the answer," Dominic muttered.

Finley shrugged and crossed his arms over his chest, scanning the room again. "I can tell you right now, some of these men have friends who have settled near Lumen. Brothers. I've heard from Rosie plenty of times that she misses the girls who settled there. You're right not to expect these men to take up your cause to protect that temple. But they may have their own reasons."

"Towns can be built," Dominic said, a little twinge of hope flickering at the back of his head.

Finley grunted, a dubious sound. "During a harvest season on top of it? You'd better take that vote now, we'll need every minute before winter to build or else we'll end up breaking a promise to Lumen."

Dominic grimaced. That was almost enough for him to change his mind about the entire idea.

"It will attach them to the place though," Finley said softly. "They'll fight harder to keep it."

Dominic stood, pushing back his chair, and for a moment, the soldiers in the room forgot to rein in their curiosity. "Meeting in the square," Dominic said, loud and clear in the room. "Gather everyone."

The men moved with a slow kind of reluctance to the door, one slipping up the stairs to find anyone in their room of the inn.

"Show of hands?" Dominic asked Finley under his breath.

Finley held his palms up and shook his head. "This is your event now. You know my vote."

THE RIDER COULD'VE BEEN ANYONE ON ANY HORSE. HE WAS ONLY a silhouette in black, sunlight bleeding over his edges, but Lumen knew with certainty who rode up to meet her in front of the temple. Gideon was out in the fields, or maybe in the woods working on his house, and Lumen considered retreating into the temple. But Dominic was a new kind of animal lately, mild and reserved, and she wasn't sure which of them was really avoiding the other.

He stopped his horse where she stood at the end of the drive and scanned the area around them. "Where's Jones?"

"Working," Lumen said with a shrug, pulling her basket of herbs closer to her stomach and turning to head for the front doors. "Where's your army?"

Dominic took a deep breath, and Lumen's head prickled with caution until he answered. "Packing. I...I've been wondering how long we could maintain the back and forth recently."

Lumen nodded. "You're wearing them down."

"Oshain and Stalor, or my men?"

She snorted. "Your men."

He grunted—a soft, annoyed sound—and she ducked her head to hide her flickering smile. "You're right. Myself too. I took a vote to the men yesterday. Gave them a choice on whether or not we should decamp from the town we took and...and move south. Focus on holding this land."

Lumen's steps paused, her eyes fixing on the temple as her head spun. Dominic's horse continued to plod forward, and he turned it slowly to face her. This time the sun was on his face, and she could see his expression properly, the scar running down his left cheek shining.

"I should've asked you first," he said, eyes wincing. "We won't be taking up any space in the temple, of course."

"The injured men will come," Lumen said.

Dominic shifted uncomfortably in his saddle. "Not if you'd prefer they didn't."

Lumen shook her head, waving her hand between them and shifting her basket to her hip. "No, you misunderstand. I'm telling you they will."

Dominic's lips quirked briefly, eyes laughing, but he forced his face to sober before she could enjoy the transformation. "Very well. We'll build new shelters if that's all right with you."

Lumen's lips pursed, and a dismissive sound escaped her mouth as she rolled her eyes. "Fine. It's not my land now." He looked as though he didn't agree, one shoulder bouncing, eyes fixed to her in a warm study. "Dominic, this plan is going to get you all killed," Lumen said, trying to wipe the warmth from his face.

"Maybe," he said.

"It's not worth it," she pressed.

Dominic nudged his horse and it came closer, Lumen reaching out to stroke along its neck. He stopped when he towered directly next to her. She tipped her head back to stare up at him, resisting the urge to pull herself out of his weighty gaze.

"Yes it is," he said.

Lumen scoffed gently and caught the flicker of a proper smile over his lips before he was riding back up the road.

"Tell your people to expect us tomorrow."

Lumen gaped at him for a long moment before a sudden and silly realization struck her and she called out. "Bring windows with you!"

Dominic's horse jogged to face her and though the sun was in her eyes, she could perfectly imagine the tangle on his brow. "Windows?"

Lumen nodded. "It's the only thing we don't have for the houses being built."

He barked a laugh and rode away, Lumen's lips twisting as she watched him. At least the men had voted, had been given the choice and weren't being forced to uproot themselves again and settle here in the country for her sake.

It was for her sake, or it was on Dominic's part, just as Gideon fought for her. She couldn't bring herself to ask directly, but he answered all the same.

Am I worth it?

Yes.

Lumen's gut twisted, and she forced her feet to march back to her home where she could find work to occupy herself with until she forced Dominic Westbrook out of her mind.

IN THE NORTH, the heat peaked at the end of the summer. Every day, sweat ran down Dominic's back and chest, either with his sword raised in training and fighting or with a scythe swinging in his arms. Oshain hadn't sent another missive yet, and apparently, the retreat to the south had been a strange enough choice to baffle them and put them on the defense again. Stalor too was growing quiet, running out of small parties to send to battle when so many of their men didn't return. It was a false peace, but it lulled any man who'd resisted the move into a temporary acceptance.

Evening fell late in the day, barely cooling the air off in time for the sun to rise in the morning again. But it was a reprieve to walk through the woods after a day in the fields and not have the burning tongue of sunlight on his neck. Gideon had turned over the house he was building to Dominic and Finley, since he spent his nights at the temple anyway. Dominic avoided Lumen, only catching glimpses of her at the edges of his vision occasionally, so brief he might've imagined them. The privacy of the house in the woods was complete and strange after so long surrounded by men. At least there was Finley around to make it feel like less of a dream.

"Hello, wifey," Dominic greeted, finding Finley putting a meal together on a rustic table they'd fashioned—it wobbled at every opportunity but was generally a useful flat surface, if not a steady one.

"Fuck off," Finley answered with a roll of his eyes. "Or I'll eat during my wanders and leave you to starve."

Dominic could manage for himself too if it came to it, and the joke was too amusing not to use when he had the opportunity. "This is a charming scene, indeed," he continued.

"I swear to Sol, Dominic, I will gut you," Finley muttered.

Dominic grinned to himself and tugged his shirt off over his head, crossing to the bucket of fresh water they kept by the unfinished wing of the house, splashing handfuls over his bare chest to wash away some of the sweat from the day.

"How was your stitching? Have you made me a handkerchief to wipe my brow as I toil?" He and Finley were forming a new kind of friendship while living together that consisted almost entirely of pissing one another off. It was an unexpected source of joy for Dominic to watch the healer's face turn red as he tugged on strands of his own hair and spat weak insults back at him.

Finley snarled and stood at the table, eyes narrowed across the room. "I have a mind to teach you—"

A knock sounded on the door before his threat could be finished, although Dominic could guess the direction. They hadn't fucked after the first time. Dominic missed sex in general, but he wasn't in the mood to surrender again, and the one time had been born mostly of many months of desperation. They might reach the boiling point someday, but in the meantime, they both seemed comfortable as friendly antagonists.

Finley's lips pressed together until they almost vanished, and he turned to head for the door.

"Wait," Dominic warned, grabbing his dagger from where it hung by the stair in its holster.

"Really?" Finley hissed.

Dominic raised an eyebrow. They were in the middle of a war, one where they had two enemy countries now.

"It's us, you fools," boomed a voice from outside. Gideon.

Dominic relaxed against the stair railing and shrugged at Finley, who rolled his eyes again and threw open the door.

Oh. *Us.* Gideon filled the majority of the doorway but tucked just behind him, falling into darkness under the cover of her black robes, was Lumen.

It was not in Dominic's nature to be self-conscious, but he did wish for a moment that he was wearing a shirt. The couple stepped inside, and Lumen moved forward out of Gideon's shadow, her eyes landing on Dominic and flicking down to his chest with a brief widening glance before dropping to the floor.

"What's happened?" Finley asked.

"We received these letters at the temple today," Lumen said, pulling folded papers from the pocket of her robes.

She crossed the open room to where Dominic stood at the base of the stairs and held them out to him. He stiffened during her approach, a reflex he'd learned long before her return, a way to control the urge to reach out and touch her. He frowned at the outstretched letters and swallowed hard.

"Have you read them?" he asked.

"No, but I know what they contain," she said. He took them from her pale fingers, and she pulled a third from her other pocket. "One came for me from High Priestess Wren."

"Come sit," Finley said, his hands fisted around the back of a chair. "There's enough food for all of us."

There wasn't really, but Dominic wasn't sure how hungry he'd be after reading these letters anyway.

"We ate before walking here," Gideon said, joining Lumen at the end of the table, his arms automatically wrapping her up in his embrace.

Dominic slunk to the table, landing in his seat and pushing the plate of food aside as he opened the first letter from Commander Becker. Finley brought a candle from the ledge around the fireplace and set it down in front of him until the words on the page shone clearly.

His scoff came almost immediately. "They're calling us 'neutral territory.'"

"Isn't that what we want?" Finley asked. He was still standing, and Dominic wondered vaguely if it had to do with the fact that Lumen was standing. Was it impolite to sit while she stood? He doubted she cared under this circumstance.

"Yes, but we can hardly be neutral while they're battering us from every angle," Dominic said. "Stalor is coming, they want a parley."

"When you say Stalor..." Finley trailed off into quiet.

"Becker and his men," Dominic said, glancing up to catch Finley wincing. "And some Solar Priest I've never heard of."

"But are they bringing an army with them?" Gideon asked.

"Doesn't say, but I won't kick my feet up and assume we're safe. No doubt they're hoping to draw me to heel," Dominic said. He opened the second letter and gritted his teeth, glancing to Lumen. She met his eyes, sharp and guarded, and he knew her High Priestess must already have warned her what was coming. "It looks like we'll be hosting everyone. Oshain's sending General Cannary and his party."

"Cannary?" Lumen breathed, and Dominic's head whipped up to watch as she paled and shrank in on herself.

Gideon grew around her, his head tipped down to try and peer into her face. Dominic's flipping stomach turned to stone at the wilt of her shoulders. Cannary must've been one of the officials responsible for her entrapment in Oshain's capital, and the man would pay if Dominic could manage it. One of Gideon's hands slipped up, squeezing over her shoulder, and Lumen gathered herself, straightening and gaining her color back.

"What did your High Priestess say?" Dominic asked.

"I think she meant to warn me, but her letter came at the same time. She and some of the other priestesses are coming as well. I don't know if Oshain asked for them or not."

"It makes no mention of them," Dominic said, tapping the paper.

"What do they really want?" Lumen asked, eyes narrowing.

"To break the stalemate I've put us in," Dominic said with a shrug. "Becker might depose me, officially, in the hopes it will shake out some of the men who've been serving under me."

"But it won't," Gideon said, with eager certainty, another squeeze on Lumen's shoulder to offer comfort. "Our men all know they fight for themselves and not for any country."

"Oshain will want us to surrender this land too," Finley said, drawing their gaze.

Dominic held still for a pause and then relented, nodding. "That was my thought too. They were sent to the temple for a reason, to prove everyone knows where we've camped." And possibly even to prove that the countries knew why Dominic had stopped fighting for Stalor, although he hoped that was only his paranoia.

"I shouldn't have come back here," Lumen murmured.

"Sweet spirit," Gideon said, half-gentle and half-growl.

"No, I mean here, the temple. When High Priestess Wren gave me the horse and the silver, she could never have expected me to try and resurrect the temple to what it'd been over one hundred years ago. And then to...to encourage any of you to- to try and hold the war..." She gasped, breaths starting to come at a rapid pace.

"You hardly encouraged us," Dominic said. He forced his expression to be hard. Lumen didn't want his compassion, and he didn't want her to carry any guilt on his behalf. He would be stubborn and uncompromising if it meant she didn't try to carry his own decisions on her shoulders. She shot a silver slitted glance at him, and he sat up straighter, aware of the way her gaze trailed down his chest, skin prickling as if it were her nails scratching softly.

"This could be a massacre, Dominic," she whispered.

"Not if they abide by the rules of war."

She arched an eyebrow. "Have you?"

He grunted. That was a fair point.

"She's not wrong, you don't know what Oshain and Stalor have already discussed together. They've clearly arranged this meeting," Finley said.

"And if it's the truce we've been fighting for?" Gideon

suggested. He turned Lumen in his arms and tipped her face up to look back at him. "Things may still turn out for the best, sweet spirit."

"Gideon, it's not just you or me here to worry about. There are women and children living in this no man's land. Colin will be here too, in the crossfire." Her voice choked and died off, and Dominic's heart tied itself in a knot. Finley's face turned away in a pained grimace.

"You can't live, expecting only bad things to come your way," Gideon said, nearly whispering.

"Not preparing for them won't stop them from arriving, Gid," Lumen said. She slipped free of his arms like water and raised her hand when he made to follow her. "I'm just walking back. Stay and make your plans."

Gideon's hands rested on his hips as he watched her leave the house into the cool dark of night. Dominic resisted the sudden urge to crumple the letters into worthless wads of paper and then toss them on a fire. He'd comb them for every last detail of information he could over the next two weeks before the officials arrived.

Gideon turned and looked at the pair of them, settling on Finley. "Go and talk to her."

"Me?" Finley said, shooting up straight, eyes growing wide. "Gideon, I think her comfort is your domain now."

Gideon's expression was mild, the slightest hints of mischief tightening the corners of his eyes. "I try to make her hopeful, and it only makes her more worried. You think like her where I can't. She doesn't want to be comforted, she wants someone to understand her concerns." When Finley only narrowed his eyes at Gideon, Gideon added, "Anyway, she shouldn't be walking through the woods alone, and Dominic and I have strategy to discuss."

It did the trick, Finley pushing away from the table and heading for the door while Dominic stared at Gideon in confusion. He waited for the door to click behind the healer.

"What are you doing, pushing them together like that?" Dominic asked. He could guess, but it seemed impossible that

Gideon might try and share Lumen's affections with another. Even more impossible was the idea that Gideon was trying to pass her off, but it still flooded Dominic's veins with a wave of sizzling anger.

"Lumen knows Finley isn't an optimist. I can't help thinking we will win this in the end, because I know I won't put down my sword until we do. She might have that same confidence in me someday, but I think for now, all she sees is me getting gutted in one of these battles."

"And you want Finley to what? Convince her that it won't happen? Because, Gideon, at this point even *I'm* not sure where we'll be by the end of the war."

Gideon rolled his shoulders and slid over to Finley's seat at the table, plucking up a spare roll and tearing it pieces, one of which he popped in his mouth as he shrugged. "I just want him to hear her. I think she'd rather someone agree with her right now than tell her it'll all turn out alright."

Dominic ground his jaw to keep his thoughts in. If Gideon knew that, Dominic didn't see how he couldn't manage it, instead of sending Finley on an errand.

"It's your relationship with the woman," he said instead, and Gideon just chuckled, grinning around another bite of Finley's roll.

FINLEY HAD BEEN SEARCHING through the woods for several minutes, wondering how he'd been talked out of his own dinner and if he really knew way his way back to the temple in the dark, when he finally got a glimpse of a pale blonde head floating through the trees. He was lucky she'd left her hood down.

"Lumen, wait!"

Her head twitched in his direction, a brief glimpse of her profile tugging at him like a fish on a line and sending him trampling through greedy briars. He half expected her to continue on. She hadn't wanted Gideon to follow her in the first place, why would he be any more welcome? Lumen didn't stop walking, but she seemed to slow and Finley caught up with her, new scratches on his pants and hands for his efforts.

"I can make it back on my own," Lumen said, staying a few paces ahead of him, chin held high.

"I think Gideon thought you might prefer the company of someone less inclined to only imagine victories in the future," Finley said.

Lumen faltered, head drooping, and Finley reached her side, finally seeing moonlight shining on the wet tracks running down her cheeks. "Shit, I'm sorry," he muttered.

Her head shook. "No, you're right. Or Gideon is. Am I really showing a lack of faith in him by wondering if I've made a terrible mistake by staying here?" she asked, looking up, face torn. All the emotions she had guarded under her usual stone while in the house with them were now carving lines in her face. He opened his mouth to answer, unsure what might come out, when she turned and began to stomp down the path again. "High Priestess Wren had faith that I was acting in Lune's interest by leaving the convent, but if she comes here and sees what my staying has wrought—"

"Peace, Lumen," Finley murmured. "You wrought peace by staying. Men have built homes. Lovers were wed."

"And the war will still come and crush it all under their boot!" Lumen cried out.

Finley would not make the mistake to catch her in his hands again, not after what it led to the last time, but he stepped closer and Lumen's nervous energy stilled for the moment. "Maybe that's true," Finley said softly, hands outstretched between them. "Stalor might hang us for treason, and in another month these homes might be empty and your temple hollow again, but Lumen...we were happy. Or if not happy, we knew why we fought, and we made the choice ourselves."

The woods around them were not daunted by their sharp words, birds rustled their chicks closer in nests above, and owl released a soft hoot. Lumen caught her breath in the stillness, studying him and letting his words sink in slowly.

"The longer we have this, the more I am terrified at the thought of losing it all," Lumen whispered.

Finley swallowed and nodded. "You could take Colin and anyone else, even Gideon if you urged him. Take them and head for the coast. Or the mountains."

Lumen huffed, a wet shaky sound, and her eyes fell shut, a few glittering tears escaping. "That's the worst offense. I don't want to run. I want to share Gideon's unshakeable faith that he can fight every man who comes to tear this away from us. Am I the greatest fool for trying to keep this?"

"Not the greatest," Finley said easily. That honor belonged to him or Dominic, willing to stand and fight an enemy back from her door, knowing they had no hope of ever being welcomed to her bed. But Finley didn't want her to survive in the hopes he might one day touch her again. Lumen was good, and the world needed her, *he* needed her or at least needed to know she existed safely somewhere. "This is home to me too now."

Lumen's eyes opened, lines of stress melting away as she smiled up at him. It was a faint twist of her lips, but outside of her temper and her passion, all of Lumen was made up of soft strokes and he knew them by heart. He had failed in their beginnings to offer her the honest truth of his feelings. And she was right in her accusations, he thought by denying her the truth, he denied her the ability to hurt him.

"I don't think the High Priestess will see fault in your work here," Finley said.

Lumen's lips pursed, and she breathed out slowly, her hands lifting and sliding into his, holding gently. "Thank you," she said, eyes shying down to the ground.

With sudden clarity, Finley felt words rising in his throat and hoped he was not making a mistake by giving them a voice.

"I love you, Lumen Fenn. I am learning to be a better healer under your guidance, and I hope a better man simply for knowing you." Her face lifted, that same stunned and still surprise written there as it had been after he'd kissed her, and he continued, voice drawn out by her bright gaze. "You treat all of us, every man and woman lucky enough to land their feet in front of you, with the same selfless care and consideration." Lumen's nose wrinkled and she parted her lips to object, so Finley squeezed her hands. "I will walk onto a battlefield every day, if it means you have somewhere safe to lay your head at night, and I am no warrior. I have faltered, I know that, but believe me when I say I will not falter again. I have no expectation, no goal, but to know that you are somewhere in the world, happy and safe."

Lumen's breath hitched, and her eyes fell shut as Finley leaned forward and left a brief press of his lips to her forehead. He made to drop her hands, but she tightened her grip and he leaned away, finding her brow furrowed as she stared up at him, lips parted but without any word.

He winced. "It isn't something you have to answer, Lumen. Only that I should have had the sense to say—"

Lumen rose up to her toes, tugging on his hands, and Finley's body followed the order even in his confusion. She released his hands only when he was bent close enough for her to catch his shoulders, dragging him down. Her lips slanted across his, swallowing his rambling words in a fierce and steady kiss. The sound of his voice collapsed in a soft groan, her taste fuller on his tongue as she dragged their lips together, hands clutching at the back of his neck. His arms circled her waist tentatively, and Lumen fell into him, his body bowed over hers.

He'd been an idiot in the past, but he thought it was a testament to his growth that he didn't hesitate in returning the kiss. She was eager in his arms, clinging and pressing closer, mouth begging from and claiming his.

When his lungs were tight with a need for air and Lumen's kisses slowed and tempered, Finley turned, sliding his cheek against hers. She panted, hot breath against his neck and his fingers tightened on her waist, afraid at any moment she would pull away and declare the kiss a mistake, or an unwelcome reaction.

"I can't dive in again," she whispered.

His chest ached and he squeezed his eyes shut, prepared to

walk away from the embrace, to swallow down the brief euphoria of the moment.

"If you can just give me time to learn you now. I don't know if I am trying to replace the way things ended with us before or..."

His heart was in his throat, and Finley turned his head as her words rang bright like bells in his head. He pressed kisses to her jaw, holding her tight against him, shuddering as she slipped her fingers into his hair at the back of his neck.

"Yes," he breathed, and since she was asking for patience he resisted the impulse to lick her throat when she shivered. He made to release her, and Lumen shook her head.

"Not yet."

His eyes opened, vision full of her hair and the faint scars on her pale skin. He mouthed along her jaw, watched her eyes flutter shut, and pulled his hips back so she wouldn't feel pressured by his arousal.

"Gideon?" he asked when it finally occurred to him. He leaned back and watched Lumen's smile curve.

"Oh, he'll be pleased to be proven right, I suppose," she murmured, eyes opening and shining like stars up at him.

Good. Gideon and he would make a worthy team in seeing to her happiness. Provided she didn't discover that her feelings for Finley were better left in the past.

"Walk me back, Finley," Lumen said.

He nodded, although it took him another minute and another handful of kisses before he was able to move to her side, her arm wrapped around his as they moved in quiet through the night.

VII
THE SETTING
SUN

A SOFT HOWL ECHOED ACROSS THE FIELD AND LUMEN'S BREATH hitched in her lungs, Colin's hand squeezing tight around hers as he twitched and shifted at her side. A breeze curled around them, cooling the sweat on her back as they held still, waiting and listening. Sheared wheat stalks snapped in the distance, and Colin hiccuped and stirred, staring up at Lumen.

She nodded, heart-racing. "Run," she hissed.

They took off, legs pumping, voices trapped in their laboring chests.

"Woods," Colin whispered, pushing ahead of her on his quick legs.

The howl again sounded, an eerie cry broken with low laughter, and Lumen grinned down at her speeding feet. Gideon was on the hunt behind them, but she and Colin would be quicker.

It had been Hans'—one of the men from the Oshain army—idea to bring back full moon festivities. Stalor and Oshain and the priests and priestesses were on their way, and no one knew if their strangely patched together community would still be standing before the end of the talks. The celebration of Lune's brilliance, of the wild illuminated night on a harvest moon, was their best distraction from the approaching worry.

Gideon howled at their backs again, a committed attempt to play the predator, and Lumen and Colin neared the edge of the woods. Lumen saw the flick of white behind a tree, her hand slipping from Colin's just before Jennie leaped out of the dark, face pale under moonlight and mouth open in a crooked growl that broke with a giggle. She caught Colin up in her arms, the boy giggling and screaming and kicking his legs as Jennie peppered enthusiastic kisses to his cheek.

"Run, Lady!" Colin screeched, grinning as Jennie dragged him into the woods. They might go and hunt together, or Jennie would carry Colin back to the temple to sleep. Either way, the boy was in safe hands for the night. Lumen dashed into the woods, ignoring the scratch and kiss of fallen branches and brambles on the ground.

She remembered a full moon celebration as a child before so many of her brothers had left for the war, before the families of the estate had traveled north to escape the war's reach. She remembered clinging to Sara Blythe's hand, slipping through the trees, the fields, and down by the lake, equally giddy with joy and wild with a happy kind of terror. Her mother, who had played the part of Lady Lune, smiling on them all from the gazebo, had eventually swept a sweaty and exhausted Lumen into her skirts and off to bed without ever being caught by those who chose to spend the night hunting.

Tonight, she suspected she might not make it to sanctuary with a predator like Gideon on her heels. There was an advantage though, Gideon had spent more time in the woods of late, but he would never know them quite as well as she did. The other advantage, of course, was that she wouldn't mind being caught.

She slowed her pace through the trees, careful to move quietly. There was a screech and a giggle of laughter far to her right, one of the women snatched into welcome arms. Somewhere at her back, a large fallen branch cracked with an echo and she bit her lip, knowing only a beast like Gideon could make a sound like that in the woods. She wove in a new direction, hands stroking down the mossy blankets covering bark. Her breath slowed in her chest, the night cooling the heat of her skin. A broad shadow swooped down from a tree, coasting through the cross of branches and down to the ground to catch prey in its mouth with a soft scream.

A muffled grunt sounded up ahead and to the left, two figures in pale clothing pressed to the trunk of a tree, skin slapping wetly. Lumen swallowed and hid for a moment behind a tree to watch the lovers, unable to make out their faces, distant enough that even the sounds of pleasure were whispers. She slipped away before she could be caught by them or anyone else. In the dark, she reached a point where even she was uncertain if she knew where she was on her own land.

Orange light flickered ahead, a trickle of relief stroking down her spine at the sight, and Lumen headed for the source. Gideon's cottage had grown into a reasonable but small house, large enough for them to share if it weren't already occupied by Finley and Dominic. She hadn't said anything to him on the subject yet, but she wondered how long Gideon would share the house or if he'd make room for her by asking the others to leave. Where would Dominic *go* if separated from the others?

There was no sign of Gideon in the woods behind her, and for a moment, Lumen wondered if she should turn around and find him. Finley had also decided to celebrate with everyone, and she'd never even seen a hint of him during the hunt.

The fire in the little house was due to Dominic then. Lumen slipped up to the back of the building, tiptoeing past the well and creeping carefully toward the window. Maybe he was already in a bedroom upstairs, and the fire was for Finley's sake.

Except there he was, framed in warped glass, a blur of black and orange. Lumen crept closer to the window. She may not have been the wild wolf that Gideon and Jennie played, but the full moon did transform her into another kind of creature, spying on others and sneaking through dark and quiet. Dominic sat slouched in a roughly made chair, legs extended towards the fire, arms back behind his head. His black hair glittered faintly, and Lumen wondered if he'd just washed like he had the night she and Gideon arrived with the letters. His chest was bare, dark hair dusting down to a thick line over his stomach to the waist of his pants.

It was rare to be able to observe him without having that fierce stare turn on her, and it gave her a moment to appreciate his form in a way she often resisted. Gideon was handsome in his broken brutality, Finley beautiful in his more delicate elegance. Dominic was both, terrifying and polished, carved like a statue and equally as impenetrable.

His hand combed through his hair and then ran back down to his face, scrubbing over his eyes. She could almost hear the rough sigh as she watched his chest rise and fall.

Escape this, she thought. Leave the sight of him before it turned into a snare on her memories, drawing out the pleasurable ones and smudging the painful. She didn't regret falling back in love with Gideon or seeing the good in Finley again, but she knew better than to think she would ever forgive Dominic Westbrook for his part in her history.

She turned away from the window and nearly screamed to find the tall figure lurking behind her, but Finley was ready, one hand covering her lips as his other arm circled her waist and drew her to his chest.

"Looking for me?" he whispered against her ear, breath hot.

Lumen nodded behind his hand, and Finley huffed, loosening his hold just enough for her to look up into his face.

"Liar," he said softly, eyes crinkling in the corners and a smile cracking. "I saw you watching him far longer than it would take to tell who was inside."

Her lips were parted against his palm, eyes wide as she took him in. The silver in his hair winked blue in the moonlight, with just a dusting of the orange light from inside warming the features on the right side of his face. As she scrambled for an explanation, Finley's hand pulled away and his head dipped, Lumen accepting the kiss with sudden and desperate relief. His lips were certainly welcome, but even better was the reprieve from his questions when she had no decent explanation for why she'd been spying on the general.

Finley's arm tightened around her waist as his teeth dragged repetitively over her bottom lip. He lifted her feet from the ground and pulled her away from the house, back into the dark of the woods. She thought they might become another pair of lovers up against a tree, and the idea sent a syrupy warmth pooling in her core. But it wasn't a tree Finley pressed her to, although the warm solid form was equally as sturdy. Instead, Gideon's large hands cupped her hips, his groin pressing to her ass. Her toes grazed the top of Gideon's boots as he held her up while Finley's hands traveled over her front, cupping mound through her skirt and then rising to squeeze her breasts.

Lumen gasped, and Finley nipped the tip of her tongue. "You'll have to be quiet, milady, or we may have an uninvited observer," he said, just a hint of his perfect subtle wickedness on his tongue.

She shivered and stretched in Gideon's arms, looking over her shoulder. Gideon's back was braced against a tree, and as a group, they faced away from the house. Dominic *might* hear her if she wasn't careful, but he'd have to come outside and go looking for them before he'd see anything. She should've been relieved, but instead, she found the notion of Dominic discovering them a dark and perverse kind of thrill. An opportunity to twist the moment from months ago when he'd fucked her with his fingers while Finley stood on and waited for them to finish.

"Do you want to return to the temple first, sweet spirit?" Gideon asked, head bending so he could suck on the flesh and muscle of her throat.

Lumen gasped as he pulled away, cool air completing the kiss on the wet mark he'd left. Finley stepped back slightly, fingers still toying at her breasts through her dress, nails scratching through fabric against taut nipples.

"Do you want me to kneel before you, Priestess?" Finley asked, already dropping down to one knee. "I can see the moon through the trees, and I feel the need to worship my goddess."

Lumen shivered and narrowed her eyes. "I might believe you were sincere if your hand weren't so far up my skirt."

Finley grinned and raised an eyebrow. "Are you not Lune's vessel?"

"I don't think this is one of my intended duties," she said, but

231

as Finley's fingers grazed at her slit, her hips rolled into the touch.

"Would you rather I play the wolf who devours you?" he asked.

Lumen squirmed, trying to get closer to his skirting touch as it traced back down between her thighs to swirl behind her knees. She and Finley had found an unsteady balance together in the week since she'd agreed to give him a second chance. It was easy to talk or to go hunting for medicines, or even to sit in silence together. It was also clear that Finley was taking care not to push her, or demand too much when they touched, when she really wished he would be more direct. Apparently, the full moon had offered him that opportunity to test the waters as her pursuer.

"Tell me what you want," Finley said softly, eyes shadowing with caution.

Lumen bit her lip, and Gideon kissed her shoulder. "Stand up," she said. "I want to be surrounded by you both."

Finley rose without a moment's hesitation, and with him came his hand back between her thighs, skirt bunched over his arm. "Kiss her, Gid."

Lumen arched and offered her mouth to Gideon, the kiss at a strange and arousing angle, mouths crooked and tongues stroking deep. Finley pulled the loose shoulders of Lumen's dress down her arms and tugged at the waist until the fabric became a corset around her middle. His fingers rubbed in a steady but simple rhythm over her sex, ignoring the way she offered herself by spreading her legs farther apart. His other hand pulled her breasts free from the top of her dress, pinning them high, fabric digging into the soft undersides. Finley's head lowered to kiss her there, gripping at her ribs. One of Gideon's hands lifted to tangle in her hair at the base of her neck, and between them she became a long, curved line, body stretched under their control as they feasted on her lips and skin.

She'd forgotten Finley's order to remain quiet, a soft pleading whine falling from her lips, followed by a low moan as Finley finally pressed two fingers against her opening, teasing her with the stretch. Gideon sucked and licked at her mouth, swallowing her noises. The lustful, wanton part of her that she'd tried to bury after running away rose up again and imagined Dominic coming out of the back of the house and finding them here like this. Finley's thumb stroked over her clit, pushing against it and swirling over the spot, his tongue mimicking the motion on a nipple until she tore away and cried out. It was like she was *trying* to lure someone to find them, wanted to be seen in all her depravity.

"Kiss," she said. She rode Finley's fingers, body bouncing and hips rolling to work herself to the edge. "Kiss each other," she repeated when Gideon began to bite and lick at her shoulder. He lifted his head, his hand leaving her hair and tugging on Finley's. Gideon drew Finley off her breast, the other man snarling as Gideon caught him in a rough kiss.

They clashed together and Lumen gasped, watching them fight one another with teeth and tongues in a way they never did with her, jockeying for control and less afraid of harming one another. Finley's fingers were urgent on her sex, pumping faster, thumb rubbing harder, and Gideon was rutting against her ass. The healer was the victor, pushing against them until Gideon was pinned between her and the tree trunk, growling as Finley fucked his mouth roughly with his tongue. Lumen had one arm over Finley's shoulder, clutching to his back, and the other raised and dug into Gideon's chest as she whimpered and shook while Finley controlled them both. She let herself rub against Gideon's arousal and wondered if he would fuck her when Finley was done or if she would ask to watch them together.

It's just the lunacy of the full moon, she told herself as the spiraling arousal began to turn dense in her core, their chorus of breaths loud in her own ears. She wanted to pretend it was the game of the full moon hunt, or the power of the two men that made her want Gideon to bend her over and fuck her until her ass was sore with the rhythm of his thrusts, for Finley to bruise and coax her into strange pleasures.

The truth was there on her tongue as she grew louder, as she intentionally pressed herself into Gideon's erection, as she watched the men suck on one another's mouths by her own demands. This was part of her. They hadn't created it, they'd only discovered how it complimented their own interests and desires.

Gideon tore away first, one rough, "Go," on his lips before Finley dropped to his knees.

Warm, wet lips replaced Finley's thumb, and Gideon's hands clutched to Lumen's bare breasts as she finally silenced her shouts before they became a wild scream. Finley sucked, fingers spearing her and curving to drive her to a shocking height of rapture she'd almost forgotten while away from him. Gideon grinned against her cheek as she thrashed and shuddered, falling under a wave of blissful, spiky warmth that exploded and then softened and flooded through her veins.

Her knees shook, threatening to fold beneath her, and Gideon abandoned one breast to hold her up.

"That's it, sweet spirit," he said, squeezing her flesh to force her pleasure to flare.

She shuddered as Finley lapped at her swollen, tender sex, cleaning her with gentle thoroughness. She pushed him away, fingers slipping through his hair, and Finley laughed, rising up and letting her skirt fall between them. He and Gideon surrounded her, tucking her breasts back into her dress and smoothing the fabric all into place as if they'd never left her exposed to moonlight.

"It's your turn now," she murmured, still too dazed to know who she meant.

"I've a mind to reward our healer for taking you apart so beautifully," Gideon purred in her ear, chuckling as she bit her lip.

Finley blushed, watching her face. "We'll take you back to the temple first," he said. "Let your head clear. There's plenty more of the night to enjoy, and I remember all too well how far I can push you before you've really had enough."

Lumen leaned into Finley's chest, savoring the way his eyes lit up and a faint smile turned on his lips. "Or maybe you were just greedy," she murmured. Gideon grinned and snorted at her side.

"Only for what you were willing to offer," Finley said, sobering.

"I remember." Lumen rose to her toes, grazing her lips against Finley's, and then let herself be tucked between the two men and ushered out of the woods and toward the temple.

THE WAY back to the house looked different by bright morning, less covered and secretive. The woods seemed more open, and Finley fought his own blush under the harsh glare of sunshine as he remembered the way he'd pushed Lumen's dress down. Anyone might've seen them. Dominic almost certainly had *heard* them.

He hadn't expected the turn the night would take, had assumed the chase through the woods and the fields would be a frivolous child's game and not a wild debaucherous fertility celebration. Lumen confessed before sleeping that she'd known as a child the hunt of the ritual was a way of confirming life and agreed it'd taken new meaning as an adult.

He celebrated *her* in the moonlight, and Gideon too for that matter. Celebrated himself for surviving this far, for earning his way back into Lumen's affection, regaining Gideon's trust. The picture of them together, Lumen moaning face down in the pillow as Gideon churned over her back, throat strained with pleasure and control, was haunting Finley as he walked back to the house in the woods.

Dominic would know or would guess, where Finley had spent the night, and Finley imagined he might somehow see the explicit moments of the night on Finley's face as he walked in.

Instead, Dominic met him on the path outside the house, shutting the door behind him. Finley froze in place, wincing against sunlight, trying to control his expression as Dominic approached him with steady heavy steps.

"Are you working as a healer today or coming out to the

fields with us? We only have a few days now to get everything in before the officials arrive," Dominic said by way of greeting, stopping in front of Finley on the path. His eyes were focused over Finley's shoulders, expression controlled and even.

"I...I can come out to the fields," Finley said. He'd left Lumen in bed, her skin pink and warm from being curled between him and Gideon for the night. Finley dropped his head, blinking away visions of Lumen before looking up at Dominic again. "Dom..."

Dark eyes flicked to his, Dominic's head cocking with a flicker of a derisive sneer twitching over his mouth. "You don't owe me explanations for where you spend your nights, Fin."

Finley's eyes narrowed. "I know you feel as much for her as—"

Dominic held his hand up. "Stop. I have even less right to care about Lumen's bed partners than I do yours. It's none of my business." He made to walk past Finley and then stopped again, sighing and shoulders slumping. The sneer softened to a dry kind of amusement. "Besides, I know Gideon would sooner break your neck than let you hurt her. Let's get to the fields. If we survive this meeting, we'll need food to last us through the winter."

Another winter here, Finley realized. If they made it. If Stalor didn't drag them south in chains or hand them over to Oshain to be hanged.

"We've been here a whole year," Finley said.

Dominic grunted and pushed ahead, his back tightening as he marched to the fields.

If I can be forgiven, can he? Finley wondered. He would never ask Lumen, just as Dominic would never ask her. She might still be better off without them, but Finley had at least learned to be grateful that she chose to let him remain in her life.

LUMEN WAS OUT GATHERING APPLES WHEN SHE HEARD THE HORSE and its rider galloping down the road at her back, heading toward the fields. She held her breath, remembered Oliver Spragg and the day he came to announce her fate. The fall was cooler this year and the day was cloudy, but she remembered the burn of the sun on the back of her neck and the cold acceptance in her veins. Now, she watched as one of Dominic's scouts rode high on the brown horse's back. He came from the north, which meant that Oshain was two days early or...

Or the Priestesses had made it to temple first. Lumen dropped the full basket gently to the ground. She could go to the fields and find Gideon and Finley, or back to the temple to face her guests herself. The first would be the act of a lover or a manor lady seeking protection, so instead, she ran in the opposite direction of the horse and rider, heading to the temple.

From the top of the hill, the white robes were clear, standing in the drive at the front of the old Manor entrance, small Colin barring the way through. Lumen smiled at the sight of him, knew by the slightly bowed figure he was speaking to High Priestess Wren, who would surely be equally amused by the boy. She rushed down the side of the hill to the back of the temple where Jennie waited by the kitchen entrance.

"There you are, I have your robes," Jennie whispered, although any eavesdroppers were on the far side of the temple.

She held out the black robes by the shoulders, and Lumen hesitated in front of them. "Do you think I *should* wear them?"

"Whatever your priestess thinks of what you've done here, you are *my* New Moon Priestess, Lumen," Jennie said, twitching the fabric in her hand. "You've done more for the people here than any distant religious figure. Put on your robes to meet them, knowing you've done your duty to *us*. We'll worry about what's next when it comes."

Lumen ducked under the fabric, hiding her smile, and Jennie settled it over her shoulders with a few gentle fussing touches.

"You are my sister whether you consider yourself one of Lune's daughter or not," Lumen said, catching Jennie's hand and squeezing briefly.

Jennie's eyes rolled, but her cheeks brightened with a blush, and she pushed Lumen inside and through the kitchen. Lumen hurried across the courtyard to the front entrance, feet shuffling softly across the smooth tile and catching Colin's ear where he stood wedged between the slightly parted doors.

"Let them in, love," Lumen said, resting a hand on his back and helping him open the two heavy doors inwards. High Priestess Wren's eyes were wrinkled with laughter as Lumen met her on the top step. "High Priestess, it's an honor."

Lumen's knees bent in a deep curtsey, the black hood of her robes dipping low in a nod of respect until soft, wrinkled finger-tips caught her beneath her chin and drew her up again to look into watery blue eyes.

"The honor is mine, Priestess, to see this temple restored and under such dutiful care," Wren said, thumb stroking at Lumen's chin.

Horses galloped up the drive, and Lumen blushed to see Gideon, Finley, and Dominic barreling up to the mingling Priestesses, panic melting off their faces. Wren turned slowly, raising an eyebrow at the three men as they pulled their reins short and came to sudden stops.

"High Priestess Wren, may I introduce—"

Wren stopped Lumen with a soft wave of her hand. "I'm

familiar with the gentlemen, sister." The old woman dipped her head to the men as they jumped down from their horses.

"High Priestess," Dominic greeted, and it was not the sharp and sure tone Lumen recalled from their first meeting on this same drive. He bowed to the women, and Lumen finally took note of the sisters Wren had brought with her. They were younger, quieter women Lumen remembered from the convent, with one exception.

Neave was waiting by a pony, eyes narrowed on the men in the drive, body leaning against the round belly of her horse. The young girl remembered the men in front of her from their own stay with her family, and while she looked suspicious, she didn't appear frightened of them.

"I have enough rooms for all of you here," Lumen offered. "Not the comforts of Fenn Manor, but ones suited to prayer and worship."

"You know that's all we need," Wren said, squeezing Lumen's outstretched arm and using it to balance her steps as Lumen led her inside.

Gideon cleared his throat on the drive, still seated in his saddle. "Do you need one of us with you, Priestess?"

High Priestess Wren waved her hands at the men. "Your Priestess is in good company, gentleman. I'd like to speak with you myself this evening regarding the other parties on their way here, but for now, I need words alone with Priestess Fenn."

Not one of them budged, and Lumen blushed and met Gideon's gaze head-on. "We're fine. We'll speak later."

He nodded, all the other young women watching with wide gazes as Dominic clucked to his horse, the three returning the way they came. Lumen wondered if the Lunar priestesses saw the men as enemies or if they noticed the same things she did, broad shoulders and tanned skin and strong thighs. She turned away and forced a smile for a nervous and twitchy Colin, who waited in the entry.

"Jennie's checking all the rooms again," he said, voice softer in the presence of High Priestess Wren.

"Would you make some tea and warm the scones from

yesterday?" Lumen asked him, adding to Wren. "We can bring them to your rooms if you'd like to rest after the journey. Or we can start a fire in the old dining hall. We've been using it as an infirmary, but I'm sure we can find chairs and—"

"Settle, Priestess," Wren whispered, cheeks filling with her gentle smile. "We are only your sisters, remember? I'm sure the others would love to rest, but I have been looking forward to speaking with you for a very long ride. Give me a room and a chair so we can sit and speak."

"Of course." Lumen led Wren out of the entry and into the courtyard. She and Jennie and Colin had done their best to scour the stone before Inda and Philip's wedding, and it was still looking bright and buffed clean after years of being left to grow mossy and dark.

Skirts rustled behind them, women whispering to one another as they turned and faced the courtyard. Amongst their soft steps and voices, another pair of feet stomped noisily to reach High Priestess Wren's side as Lumen guided her around the archways.

"Hello, Neave."

"I recognized those men who were here, and the boy you have," Neave said, instead of answering Lumen's greeting.

Lumen swallowed and glanced at the girl who was staring back with narrow eyes. "Yes, they came here after moving on from your Manor."

"You believe Lune wanted you to come back for them?" Neave asked.

Lumen hummed with thought. "I believe she wanted me to come back, and they were part of that. But not all."

"If you hadn't saved them, Stalor would be gaining ground in Oshain," Neave said, following them up the stairs to the rooms above. "The big one broke the hands of one of his own men for trying to grab me as I was serving food."

Lumen's steps faltered, and Wren's hand squeezed her arm.

"They aren't *good* men," Neave continued. "But I never thought they were as bad as mother said. It was her that told Imogen to waste her virtue, not them."

Lumen pressed her lips together. She'd had the order from Dominic himself, but Neave didn't need to hear that. Sometime over the summer, she'd stopped wondering what would've happened if she'd refused Dominic's threatening choice and accepted the ugly reality that already passed. Dominic Westbrook had committed unforgivable acts, and now in spite of all that, they were allies.

"There's something I'd like to show you," Lumen said to Wren as they reached the upper hall. She turned them to the large open room her father had made his study, and she had destroyed and transformed back into a room of prayer.

Wren stopped short in the doorway, eyes full and wide in wonder, Neave's breath catching as she peered around Lumen's waist. The mural painted on the wall had been chipped and broken after they'd finished tearing out the shelves, but there was enough there to work as a guide. Lumen had fashioned some usable stains and filled in the dancing constellations of indigo and silver that swirled from one dark side of the room and blended into yellows and reds and golds on the other.

"I thought it was for the full moon, but it's older than that, isn't it?" Lumen asked.

"A painting from the original Sol and Lune temple," Wren whispered, stepping slowly into the heart of the room. "I'd hoped seeing the tapestry might inspire you."

Lumen bit her lip, chest squeezing. "Did you? I was afraid… afraid I'd done wrong in staying here."

Wren spun on her heels, surprisingly nimble, and her gaze flicked between Lumen and Neave before settling on the girl. "Neave, child, go and find me a room before the younger girls snatch them all up."

"The best bed is across the way," Lumen said, pointing through the arches. "And there's a good fireplace there too."

Neave's lips twisted, and Lumen was sure the girl knew she was being excluded from whatever conversation came next, but the temptation of a bed and a fire was enough and she took off, racing around the curving hall.

"Come here, Lumen," Wren said, crossing slowly to a chair

and easing herself down. Lumen joined her, kneeling on the floor in front of the High Priestess' feet. Wren huffed and took Lumen's hands in hers, cool and soft with little nicks and callouses from her life of work. "Tell me what's happened here since you arrived."

Lumen took one deep breath and tried to hold it in her lungs as if it could prevent the sudden outpouring of words, but the confession came in a rush.

Flushing out the poison in the army, returning to the Manor to refashion it into a temple, going back to healing broken soldiers, the army's new determination to halt the progress of the war. Lumen stumbled around her thoughts of Gideon and taking him back into her bed, avoiding spilling everything out to High Priestess Wren, although the woman's lips twitched as if she could guess. Lumen continued, telling her about the growing numbers of men from both Oshain and Stalor, the new moon prayers, the wedding, the harvest, and the full moon rites in the night.

High Priestess Wren's smile was wide as Lumen finished. "I'd forgotten how lively our faith could be in a community. Sometimes I think our convent is too removed, sterilized from the people we should be celebrating with," Wren said.

"I thought I wanted the silence there, but I missed worshiping with others," Lumen admitted.

Wren hummed and nodded. "If I'd realized your capacity for nurturing faith in others, I might've made you stay with us longer. It's better that you're here, seeding our belief and practices in unlikely ground."

Lumen's brow furrowed as she considered the words. "It was never an *intentional* effort to lead anyone to Lune if I'm being truthful."

"Of course not," Wren said with a shrug. "You offered the sanctuary you saw was needed. You gave worn men time to remember themselves off a battlefield, to decide what they wanted to fight for. And you did so without any calculation on your own part so they knew their actions were their own."

"If anything, I advised against it," Lumen said with a sigh. "What's going to happen?"

Wren's lips pursed, and she puffed out a breath of air. "Who's to say? It's been decades since Stalor and Oshain's leaders even bothered to meet with each other. They've let their armies make motions, and now their armies are starting to turn against them. They'll try to rein them in. If they can't…"

"They'll try to burn them out," Lumen finished in a whisper. Wren stared down at her and nodded slowly.

"Of course. Their lives were always forfeit in the war, Priestess Fenn." Lumen nodded and made to stand, but Wren's next words sent her back to her knees. "It bothers you that he fights for you."

Lumen gasped and shook her head. "That isn't—they don't all…"

"Not all. But he does, and likely those other two that raced here to guard your door against an old woman in white robes," Wren said, smirking.

"I think…I think he sees it as a kind of penance," Lumen said, and frowned.

"It's no one's decision but yours to open your doors to these soldiers again, just as it's no one's decision but his how he chooses to make amends. At least you've inspired that much," Wren said.

She stood first, and Lumen scrambled to follow. "Then you think Lune would still approve of my being here? It's not wrong that I wear the robes?"

"You've done more work here in a handful of months than most Priestesses will do in their lifetimes," Wren said. Her eyes narrowed and she lifted her hands, taking Lumen's face and turning it to the side to catch the light. "You may not always be the New Moon Priestess. Her shadow is fading, and I see more of Lune's glow about you now. But you will always be one of her daughters. Trust your instincts, Lumen." Her hands lowered and her shoulders sagged. "Now, take me to a bed. I'll have a word with Westbrook, but first, I think a nap is in order."

Lumen and High Priestess Wren found Neave asleep in the

room, spread out as far as she could stretch over Lumen's mother's bed.

"If I didn't suspect the danger coming, I'd be tempted to leave her here with you," Wren grumbled, tottering over to the bed and pushing the girl aside enough to make room for herself. "But then again, she does know how I like my tea."

TREAT HER LIKE YOUR POLITICAL ALLY, NOT WHAT YOU'RE HERE TO
protect. The High Priestess' words rang in Dominic's head as he
stood at Lumen's side, watching the procession of carriages and
horses moving sedately up the drive to the temple. Stalor's flag,
Sol's too, and even Oshain's colors, one by one in bright and
shining paint, clear and pointed luxury. The small collection of
men he had waiting on the sidelines—from both Oshain and
Stalor's ranks—wore scowls and dark gazes as they watched the
arrival. Where had the money for carriages been while armies
had scrounged for scraps and stolen their dinners?

High Priestess Wren stood on Lumen's other side, their
hands folded together. The two women were an unusual
contrast, one young and straight-backed and shrouded in black,
the other old and bowed and gilded in white and silver. He
discovered the night before that he liked Wren. She was plain
spoken, and she saw directly through him in a way that
reminded him of Lumen and her slicing glances.

*If they know she is precious to you, she will be the first they
condemn. Respect her, but never shield her in front of them.*

Dominic held his hands fisted behind his back and his eyes
slid to Gideon, who looked barely restrained by some kind of
invisible rope. Finley chose to remain at the house and out of the
way. He was only their healer and he'd been the one to kill
Cantalion, the worst of their offenses against the Stalor army. At
least it was one less man who might not be able to refrain from

reacting on Lumen's behalf. Dominic barely trusted himself, and while Gideon was calming by her influence, he was still an unpredictable man.

It was the Solar priests who arrived first, Colin and Mitchell jumping out of line to tend the horses. High Priestess Wren gave Dominic a warning twitch of her head when he made to step down from the stairs, and he froze, letting her and Lumen make their way to the drive. A tall, powerfully formed man stepped down from inside the carriage. He was dressed in colors of heavy gold and rust-red blood, a cable knit coat over a glossy tunic and woven pants. His skin was a darker shade of olive-brown than even Gideon's, head shaved bald and painted in red swirls and sun rays.

"Father Wesley," Wren said, head dipping.

"High Priestess Wren," he said, bending at the waist to the older woman. He rose, took one scanning look over Lumen in her black hood, and repeated the deep bow, lips pursed and eyes narrowed. "Priestess."

So Lumen's role as New Moon Priestess was almost as significant as Wren's. Interesting. Which meant any deference Dominic showed her would be respectful rather than suspicious. That was a relief, considering he couldn't bring himself to act against her now.

The Solar Priest straightened and stared above the two women's heads to Dominic. "Westbrook," he offered, clipped and hard.

Dominic smirked in answer. Stalor had taken his title, and this was how they wanted him to find out, from a priest in a faith he didn't follow.

"Father Mott couldn't make the trip?" Wren asked.

Dominic watched Lumen's shoulders, pinched and high under robes, as the priest explained that the head of the church was too busy to make the trip north for the meeting. More likely the man was too infirm or too lazy, Dominic thought. Another pair of priests, younger twins—whose movements seemed to work like a mirror of one another—exited the carriage and it pulled away to make room for the next in line. Dominic descended the steps to greet the Stalor army generals, his hands twitching with the urge to rest on Lumen's shoulders to try to soothe her. It was so far out of the realm of his responsibility to her, let alone Wren's advice to him on how to treat her, but it still made his knuckles ache to resist.

The priests made room, and Lumen held her ground as the next carriage rode up, barely stopping in front of a stone-faced Gideon. Dominic held his breath, steeled his expression, and tried to force his body to relax. He'd served under Commander Becker before the man's promotion, had learned brutality and control of army ranks from the man, although Dominic had been better at strategy and more daring in warfare. At the time, he'd looked up to Becker, no matter how cruel the man chose to be. Briefly, he'd felt his own promotion to general as a kind of favor, almost even paternal. Now he knew that Becker only wanted to be off the field himself. He'd successfully beaten mercy out of Dominic, made a general who was both ruthless against his enemies and his own men, and taken his promotion back to the Stalor war office.

He almost didn't recognize the man who descended from the carriage, the structure actually sighing as the heavy man unloaded himself. Stalor claimed war in order to help its people prosper, but by the look of Becker—swollen and red-faced and glassy-eyed—prosperity was achievable if you had the power to claim it. His hair was light and yellow with age, once a fiery shade of red that he'd combed with the blood of battle, and he glared at Dominic with eyes traced in fine red lines. Dominic wondered if he'd taken up a drug, like Finley had, or only a great deal of drinking.

"I have half a mind to kill you here on the spot," Commander Becker said to him. The man may have lost the strength he'd carried while still fighting, and the color in his hair, but his voice was every bit the threatening hiss and growl Dominic remembered from his youth. On reflex, Dominic's eyes fell down to Becker's now widened hips, expecting to see the long black whip the man had used to discipline his men. Instead, there was a golden flask, and Dominic lifted his head wearing a tight smile.

"Likewise, Commander," he said softly.

The company standing on the drive was silent, and Dominic's heart stuttered as Lumen shifted, her shoulder sliding in front of his chest. What was she doing? Defending him? *Intentionally?*

Becker tried to draw himself up, but his years of idleness and pampering left him stiff and weak, and Dominic found that he was taller than the man now. Becker's chest puffed and his eyes burned, head drawing back.

Out came a loud honking laugh, and Becker's body sagged. He leaned forward, clapping his hand roughly against Dominic's immoveable shoulder. "You stupid, brave, bastard," Becker croaked, heaving on his next breath, head shaking.

They had to step back collectively so he could make room to let the rest of the carriage out, a handful of officials Dominic had never met or heard of, who looked as though they'd probably bought their way onto Becker's committee rather than earned it.

Colin guided the Stalor carriage toward the stable, and in its place came a modest but long gray and green structure on three axles. With Becker close at his side and the Solar priests watching, Dominic couldn't look at Lumen on his left, but he'd become so aware of her in the past year he was sure he detected the softest flinch, the faintest catch in her breath, as the carriage emptied of passengers.

General Cannary was easier to pick out, shorter than Dominic expected, but harder too. He had a pale and sharp gaze that fastened immediately on Lumen, as did the other members of the party. Lumen didn't duck or hide under her shroud, but Dominic detected a kind of empty haze in her stare as she met their eyes as if she'd retreated mentally.

"Miss Fenn," Cannary said, soft and cold.

"Priestess," Wren corrected simply.

"Was that paperwork filed?" asked a woman in a severe black gown.

"It was," Wren said, raising an eyebrow. "Although, you know I do such things as a courtesy and not a requirement of your law."

"And did you know she was a prisoner who escaped Oshain's custody when you gave her sanctuary?" the woman pressed.

Lumen remained frozen between Dominic and High Priestess Wren, and it was a painful test of his resolve not to shelter her, or at least push her to Gideon who would be a welcome refuge.

"It's never been a matter of our concern where women come to us from. Priestess Fenn was undeniably chosen by Mother Lune for service," Wren said.

She would make a good general, Dominic thought absently, watching the older woman. Or she was simply better at hiding her emotions than he'd expected from a priestess. Cool and impenetrable Lune chose her mouthpiece well in Wren.

"I've made some rooms available for your use, although some of your parties may have to camp," Lumen said, her voice smooth and steady, rising from beneath the shadow of her dark hood.

"How accommodating…Priestess," General Cannary offered with a brief dip of his head. "Perhaps we did you a favor in your captivity. New Moon Priestess is quite the honor to bestow on a woman so young."

Dominic wanted to put his knuckles in the older man's face.

"I'm afraid I can't afford you all the credit for my losses in life, General," Lumen said.

Dominic fell back a step, the punch he'd been fantasizing over landing in his own gut at her words. He would take that credit, he assumed. Lumen turned, head tipping and eyes flinching as they met his. He took it as proof of her meaning until her sleeve brushed against his arm, fingers running over the back of his hand and then vanishing. It was so rare for her to touch him now, and it drew out needle pricks of awareness on his skin. He didn't know if it was an accident, or reassurance, or apology, only that he couldn't show any sign of the touch, no matter how badly he wanted to catch her hand in his.

"This way, please," Lumen said, without glancing back at anyone.

High Priestess Wren took his arm and shot him a subtle, chiding glance as they made their way inside.

"WHAT THE FUCK do you think you're on about out here?"

Dominic glanced down at the hand squeezing tight around his arm with a strange flicker of relief. Finally, after a day wasted in political niceties—absurd for two countries in the midst of a decades-long war—someone was speaking the truth. Unfortunately for him, it was Commander Becker, looking as though he needed a refill on his flask—his upper lip and forehead dusted with sweat, face alternately clammy pale and flushed red.

"Undermining you," Dominic answered, eyebrow ticking up in challenge. "Abandoning my position for Stalor."

"Treason," Becker hissed.

Dominic glanced around the stairwell. It was evening, and Lumen had arranged a modest meal for the visiting emissaries, although he thought she ought to have simply let them starve. Everyone had taken to their rooms for the night, and Dominic had intended to make it look as though he was leaving. Not that he planned on leaving Lumen here defenseless. Becker may have grown slovenly, but he was still brutal, and General Cannary and his cronies were clearly snakes. Dominic wouldn't even put it past the Solar priest to try and eliminate any of the Lunar women. Sol loved his worship dressed in blood.

"Yes. Treason. I turned my back on Stalor, who turned its back on its people ages ago," Dominic answered, not bothering to hush his voice.

"Conquering Oshain would *save* Stalor!"

"Unseating the officials who claim every ounce of land and wealth and influence would save Stalor. Conquering Oshain would only make the rich richer and *you* drunker."

Becker made to grab him by his vest, but was too slow, Dominic dancing out of the way with ease. "If this is about that frail little priestess of yours—"

"It's not," Dominic said, perhaps too quickly. It wasn't. Not for all the men who chose treason over continuing the same exhausting pattern of war. Maybe for him.

"You're going to see every man behind you killed for this insane effort of yours," Becker warned, head shaking. "You have one chance left to turn this around, to not waste valuable lives."

Dominic scoffed and shifted on the steps, squeezing past Becker until he stood above the man. "You're trying to reason with me, but you forget the way I watched you spend your own soldiers onto our enemies' swords, or under your whip when a man was too tired to march. Stalor doesn't consider its soldiers valuable," Dominic said. He narrowed his eyes. "How many men do you even have left? A couple thousand?"

Becker's face flinched, and Dominic grinned and pushed, driving the man to stumble down another two steps. "Not even that, eh?"

"It's more than Oshain can boast. More than *you*," Becker growled.

That was certainly true. They'd reached just nearly one hundred men living on the old estate. It was a decent size for the standard battles they'd been fighting, but it only made up a fraction of Stalor's full army.

"And who do you think they'd fight for if given the choice?" Dominic asked.

"Arrogance will put you in your grave, Westbrook," Becker muttered. "I wanted to believe this was some plan of yours, to throw Oshain off its guard. But you really have just given up. I had an offer I was meant to share with you, but now I'm not sure it's worth it." Becker hummed and shrugged, eyes slanting out of their corners to watch Dominic as he stepped down, feigning disinterest.

"Do you think I'm just an ass you can dangle a carrot in front of and I'll make to bite? The only offer I'd accept from you is Stalor's permanent retreat from this territory."

Becker scoffed and shook his head. "You're a dead man."

Dominic waited, back to the curved stone wall, until Becker had finished his descent from the stairs. Either Becker had been visiting the Solar priests who'd been placed on the second floor or someone from Oshain like Cannary. The opposing forces might make a temporary alliance to stamp Dominic and his men out. Or they might see past his best attempts to disguise his motivations, and target the real catalyst of the situation.

Dominic put High Priestess Wren's advice out of his mind for the moment and scaled the rest of the stairs, heading for Lumen's bedroom. He knocked as lightly as he could on the door and held his breath. It wasn't Lumen who opened the door, but one of the former Oshain soldiers who'd joined their ranks, and for a moment, Dominic's heart went cold. The man nodded his head once and stepped aside to reveal...again, not Lumen. Irritation sparked like a match in his chest as he saw Jennie's red hair resting on the collar of the black robes.

She rolled her eyes at Dominic, and pulled the hood up over her head, hiding her face and gesturing for him to lead the way out of the hall as she followed.

"Might've known you'd come," she whispered.

"Where is she?"

"Sent her to Gideon and yours," Jennie said, barely audible, careful not to share the words with anyone who might be listening on the other side of one of the doors.

His heartbeat steadied, and he nodded. "Alone?" he mouthed.

"Better out there than in here with the snakes," Jennie said, shrugging under the cover of the robe. "Colin went. It was Wren's idea."

Colin was no serious protection, but if he and Lumen were careful, they might make it through the woods without anyone seeing them or at least recognizing Lumen.

"You'll be fine for the night?" he asked as they neared the stairs by the kitchen. He'd go out the back and see if he could catch up with Lumen before making it back to the house.

Jennie's face appeared briefly beneath the hood, surprise in her eyes, and then she ducked and hid herself again. "I can take care of myself. But Harvey will be near too," she added more softly.

He nodded and stopped at the top of the steps, turning to stare at the rooms housing High Priestess Wren.

"She's being watched over by Mitchell," Jennie said. "You're not the only one with strategies. Go on. We have the temple taken care of for the night." When he didn't move, Jennie nudged his back briefly and whispered. "Wren sleeps with a dagger, apparently, and I don't think she's the only one."

Dominic ducked to hide his smile and headed down the stairs. If the priestesses were armed, then Lumen's allies were likely safe for the night. He'd given his orders to his men to keep an eye on their visitors, and not allow them any opportunities to break the temporary truce, but he would never trust men like Cannary and Becker to keep their word. Just as they would never trust him.

Lumen and Colin made slow and quiet steps through the woods on their way to the house. It was a relief to leave the temple for the night when the rooms were full of enemies, but the night sounded hollow in her ears, full of suspicious echoes. Without a word to Colin, they held onto one another more tightly, made softer and more careful steps. Were those eyes she felt hammering between her shoulder blades or was it the rhythm of her own anxious heartbeat?

She wished Gideon had been able to wait for her at the Manor and walk her back, but they were doing their best to keep from appearing to protect her. Truth be told, Lumen hadn't felt the demand for that protection quite so much as she did now. Jennie had given her a simple brown cloak to walk in, enough to hide her more noticeable hair color, and Lumen was longing for those black shrouding robes of her priestesshood.

Colin paused on the path, body trembling and eyes darting over the darkness. Lumen held her breath and searched the woods around them. Her own eyes still favored night, saw shadows moving at the corners, but then only still trees when she turned to look. She was stepping slowly in a circle when one of the shadows rushed to her. She opened her mouth to scream or tell Colin to run, but not before a hand landed firmly over her lips, an arm latching around her waist and dragging her to a firm body.

She knew him at once, that rich scent of him on his skin, salt and spice and musk, and she softened, staring up at Dominic's dark and furious eyes.

"It's me. Colin, come here, stay close," he hissed. His hand slid from Lumen's lips, brushing over her cheek and then she was released, feet stumbling to steady herself. "Wait here?"

Lumen nodded. Dominic's eyes were over her shoulder and he lifted one knee, reaching into his boot and passing her a knife, folding her fingers around the hilt. His eyes skimmed once over hers, a warning or a reassurance for either of them and then he pushed Colin to her hip and headed into the shadows.

"What's he—?" Colin began in a hiss, the question cutting off with a gasp as a branch snapped and one shadow broke out from behind a tree in the shape of a man, making to escape from Dominic's chase.

Lumen's fingers tightened around the hilt of the knife in her hand. Dominic was following the man who'd been watching them, but even from here she could see the way he had to pause and watch and listen to keep up with the stranger's weaving movements, where she could see him clearly.

"Lady," Colin said, sensing Lumen's muscles tensing.

"Follow, but stay back and shout if you see anyone else," Lumen said.

Colin took off at a run with her, dashing close on her heels as she cut through brush, following a quicker angle.

"Stay back!" Dominic growled from her left, but Lumen ignored him. He didn't know how close she'd come to gutting him the night she met him, that there would always be a part of her half-thrilled at the thought of sinking a blade into a man threatening her.

The shadow wasn't keeping track of his direction well enough, curving slowly to his right, and with her heightened eyesight Lumen was able to catch up to him from the front. Running as fast as she could, heart pumping, she nearly collided with the man, knife raising quickly and nicking the underside of his chin. His own blade dug its tip against her waist, dulled by layers of fabric.

They were both panting, eyes wide, and Lumen took a moment to study her opponent. Of the two of them, she was the one whose dagger would do the most damage if it sank any deeper. The man was unfamiliar, with a forgettably plain face. His coloring was light, a few strands of blonde or gray hair peeking out from beneath a knitted cap. He looked northern, although he might've come up with Stalor for all she knew. Finley didn't have the same tan as Dominic and Gideon either.

Dominic reached them, breaths huffing, and struck like lightning, whipping the man's arm behind his back and twisting until the dagger he'd held dropped to the ground. Lumen kicked it in Colin's direction.

"I told you to wait," Dominic hissed at her.

Lumen hitched an eyebrow at him as he wrestled the stranger into his grip. "Well, you're welcome," she said.

"Go and get Gideon from the house," Dominic said to Colin. "Stay quiet until we know we're alone for certain."

Colin nodded, grabbed the knife from the ground, and went running back in the direction they'd been heading to start with. Dominic kicked the knees out from the man they had cornered without warning her, and Lumen stepped back a moment too late, the knife scratching a red line on the underside of his chin, blood dribbling slowly down his throat.

Dominic ripped the hat from the man's head and dug his fingers into his hair, tilting his head back to get a better look at his face. "Who hired you?"

The stranger hissed but fastened his teeth in a snarl and refused to speak.

"You think he was...paid to come here? To kill you?" Lumen asked.

Dominic frowned, and the man in his grip scoffed. "You. I was here to kill you, Priestess," the man said, trying to spit at her feet, but instead only mixing it with the blood on his throat.

Dominic growled, but Lumen found a calm, cool center expanding in her chest, the weight of Lune at her back. "Cannary," she said.

The man—the assassin's face stilled and went blank, and

Lumen stepped back and out of his sightline, moving to stand at Dominic's tense shoulder.

"What will you do?" she asked.

"Question him. Kill him," he added after a brief pause, eyes sliding to her as if to check her reaction. "What would you have me do?"

She didn't know. Would General Cannary and his company be deterred by losing one man on the errand? Probably not, and Dominic and Gideon and Finley would waste energy protecting her from further attacks. She'd thought their mission to stop the war around her land was an impossible goal, but if it worked and brought an actual end to the war? That was...that was powerful, that was worth something. She wanted them to succeed. Cannary needed to believe she was more than just the precious object these men fought for. He needed to fear her.

"Hold him still," Lumen said. She looked and found Dominic's stare on her and waited for him to nod in agreement.

She stepped in front of the man on the ground, closing her eyes and waiting until cold rinsed down her bones, her hands stiff and icy, her heart slowing. Lune draped over her shoulders, rattling in her head, whispering through her thoughts all the punishments she could give, all the mercies she could grant. She could take the man's breath from his lungs, freeze the blood in his veins, bury a hunger in his stomach that could never be satisfied.

Lumen wanted him vulnerable, weak, fragile, and at the mercy of the world, the way she'd felt as she'd been carried to the cell where Cannary kept her for weeks. She raised her hands to his face, and Dominic caught his breath and held him tighter in his arms as he started to thrash. She pressed her thumbs gently over his eyes, and two fingers over his ears. Deep silence rushed in her ears, black night behind her eyes, and the man in her grip gasped and moaned, shaking under her fingers.

"What are you doing? What are you doing?! Let me go! Let me—"

Lumen's heart hammered in her chest, a tickling rush running up her hands and into her wrists, the sensation of her theft tangible. She released his head and found empty white eyes staring aimlessly out of his face.

"Sol's fire," Dominic whispered in horror and awe.

Lumen moved out of the man's reach, watching him, the way his head rolled on his shoulders, searching and searching and never finding.

"Please," the man whispered.

"Release him," Lumen said to Dominic.

"What?"

"Release him," she repeated.

"Please. What have you done? Please, please, I can't see. I can't —" His voice was too loud, rising and pitching in panic.

Dominic let go of his grip on the man's wrists and hair, and Lumen led him out of reach by the elbow. The man landed on his hands and knees, fingers digging through leaves, head still turning turning turning and searching.

"Please. Please. What have you done?" His voice grew louder, the blind volume of someone unaware of their own voice. He leaned back on his heels, hands raised and groping at the open air.

"Lumen!" Gideon growled, footsteps crashing through the woods.

"Here," she called.

"He's blind," Dominic breathed, staring slack-jawed at the man on the ground.

Gideon arrived, sword drawn and face furious, eyes immediately landing on the man whimpering and crawling, searching desperately for someone to grab onto.

"Don't!" Lumen cried before Gideon could swing his blade against the man's neck. Finley was skidding to a stop behind Gideon, his hand linked with Colin's, and the three of them gradually absorbed the picture of the man.

His breaths hiccuped, and Lumen pushed herself and Dominic out of the way as he crawled in their direction.

"Where are you?" he whispered. "Just kill me. Don't leave me here. Please, where are you?"

"He can't hear us," Lumen said. "Take him back to the temple. Leave him where General Cannary can find him."

Finley cursed softly, watching the man crawling, his gaze rising slowly up to stare at her. His face hardened then, and he stepped forward.

"No, let me do it," Dominic said. He turned to Lumen and squared his shoulders. "Let them take you inside, Priestess?"

There was a thin vein of caution in his voice, and it took Lumen a moment to realize that she was still surrounded by the sharp shield of the Dark Goddess' protection. It melted away as soon as she realized, and across from her, Gideon sighed, sword lowering.

"Come here, sweet," he said.

Lumen shivered, eyes sliding to the man she'd stolen from until Dominic stepped between them.

"You would not have been the first life that man took," Dominic whispered. "Go to the house. I will take him to the temple."

"No more than he deserved," Colin whispered to Finley.

The assassin was panting on the ground, the occasional animal whine rising up from his throat. Lumen's rage had been cold and brutal, and even now she didn't regret the power Lune had gifted her with to steal the man's sight and hearing. It was only that she didn't understand how much of the decision had really been hers, just as when she'd encouraged the wounded soldier to pass on in the village, or when Lune sent her to hear the Mallen women plotting.

Gideon skirted around Cannary's hired man, and Lumen raised her arms, ready and grateful as he scooped her up against his chest. He sheathed his sword and then hiked her higher in his hold. "Tired?" he asked.

Lumen softened and slumped over his shoulder, hiding her face in his neck. He carried her to Finley and pulled her down, kissing both her cheeks. "I'm going to make sure Dominic doesn't get himself killed on that delivery, is that all right?"

Oddly, Lumen found herself soothed by the declaration and let herself be passed into Finley's hold. Dominic had appeared at the right moment, and while she'd dealt with the man on her own terms, she could admit that his presence had been partly responsible for her courage. She squeezed Gideon's hand, and Finley's arm covered her shoulders and drew her to his side, lips brushing across her forehead.

"Be careful," Finley offered the men.

Lumen heard the gasp and sob behind her back as Finley and Colin guided her away from the scene, the pleading hisses and scuffing footsteps heading in the opposite direction.

"Does it hurt, Lady?" Colin asked, holding her hand gently.

"No," Lumen said, although the thawing of her bones did burn under her skin. "I just..." She didn't know how to finish the sentence. It exhausted her, not just in some unexplainable magical way, but emotionally, as if she were being manipulated to a purpose, something she grew increasingly tired of.

She wanted to be devoted to Lune, to do her bidding, but when the commands came forcefully, Lumen had a harder time sorting out where her own will began and ended. She looked back over her shoulder and through the dark, the silhouette of Dominic's shoulders was clear, laden down on one side by the man she'd cursed.

Witch, she thought, in Dominic's voice. As if she'd called to him, his head turned, searching through the dark with an open gaze for her. She didn't know if he could see her from that distance, she only knew that it wasn't fear or suspicion on his face, but concern.

Finley let Colin fuss over Lumen when they made it back to the house, taking her upstairs and settling her in a room that smelled like all three of the men of the house in a confusing but appealing mixture.

"You're not frightened of me, are you?" Lumen asked the boy.

He stopped wrestling the blankets over her shoulders and sat back on his heels, eyes wide. "Frightened? Gods no, Lady. I'm proud. I hope those generals and priests piss their pants when they see how strong you are. And I'm grateful that Lune gives you this power. That she has the good sense to love you as I do."

Lumen covered her eyes with a limp palm, her watery smile

appearing below. "Colin, there isn't a man in the world with a stronger heart than yours."

Colin huffed and wrinkled his nose at that, pressing a brief kiss to Lumen's cheek before leaping down from the bed and rushing out of the room. "You hear that?" he asked Finley in the hall. "Do better."

"I'll do my best."

Lumen was grinning as Finley slipped into the bedroom, shutting the door behind him. When her smile began to slip, he shook his head.

"Don't do that. Not on my account. I agree with Colin. None of the science they claimed to teach me ever did as much good as your healing," Finley said, shrugging off his coat and leaving his shoes on the floor. Lumen scooted to the center of the oversized bed, and Finley crawled in to lie at her side.

"There's more science in herbs than I think you realize," Lumen said. "And none in what I did to that man tonight."

Finley hummed and rolled to his side to face her, combing stray hairs back from her face or taking the excuse to touch her. "There was justice in it. And I suspect there will be a...shift in how our enemies see you, which is enough for me."

Lumen had thought as much before she acted, now she dreaded seeing the proof tomorrow when she returned to the temple. Her stare trailed down to Finley's throat, an oddly appealing spot she enjoyed inspecting, and she scooted forward to press her face to his skin. His arms circled her back, cradling her against his chest.

"I don't want to sleep until Gideon is back and I know they're safe," Lumen said.

"Fine."

"Do you think the war will end?" she asked. Her lips were running over his throat, with every word and she smiled as he swallowed hard. Sooner or later, Finley's control would break and he would consume her, but tonight was probably not the night for that moment.

"I think you will survive," he said. "That's enough for me."

Lumen frowned and arched to catch his gaze, her hands

fisting in the weave of his shirt. "No. Not for me. Not if I'm alone again, that's not what I want."

Finley's brows rose, and he closed his arms tighter around her until the only space between them was the press of their clothes. "Then we will have to survive together."

His head tipped to hers, lips sliding over hers, and Lumen sighed into this kiss. Finley was never impatient when it came to a kiss, and for all of his anxieties, he knew exactly how to soothe her nerves away with slow and gentle caresses. Lumen happily settled into the steady and relentless rhythm, the passing back and forth of affection, trying not to lose her patience and drag Finley over her.

Her skin felt more solid, more her own, the longer he touched her, and gradually, his weight eased over her, not impatient but comforting and real. When the house rattled softly with the opening and closing of the front door, Finley held her pinned in the bed.

"Stay. He'll be up," he said.

Sure enough, Gideon arrived within a moment, the tangled brow smoothing away as he spotted them in bed. Finley dropped a kiss to Lumen's nose and then slid over her to the opposite side of the bed, making room for Gideon.

"Are you well?" Gideon and Lumen asked at the same moment.

"Fine," Lumen said. Her tongue itched to ask if Dominic had come back with him, and she fastened it between her teeth.

"We left him in the courtyard and made it out the back before he began to shout for help," Gideon said, tearing his shirt off over his head and then shuffling out of his pants. He jumped into the bed, diving under the covers and then frowning. "Why are you all fastened up in your dress?"

"Colin tucked me in."

Gideon grunted at her answer, and Lumen smiled as he shimmed it up over her head with a few helpful tugs from Finley, until she was in only her shift. "Come here, sweet spirit. I need to feel you safe."

She needed it just as much and slid into Gideon's arms,

pleased when he seemed content with cuddling her up and making room for Finley at her back.

"I'm glad your Goddess gives you such good defenses," Gideon said. "You may need them again before we have settled the matter."

Lumen wondered if he meant the war or just the meeting of the officials taking place. Finley kissed the back of her neck, and she decided not to ask.

DOMINIC HAD BEEN WAITING WITH A PERVERSE KIND OF PLEASURE to see Cannary's face as Lumen walked into the large, painted chapel the next morning. And it *was* satisfying—the man grew paler and his nostrils flared at her entrance. Dominic and Gideon hadn't waited to watch the assassin be discovered, but he had no doubt that one way or another, Cannary was aware of exactly how a hired killer had suddenly lost two of his most valuable senses. But it wasn't General Cannary whose control broke greatest. It was the severe and pale woman in her black gown, rearing back with wide eyes fixed to the shadow beneath Lumen's hood. As if she hadn't been entirely convinced Lumen was still alive.

Dominic was tempted to leap across the table and throttle the woman's neck in his hands. Instead, he waited, fists wrapped around the back of a chair, for Lumen to reach his side. He pulled the seat out for her, and she reached up, flicking back her hood and letting it drape over her shoulders. She was incandescent, the sunlight filtering to the far side of the room, just enough light to catch in her hair and make that ghost pale skin of hers shine. Dominic forced his gaze down to his knuckles to keep from staring, guiding the chair into the table as she took her seat. He did the same for High Priestess Wren, finding it a little easier to breathe with someone between him and Lumen. Gideon forced a chair on Lumen's other side, having refused to spend another day pretending not to guard her. It hardly mattered now. No one would suspect any powers but Lumen's in blinding a healthy man.

"I hope today we can dispense with diplomacy and you all might arrive at the real matter that brought you here," Dominic said as the rest of the officials and religious figures found their seats.

Commander Becker scoffed, but Cannary dipped his head in Dominic's direction.

"You and your men are attempting to stand in the way of forces greater than you."

"Attempting or succeeding?" Dominic asked, affecting a casual lean he knew would irritate the older man. He knew how to behave in a court of this company, playing at respect, but he liked his roguish character and wanted Cannary to see he didn't give a shit for the game of chess Stalor and Oshain seemed determined to continue.

Becker growled and leaned forward, face already blooming red in color. "They stole our land, our best ports, and sent our country into poverty!"

"That was over a century ago," Cannary's woman said with an irritated wave of her hand.

Dominic turned to her and arched an eyebrow. "A century is a long time for a country to go hungry."

She opened her mouth to speak and paused as General Cannary's head twitched in disagreement. Oshain would let Becker ream him out first.

"Stalor has reclaimed its land. If you continue to push there will be no men left to work it," Dominic reasoned.

"You swore your life to your country, boy, and if you refuse to keep your word that life will be taken from you by your country."

"I have given Stalor over twenty years, over three-hundred miles under my leadership, and plenty of lives were sacrificed by my hands. My service is complete now, and I dare you to try and make any further claim." He'd meant the words as a disguise. For so long, his goal had been to protect Lumen, to make amends for the wrongs he committed. But Lumen Fenn was a creature far beyond needing his protection now, and the speech he'd made was more than a disguise. It was a relief to speak thoughts he'd barely made room for in his own mind.

"You think you want peace?" Becker spat on the table in punctuation. "Men like you rot in peaceful times. You're a clever blade, Westbrook, nothing more."

"So be it," Dominic said. It had already occurred to him he might wither without war, and he was willing to find out.

"Becker, you speak of the past, of Oshain's old victories, and you neglect to mention the millennia of aggression that came from Stalor before. Stalor burned our villages, stole holy silver from the mountains," Cannary said. "If your retaliation now is justice, what was ours a century ago?"

"Stalor was destined by Sol himself to conquer," Father Wesley said, his eyes above the heads of the gathered party, studying the walls of the chapel with a frown on his lips.

Wren made a soft dismissive 'pft' on Dominic's right, and he fought his grin.

"Even now, Stalor and Sol's men take ugly liberties on our people," the dark woman spoke with a snarl. "Destroying our communities, defiling our good women."

Dominic bristled, but it was Lumen who answered her. "My care could hardly have suffered worse than it did in Oshain's own hands."

"Your case was an...unfortunate exception to our process," Cannary said to Lumen with a slight dip of his head.

"Oshain is no less guilty of unfeelingly using its people as a tool," Dominic said, more to draw the eyes of the room away from Lumen than anything else.

General Cannary frowned at him, gray beard twitching. "Are we expected to lie back and allow Stalor to mount us?"

Gideon growled and Dominic swallowed, aware of the suggestion of the words. He had done as much to Oshain's women, yes, he remembered. He regretted, the self-disgust a strong acid running through his mind at every hour.

"I am not surrendering. Not myself, my men, or this territory. Whatever conclusion you hoped to see in this meeting, that is the only answer I have," Dominic said, voice flat and blood simmering.

General Cannary gave him a soft, amused smile, even as Becker snarled a curse down the table. "Do you really think you and your men can stand against two countries and their armies, Westbrook?"

"Do you think we can?" Dominic asked, leaning forward and resting his chin on a fist. "You must worry, or you would not have come here to try and persuade me to step back." He watched as Cannary and Becker shared a brief and accidental glance of worry. "Ah. I may end up dead, but you know it will be costly. Perhaps so much so, your armies won't stand by the end. That suits me fine," Dominic said and found he was being honest.

Cannary and Becker picked up their arguments again, which country had committed what crimes, and who had the most right to land and wealth. Dominic sank back in his chair and let the words run past his ears.

FINLEY WAS FUSSING WITH A TINCTURE, trying to make something new that Lumen might approve of for treating lung infections when voices echoed from the courtyard outside. He looked up at the window, judging the falling light outside and the hunger in his own stomach. It was late afternoon, which meant Dominic and the others had spent a solid six hours arguing around a table. It was a miracle an actual battle hadn't broken out already, and it meant Dominic and Gideon were better at diplomacy than Finley would've guessed.

The door creaked at this back, and Finley expected Lumen's soft tones or Gideon's growl.

"Looks as much like a witch's lair as I might've imagined."

Finley spun and frowned, hand finding a small trowel on the counter that was meant to measure pastes out but might be used to gouge the eyes of an enemy. He tucked it behind his back and straightened as Commander Becker's gaze traveled over the hanging herbs and darkened bottles lining high shelves.

"Commander. Were you in need of...healing?" Finley asked, annoyed at how transparently nervous he sounded.

Commander Becker scoffed, face twisting in a derisive snarl. "I know better than to accept such an offer from my enemy, even if I were ill."

Finley didn't respond. He may have taken a vow to heal, but Becker was right, he wasn't above breaking it in this case. Lumen was noble in that way, but Finley preferred to be open to all possible defenses. Becker's eyes moved down from the beams above as he walked deeper into the workroom, taking in Finley opposite him with a thorough study.

"You don't look like him," Becker said. "But I caught a glimpse of your mother once when we met on the field, and I suppose that her resemblance would've been stronger. If she'd lived."

Finley's throat constricted as if Becker had tied a rope around it and yanked with a sudden ruthlessness. Commander Becker knew his father. And...his mother was dead.

He'd always chosen to believe she'd been a maid who'd ended up in bed with a wealthy employer, maybe even was still working for a family somewhere in Stalor. He had no fantasies of ever making a connection with his family, but somehow, the finality of knowing she was long since gone from the world was an unexpected wound.

Becker hummed, eyes narrowing, and Finley tried to bury his reactions before the man read too much. "I suppose you don't know. She was northern. Your father snatched her up out of her house during his time in the army. Carried her about with him. Luckily, she died in childbirth before he might've taken her back home to disillusion his young wife too soon."

It was too much, too much information unbidden and all at once. Dominic thought Becker was a brute of a man, but Finley was sure this was pure cunning without force.

Becker stopped in front of him, reaching into his padded vest and pulling out a thin envelope, holding it in the air between them. "From your father," he said.

Finley took it in a reflex, and the fine edges of the paper seemed to burn at his fingertips. He waited for Becker to leave but the large man remained, watching expectantly, and Finley couldn't think of the words to dismiss him, not with this in his hands and Becker's sudden dumping of information running circles in his head. He tore the letter open and read the familiar hand.

My son died in battle not long ago, and I find there is a place for you here. An inheritance far outside the expectations I'd had to give you. Quit your position in the army, whatever you still claim of it, and return south with Commander Becker. I've secured your pardon, provided you agree to a statement that Westbrook forced your continued service.

Safe travels.

X

X, Finley thought, frowning at the letter. He'd seen it before on his mysterious father's biddings. A veil of secrecy to keep Finley in his place as the bastard, rather than the son.

"You're not his only bastard, you know," Becker said. "Just the one who turned out the best. Not that that's much to boast of, considering where you ended up."

Finley frowned at the words on the page. They told him little he hadn't already known. A man who could pluck an orphan out of poverty and put him through school, and then shove him into the army's service, was certainly rich or powerful enough to buy that same son a pardon from treason. Finley would be some rich lord with enough time if the letter wasn't a trap, which he suspected it wasn't. No one knew he killed Cantalion but the men who fought at his side. It would be easy for him to look like the meek healer who'd only done as his crazed general commanded.

He'd left a candle burning on the counter so he could heat oils in his tests, and he turned to it now, letter in his hand. He set the page on fire, watched bright orange and golden flames lick at paper, eating up plain words in a handwriting he'd come to loathe. He dropped the page into an empty stone tray before it burned his fingers.

"I'm afraid my father, whoever he is, will have to settle his hopes on one of the less impressive bastards," Finley said mildly, turning back to Becker with the bright fire still burning at the corner of his eyes.

Becker tutted and shook his head, humor on his lips. "You'll be strung up with the rest of them now, boy. If you'd thought it through a little better, you might've dragged that pale priestess of yours home with you, just as your father tried to do. At least she'd've been safe in your fine house in the south."

Finley smiled at Becker's goading. "She'd have slit us from cock to crown on the ride south, Commander."

Becker paled at the threat, brow furrowing as he cleared his throat, eyes twitching. Good, let the disgusting man think twice about Finley's *pale priestess*. It might've been an exaggeration of Lumen's abilities, but Finley was sure he'd have a fate equally bad if he tried kidnapping Lumen as his northern conquest to carry home.

Finley waited until Becker took his halting heavy steps out of the workroom before finally releasing his held breaths. He turned and looked at the smoldering ashes on the stone, just a few crumbling letters here and there scattered. *Let that be an end to it*, Finley thought, and he opened the window to toss the ash out into the sky.

LUMEN DECIDED NOT to sit in on the second session of discussions for the day. Partly because it made her stomach turn to hear them talk, even Dominic as he played careless about his own odds at living. And partly because she thought Gideon was likely to break his own bones with how hard he fisted his hands as the men alluded to her in passing. There seemed to be two axes in the discussion. One was Stalor and Oshain's endless history of war, and who was owed what from their last round of battle. The other was herself and the land Dominic had claimed.

Perhaps if she removed herself from the room, the conversation might move in a new direction. Either way, she was relieved not to be trapped listening.

She and Jennie were preparing another meal—something suitably scant to keep their guests from feeling too welcome, without denying them so much they felt the need to steal it directly—and Lumen rushed across the courtyard, heading for the stable to see if Colin had gotten enough milk to make a cream sauce when she found Father Wesley staring through the open doorways and windows at sunset. Her steps slowed as his head turned to face her, the question digging lines over his smooth forehead.

"It's interesting isn't it?" Lumen asked, turning to look down the hall of the small new moon chapel where the moon was visible out the narrow blue window. "Did you know it used to be a temple devoted to both God and Goddess?"

Father Wesley searched her face and then shook his head once. "Then the painting in the chapel upstairs is…"

Lumen shrugged. "I did my best to restore it when we found it behind the old bookshelves. But yes, it was there originally."

"A balance between Sol and Lune," Father Wesley mused with a slow tongue. His gaze narrowed on Lumen. "Surely you don't mean for that balance to echo between Stalor and Oshain's armies?"

"Father Wesley, I think Commander Becker is as dedicated to Sol as General Cannary is to Lune," Lumen said with equally careful speech. "My loyalty is to my Goddess and to my fellow mankind."

"And you approve of Westbrook building an army to fight both countries?" Wesley asked.

Lumen's lips pursed, and her eyes strayed up to the balcony as if she might find Dominic looking down on her. Gideon was out gathering eggs, the Priestesses were in prayer in their rooms, or snooping maybe, and Jennie and Colin were in the kitchen together. There was no one to hear her conversation with Father Wesley, but she found herself speaking with an honest tongue all the same.

"I don't know that fighting will ever bring an end to war,"

Lumen said. "But I believe that I have a duty to offer healing and care to men and women who are tired, as I am tired, and who have suffered as I have or worse."

Father Wesley huffed, offered her a false smile, and looked down his nose at her. "Do you think you know your Goddess so well?"

Lumen found that drawing Lune closer was a simple thing as if she'd taught herself the skill in the same way she'd learned to flip a pancake for Colin or thread a needle to sew a man shut. Lune's touch weighed on her shoulder, a cold ache in her chest, and Father Wesley's smile faltered as he stared at her.

"Yes. Do you know your God? Is his thirst for blood so unquenchable? If Stalor ever conquers Oshain, where will he have you turn next, on yourselves? Or has your church confused sweat and toil for blood and conquest?" Lumen left the priest in silence, her feet moving beneath her without sensation. She made it out to the drive, the sinking sun hitting her throat before Lune retreated. Lumen threw her hood back and gasped for breath, staring into the bright fire of sunset, the sky bleeding on the horizon as her heartbeat steadied in her chest.

ON THE THIRD DAY, STALOR AND OSHAIN STATED THEIR TERMS IN plain language. Dominic, Cannary, and Becker were alone at the table for once, and Dominic remained silent as they laid their offers out, dangling soft temptations on their lines in the hopes he might choose to comply. He didn't believe either one of them, didn't believe the quiet bargaining of the conversation, gentle words twisted to make bloody acts seem less threatening. Anyways, it wasn't his decision to make alone.

Dominic found Lumen, Finley, and Gideon together at the house, waiting for him. Jennie was keeping up the nighttime illusion of being Lumen, although Dominic had doubled the watch duty and no further attempts or assassins had been discovered.

"If I were you, I'd have cut their heads clean off their necks by now," Gideon greeted him. He sat in a large chair, with Lumen tucked against his side. She was almost swallowed by his vastness but appeared content surrounded by him.

"I considered it," Dominic admitted. He shrugged out of his plain coat and took the empty chair by the fire, combing his growing hair out of his eyes. "Not sure it would leave us in a better position though. We...*you* have two offers," he said, looking at Lumen who stiffened in surprise.

"What do you mean?" Finley asked, leaning forward onto his elbows.

"I can turn myself over to Stalor, they will resume the war as before, and the temple will remain untouched," Dominic said.

"You'll be hanged," Gideon growled.

"Or worse," Dominic agreed. Probably worse. Becker would enjoy the show.

"And the men who've made homes here?" Lumen asked.

"They'll have to choose a side to serve," Dominic said.

She scoffed and leaned deeper into Gideon's side, his arm tightening over her shoulder. "Do you really believe she'd be safe?" Gideon asked, ignoring Lumen's irritated stare.

"Not especially, but I didn't think it was my choice to make," Dominic admitted.

"It's still not your decision to make, just as it's not mine," Lumen said stiffly, eyes narrowed. "I understand that here, in this room, you've made your decisions based on...on me, but it's not the same for the others. They want this war to end. You can't break your word to them," Lumen said.

"You said there was another offer," Finley said.

Dominic nodded, head ducking to avoid Lumen's gaze as it burned over his face. "We join Oshain's ranks. Gain back one hundred miles. Lumen and the temple will be protected." It was the more tempting of the two for Dominic, although he hated Cannary and his poisonous compatriots. He must not have been alone, because Gideon and Finley were both quiet with thought in the wake of the declaration, and Lumen looked over each of them, her frown growing by the second.

"No," she said.

"Your own people would be less likely to act against a Lunar temple," Dominic said. "And one hundred miles is not so far. We might've gained it within a year."

Gideon's hand curved around Lumen's arm, turning her to face him with a sorrowful expression. "It might be our best chance at surviving, sweet spirit. Of having summers and holidays and full tables of family together."

Dominic's chest ached, and he swallowed down the bile in his throat, the sweet words making him want to run to Cannary now and agree to the offer.

"I don't care about Oshain and their land, I don't care about who is right and wrong in this war," Lumen said. "I care about you, and I care about the men and women who've come to us desperate for change and for peace."

"Be realistic, Dom," Finley whispered. "If you gain one hundred miles for Oshain, they'll want one hundred more. All you'll accomplish is turning the tide in Oshain's favor. No one will be free."

Dominic looked at Lumen. She might be free, although if Gideon and Finley followed Dominic into battle, he might cost her happiness with them too.

Lumen met his stare with a warning glare. "No, Dominic. Pretend I don't exist for a moment."

It pains me to, he thought. "I would rather stand our ground here. We have a week to decide, and I'd use it to let the men make their choices about where to stand, and prepare for everything they can throw our way."

"I don't relish the thought of helping that bastard Cannary," Gideon said with a dip of his head.

"I'd happily watch Stalor burn under its own efforts," Finley added, pushing back into his chair.

Dominic frowned and watched Lumen. "And if you could keep your men, keep Colin and Jennie? I could take men willing to fight, Oshain would never know who was here, it's me they're after."

Lumen shot up from her seat, cheeks blazing and eyes sharp. "Enough, Dominic. You're not rescuing me by throwing yourself into service for Oshain or letting Stalor hang you." She stormed to the stairs, and Dominic swallowed hard, watching her pale braid beat at her back as she stomped up to the bedroom.

"You didn't really think she'd agree, did you, Dom?" Gideon asked, head tipping and faint smile curling. "Our lady?"

Dominic ignored the tightness in his chest and turned to the fireplace, Lumen's blazing stare brighter than the flames he fixed his gaze to.

"I wish you would stay longer," Lumen said, holding High Priestess Wren's hand in hers. The emissaries had left in their coaches at dawn, and it'd been a weight right off her own heart to watch them go, but now the heaviness was returning as Wren prepared to leave.

"I'll get in your way," Wren said, with a soft smile. "And besides I'd better return to the convent and be sure the refugee women haven't caused any extra trouble in my absence."

"She means my family," Neave muttered where she waited by her horse.

"I have half a mind to leave her here with the others," Wren said in a whisper to Lumen, shooting the young girl a teasing glare.

Of the five priestesses Wren had brought with her, three were staying with Lumen at the temple. It was an offer she would've refused if High Priestess Wren had given her any choice. "I don't disapprove of your company here, dear, don't misunderstand. But you could use more hands to make this place shine, and you'll need more help when the fighting starts in earnest," Wren had said, her arm locked with Lumen's as they took a walk over the rolling property surrounding the temple.

"If the war ends…" Lumen said, smiling at Neave, the hopeful words clumsy on her tongue before she trailed off and shrugged. "Jennie enjoys Neave's company. She'd be welcome if it were safe. Are you sure the others should stay?" She tried to speak softly but one of the younger priestesses, Adelaide Nemory, overheard and rushed forward.

"High Priestess Wren told us the risks, and we still volunteered, Priestess. I lost all my family in this war, and my home far south of here was burnt. The convent was my last hope, but I don't want to spend my entire life in the mountains. I want to do Mother Lune's work amongst her people," Nemory said. She was pretty, hair a deeper shade of gold than Lumen's and eyes a springy green. Lumen had already demanded assurance from Gideon that the priestesses would never be harassed by the men, but she thought she'd seen Nemory making plenty of study of the available soldiers on her own.

"Not all of us were meant to pray in seclusion," High Priestess Wren said softly. "Some women have to make work in the world, see life and death hand in hand. If they change their minds…"

"I'll make sure they make it back safely," Lumen agreed. It was the best she could do.

Wren seemed more than satisfied, squeezing Lumen's hands in hers and dragging her forward to kiss both her cheeks. "I hope you see one day how much change you have wrought. In this land. These men. Yourself," Wren whispered in her ear.

Lumen stared after the High Priestess as she was helped onto her horse, the remaining members of her party following close at hand.

"I heard Father Wesley saying the armies plan to strike in a week if General Westbrook doesn't surrender," Priestess Nemory—Adelaide said.

Lumen opened her mouth to say that Dominic wasn't a general now, and then realized that he was to his men and that was all that mattered. "That's true."

"I've never done any healing before," Adelaide said.

Lumen took a deep breath and turned her back on the road and the retreating women. She forced a smile on her lips and took a longer look at Adelaide and the other two women. They weren't younger than her, she realized. In fact one, Hannah James, was probably closer to thirty, but they *felt* younger to Lumen. In the past year, she was fairly sure she'd aged fifty years at least.

"Then we know how we will keep ourselves occupied as we wait," Lumen said with a nod. "Healer Brink and I will show you all our methods so you're prepared. As much as possible," she amended. There would be no preparation for seeing their first wounded soldier, except a good bucket to heave in if the sight of blood made them sick.

LUMEN AND FINLEY watched each other from opposite ends of the dinner table as the temple's new occupants pestered Jennie and Colin with questions about the people in the growing village, the numbers of men who were injured, the number of battles already fought. Finley was as welcoming to the priestesses as he had been of Lumen initially, which was to say snappish and withdrawn, although he relayed information without too much prodding. She'd sort his mood out later when they were alone. It probably wasn't much of a secret that Lumen had a relationship with the healer—and Gideon too for that matter—but she didn't intend to flaunt the fact. Especially not as Adelaide Nemory quizzed Jennie on every man under the age of fifty.

Jennie flicked a swift glance in Lumen's direction, amusement and concern mixed together, and Lumen wondered if it was too much to ask Jennie to teach the women some of the ways they might protect themselves against men, or pregnancy, or both.

"But the general, he's very handsome," Adelaide said with a soft giggle.

Lumen's fingers fisted around her fork in a sudden and painful clench, and she stared at her own hand in shock.

"Nah, he's a beast," Colin said easily. "Gave Lady her scars."

"Colin," Lumen chided softly.

He lifted his chin and squared his gaze on her. "It's true."

Adelaide was staring at Lumen's face with a horrified awe, lips parted. "But I thought he fought for you."

Lumen's cheeks heated with a burning flush, and the leg's of Finley's chair screeched against stone as he stood from the table. "Westbrook fights for his men, just as we fight for him," Finley said, turning his back to the table, and rinsing his dish quickly in the bucket. Adelaide and the others didn't look entirely convinced, and Jennie tipped her head to Lumen, a soft encouragement to escape the scrutiny. Colin sent her his own look, a comical grimace of apology she accepted with a smile.

"Priestess Fenn, if we might have a word before I leave," Finley said.

Lumen sighed and stood from the table, and Finley took her dishes out of her hand, dropped them into the water, and then brushed past her, shoulders tight with anxiety.

"I'll see you all in the morning," Lumen offered the room, pleased that Adelaide contained her whispers until she and Finley were out of hearing range.

He was waiting against the arch of the stairway, head tipped back and eyes shut.

"The first battle is going to come as a shock to her," Lumen said, tucking her hand into his.

Finley hummed in agreement, head lolling in her direction and eyes opening slowly with exhaustion. "Come back to the house?" he asked.

Gideon would be there, but so would Dominic, and Lumen wanted privacy if she was going to spend the night next to one of her men again. She shook her head and then stepped onto the first stair, hiding in the arch. Finley followed her, bowing over her, a soft smile growing as his hands circled her waist.

"I'll kiss you goodnight," he said, bending.

Lumen skipped up two steps, missing his offered kiss, and smiled at his baffled frown. She tapped at the line that appeared between his brows and then slid her fingers into his hair, rifling it into an untidy mess.

"I've decided something about trust, I think," Lumen said, letting her fingers trail through his hair down to the back of his neck, guiding him stumbling up the steps. Finley's eyebrow raised in question, and she continued. "It does not grow on its own, but is granted."

Finley's eyes clouded, and he resisted her pull. "I broke yours."

Lumen sighed and stepped down, tipping her head to press her forehead against his. "Yes, once."

Finley reached up, pulling her hand from the back of his neck and raising her wrist to his lips to suck a soft kiss over her pulse. "I won't again."

Lumen tugged her hand, catching his with it and returning

the kiss at the edge of his sleeve cuff. "Good. Because mine is given. Do I have yours?"

Finley's heavy mood broke with his smile, and he stepped up until he and Lumen were pressed chest to chest and nose to nose. "You absolutely do."

"Then come with me," Lumen said, turning and pulling him up the stairs before he could capture her in his arms.

Finley huffed and followed her to her new bedroom, the one she shared with Gideon and him briefly, and he paused in the doorway. "Are you certain?" he asked, his lean lines filling the frame of the door, the pink glow of sunset lingering in the courtyard behind him and painting the stone of the temple. "Because, Lumen, I know now that I could never, would never, be able to abandon you again."

She considered teasing him, but Finley was more serious than Gideon and he deserved her sincerity in this moment, although she chose to give it in a playful way. "I am certain that I would tie you to the bed before I let you leave again."

Finley's eyebrows rose at the declaration, and he stepped inside, shutting the door behind him. There was no fire to warm the room yet, and no candle burning, only enough light left from the dying sun outside for them to see each other. "Is that what you'd like? Am I to submit to you tonight?"

He stalked forward, and Lumen knew how quickly he could turn the tables. Finley was an anxious man, yes, and often insecure, but when she surrendered herself to him in bed the gift of control transformed him. She had missed those pleasures and the freedom of throwing herself into his hands, but tonight she wanted to savor him as well as force him to be on the receiving end of her affection.

Towering over her, lips pursed and ready to give her a command she would thrill at obeying, Lumen halted Finley with a soft hand on his neck. "Undress and put yourself on the bed for me to look at," she said. A soft sound choked in his throat, and the simmering power he wore during sex cracked to reveal his nerves. "It's your choice. If it's too uncomfortable, then I'll be yours tonight—"

"No, I... Yes, Priestess," he said, sucking in a breath, eyelids hooding his warm stare.

Lumen curved around his side to watch him shrug his shirt off over the back of his head. The planes of his back were more defined after months of training and helping in the fields and on Gideon's house for them. He was still the same beautifully sculpted arrow of muscle, even sharper now. He twisted and smiled as she stared, long fingers going to the fastenings of his pants.

"What will you do with me?" he asked.

Lumen bit her lip and stared at the arching lines of his hips guiding down to his long cock, still tucked away and twitching against fabric at her attention. She hadn't decided exactly where her control would lead them, especially not when her body already throbbed for Finley's attention. "Don't stop," she said, watching his hands hold the waist of his pants around his hips.

Finley blushed, his shaking sigh audible in the quiet. He stepped out of his trousers, and Lumen stifled a giggle as she saw his plump ass and fought the immediate urge to smack it. He slid onto the bed, hands behind his head and ankles crossed, his cock growing stiffer without a single touch. Lumen stepped to the foot of the bed and stared up the length of him, slowly crawling onto the mattress.

"Won't you undress?" he asked.

"Grab onto the headboard," she said, ignoring his question and sitting up on her knees next to his thighs. She reached back to his calves and tapped one. "And spread."

Finley's cheeks were bright red, and Lumen's heart was heady and thumping with the power she held. His hands slid out from under his head, wrapping around the headboard as she had done for him ages ago. She scooted aside as he spread his knees, and tipped her head to stare between his legs, realizing she'd never had quite such a good look at a man's privates before, although they'd certainly had their fill of staring at hers.

Finley was embarrassed, his body tense and covered in a blush, but his cock was fully engorged and weeping fluid.

283

Lumen leaned forward, dipping her head, and took a quick lick from the swollen, leaking tip of him.

"Gods, Lumen, fuck! It isn't right that I can't touch you after all this time," Finley rasped through gritted teeth.

Lumen scoffed and smiled, her puffed breath sending Finley's cock kicking at the air. "You've touched plenty these past few weeks, Healer Brink. Be patient."

She considered undressing but knew that if she did, nothing would stop her from mounting Finley and riding him to their quick finishes. And she wanted to draw out his agony as much as possible for once. She shed her black robes, folding them and resting them out of the way, and then picked up her skirts to settle herself on her knees between Finley's legs. His chest was rising and falling at a rapid pace, although his arousal had begun to flag without her touch.

Lumen considered the catalog of all the pleasures she'd received, and the ones she'd witnessed between Finley and Gideon recently, and made her choice. With a quick and thorough suck of her own finger, which Finley watched with growing eyes, she slid it between his cheeks, burrowing for his hole and discovering it quickly. Finley arched at the touch and bellowed a wordless cry, Lumen tutting and smiling.

"Hush. The priestesses will hear you."

Finley laughed, panting, and then groaned and squeezed his eyes shut as Lumen worked her finger in a knuckle deep. "You're far too wicked to be holy."

She was inclined to agree, but instead of answering, she bent her head and pulled the rounded tip of Finley's cock between her lips, sucking and lapping at the spot, rolling her bottom lip against the underside. With her free hand, she rolled his sac, massaging it with calculated pressure that made his thighs shake. Gone was the man who knew how to wring handfuls of orgasms out of her, replaced by a whining and desperate creature who worked himself between digit and mouth. She was careful to give him very little of each, just enough to hold him at a painful plateau of pleasure that demanded *more*, a word he quickly began to chant amongst repetitive praises and her name.

Finley's heels dug into the mattress, his hips rocking and bouncing beneath her. "Please, Sol, Gods, fuck, Lumen, please!"

Lumen pulled away, drawing in a quick breath and then pinning Finley's knees to the mattress in an open position. She kissed at the crease of his thighs, his cock begging at her cheeks, and then down to his knees and back up again. She skipped his arousal, pinning it between their bellies, and laid herself over his chest to suck on his tongue as he thrashed beneath her, all his whimpers and groans kept quiet under her orders. He started to fuck the stomach of her dress, and Lumen grinned and lifted herself off him, rising to her knees again to survey her work so far.

His gaze was glazed, lips shining with her kiss, and there was a small dab of sticky fluid on his stomach, his cock red and angry for touch.

"Is it too much?" she asked.

"No," Finley said, head shaking quickly. "You are far too good at the game. More."

Pride burned like fire in her chest and her cunt, and Lumen wondered briefly if this was how men felt when they conquered women in their beds. She ducked down again, sucking her teeth and lips around Finley's flesh on his throat and collar and chest, leaving dark wet marks to stake her claim. Finley moaned and bucked, a light sweat breaking out over his chest that she licked away and spread over her lips. His hips still surged, cock scratching a pathetic itch against the fabric of her skirt, and Lumen continued her way down until he bumped and begged at her throat.

Gideon was too thick to hold in her mouth for long stretches of time, although she could make him weak on licks and kisses and her hands alone. Finley was easier to take, the perfect size to fill her lips and press to her tongue, long enough to hit the back of her throat and still hold in her hand. His groans grew louder, but he held himself still for her assault, and this time when she pressed a slick finger to his hole it seemed to take her gratefully.

"I'll come. Gods, Lumen, you'll undo me," Finley hissed. She started to pull away, and he whined and gasped out, "Pinch tighter around my base. Yes…" He made a broken sound as Lumen tightened her hold and pulled her lips off of him to catch her breath.

Lumen sat, bent, body aching for touch, and stared at her triumph over Finley. His body was taut, pulse pounding visibly in his arched throat, lips parted up at the roof of the bed, hands clamped tight around the headboard. Gods, he was going to break it if she kept up her work. Her own inner thighs were dewy with desire, and Lumen had a wonderful taste of control, but now she badly wanted the feeling of Finley stretching and filling her.

"Hold yourself so I can undress," she said, a little breathless.

Finley was fast, his hand taking an even rougher grip of his base, the other diving into his hair and tugging hard as if to distract himself from the pleasure.

Lumen threw her clothes off over her head with a rough efficiency and then climbed over Finley's chest, lowering her breast to hover above his lips. "Kiss," she said, although he was surging up, a hand bracing on her spine before she'd even finished the word. She moaned as his mouth wrapped around her nipple, suckling and licking until it tightened to a painful tip. She pulled herself free, and Finley was quick to shift and repeat the process on the neglected breast.

Lumen reached between them, guiding the head of his cock to her soaking core. Finley crashed to the pillows with a strained moan as she sank down, marveling at the way his length seemed to go on and on inside her before finally bottoming out.

"Can you wait for me?" she asked, rising and falling on his length experimentally. Gods, he was longer than Gideon and her body had forgotten the difference of sensation, Finley's pressure sharper and edgy.

"Yes," he hissed, reaching for her hips.

Lumen shook her head, and he paused. "Hands in the sheets. You'll break the headboard."

Finley swallowed hard, every muscle in his body coiled tight to keep himself from fucking her from below. One of his hands reached for hers, braced on his chest, and dragged it up to his throat, his eyes holding fast to hers. "Will you hold here? Tight?" His fingers guided hers in place, and Lumen's heart stuttered in her chest. Finley smiled, tense but sweet, eyes softening. "I trust you," he said.

Lumen slowly settled herself, sinking down his length, hand pressing carefully to his throat, and Finley gasped, eyelids fluttering and cock throbbing inside of her. She rode him slowly, Finley's hand still covering hers on his throat, coaching her through the tight grip and the slow release in a pulse that seemed to echo inside of her. They were sharing the control now, but Lumen didn't want to stop, wanted Finley to teach her how he liked to be used in this way as she'd given herself over to him with his careful coaching.

Her breath held as his did, and she gasped when he did, body rocking faster by every minute, hips trying to grind against him to find that lovely scratching, swelling bliss that always threw her over.

"Fuck me," Lumen whispered when her thighs burned and her body ached for Finley's power.

He grunted, hips rising, and the deeper thrust made Lumen cry out. The bed creaked as their pace raced, bodies crashing together desperately. Finley's hand in the sheets slid between them seeking out Lumen's clit, and she gasped and ground into the touch, finally losing herself to the rhythmic craving of wanting more.

"Oh gods, yes! That's it. Finley, yes!" Her voice was tight and high, head thrown back and her own hair tickling down her spine. Her thighs shook and burned, and her body began to jerk as the crest of pleasure rose up her spine.

Finley's hand ripped hers from his throat and together they twisted, his shout ragged and loud, body bucking fiercely beneath her as he filled her with steady streams of heat. Lumen shook and tried to wring more pleasure from between them even as she collapsed down onto his chest, fingers digging into his chest to steady herself in the onslaught. Finley's arms wrapped around her back in an attempt to keep her from squirming away, granting her a few final soft thrusts until they both went limp.

Heat still swirled in Lumen's skin, her body trying to suck another gasp from Finley's cock, and he hissed as her after-shocks stirred over his length but kept her in his grasp. Lumen's face was tucked into his throat, eyes fixed to the mark of her fingers growing red on his skin. Finley's head turned, nose nuzzling against her cheek.

"Don't stir," he said.

Lumen smiled and nodded, and Finley soothed her uneven breaths with steady strokes of his hands up and down her back.

"I should've handed you control from the beginning," Finley mused. "You are exquisite in the throes of power, as much if not more than when you surrender."

"I wouldn't have known where to start then," Lumen said, nipping at his pulse and making his cock twitch as it slowly relaxed out of her body.

"Knock, knock." Lumen was glad Gideon announced himself because she was still too weak to move. The door creaked open and shut quickly, and a warm chuckle sounded by the door. "Thought I might find you like this. May I join you? Hate to sleep alone now."

Lumen made to move off Finley's chest, but he held her fast. "Gid, do you think you have it in you to make our girl gush on your cock?" Finley asked.

Lumen gasped and stirred enough to lift her face over Finley's, who tilted her chin and caught her lips in a kiss as Gideon growled, rustling fabric off his body.

"I want to hold her as you make her come, see her face as she falls apart again," Finley said.

Lumen caught a brief glimpse of Gideon as he prowled to the bed while kicking off his pants. His weight sunk the bed between her thighs, and Lumen twisted her head to watch, open-mouthed, as he pumped his cock to life with his fist.

"You know I like them wet and ready," Gideon said in his darkest rumble.

Lumen swallowed and whipped her head to stare at Finley, who grinned, eyes shifting to a brighter green. "My turn," he whispered.

"IT HAS SUCH A STINK TO IT, PRIESTESS FENN," HANNAH—Priestess James—said as she lifted the lid of their fresh barrel of cider vinegar.

"It does," Lumen agreed with a laugh. "But it does a great deal of good, regardless of the smell. Just give it a good stir, and we'll get back to the others. It should be ready to dispense as needed in another week."

Five days had passed since Stalor and Oshain took their leave of the temple. Another two days and their war would begin in earnest. Lumen fisted her hands in her sleeves, the countdown a constant presence in her thoughts. If she went to Dominic now and told him to hand himself over—to either side—she knew he would, and that it might buy them a few more months' peace, if not longer. She couldn't bring herself to ask, even though it meant Gideon and even Finley might march to their deaths, her own sure to follow not long after.

"Priestess?" Hannah prompted gently.

"Lady!"

Lumen shook herself and stepped out of the kitchen to find Colin racing through the courtyard. She caught him against her skirts, indulging in a brief comb of her fingers through his hair before she read the plain message on his troubled face.

"Oshain's coming down from the north, Lady," Colin gasped. "The men are getting ready to meet them. Think I saw Jones riding this way."

291

Overhead, a door shut and Finley stood, framed in the arches above.

"Two days early," Lumen said, too softly, but Colin and Finley both nodded.

Finley disappeared, and his footsteps clapped down a stairwell until he reappeared in the courtyard. "They'll need a field medic."

Lumen wanted to shout, object, race to Finley's side and hold him tight so he could not leave. He crossed to her slowly and brushed his hand against her shoulders. "Walk out with me to speak to Gideon, Priestess, and then ready the infirmary."

She nodded, a wooden jerking gesture, and Colin wrapped himself around Lumen's hips for a moment before taking off, his hand in Hannah's to find the other women.

"Don't think too far ahead, Lumen. We've gone to battle before," Finley murmured, a coaxing hand guiding her through the courtyard and out to the drive.

"I know," Lumen said, her voice too much of a whisper. She took a deep breath and pushed her shoulders back. "I know. So much has changed so quickly."

Out of sight of the others—although could it really still be any kind of secret what this man was to her—Finley paused and drew her to his chest. His lips caught hers in a brief and thorough caress, and Lumen clutched to the collar of his black coat, forcing herself to step back and not cling to him as the moment ended. Horse hooves beat on the gravel outside, and together they turned to meet Gideon.

"Good, you've heard," Gideon greeted, jumping down from his horse. He made quick strides to Lumen, catching her chin in his hand and tilting her eyes to meet his. "You could make it to the convent if you left with the others now."

Lumen glared up at her lover, her heart pained with unbearable affection. "Not a chance."

Gideon's grin was crooked but half-hearted, and he ducked his head as she rose to her toes, their own kiss full of conquest and surrender in equal turn.

"Love you, sweet spirit," he whispered.

"And I love you, my warrior," she said. She let herself fall into the warm amber of his gaze, sunshine blooming sweetly in her chest, and then Gideon skimmed his lips against hers and backed away.

"Pray to your Goddess for us," Finley said, kissing her forehead. He'd readied his own horse while Lumen and Gideon had embraced.

To Lune and Sol both, Lumen thought.

"Go inside and get to work," Gideon said with a tender bite in his tone. "Don't stand out here and watch our backs as we go."

"I'll bring him home whole," Finley said, lifting himself into the saddle.

"And I him," Gideon added.

She tried to think of something sweet to say, something good so that they would know she believed in them, in their return. But her throat was bound with worry, and she was still a terrible liar. She remained on the bottom step, watching their backs as they turned to ride away, hands clutching at her broken and uneven heartbeat.

GIDEON ROARED into the face of the man before him, their swords crossed between them. Both blades dripped red, Gideon's opponent's own face coated in the color from a head wound. Their arms shook with the strain of holding position. Gideon's boots slipped in the muddy, ruined ground beneath him.

For Lumen, he thought, the day's endless refrain of his thoughts, and then he tore his sword away in a long arc before driving it forward and into the man's belly. The man fell back with a slippery stumble, and Gideon skipped out of reach as the Oshain soldier made a last feeble swing of his blade, hoping to catch Gideon by the ankles.

Gideon left him bleeding on the ground, hoping the soldier wouldn't get up again for more. He was growing old, or tired, or both, but the battle dragged on by a slow heavy drumbeat. They were outnumbered three or four to one, which was hardly a surprise. Oshain had gathered its army and struck early and with rare force. Easy to do when Stalor was happy to turn their backs and leave them to it, Gideon supposed.

He scanned the field, relieved to see that despite the long hours of fighting, their ranks still seemed to be standing. For the most part. A flash of tarnished gold, the Stalor armor made dark, caught Gideon's eye, and he watched as Dominic Westbrook ducked and skidded in mud, falling to his knees before an Oshain soldier, arm unable to lift his own sword.

Gideon surged forward with a roar, barely meeting the sword with his own before it landed on Dominic's throat. He took on the fight for his friend, and with it another handful of soldiers who'd seen the weak opening of General Westbrook. With a moment to breathe, Dominic changed sword hands, rising on weak knees and joining Gideon in battle.

"Get to Finley," Gideon ground out. "Your shoulder—"

"I know," Dominic growled.

Dislocated shoulder or not, Dominic dispatched two of the men who surrounded them on his own, and a few more turned to find weaker targets than he and Gideon.

"We're going to lose," Dominic breathed in the beat before the next blade swung.

Gideon grunted, refusing to agree, but aware that as brave and loyal and determined as their men were, no one could last four to one for much longer. Not even him.

"Get your shoulder fixed. Get off the field," Gideon repeated. He couldn't leave Dominic to his own devices like this. Oshain would descend upon his friend like vultures to a feast.

"I'm not leaving my men in a fight like this," Dominic roared, chasing after a running enemy.

Gideon raced with him, and together they beat back a crowd who'd gathered around two of their own.

"Arm looks bad, sir," one of their men said.

"Fuck off," Dominic spat, and Gideon snorted and focused on his next target.

He was staring to the north, through the thin mix of green

and brass uniforms, at a dark line on the horizon of a hill. "Fuck," Gideon breathed as the line became a mass, running down the crest.

"Is that—Gods, are there more?" Dominic moaned.

Lumen, Gideon thought, but it was not his rallying cry, but a mournful exhalation. He would never make it back to her. Not unless he ran there now like a coward, and then what good would it do? Oshain and Stalor would catch up to them.

"They're un-uniformed," Dominic said, before being drawn into battle.

Gideon's eyes narrowed, and he knocked past two soldiers. Dominic was right. The swarm of men, another four hundred at least, weren't wearing colors, although a good few had makeshift armor. He watched, stunned, as they reached the backs of the Oshain soldiers. One man, older with a graying beard and a tightly knitted cap on his head, pulled a uniformed soldier off the back of one of Gideon's own men, punching him squarely in the nose and throwing him to the ground.

The new men bled through the army like water, one refrain roared in repetition upon their lips.

"For Oshain! For Oshain! For Oshain!"

A body appeared at Gideon's side, and he readied to toss it off, but it was only a breathless Dominic, holding his twisted shoulder and watching the strange tide of men with baffled awe.

"Who are they?" Dominic asked, as if Gideon might know.

Just ahead of them, one of the Oshain soldiers met a man in a sudden burst of movement. A dagger was at the soldier's throat, a sword at the belly of a scarred young man with a missing ear. The two stared at each other with wide eyes, the soldier in green gasping at the sight.

"I thought you'd died."

"Nearly did in hospital."

The sword wavered between them, but the dagger never faltered. "Will you kill me?"

"No, but one of the others might."

The men stared at one another, eyes locked, and the dagger

dug into the other man's throat as the soldier tore his helmet away, blond hair damp with sweat and matted to a young face.

"Enough, brother," the soldier whispered, sword landing in earth.

Gideon turned away as the young men embraced and searched the field. Most were still fighting, still locked in battle, but the two behind him weren't the only ones who recognized faces from home.

"Get to Finley, Dominic," Gideon said, watching as the Oshain army realized its new and terrible odds in the battle.

Allies from the most unlikely place had arrived, Oshain's own sons and fathers turning the tide against each other.

⸎

LUMEN STOPPED in front of the bedroom door, listening to the growling tones emitting from within, and took a deep and steadying breath. She pushed inside to find Priestess Nemory attempting to fuss around Dominic Westbrook as he tore himself free of his own shirt.

"Enough, pest, leave me be!" Dominic snarled at the young woman, spinning on his heel. His voice died, eyes popping, as he discovered Lumen in the room. His skin was pale and shining with sweat, his face bloody and his right arm hanging from his shoulder in a terrible way.

"Sit," Lumen said, pointing to the chair.

Dominic parted his lips and shut them just as quickly, Priestess Nemory hiccuping a soft whimper at his sudden obedience.

"Priestess Nemory, hold him there. No, by the other shoulder. Dominic, find something to bite down on," Lumen continued, crossing to him.

He pulled his belt from his pants with a quick flash, barely stuffing it folded between his teeth before Lumen gripped his elbow in one firm hand.

"Tighter, Adelaide," Lumen snapped, and Dominic growled and then roared, straining as Lumen rotated and reset his shoulder with a quick and brutal determination. His boot stomped against the floor as he caught his breath, and Lumen shooed the other priestess back. "Thank you, that will be all for now."

"I could—"

Dominic spat the belt to his lap and barked out, "No!"

Priestess Nemory scurried from the room, and Dominic sagged in his chair as the door shut behind her. Lumen remained standing over him, folding her arms over her chest as she surveyed him. His armor was abandoned on the bed, bent and dented in new places, and he had the bruises to match forming on his chest.

"What happened? Where are the others?" she asked. Finley had arrived with a party of injured in a cart, Dominic West-brook included, and together they'd been so busy that Finley barely had the time to spare to offer her a kiss and reassurance that Gideon was well and would return soon.

"On their way shortly," Dominic said, an echo of Finley's words. "We were close to losing the battle when a…an army of Oshain men arrived. Not soldiers, just…men," he added, frowning up at her.

"They fought for…"

"For themselves," Dominic said with a raised eyebrow that stuck with dried blood.

Lumen sighed and crossed to where Nemory had left a bowl of steaming water. There was a full bath warming by the fire too, and she wondered what trouble Dominic would give her to put him in it. She took a clean rag and carried it back to him with the warm bowl. He reached for the cloth and then paused as she stepped away.

"I can do it," he said. "I can manage my arm now too."

Lumen ignored him, wiping the cloth over his face and making him hiss at the hot water. "Your eyes look strange. Are you nauseous?"

"It's just pain," he grumbled.

"And your hearing?"

He was quiet for a longer stretch. "There's a…ringing."

"This blood is from a hit on the head?"

He tried to nod and then stopped immediately, eyes sliding shut and face paling further to a greenish shade.

"You need to be watched until it all passes," Lumen said, some of the fire of her mood passing. "Tell me more of what happened on the field."

She cleaned the blood away, slightly appalled by the sheer amount of it before she found the actual wound. It wasn't too deep and didn't appear to need stitches, but she treated it carefully to keep it from bleeding again. Dominic remained silent for most of her treatment, his eyes drifting in her direction before forcing his stare away again.

"Gideon was trying to get me to leave the field when the new army arrived. Oshain was the only one wearing any proper uniform, and these men aimed right for them. I made it back to Finley, added a wound on the way," he said, pointing to his head. "One of the new men was brought to Finley with a wound, and he said they'd heard rumors of us in the Oshain army and decided to join the battle to fight for an end to the war."

Dominic's voice grew soft and slurred as he went on, and Lumen tapped his chin, shocking him into alertness with her touch. "So we won," she said, marveling over the thought.

"*They* won," Dominic said, trying to shrug and then groaning. "They want to hold the northern border, and I'm more than happy to let them."

Lumen left his head and moved away from him, perching on the bed, aware of how his eyes tracked her. "You need to soak in the warm water." He looked to the bath and then back to her, and she raised an eyebrow. "I can turn my back if you require modesty," she said.

Strangely, Dominic blushed and ducked his head, so Lumen shifted herself to face away from the tub. "Don't you have healing to do elsewhere?" he asked, groaning as he rose from the chair. He stepped out of sight ,and Lumen held her breath and watched his shadow undress on the wall.

"You're the last of my patients," she admitted. "And since

you're too terrifying to leave to the other priestesses, I'll have to guard you myself."

Also, she wasn't entirely certain she wanted Adelaide Nemory fawning over him, although if that was for Adelaide's sake or Dominic's, she wasn't sure.

Legs stepped out of pants, and Lumen's head tilted at the blurred dark outline of Dominic's form cast against the wall. He dipped one leg into the tub, water sloshing quietly, and then hummed. When his shadow wobbled, Lumen shot up from the bed, reaching his side and steadying his arm through the dizziness before he landed on his face. His skin was hot in her hands, and his face turned away as she helped him into the bathwater.

She was surprised by how familiar he looked. She'd spent so long forcing herself *not* to think of him, that the sight of him naked at her side again was only startling for how much she remembered, from scars to freckles to the curl of his dark hair as it ran down his stomach. Lumen crouched at the side of the bath as Dominic settled himself in the water.

"You shouldn't be the one stuck tending me," he said.

Lumen smiled and rolled her eyes, propping her elbow on the ledge of the tub and staring past his shoulder to the blank wall. "I'll survive, Dominic."

He sank into the water, sighing as it covered his shoulders and rose to his neck. His knees sat high and glistening with water, and Lumen kept her eyes carefully away from his bobbing length.

"Did you love me ever?" he asked, so softly Lumen thought she might reasonably pretend she never heard the words.

The room went still and quiet, a warning ring chiming softly in Lumen's ears. Dominic was suffering a head injury, and now was not the time to reminisce moodily on their history. Or perhaps it was their *only* time to discuss what had happened.

"No. I don't think I could have," she said, thinking of their first night together, and the moment he cast her out of his bed. He nodded, prepared for her answer. "Did you love me?"

"No, Lumen. I don't think I could have," he echoed, head tipping to her, eyes aching as his stare traced the scars on her cheek. The words twisted to a new meaning in his mouth. "If I had, I would never have been able to…I made everything wrong from the start."

Lumen was at risk of splitting in two, unable to catch a breath. "I think your head injury might've been worse than I realized," she said, half-heartedly teasing.

"I won't speak if you'd rather. But if we are going to talk, let's be honest with each other," he said. She'd forgotten the sound of his voice when he wasn't snarling or trying to intimidate, it was almost melodious in tone.

"Very well." She shifted to face him, stamped down the odd clench of her heart at the picture of his head tipped back, gaze warm on her face. "I don't want you to fight this war for me."

"Too late," he said, blinking slowly, lips soft in a barely-there smile.

"I don't want you to *die* for my sake, Dominic," she said, fingers clenched around the edge of the tub.

He swallowed and sobered, dipping his head once. "I understand. For what it's worth, if I'd died today it would've been for my men so that they knew I stood beside them until the end."

Lumen sighed, the declaration was an awful breed of comfort that could only be offered in war.

"I never believed in the Gods until you," he said, drawing her gaze back to his face. "I flew Sol's flag under orders, but I knew He didn't give two shits about me, about my men. And then…" Lumen could barely stand the softness of his expression as he stared at her. He smiled and continued, "There is no denying divinity in your presence, Lumen Fenn."

She swallowed and resisted the urge to leave the room. "What did you put your faith in then?"

"Myself, my men. Now you. I would worship you like you do your Goddess, if you would let me."

Lumen sagged and shook her head, turning to face the wall again. "You mean you would touch me if I would let you. I don't touch the moon when I worship her, Dominic. Worship doesn't take permission. It takes sacrifice."

He hummed, and Lumen bit her lips between her teeth. She

had just told Dominic she didn't want him to die for her. She looked at him again and forced honesty to her tongue. "I know you are sorry, Dominic. You've done enough now. Let that be the end of it."

One hand rose from the water, warm fingertips tracing over the marks he'd left on her cheek. "We both know that will never be true," he said. He glanced to her parted lips, the first warnings of a sob rising in a shaky breath from her chest. "Go, you can't stand to be here."

It wasn't true, she could've bared it a little longer, even with all the painful, gentle talking between them, but Lumen pushed up from the floor and raced to the door. She would send Finley to watch over Dominic, that would've been so much wiser from the start.

Gideon was pacing down the hall as she escaped, and his expression darkened from a triumphant grin to a terrible storm as he saw her. Lumen threw herself against his chest, stopping his momentum as she wrapped her arms around him. He smelled of sweat and blood but he was whole and here, a perfect beacon of safety.

"It's nothing," she said against his chest, before he could ask.

She tipped her head back, tears swallowed before they could break loose, and Gideon studied her with an awareness most wouldn't have believed he possessed. He relaxed slowly, hands cupping her shoulders and pulling her up to his lips for a soft kiss.

"You're sure?"

She nodded and pressed her cheek to his, her heart slowing and steadying the longer he held her. Oshain was held back for another day. The people she loved were safe for another day. And Dominic Westbrook, though it left her reeling and uneven to think it, was becoming someone *kind* in her thoughts.

Finley frowned at the swelling around Dominic's shoulder, pressing it carefully and watching the tick of muscle in the other man's jaw.

"You shouldn't even be going out on the field," Lumen murmured. She was tucked against Gideon's chest, his arms crossed over her chest, and Dominic refused to look in her direction.

Gideon had warned Finley that something passed between the two, but neither of them could get anything out of her but a puff of breath and wave of her hand, dismissing their questions. She wasn't avoiding Dominic, and he seemed every bit as shy of her as he had since her return, so Finley was willing to let it pass.

"You certainly won't be able to use your right arm," Finley conditioned, catching Dominic's eye.

Stalor would stand at their southern border tomorrow, he knew better than to think Dominic might stand down in the fight.

"I'll strap it," Dominic said with a nod.

Finley caught the collar of Dominic's shirt and pushed it back up over the healing shoulder.

"Wait," Lumen said, sighing and slipping free of Gideon's arms. She pulled a small jar out of the pocket of her skirts and passed it to Finley. "I figured you'd say that, so I made this. It should help the healing and the pain."

Gideon and Finley caught each other's gaze as Dominic grunted. Lumen was softening to him, but how much? Finley would have to be sure Gideon didn't meddle again this time. In the unlikely event that Dominic and Lumen found steady ground between them, it ought to be of their own making. Or maybe he was just nervous at the idea of Dominic having some claim on her affection again.

"Thank you," Dominic managed, as if someone had dragged the simple words out of his chest on the end of a dagger. Dominic turned to Finley as he opened the jar and applied some of Lumen's salve onto his shoulder beneath his shirt. "You should stay here tomorrow. We'll be near enough to bring you any men well enough to be saved, and it'll keep our healer out of danger."

Finley grimaced, glancing at Lumen and then back again. "We'll see."

Dominic's brow furrowed, but it was Lumen who spoke. "See? How so?"

Finley swallowed, Gideon tipping his head behind Lumen's back. "I think I should be on the field tomorrow," Finley said.

"Out of the question," Dominic barked.

"Why?" Lumen asked softly.

"There'll be no rebel force rising from Stalor on this battle, and the men from Oshain want no part in the fight. We're going to need every available sword as it is," Finley said, staring down at Dominic first and then looking to Lumen. "Dominic's right that men can be brought here, and you and the others are more than capable of taking care of them. It's as important to me as anyone that we succeed tomorrow, and I want to carry a sword to help ensure it."

"He's ready, Dom," Gideon said, as his hands soothed over Lumen's shoulders. "I trained him myself."

Finley was more concerned with Lumen's reaction than Dominic's. He couldn't really *stop* Finley from walking on the field, not in all the chaos.

Lumen stared at him for a long pause and Dominic sat stiffly, probably waiting for her to refuse. "Come on," she said eventually, holding out her hand for his. "Let's go to bed."

Finley took the offering, smoothing her palm against his, folding his hand over the back of hers, and Gideon settled his arm around her waist as together they headed for the door of Dominic's borrowed bedroom. Finley looked back to their general, his friend. "Tomorrow," he said.

Dominic nodded once, eyes dark and lips pressed firm in a grave line.

BLOOD IN THE SKY ALREADY, Gideon thought, frowning at the red-streaked clouds combing through the tops of the trees behind the temple.

"The infirmary is ready," Finley said at his side, Lumen wrapped in his arms and pressed to his chest. "But that doesn't mean you should pace the halls until you hear news."

"The women, Gretchen and Inda and the others, are all coming here. We'll pray in the chapel," Lumen said.

Her eyes had been shining with tears she'd refused to let fall since the night before when Finley announced he wanted to fight in the battle. Gideon hated to see his sweet lady cry, but he thought it might be almost worse that she could bind herself up so tightly that not a single drop spilled over.

"We'd be lucky to have your prayers," Gideon said.

Carefully, Finley passed Lumen into his arms, her body soft and nearly limp in his embrace. Her face tilted up to his, and he took comfort in the sharp slit of her gaze. "No theatrics," she said. "Be safe."

He grinned, the expression tight and uneasy on his face for once, and nodded. He wanted to ask what she would do if they failed, if he and Finley died in battle against Stalor, but he didn't want to worry her or to show a crack in his resolve to win and return safely.

"My heartbeat," he whispered, bending to kiss her.

Her strength surged, arms tight around his shoulders, hands clutching him closer. "My love," she said against his lips.

Gideon's heart swelled in his chest, with pride and devotion and worry and sorrow. He kept Lumen there, trapped in his arms until he could school his expression. He wouldn't falter in front of her, not if he could help it. Lumen's love was a blessing he felt he had yet to earn, but he soaked it up like sunlight, an odd comparison for a Lunar priestess.

Their arms slipped free at the same time, Finley already on his horse, hands shaking around the reins. Colin was ready, clutching Lumen's hand in his as Gideon stepped away. Dominic rode slowly out of the stable, his armor tarnished to black, as they'd all done to distinguish themselves from the Stalor soldiers.

Gideon held his horse still for Dominic's approach, found himself growing tense with the fire that ran through his blood before a good battle.

"You could take her and run. I wouldn't say a word," Dominic muttered to him and Finley.

Gideon laughed and shook his head. "I like my balls attached, thank you," he said, nudging his horse and starting forward. "Time to meet the men on the field."

THE CHAPEL HELD A DREADFUL SILENCE, even with the whisper of skirts and the soft sighs of women restraining their tears. The weight of their joined prayer was like a boulder pinning Lumen's back in her deep bow to the statue of Mother Lune.

For the first time since she was a little girl, Lumen put words to her prayer, her lips moving in a silent speech.

"Cover them, protect them, Mother Lune. Bring this war to a halt. Give us peace. Bring this endless battle to an end. Cover them. Protect them. Shine on them, Mother Lune." The thoughts continued unbroken until her lips were chapped and her body numb.

They had begun their prayers at morning, to a red sky and

the sound of horse hooves on the road. Hours passed with impatient tedium, minutes seeming to slow to spite their wait. The battle might last days if the men held out, or it might end in a matter of brutal hours. As the light changed, Lumen knew she would remain on the floor until some word came.

"I cannot lose them," she begged in silence. "I cannot lose anyone else. Please, Mother Lune. Bring them home. Cover them, protect them."

A headache throbbed through her, running up from the base of her spine to behind her eyes. She squeezed them shut and pictured Gideon and Finley by moonlight, but the sight of them was pale and frightening. By sunlight, they became gory in her head. She tried to pull up her vision of the New Moon Goddess, of Lune draped in black, tried to draw out some of the mysterious power the Goddess gifted her, but it wouldn't come, until a steady piercing beat of pain throbbed in her bones.

I've already taken all she can spare for me, Lumen thought, lips still moving in a strange and mute mimic of speech. Outside the temple, an uneasy, howling wind picked up, carrying a whisper of moans through the trees to rattle the glass panes of the chapel windows.

Some untold number of hours into the day and footsteps scuffed against stone at Lumen's side. "Lady? Lady, I think you need to see this."

It was the fear in Colin's voice and not his words that roused her, her arms groping blindly to catch his hand in hers. When she opened her eyes, it was to a strange light in the room, gray and yellow like the world had aged and faded. Colin's gaze was fixed out the door of the chapel and he tugged Lumen to standing, letting her rest her weight against his side.

"Come outside, Lady," Colin whispered, even as the other women in the chapel shifted and woke from their own deep prayer. Jennie had been at the back of the room, and she stumbled down the hall ahead of Lumen, stopping short in the archway with a soft, brief gasp.

The sun was black and blinding in the sky, and the world was the wrong color. There was no wind, no sound of birds, and not a single cloud in the sky, just the strange and eerie shade of tarnished silver. The moans and howls she'd heard were not coming from the trees at all.

"Cover them, protect them," Lumen chanted in a whisper, staring up at the blotted out sun with a horrified pit growing in her stomach. "Colin. I have to go to the field."

"Don't, Lady. It ain't safe. Don't think this changes that any," he said, a slight whine in his tone. His head ducked and pressed to her side to keep from seeing the awful picture of the sky.

Lumen tore her own eyes away although a ring of blue light followed in her vision. She crouched in front of Colin and cupped his face. "Stay here. Keep the others too. Try not to look outside. I love you, darling boy."

She kissed his cheeks with rough presses of her tired lips, and he held tightly to her wrists for another moment before releasing her. Lumen ran through the courtyard, the murmur of women fading behind her as she headed for the stables. Her body was numb and aching at the same time, her shadow shifting eerily on the ground in front of her, squat and wavering. Sosha was quiet in her stall, her head ducked down as if she too wanted to avoid seeing the vision of the dark sun, but she let Lumen saddle her and lead her out of doors.

"I'm sorry to make you come with me, but I need your help," Lumen whispered, soothing the shivers off the horse's neck and then pulling herself up onto the saddle. Her hands and legs shook, head spinning dizzily with the movement.

Lumen was no skilled rider, but she pushed Sosha down the road as fast as she could, ignoring the bruising pain of her own poor seat, the strange burn of cold sunlight on her skin. The howls, agonized and animal, grew louder as she rode, and bile swirled up Lumen's throat at the eerie sounds.

Had Lune punished her? Had she asked too much? Or was this Sol's revenge for their backward war?

She reached the battlefield, a chorus of men's screams burning against her ears and a sea of gold turned gray under the black sun, images of the sky's distortion reflecting off breast-plates like stars. There was no blood in her veins, no beat of her frozen heart, as she stared at the ugly vision. This was not battle, it was carnage. Lumen watched, horrified and riveted, as one man peeled away his Stalor armor and threw himself onto his own sword. Sosha nickered anxiously beneath her, and a stallion broke free of the waste of the field and took off for the woods without its rider.

Lumen lowered herself from the saddle, head pounding and knees trembling, tying Sosha safely away from the battle. She seemed drawn forward into the scene by a needle-sharp hook in her gut. Madness was painted over men's bulging eyes and hanging mouths, their hands bloodied as they clawed at their own faces. They parted as she reached their edges, falling away from her with high pitched screams, the sounds of rabbits dying in traps. She caught her own reflection off of one man's armor, hooded with ghastly pale skin and red lips stretched open in shock. There were bodies on the ground, faces buried in mud, and one man tripped over another in his haste to escape Lumen in her black robes. He landed there on the ground, sobbing like a child, fists thumping in mud and tearing at his own hair.

She found Dominic first, the first person she recognized, the first sign of hope that anyone she knew was left. His face was stretched in a grimace, eyes wild as he chased men in one direction and then another, teeth bared in a snarl. The calculating general was gone and in his place was a feral, frightened creature.

"Dominic?" she called, barely audible over the screams around her.

His head whipped in her direction, blood spattering from the end of soaked strands. Even blood looked brackish and dark by this light. Lumen held out her hands as she approached him, her heart hammering.

"Dominic, come here," she said as his nostrils flared and his eyes fixed to her mouth. He didn't approach, but he held still as she wove through violence, holding her gaze to his face so she wouldn't see the awful things that took place around her. He was heaving, panting, a soft growl still vibrating from between his teeth, but the sound stuttered as she reached him, her hands taking his face in her hold.

He shuddered and swallowed, and Lumen used the sleeves of her robes to wipe the blood off his skin, pushing the hair back from his face. He groaned and shook and stood straighter, eyes blinking slowly, tears leaking red down his cheeks until his gaze was clear.

"Don't look up," Lumen said before he could see the sun blocked out in the sky again.

"Lunacy," Dominic said, slow and slurred. "I saw the moon rising as the battle began."

Lumen glanced up at the sky, lips parted. Lune. *Gods*. She had risen to cover the sun.

Cover them, protect them.

Lumen made the mistake of looking around, seeing a Stalor soldier slit his own throat, dressing his chest in a flood of gore, and tore her stare back to Dominic's. His brow was furrowed and he pressed his cheek to her palm, his wet and sticky hands raised to hold hers.

"What do we do?" he murmured.

"Get off the field. I'll calm them," Lumen said.

Some of the insanity must have lingered because Dominic didn't object, only nodded feebly and nuzzled once into her touch before stumbling past her.

One by one she settled the remaining soldiers from either side, a look into their eyes seemed to be enough to calm the worst of the mad fits. She pulled Finley off a fallen man, her eyes squeezed shut as he stabbed the body over and over with a low moan, and turned him away so that when he returned to her he didn't see his own work.

"Luuuumen," Finley whimpered, raising bloody hands to try and run them over his own face.

Her robes grew heavy with blood, the hems of her sleeves soaked. She pulled Finley to her, cleaned him as best she could and waited for his trembles to ease. *What have I done?*

"What have I done?" Finley whispered in her hair.

"Nothing," Lumen assured him, this was between her and Lune now.

The battle was breaking on its own, and the light of the field was changing, warming, and settling out of the unnatural metallic tone. Lumen checked the sky and found a bleed of sunlight, still oddly distorted but less troubling than the smear of black that had taken its place.

Finley was more reluctant to release her. "I have to find Gideon," she said.

He nodded but clung to her, stained face pressed to her hair until she untangled him from around her waist and pushed him in the direction to where Dominic was collecting their small army.

The southern edge was filled with red and gold, Stalor's army impressive in its size, even as their numbers piled over the ground. The living stood off the field with faces now frozen with revulsion, their eyes tracking her.

Gideon held the last of the Stalor army, a good ten men still fighting, locked in battle. He carried no sword but swung a man from his fists, beating him against another. Lumen swallowed the sobs in her throat as she made her way to her lover.

"Gideon!" she screamed, nails digging into her own palms. "Gideon, stop this!"

Four of the Stalor soldiers escaped Gideon's ring of terror, and two were already dead. The rest seemed to skitter away as she neared, and Lumen reached for Gideon in all his rage before he could chase them. He turned to her, coated in red and brown, and bent to roar in her face, the sound broken and rattling as if his throat were tired from hours of work.

"Gideon, come back to me," Lumen said, holding tight to his wrist, letting him drag her into his arms. Her warrior would not be lost, although Gideon had always carried a kind of madness willingly into battle. "Come back, my love."

Gideon snarled, frowning, his arms crushing around her ribs. She returned the embrace with the last of her strength, his hot breath rough against the top of her head. Gideon's feet stumbled back, and Lumen sighed as his nose pressed to her hair.

"Sweet spirit?" he rasped.

"Walk north, Gideon," Lumen said.

He took two steps, still clutching her against his chest, and paused, body turning as he surveyed the scenes.

"Gods. What happened here?" Gideon asked, his words torn with an exhausted voice. "Lumen, what are you doing here?"

"Walk, Gideon," she said, tears thick in her throat. "The battle is over."

⸜

SOL AND LUNE remained side by side in the sky as their small army marched home, Sol slowly sinking rightfully down toward the horizon. The Stalor army retreated from the field without a word, but as madness cleared, Gideon and Dominic and the others returned to gather their fallen men. There was few of their number compared to Stalor's, but with one glance at the handful of faces, Lumen already dreaded going back to the temple.

Lumen and Gideon shared Sosha, his own horse having run off during the battle. "After we saw the moon cover the sun, I think," Gideon said, whispering from his sore throat.

Those who weren't dead bore superficial wounds, scratches of their own nails, a few stab wounds. Finley's foot was twisted and swollen inside of his boot.

The road led them toward the frozen, hanging moon, and Lumen shivered at the sight of what she wrought, even as it glowed full and innocent in a blue sky.

No one spoke a word, the men either relieved for their sanity or shaken by the temporary loss of it. They returned to the temple to find Lumen's three priestesses in the drive with faces lifted to the moon, eyes closed and palms open. Behind them, the rest of the women of the village waited, wearing worry like bridal veils.

One by one, each released a soft gasp of shock and joy as they spotted their lover in the crowd. Lumen watched as Jennie rushed forward to meet an older man in the mix, the two taking hands but no more.

"Philip?"

Lumen's eyes dropped to her stained hands, her stomach turning.

"Philip?" Inda called. "Where is he?"

Gideon dismounted and pulled Lumen down after him. She found Jennie through the faces around them, their eyes meeting as Inda called for her husband. Lumen shook her head, blinking through the flooding tears, and Jennie sighed, her smile falling away.

"He's here, lass," one gentle soldier offered. "I'm so sorry."

Lumen wished she could've raised her hands to her ears, never heard the low moan as Inda finally saw Philip's body in the cart. Her own heart fractured for the young woman, legs crumpling, and bitterly sorry for it as Gideon caught her.

It was Jennie who reached Inda in time to catch her.

"Nooo. *No, please.*" Sobs broke through pleads, a high keening sound echoing in the quiet of the crowd. "No. No. No," Inda chanted.

Salt coated Lumen's lips, stinging where they were still raw. "Take Finley inside. Organize the women," Lumen said to Gideon. "I must stay with the priestesses."

He kissed her once, the flavor of copper rich between them, and they parted. Lumen reached Inda on her knees in the drive, Philip's body brought down from the cart so she might hold him once more. Jennie sat on one side, and Lumen lowered to the other. She pushed curtains of Inda's dark hair out of her face, tear tracks clinging to strands on her cheeks.

"Oh, Lady," Inda moaned, broken with hiccuping sobs.

There was nothing strong enough to say, so Lumen only reached and held Inda in her arms as she cried until the men around them dispersed, one finally brave enough to wrap up Philip again and carry him away.

"I cannot," Inda cried against Lumen's throat, her tears washing down into the collar of the black robes. "Oh, Lady, please. Please, not him."

SOL RETREATED beneath the horizon without argument, as docile and trustworthy as a favorite dog. Still, Lune's face shone in the sky, mocking Lumen and her prayers. The priestesses remained, the night deep already, the healing army tucked away inside the temple and their own cottages. Jennie had taken Inda to her own bed with a sedative. Gideon and Finley watched over Colin without her.

Lumen wanted an audience with her Goddess.

She ignored her turning stomach, still queasy from the sight of the battle and thorny with hunger. Adelaide and Hannah and Cora lay piled together on the steps sleeping, and Lumen suspected they might've gone inside already if it weren't for Lumen remaining in place. Her back ached and her legs were weak, but if there was one thing she knew her Goddess savored, it was her devotees enduring pain.

Eventually, when the temple was silent and the stars were bright, gradually, Lune began to sink in the sky. It was as if Lumen had pushed forward the hands of a clock with her praying, and it refused to tick until the correct hour was finally met again. She measured its travel to reassure herself that nature might be restored.

It was at the top of the oak tree. Now it was below the thickest branch. Now it rested in the valley of the hills on the horizon.

Lumen sighed, prepared for sunrise at her back, and stared at the glowing moon nestled against the turn in the road. The glow burned against her eyes, brighter the longer she stared. It did not shrink or vanish, but grew taller, and then obviously closer. Lumen's fists clenched at her side as the moon on the road sharpened out of a bright blur and into an approaching woman.

Not shrouded Lune in her black veil and her wolf's muzzle. Not the New Moon Goddess who had guided Lumen to this point.

Mother Lune in silver glory, a neutral smile on her lips. She was tall, beautiful in a plain way, with a broad face similar to

Lumen's own. Lumen met the gaze of her Goddess head-on and wore every emotion that burned through her plainly on her face. Betrayal, hope, relief, anger, resentment, and love. Every breath she took as Lune approached filled a chest swollen with a sweet ache. Silver tears dripped down her cheeks and over her chin.

Lune stood before her, eyes made of stars, touch a stinging cold, whisper-white hair flowing beneath her pure gray hood. Lumen's hands were held in smooth, strong grips, the flesh beneath her fingers as soft as her own, but as dense and cold as silver.

"Enough," Lumen rasped. Hadn't she done *enough*?

Lune pulled her closer, drawing Lumen against a body that was vast and suffocating, surrounding her in full silken robes. The Goddess' cheek was smooth as stone against hers, her lips the scratch of a knife against Lumen's cheekbone. There was no wave of peace, only a growing pressure of blissful pain, the overwhelming fullness of emotion and thought, deeper than Lumen could hold all at once.

She gasped as Lune released her, landed on her knees as the Goddess backed away. Cold fingers stroked against her forehead and Lune bowed slightly before turning her back and retreating swiftly up the road.

The night settled to morning as she vanished on the horizon, birdsong carrying up from the trees for the first time since Lune had darkened the sky. Gravel shifted behind Lumen, and gentle hands pulled her to her feet, Hannah James blinking blearily.

"We had better go inside, Priestess," the woman said.

Lumen thought she might've swallowed her own tongue but she nodded, held in the other priestess' arms and led gently to the steps where the others roused and stumbled inside. The moment with Lune had been hers alone, the gift of her connection with Lune equal parts a curse and blessing.

Lumen carried herself inside and up to her usual room, sighing as she found Gideon and Finley asleep in the bed. She was still dirty with men's blood, but there was a clean bowl of water waiting for her. Lumen undressed, washed, and scrubbed herself raw, the vision of Lune's smiling face burned into her mind just as the outline of the black sun had been earlier in the day.

She crawled between her lovers, her breath catching as they sighed and caught her, clasping her in their arms and shifting closer. Lumen's tears landed on Gideon's warm chest, and Finley combed his fingers through her tangled strands until they fell down into sleep's embrace together.

VIII
THE RISING
MOON

A SPRAY OF BLOOD, THE COLOR OF TAR. THE HOWLS OF WOLVES IN HIS ear. The snarling faces of monsters surrounding him, dragon scales blinding and reflecting the black sun.

The shrouded Goddess parting the crowd like water, reaching her bone-white hand out for him...

Dominic swallowed, head twitching on his neck as he tried to shake out the memories of the battlefield. He'd spent the day on the harvest, filling carts and baskets with their stores for the winter until his back screamed for respite and his hands were black with earth. The first snowfall would arrive in the north soon, but they would be ready.

Dominic's feet stumbled, an onion bouncing out of the cart and onto the ground, as he neared the back of the temple. Lumen was outside, hanging laundry on a line as a group of soldiers washed and swam in the cold lake. She had her back to them, blonde hair running a long line down her back in her usual braid. She bent and pulled her black robe out of a basket, shaking it loose and hanging it over the line. Off of her, the dark fabric looked coarse and simple, bearing no resemblance to the ominous figure she cut inside of it, or the threatening shroud from the battlefield the men whispered of while farming.

Some of the men from Stalor's army—less than two dozen and most of them injured—had made their way back to the temple, surrendering their swords to Dominic.

"Better to take our chances here than return to the capitol," one had rasped before Finley guided him to a chair to be seen to.

They shivered as Lumen passed them in the halls of the temple while they recovered, her hood up to hide her face, but out here they watched her. Dominic suspected they didn't even recognize her as the New Moon Priestess they all feared.

He gathered the onion up from the ground and pushed the cart forward to meet her in the grass.

"For the temple," he said. "I've already taken another to the house in the woods."

Lumen smiled at the overflowing collection of food to be pickled and canned and stored away. "We did better than I ever expected," she said.

"Harvey thinks we might have another smaller harvest in a week or two," Dominic said, turning to watch the men in the lake, wary that some of the strangers might take an interest in Lumen. But they seemed occupied and paid neither him nor Lumen any attention.

"Is Colin at the house?" Lumen asked, and Dominic nodded. He'd left the boy there with the delivery of food. "Good. Help me unload this and then I'll walk back with you?"

Dominic stiffened, struck by the offer. Or was it a command? He grunted, eyes on Lumen's twitching lips, and then pushed the cart closer to the door of the kitchen.

"There's an open barrel in the pantry for the onions, I just cleaned it out. The rest can be put on shelves, and Jennie and I will organize it tomorrow."

He followed her orders, a stray priestess in the kitchen squeaking at the sight of him. He suspected it was the one he'd snarled at when his arm was injured, but he hadn't taken much notice of her then and he didn't intend to now, especially not with Lumen watching him.

Lumen buzzed and flitted around him, and Dominic's gaze found her at every opportunity it could without being detected. She was much the same as she was the day he'd met her, healthy and sunburnt, harried and wearing dirt and stains on her skirt.

And so much had changed too. The scars he'd left on her cheek, the way she pushed about her business without ducking her head or watching him out of the corner of her eyes.

She'd been afraid of him when he arrived at her Manor and he hadn't seen it, hadn't known her well enough to read her curiosity and her worry. Now he was nothing to her, not a threat or a looming monster or a lover.

"Good," Lumen said with a shrug, smiling at her full pantry.

Dominic's own lips quirked at her happiness. "And this year, you won't have soldiers eating it to empty before you can blink," he said, not really thinking the words before they came out of his mouth.

Lumen only snorted and shook her head. "We'll see. I've seen the way you all ration. Come on, let's go."

They walked back in relative silence that Dominic expected to feel oppressive. Except with every step they took, the heaviness seemed to be absent. Lumen picked a few stray herbs, skipping her usual lectures she offered Finley on their uses, and Dominic swallowed repeatedly as he searched and failed to find something to say.

The house was fragrant with cooking as they arrived, a hearty display of roasted vegetables and fresh bread spread out over the table.

"There you are!" Gideon greeted, a massive grin spread over his face, almost as huge as the spread of food they'd cooked from the new store of supplies. "Thought we'd have a little feast to celebrate the bounty."

Lumen raised a wry eyebrow at Dominic as he frowned, and entered the house to cross to Gideon. She rose to her toes and pressed a soft kiss to his mouth, and Finley rushed to pull her out a chair at the table, catching a kiss of his own.

Dominic needed to find a new place to live.

LUMEN SWALLOWED around her own tight throat, icy rain chilling the black drape of her robes as she stood in front of the slowly filling graves of the fallen soldiers. Jennie held a softly weeping Inda against her chest as they stood in front of Philip's burial site. The majority of the army was out for the funeral, although Lumen had overheard Dominic and Gideon discussing the rotation of scouts they kept on watch around their small borders.

Over a week had passed since the battle against Stalor. Reasonably, Lumen knew it would take time for the army to retreat and regroup, and more time for Dominic to hear word from the south. Still, she wished for everyone's sake they might *know* when the next strike would come. Or maybe there would be no warning.

"We give these bodies back to the earth, to be watched over by their friends and family, by Sol and Lune, by the ground that cradles them in their rest," Lumen said, wary of how loud her voice carried in the quiet.

Men shoveled dirt into the graves with a slow and steady pace, passing the shovels to the next in line as they tired. The time passed in quiet, sniffs and whimpers from the grieving, and shivers from everyone beaten by the growing cold.

Inda would return to the temple, escorted by Jennie when the graves were finished. She'd given up the small cottage she shared briefly—far too briefly—with Philip. Dominic had taken it instead, vanishing from the house in the woods she shared with Finley and Gideon and Colin when she wasn't at the temple. It was an awkward rotation, but it made Gideon's home slightly less stifled with the unspoken tension between them.

Lumen's teeth were clenched to hide their chatter by the time the burial was complete. She knew she should go back to the temple to check on the other priestesses, on Inda, and to put away her black robes before going back to Finley and Gideon, but she was desperate to get out of the wet garment and be warm again. And there was no work left to do in the kitchens or the fields. The cold, rainy day would push everyone into their homes for warm fires and quiet mourning.

She waited until the crowds had retreated, her men waiting

for her at the edge of the tree line near the old graveyard, and decided she could make an exception for the somber day.

"You're freezing, sweet spirit," Gideon rumbled, taking her stiff hands in his fiery grip.

"All I want is to change out of this robe and sit by that great fire of yours," Lumen said with a nod, forcing a weak smile for Colin.

"Will Inda be all right, you think?" Colin asked, slowing and wedging himself between her and Finley, who surprised Lumen by taking the boy's hand in his, scuffing cold fingers between his palms.

"In time, yes," Lumen said, although she wondered.

She had lost loved ones, lost family, but looking at Gideon she wasn't sure she would've survived losing *him* in the recent battle. Or Finley, if he had gone onto that battlefield for her sake, and then not come back. The war had taken so much from everyone in its long and unending stretch across the land. Lumen had thought she'd met her limit of suffering last winter. Maybe by continuing to heal, she continued to risk having new pieces cut out of her.

Gideon raised her hand to his mouth, absently kissing the back of her knuckles as they walked home. Lumen swallowed, pulled all three closer to her, and decided that risking sorrow was worth gaining even small hours of love.

LUMEN STOOD at Jennie's side at the harvest feast, the village gathered together in a warm crowd inside of the temple, a bonfire at the heart of the courtyard, and the dining room tables loaded with food. Across the fire, Harvey Evans watched Jennie with a fond hunger in his gaze.

"He seems steady," Lumen said, catching Jennie staring back at her beau.

Jennie blushed and ducked her head, and then turned her back on the man across the way altogether. "He is. Maybe too much," Jennie said with a careless shrug that Lumen didn't believe for a moment. "He's tried to convince me to move into his cottage with him."

"Ah. And you don't want to?" Lumen asked, trying not to sound *too* curious, knowing it would only convince Jennie to throw the subject away.

"The temple is a great deal of work and cleaning, but I don't know that one man and a small cottage will be much less with the way they carry on," Jennie said, rolling her eyes. Lumen continued to stare at her until Jennie huffed and added, "I'm worried for Inda."

Lumen hummed at that and nodded, scanning the crowd, but knowing that Inda was certainly upstairs alone in a bedroom where Lumen had last seen her pretending to sleep before the festivities started. "I am too."

"No, I mean...if I leave the temple and live with Harvey, who will Inda have here?" Jennie asked.

Lumen frowned and opened her mouth to say 'me,' but Jennie raised an eyebrow. Lumen spent her days in the temple, but almost every night since the last battle had been spent at the house in the woods in the arms of Gideon and Finley. All three of them had nightmares, and it settled Lumen to be pressed between them when she woke with visions of slaughter in her head.

"I should spend more time here," Lumen said with a sigh.

Jennie's lips pressed together, eyes narrowing. "Actually, Lumen, I'm not sure you should. Or not for Inda's sake."

Lumen frowned, but the understanding sank in painful and slow. Lumen held some blame for Philip's death. For the shift in the war, but also the strange behavior of the moon the day of the battle, the insanity of the men.

"You're her friend, and she knows that," Jennie said, patting Lumen's back. "But the mind takes ugly turns in grief and it's better to let them pass."

"Of course," Lumen said, nodding and sighing.

There was a reason why she didn't wear the black robes

around the temple lately, the way it stirred fear in most eyes she passed. In those robes, she was a figure of suffering and loss, of dark and impossible power. At the house in the woods, she was only Lumen, and she was surrounded by those she loved. She sometimes dreaded coming to the temple at all.

"I know myself," Jennie said with a sigh as if the notion wearied her. "If Harvey is constant, I'll give in. But I'll make him wait a while yet, I think."

Lumen grinned at that, and Jennie tipped her mug of cider to her before leaving the shadow of the arch they stood in. Lumen studied the crowd in the courtyard, watched Colin running with the Ramsey children around the hall, found Finley sitting and laughing in a circle of soldiers from mixed and muddled companies. Gideon was missing somewhere, probably trying to fill another plate to coax her into eating, and she wondered if she should be concerned by the almost obsessive way he lavished attention on her gradually softening thighs.

She spotted Dominic across the way, through the glow of tall flames, and he was watching the group with equal study. Their eyes found each other through the fire and held, a peaceful stare between them for once, but one that seemed no less loaded if the slow warmth in her stomach was any indication. He rounded the courtyard, and though she knew he was coming to speak to her, Lumen remained in place waiting for his arrival.

"Are you happy?"

Lumen was startled by the intensity of the question, the fold of his brow as he asked it, the grip of his gaze. It wasn't an accusation, but something he *needed* to know.

Lumen forced her eyes to tear from his, so she might catch her breath and then found her answer as she gazed around the space and saw the ease and comfort that filled the temple.

"Tonight I am," she said.

He was silent in response, but from the corner of her eye, she saw him lean against the pillar opposite her own, his own eyes traveling out over the courtyard.

"I want you to be happy."

Pressure built in Lumen's chest and she breathed through it, although the echo of the ache remained in her heart. "I know you do, Dominic."

And she did. She had *known* it, even if she didn't often think the words. Dominic cared for her in his strange, removed way. She didn't know when it began, and she suspected they both knew it started long after he'd forced her to his bed.

"Lumen."

The soft rasp of his voice, the scrape of his boot against stone, the breeze of his sigh against her shoulder—all these things were twice as loud, as noticeable, as the bright revelry around them. Her head turned to face him against her will, and she didn't recognize the man before her.

No frown, no smirk, no sneer, no glare, no half-lidded gaze of desire. Dominic's expression was entirely open, plain with honesty.

"I have words I wish you to hear, that I have no right to ask you to listen to," he began, "and if you turn and walk away, I swear I will not follow and I will never approach you again."

She swallowed, and Dominic was tense, breath held. Lumen dipped her head once, unable to blink or turn away, and he sagged with a ragged sigh.

"You owe me nothing, and I ask *nothing* of you. But I owe you everything, Lumen. Every remaining minute of my life is yours, not as a burden or responsibility, but as..." He struggled, stepping closer and then back again. "As you see fit. To be ignored, or turned against your enemies as a sword, or to be banished from you if you wish it."

Lumen was pinned in place, in time, not by his voice, but the molten warmth of his eyes. He offered himself but she felt *captured*, and she wished Gideon would come and throw Dominic away, to break the hold he had on her.

"I came to you enjoying the game of conquering, relishing the pattern I'd learned and adopted for myself, and I continued on long after the moment I realized what it cost you to be trapped in the motions with me. Even after I *cared* that you suffered, I continued," Dominic whispered, and one or both of them leaned in to keep the words private between them. Glass covered his eyes, wavering and threatening to shatter to tears. "I am so sorry. I seek no forgiveness, there is none. Only know that here, I surrender to you."

They remained a foot apart, and Lumen longed to reach for him, to grip him in her hands and...

Throttle him maybe, for stirring up pains that she tried so hard to let settle, like muck at the bottom of the lake. To force forgiveness on him in the hopes it might bury their connection for good. To simply hold him, because he knew a part of her—a fragile, broken part that he had crushed himself—that no one else could ever really touch.

Dominic bowed, a slight tip in his waist, a grimace of agony finally taking over that shocking openness, and then left her there in the archway, drowning in a maelstrom of emotion and memory.

When she finally thawed, Lumen pushed herself out of the courtyard, through the kitchen and out to the yard. She gasped for air, hands pressed to her rib cage, certain that he had torn something from her. Her knees sank into grass, and Lumen swallowed lungfuls of air, a strange kind of panic racing through her. She didn't fear Dominic's rage, or his passion, or his cunning.

She feared his devotion.

She believed him. He was hers in his mind.

Banish him, Lumen thought. *Strangle him. Make him a slave for your own gain.*

The last thought troubled her the most. It involved *keeping* him.

"Lady?"

Lumen startled and turned, Colin in the doorway to the kitchen, sweaty with playing, grinning ear to ear. He looked up at the sky instead of Lumen and found Lune hanging above.

"She's beautiful tonight, isn't she?" he asked.

Lumen turned and tipped her head back. Lune was a thick white crescent, a brilliant celestial grin in the sky. Lumen thought the Goddess might be mocking her.

I took everything from you, and now see what I have offered in return. What will you do with it?

"Beautiful," Lumen murmured, bundling Colin against her side as he joined her, and burying her face in his hair as he smiled up at the moon.

"You've seemed troubled recently, Priestess," Priestess James—Hannah—said to Lumen as they carried baskets of late-season apples to the temple.

They reached the edge of the wheat field, rounds of hay tied together the last of the summer harvest to be brought in. Men were out, running and whooping over the land, and it took Lumen a moment to realize they were *playing* and not fighting.

"Is it the threat of more war?" Hannah asked.

No, Lumen thought, staring out at the roaring men. Her eyes landed on Dominic, his mouth spread open in a grin as he raced down the length of the field, overtaking Colin and catching the cackling boy under his arm like a sack of potatoes. *No, it's not war. It's him.*

She pulled her eyes away from Dominic and found Gideon in the group, grinning and waving at her, and it cleared some of the troubled fog out of her head regarding Dominic.

"The war, the winter, the village," Lumen rattled off, and then huffed a soft laugh at Hannah's shocked expression. "I collect worries, Priestess James."

"You think there will be more war?"

Lumen frowned as she watched the game on the field, the rough laughter of men carrying through the air. They'd gained more new men in the battle with Stalor than they'd lost, while Stalor's own numbers had diminished significantly, succumbing to the madness. If what Dominic said was true, that Stalor had sent their full numbers to crush them, it was possible they would have a long break from the battles before Stalor could rebuild its army. Somehow, that didn't reassure her. Cannary and Becker were determined men, and the insult of Lumen and Dominic's survival was certain to irritate them.

"I think we haven't reached peace yet," Lumen hedged. She glanced at Hannah then, seeing the woman's frown. "How are you, sister? Do you miss the convent?"

"I miss some of the sisters, but I prefer the work here," Hannah said. "Even after the battle...I feel useful here."

Lumen smiled at that and nodded. It was the same reason she'd returned to the temple, felt herself grow stronger with every week. Life was returning to this little pocket of land, and even though the Manor was no longer her home, the woods around it and the hills and fields felt more comforting than they ever had while she was alone.

"Do you plan to stay a priestess?" Hannah asked.

Lumen's footsteps stumbled, and she stared at the other priestess who blushed. "Stay...what do you mean?"

"It's only that you have—" Hannah glanced at Lumen and blushed. "I don't mean it as disrespect, Priestess Fenn, but you have *men*. And a home to spend your evenings in. That's no prevention to being a priestess, of course, but—"

"But it is uncommon," Lumen finished for her. They passed the field, voices at their back, and neared the side of the temple. "I hadn't considered..."

Except that was a lie. Lumen *had* considered giving up her black robes plenty of times since the battle with Stalor. They were no longer a comforting weight, but an oppressive one that seemed to act as a barrier between her and the life that surrounded her, the one she found herself wanting more and more to participate in.

"You will always have a place with us," Hannah said when Lumen fell into silence. "I only wondered if you would be relieved to move on."

"Maybe," Lumen said, more to herself. Her brow furrowed.

"It would be an awfully short term as New Moon Priestess if I did."

Hannah hummed and shrugged. "New Moon Priestesses don't usually stay in the black robes for long. That's not the way of Mother Lune, is it?"

Lumen let her steps carry her to the kitchen doorway faster, a baffled understanding sinking over her. Even Lune only spent one night in dozens hiding her face. She'd been the New Moon Priestess when she needed the shroud. She could move on, grow full again in life.

It had been Mother Lune who'd come to her on the road, not the Dark Goddess.

Lumen paused upon entering the kitchen, eyes adjusting from the bright sun outside. Jennie and Inda were in the kitchen together, cutting mushrooms to be brined and canned now that one of the soldiers had smuggled them salt from the coast. Inda was listless at the table, knife moving in an irregular rhythm, her thoughts no doubt deep in the grave with her husband. She sat in the shadow of the corner, and it struck Lumen suddenly that she no longer saw the shadows as brightly, that daylight was bearable and familiar again.

"Leave them there, and we'll chop them next," Jennie said in greeting.

Inda looked up, setting her knife aside, and her expression was clouded as she took in Lumen. A smile came on slowly, forced and stiff, but she raised a hand, palm up. Lumen set the basket on the table and crossed to Inda, taking the woman's hand and framing herself around Inda's back. Lumen bent and kissed the top of Inda's head, felt the dark-haired woman sigh against her stomach. Lumen made sure never to ask if Inda was well because she knew she could not be, it was obvious on her face. Jennie smiled at them together and continued her work.

"I'll come and help you in a moment. There's something I need to do first."

"No matter," Jennie said with a shrug, and Inda echoed the thought with a hum.

Lumen left, cutting through the courtyard to head upstairs to her room, hoping that the instinct spurning her forward was not a mistake. *Instincts and divine pushes have seen you this far*, she thought.

The black robes were draped over the chair in the corner of the room, shapeless and innocent looking in their neat fold. Lumen lifted them from their resting place, the weight of fabric like lead between her fingers. Donning the black robes exhausted her, and she hoped she wasn't simply passing a burden onto someone who already carried too many. But they'd been a comfort and a shield when Lumen first wore them, an offering of power to protect herself and those she cared about.

Lumen left her room, robes in hand, and moved to the next room, her former one where Inda now slept. The bed was made, and the sunshine pouring through the window was familiar, but otherwise, the room clearly belonged to someone else. Lumen's time in the Manor as it was had ended.

She laid the robes down at the foot of the bed, smoothing away any wrinkles, and left the room.

"Do you mind if I go and check my traps, Lady?" Colin asked.

Lumen's arm was around his shoulders as they followed the now beaten path leading back to the house in the woods. A curl of smoke was visible in the trees, a fire going for dinner already, and there was still a good amount of light left in the woods. Lumen bit her lip, looking down at Colin.

"Only the ones nearby," Lumen said, arching an eyebrow. "I know you have ones outside our boundaries. I'd rather you checked those when you had someone with you."

"I'll stay between here and the village, and no further south," Colin agreed readily.

Lumen sighed and nodded. "Fine then. Back by dark."

Colin dashed away, and Lumen snorted at his urgency. Colin shared the prizes of his hunting with Sarah Blythe and some of the lonely soldiers, and Lumen couldn't refuse such a selfless impulse, even if she knew part of his motivation was pride at a growing skill. It was a useful one and had helped her survive early weeks on her return.

She continued the rest of the way to the house on her own, slowing as voices sounded softly from inside.

"And the new men from Stalor?" Finley asked.

"Apparently trustworthy," Dominic answered from inside, drawing Lumen's steps to a halt. Dominic rarely visited, and Lumen was never able to force any news out of Finley or Gideon. Now was an opportunity to learn what they knew for herself. "They've made no move to reach to anyone outside the village, and seem surprised and relieved to be accepted."

"But you think there's more to come," Finley said.

"I…I don't know if I'm so used to war I can't imagine the end of it, or if I know Stalor too well to believe it will quit after one try." Dominic's voice was so low, Lumen almost couldn't hear him and she crept softly closer, ducking beneath the windowsill and feeling like a child for listening in.

"If they come back, we'll win again," Gideon offered easily, and Lumen rolled her eyes at the silence that followed, knowing she was not alone when it came to doubting the lovely giant's optimism.

"One thing we know is that Stalor's army is good and terrified of Lumen. Or of what they *think* she is," Dominic said. Gideon scoffed, and Dominic stopped him. "This is good news. Even if Becker still has it out for us, they may leave the temple be."

Quiet fell, and Lumen was about to move from her place of hiding when Gideon spoke again.

"You love her."

Lumen was already crouching, but she felt the earth go out from under her, the sense of crashing sinking and jarring through her bones at Gideon's statement.

"Of course," Dominic said, and she could perfectly picture his irritated expression at speaking, face turning away from the others. "It changes nothing, Gideon."

"Agreed," Finley said in a tight tone.

"Oh, come on, the two of you!" Gideon laughed. "This is Lumen. She has suffered—"

"At my hands," Dominic grunted.

"—withstood every loss, saved our asses at every opportunity. She bears the weight of every man and woman that joins us. Lumen deserves every ounce of love that can be laid at her feet."

The woods were growing dim the longer she remained outside, but Lumen was frozen in place, tempted to both strangle and kiss Gideon for his speech. She knew that he loved Dominic, that their lives were entwined so deeply in history they could never be untangled. She'd worried at first that by holding onto Gideon, it meant she was forced to always have Dominic not far from hand. Now, even after Dominic's maddening words at the harvest feast, she could make peace with Dominic's presence in her life.

I trust him, she thought, blinded by the realization. He was loyal, especially to her. Ever since rescuing her from Oshain's prison, Dominic had done everything she'd asked of him and more.

"Gideon," Finley warned.

"It's not that simple, Gid," Dominic said, sounding weary.

"It is."

"It's *not*," Dominic bit out. "She...I can't force her into- into accepting me just because I care for her. And she has you two, doesn't she?"

"Yes," Finley said. Lumen smiled at his determination to draw an end to the conversation. "Gideon, leave it. Lumen is happy, and Dominic is right. If you push this, we'll be back to the start of everything all over again."

Gideon's expression was hidden, and conversation lulled between the men. A chair scraped on the floor and Lumen shot up and headed for the door before Dominic left the house and possibly found her eavesdropping. She stepped inside to find that it was Finley after all who'd stood, bringing a steaming skillet of food from the fire to rest on the set table.

"There you are," Gideon said, relaxing in his chair, a smile stretching over his lips at her arrival.

Dominic's chair squeaked as he stood from the table. "I'll leave you to your dinner."

She couldn't force herself to look at him, head too muddled with what she overheard, but she raised her hand to stop him. "Stay and eat. They prepare too much food, and you'll be saving me a sore stomach if you join us."

"Just like to see you healthy," Gideon purred as Lumen reached him, her arms going around his neck as she bent for a kiss. She considered strangling him for trying to meddle while she was so close to his throat too.

Out of the corner of her eye, Lumen watched Dominic struggling to make up his mind, turning to the door and back again.

"Sit," she said.

He sat, hands landing flat on the table in front of him.

As you see fit, she thought. Staying for dinner was probably not part of his intention, but she wanted to see how he behaved. Not as a test, but because they'd spent so little time in each other's company since he'd banished her from his bed in a moment of anger. Was he still temperamental? Still guarded? Did he still laugh and smile, and always seem surprised when he did so?

"Where's Colin?" Finley asked.

Lumen slid into her seat next to Gideon's, clearing her thoughts. "Checking on his traps. He should be back before the food's cold. What was the game you played in the field?" she asked, turning the conversation.

Gideon grinned and laughed. "Just a bit of Mob. Do you play it up here?" Lumen shrugged and pressed her smile as Gideon puffed and began to explain the rules.

Dominic relaxed in his seat as Finley served them, cracking a smile as Gideon relayed the game's outcome. Lumen couldn't follow a word of sense in the mess, but she agreed to watch the next match and cheer Gideon on.

Dominic had just finished building the logs for a fire, after waking up shivering in his cottage bed, when a knock sounded on the door.

"Who is it?"

"Colin."

Dominic stared at the door and then stood from in front of the fireplace like a shot. "Come in. What is it? What's happened?"

Colin came in, peeking slowly around the door and then sliding inside, frowning at Dominic. "You think I'd knock if something was wrong?"

Dominic raised an eyebrow and shrugged. "I couldn't think of another reason why you'd come." Unless the boy just felt like snooping, but it was far too early in the morning to be bored already, surely?

"Oh," Colin said, spinning in a circle on one foot and then stopping to look up at a puzzled Dominic. "Will you come check my traps with me? Lady says I can't go to the ones south of us alone. Usually, Gid goes with me, but he and Lady are still in bed—"

"Fine," Dominic said, not sure what might come out of the boy's mouth next.

"Thanks. You can have some of the meat."

Dominic glanced at his thinly stocked larder and nodded. Meat would be good. Lumen pressed him to stay for dinner when she caught him at the house in the woods, and he tried not to accept more than a couple of times in a week. It was getting colder as fall threatened to turn to winter, and her table was always more appealing than his own, company included.

He gathered his coat, the old red wool of his uniform now dyed black and stripped of decoration, and joined Colin by the door. Colin looked him up and down and frowned.

"You should ask Widow Blythe to knit you some mittens," Colin said, raising his own hands stuffed in wooly mittens.

Dominic snorted and shoved his hands into his coat pockets. "Maybe I will. Lead the way."

"You eat your breakfast?" Colin asked.

Dominic laughed at the boy's order of inquiry and shook his head. "I only just got up. I'll manage 'til the afternoon."

Colin sighed deeply and pulled a roll from his pocket. "Here. Have one of mine."

Dominic's lips twitched, but he accepted the offer and followed the boy out of the cottage, grabbing his holster with his knife to sling over his shoulder on his way out.

"Why do you keep traps so far from home?" Dominic asked, taking a large bite out of the filled roll.

Lumen was a master of healing *and* spicing food, and his mouth salivated for more immediately.

"Cause if I take too much from just one area, there won't be any left," Colin said, weaving lines ahead of Dominic down the lane toward the woods. "Better to spread out farther. Rotate where I hunt from."

Dominic hummed in understanding and tugged his coat closed after licking his fingers clean.

"What do you do now that you're not a general?" Colin asked.

"Mitchell and I've been putting the mill back together so we can ready the grain before it goes foul," Dominic said. He wasn't quite *not* a general yet, he thought. But he wasn't really one either.

"So you'll be a farmer?"

"Maybe," Dominic said. "What will you be?"

"A hunter," Colin said, glancing over his shoulder with a

dubious glance as if Dominic hadn't been paying attention. Ah, of course. Dominic hid his smirk. "I didn't really like being a spy," Colin continued.

Dominic swallowed and caught up with the boy, following his side to side stride until Colin grinned. "Neither did I when I was young," Dominic said. He nodded at Colin's look of shock. "That was my job when I first signed up. I was lousy at it though. Kept falling asleep."

Colin guffawed and shook his head. They were out of the main cluster of homes, a few older houses still left near the road through the woods. "We'll have to be quiet in the woods. Gid made me a slingshot, and I want to see if I can catch anything," Colin said.

Dominic nodded gravely and then tipped his head. "Why ask me to come with you?"

"Lady trusts you," Colin said.

The simple words, said plain and without inflection, stole Dominic's breath from his lungs. Reasonably, he had some inkling that Lumen no longer thought the *worst* of him. She let him sit at her table, after all. And maybe Colin only meant that Lumen trusted him not to let anything happen to the boy, which of course he wouldn't. Still, his heart thumped like a drum in his chest as he followed Colin underneath a canopy of branches.

A breeze stirred, and copper leaves fell around them, the sun rising high enough to glow on their backs.

"I put the first one by a great big rock," Colin whispered. "When we see that, we'll be close."

Dominic nodded, but his eyes scanned the woods for life rather than rocks. One of the soldiers from Oshain still scouted the area around them, but with no word for over a month, and nothing spotted so far, Dominic had let him slow his tracking the area. Stalor was likely licking its wounds and searching for a new method of attacking him.

They were well south of the last house before Colin studied their surroundings in earnest. So far that Dominic wondered if he shouldn't mention to Lumen the boy's full range of hunting. If they could afford to do with less meat, it might be better to keep Colin to a tighter area, closer to safety. At least for the winter.

And it was not the 'great big rock' they found first at all, but the sound of men's voices through the trees. Dominic caught Colin by his collar as the first notes were carried closer on a breeze. He covered Colin's mouth with his hand before the boy could shout and knelt low, raising his free hand to his own lips to ask for quiet. Colin nodded quickly, eyes growing wider as another bout of muffled conversation reached them.

Gold flashed under a ray of sunlight, and Dominic hissed through his teeth, Colin gasping behind his palm.

"Stalor," Colin whispered.

Dominic nodded and released the boy, spinning him so they were face to face. "You run back to the others, send Gideon and whatever men you find along the way. Yes?"

Colin's head bobbed quickly, and he was dashing down the path as soon as Dominic loosened his hold. Dominic pulled his knife, debating on whether to follow Colin or run to catch the soldiers off guard. A branch cracked, and the conversation of the Stalor soldiers died, allowing Colin's beating footsteps as he ran away to echo through the woods.

"Catch that boy!"

Well, that settles it, Dominic thought, standing and rushing forward, knife drawn high in his fist. The soldiers would have better weapons, so he'd have to grab one as quickly as he could to stand a chance. He withheld his roar as he ran, listening to the small party shout to one another.

There were less than ten Stalor soldiers camped together in the clearing. Two had bright armor plating on hand—only one had managed to put it over his shoulders before being spotted. The rest were dressed in dark colors, weapons at the ready and full bags of supplies waiting on the ground. These weren't men who'd refused to return south after the last battle, but a party sent for a new mission. Probably one involving stealth, judging by their dress.

"At the ready!" the armed soldier cried to his numbers.

But they weren't well trained, and one young man—painfully

young, Dominic thought, throat squeezing—jumped forward to attack Dominic first. Dominic stepped out of the way of his extended sword, catching the man by his throat and twisting him, boot slipping over leaves and ankle cracking, until he had the soldier's back to his chest. He swiped his knife across the man's throat, a gurgling cry rising and a rush of warmth flooding over Dominic's sleeve.

He stole the sword from the young man's shocked hand and let him drop to the ground, swinging the new weapon just in time to block a strike.

"Now, now!" the commander shouted.

Gods, they were all so young, likely barely trained. Regret was thick in every slash of Dominic's knife and thrust of the sword as they converged on him.

Seven more, he counted. *Now six*, as one fell to his knees and Dominic struck him hard over the skull with the butt of the sword. They were too close to him, all trying to attack at once, and their own blades crossed and crowded one another as Dominic danced and dodged out of the way, timing his strikes to catch them at their weakest.

Still, it was six to one.

Dominic grunted as a blade caught his side, leaned into the knife briefly to surprise the soldier with his own deeper stab in his opponents belly, and then pushed the man aside to gain some breathing room. One, smart enough to see the error of their cluster, tossed his sword aside and caught Dominic by his collar, spinning him so fast Dominic barely caught the glimpse of the fist before it met his cheek. Dominic stumbled, the woods turned wrong-ways for a moment, and shouted as a sword hit his shoulder. It didn't dig deep, but the force was enough to send a brilliant shock of agony into his bone.

He ran, gaining ground more by luck than anything and then turned, catching his next attacker with a knife to the throat.

Five, he counted, knowing with a grave certainty that their numbers were still too high.

"Ochers, Welks, grab him!"

One leaped forward to follow orders, but the other hesitated, eyes wide. Dominic took the opportunity, grimacing through the screams of the man who made to grab him.

Four.

The remaining men charged for him and Dominic tightened his grip on his weapons, metal slick with blood.

Just hold them here, he thought, even as he knew *he* was the reason they'd come. His death was all they needed. And they would likely succeed.

Dominic growled as he was tackled to the ground, roaring as another blinding pain flashed up his right leg, and wrestled for a grip, any grip at all, to turn the tables again.

"GID! GID! LADY!"

Lumen's heart stopped at the piercing scream echoing through the woods, and the plate in her hands dropped to the table. Gideon's steps thundered down the stairs, and Lumen ran out of the house, eyes searching the trees for Colin, passing him over twice before panic settled enough for her to see clearly.

"Lady! There are Stalor soldiers in the southern woods. Westbrook's holding them off. Gideon!" Colin paused, bending and shoulders heaving with his pants.

"How far?" Gideon asked, rushing to the boy and landing on his knees to take his shoulders. "Are we faster or slower to get horses?"

"Faster," Colin managed. "It was a handful of men. Maybe a dozen."

Lumen passed them on the path, legs pumping at a sudden race she didn't even know she possessed. "Colin, you stay *here!*" she shouted, glancing back for just a moment, long enough to see Gideon start after her. He was slower, but not by much.

"Lumen, you can't fight them!" Gideon growled at her back.

No, but Dominic against a dozen? Men would be injured, and Lumen tried not to think of *who* those men might be.

"Go and get men. I'll get horses," Lumen shot over her shoulder. There was a brief huff, and then Gideon's running steps turned toward the fields.

Her thighs were weak before she reached the temple, calves numb with effort and chest burning.

"Jennie! Inda! Priestess!"

It was Priestess Nemory who appeared in the doorway to the kitchen first, lips parted in shock as Lumen came running up, feet beating against the cold ground. Lumen nearly crashed into the other woman.

"Horses, saddle them. Where's Finley?"

"Healer Brink is in the workroom," Nemory said. "What's happened?"

"Ready the horses," Lumen snapped, scowling as the young woman scurried out of the kitchen and through the courtyard. Lumen followed her and then stopped below the archways, cupping her hands around her lips. "Finley!"

"Lumen, what's happened?" Jennie called at her back.

The door to the workroom creaked, and then Finley appeared above, brow furrowed.

"Stalor soldiers south of here. Just a small party, but Dominic's holding them off, Fin. Grab everything you can. Bandages. My stitching kit. Anything we can use to sterilize him there."

Finley blanched but disappeared back into the workroom, the sound of activity rustling through bottles and drawers clear from above.

"How many men?" Jennie asked, following Lumen as she moved toward the temple entrance to help Nemory in the stables.

"Colin thinks less than a dozen," Lumen said.

Jennie puffed a breath. "If he's *holding* them…"

"I know," Lumen said. She was cold, stone again, refusing to think ahead. They needed horses and she needed supplies. They would ride to find Dominic under the assumption that he was still alive. Even if that…

Even if it seemed impossible odds.

Nemory had Finley and Gideon's horses already saddled

when Lumen joined her, and Lumen had to bury the urge to snap at her for not saddling Sosha. She could do that herself, and Gideon would have his fit when he saw her riding with them. So be it.

You'll find him dead, that dark voice warned in her mind. *And there may be enemy soldiers left standing when you get there.*

Finley made it to the stables, shoulders burdened with heavy bags, just as Lumen had finished saddling Sosha. He reached her, grasping her waist firmly in his hands as she prepared to seat herself.

"Wait," he said, stepping in close and speaking only for her ears. "Just wait for Gideon."

Lumen took a deep breath, and with it came a surge of worry so thick it seemed to fill her vision with black, threatening to swallow her under. She wavered, and her back pressed to Finley's chest as she steadied herself. He pressed a kiss to her temple and Lumen nodded. If there were any Stalor soldiers left, Gideon would need to chase them off before she could get close enough to see to Dominic. It was a simple fact. She rolled her shoulders and Finley released her, passing her a bag of supplies and then taking the reins of his own horse and Gideon's.

They led the horses out to the drive and then up to the road, and Lumen sighed at the sight of men running in their direction, Gideon at the lead. She pulled herself up onto her seat and Finley followed suit, riding close at her back as she nudged Sosha forward, skirting around a scowling Gideon.

"You follow my orders," Gideon barked at her back.

Lumen kept her pace slow until Gideon was overtaking her at a gallop, the rest of the men joining them. Sosha didn't wait for her urging, or maybe Lumen was squeezing her in tension without realizing it, but she leaned forward and let her horse carry her faster, heart still jumping.

The woods were loud as they rode, but it was not the sound of swords clashing or men shouting, it was bird cry heavy in the trees.

"Look for a great mossy rock to the right of the road," Gideon shouted to the others.

Lumen knew the rock, and she pleaded wordlessly with Sosha, who beat her hooves harder and wove her way through the men.

"Stay with me," Gideon warned her.

"I am not helpless," she said, and he grunted something that might've been agreement or denial for all she knew.

There was no sign of men beyond the rock when they neared it. Lumen wondered if Dominic had taken the Stalor soldiers on a chase and if Gideon or the others might be able to track them.

"Dom!" Gideon called as they pulled their horses to a stop. He jumped down and ran forward into the trees, probably determined to find the scene before Lumen did.

She followed him but held back, let the other men rush ahead of her slightly, her stomach turning with a queasy swoop as they searched the ground. Southwest of the great rock, Gideon stopped and raised a hand and their search party went quiet.

"Here," he called. "Come quick, sweet spirit, Finley."

Finley was at her side and together they ran forward, a dense metallic fragrance growing heavy as they ran. Lumen found the men on the ground with a numb acceptance. One stranger, dead. Another. Another.

Dominic in the midst of them, brow still tangled with fury, a wet wheeze rattling from his chest and a splash of blood on his lips. They twitched, and Gideon crouched down, bending his ear to catch the words. Gideon stiffened and stood, searching through the woods.

"He says two more. You two see what you can do with him," Gideon said to her and Finley. "Mitchell, Reaves, Evans, you watch our healers. The rest of you, follow me."

Lumen remained stiff, staring down at the fallen figure of Dominic Westbrook as Finley landed on his knees in the muck of blood and leaves and dirt. Dominic was soaked in blood, his coat wet and sticky with the substance, and Finley huffed as he peeled the garment off Dominic's shoulders. Dominic groaned, eyes widening, and Lumen roused from her stupor, joining to help Finley.

"I can't tell where his injuries are yet."

"His leg is twisted," Lumen said. "You cut the pant back. I'll sort out his chest."

Dominic's chest heaved with a handful of breaths, a weak moan holding in his mouth, and Lumen winced with him as she pulled away his coat. She dragged a cloth from her bag and found a slash through the muscle of his shoulder, pressing it to the spot. Dominic arched briefly, a silent cry trapped in his throat, and then his eyes rolled up in his head and he sagged, collapsed under the pain.

"Someone hold this here for me," Lumen said, and Harvey Reaves rushed to help her.

"His shin is fractured, and his knee is twisted," Finley cataloged. His breath was shaky, and he continued in a quieter tone, "Lumen...this is a great deal of blood loss."

She pressed her lips tight and refused to look up at Finley's stare. Gideon came stomping back, breath panting and blade bloody. "Caught 'em. Is he dead?"

Lumen flinched at the question, her fingers slipping in Dominic's blood over his weak pulse. "No," she said.

"Not yet," Finley added.

"Hold this here," Lumen said, clasping more cloth over Dominic's wounded ribs.

Gideon shook his head at Mitchell, who stepped forward, taking the place at Lumen's side himself. His hands covered hers, pressing down as she asked, and Lumen's fingers trembled over Dominic's chest, searching for another wound to staunch before she could begin her work of mending.

"Sweet spirit," Gideon murmured.

"Don't," she said, voice tight and eyes blinking.

"You'd be doing him a mercy," Gideon continued. "As you did another soldier before."

Lumen's head whipped up, eyes startled and heart breaking as her head shook. Gideon wasn't being callous, his eyes were glassy with unshed tears, head tipping in a pleading stare.

Could she leave Dominic to die? Was this what he was meant for when he vowed his life in service to hers? To die in the woods after protecting her yet again? Protecting Colin?

"I can't," she whispered, words cracking.

"Can't?" Gideon asked.

"He's right, Lumen. This may be too much damage to save," Finley said.

She swallowed and stared down at Dominic. There was another long scratch on the inside of his right arm, his sleeve torn to reveal the bleeding flesh. Lumen covered it with her own hands, felt the hot, uneven pulse against her own skin. He was fiery, as always. Sunlight shone on him, warped by tears floating in her own eyes. She searched for that heavy weight, the sinking she'd found in the soldier on the edge of death, and gasped when there was a snagging claw instead.

Dominic wasn't ready to die, and no matter what he was to her, and what he was not, she was not prepared to let him.

"No," she said, sniffing and blinking her eyes clear. "Someone pass me my needle and thread."

Finley sighed and shook his head, and then got up to retrieve the items. "He may not make it through the mending," he said, more as a warning than another attempt to coax her into quitting.

Lumen hummed and took her kit, hands steadying with the force of her decision. If she knew Dominic, he would live. Just to spite Stalor. Just to please her.

"He'd better," she said, loud enough for Dominic to hear her.

THE FIRST THING HE REMEMBERED WAS IRRITATION, WHICH WAS fitting. It was a mood he often indulged in.

Everything was too bright, too hot, too heavy and stifling. *Sol's punishment*, he thought. He tried to move, and pain split through his body like an ax. Shards of glass sliced through his throat at his groan and Dominic collapsed with a feeble whimper.

Ice coated his lips, the contrast to boiling heat so sudden and relieving he sighed. Water melted onto his tongue, evaporating against the fire scorching his mouth. Cool stone stroked against his forehead. Musical notes rang near his ear and the light dimmed.

Lumen. He saw her—or imagined her—for a brief moment, cast in silver and gold. Looking down at him with a slight fold of worry between her brows. The brilliant light was swallowed in complete dark, and Dominic sank under again, thoughts passing to nothing.

"HE'S A PATCHWORK OF PROBLEMS," Finley groused, arms folded across his chest as he watched Lumen attend a delirious Dominic in the spare little bedroom of the house. Gideon leaned against the opposite wall, quiet and pockets stuffed with his fists.

"Infection. Anemia. Fever. Fractured bones. He'll have bedsores too if he doesn't wake up soon," Finley rattled off.

"He'll die?" Gideon asked, receiving a brief glare from Lumen as she changed out old bandages for fresh ones.

Finley huffed. "Gods, I don't know. If it were anyone but her, I'd say yes."

Gideon took Finley by the elbow, pulling him to the stairs and then down to the main room of the house. "Are you worried he'll die anyway, and she'll be hurt? Or are you jealous that she cares enough to save him?"

Finley scowled at Gideon, jaw ticking, and then made an exasperated grumbling sound and turned to collapse in the nearest chair. "Both, I suppose. Don't think I've forgotten the way you encouraged him. Do you really think that's wise, Gideon?"

Gideon hummed. "If it makes her happy, then I think that's wise. And I wanted to see if he jumped at my permission when it's her interest that matters," Gideon said, shrugging at Finley's gaping expression. "Don't worry about conflict with Dominic right now, Finley. Just hope he survives. That's what matters to her at the moment."

The floorboards creaked overhead, and Gideon left Finley stewing to go and check on Lumen. She was shutting the door behind her and leaning against the wall as he reached the top of the stairs.

"You need to rest," he whispered. It'd been days since they brought Dominic back from the woods, and she'd mostly taken naps in the chair of the spare room in between nursing.

Lumen nodded, sagging slightly, and Gideon rushed to scoop her up against his chest. "I do," she murmured. "I think the fever is easing. He's drinking water. I just need to see if Finley will keep an eye on him."

"He will, sweet spirit," Gideon said, carrying her into their room. "I'll go and see to it myself if you'll get into bed."

Lumen hummed in agreement, and Gideon set her carefully down at the end of the bed, helping her wrestle out of her dress when she got an arm stuck in her sleeve.

"Will you lay down with me 'til I sleep?" Lumen asked.

Gideon smiled as he watched her wiggle backward to slide beneath the covers. No matter what Finley worried, Gideon knew that his place in Lumen's heart was fixed. Dominic could no more shake Gideon loose of her than he could rid himself of his own love for the woman.

"Course I will. Let me have a word with Fin and I'll be back in a moment," Gideon said, draping her dress over a chair and then going out to the hall.

Finley was coming up the stairs with a bowl of fresh water and an irritable scowl on his lips.

"I'll keep an eye on him," Finley said before Gideon had to speak a word.

Gid grinned and patted his friend on the shoulder. He ducked back into the bedroom and turned to find Lumen curled on her side, eyes shut and breath puffing softly between parted lips. A contented purr echoed in his chest, and he toed his boots off as quietly as he could, sliding into the bed and gathering her limp and languid form to his chest.

CHILLS AND FEVERS, daylight and black night, consciousness slipped in and out of Dominic's grasp for days with an oily evasiveness. He woke again, head pounding and skin itchy and stinging. He tried to move, and his body gave one complicated cry of complaint after another.

"Settle."

The word was powerful in her voice, and Dominic's body gave out gratefully, eyes opening to find Lumen entering the small narrow room he was caged in. She held a steaming bowl in her hand, and the mattress sank at his side as she sat beside him. She rested the bowl in her lap—fragrant broth sloshing slightly —and reached a hand out to rest on his forehead, stroking it down the side of his face. Dominic's eyes shut, body trembling at the touch.

"Your fever is down."

"How long?" Dominic asked, a cough following quickly at the rough texture of his own throat.

Lumen settled the bowl on the floor out of the way and then stood. "Eight days. Put your arms around me and don't use your right leg. I'll help you sit up."

"You should've left me in the woods to die," he rasped.

He meant to resist her efforts to help him but when she leaned in close, arms circling his bare chest to his back, he found himself drawn to her. He hadn't been this close to her since they'd had that awful moment in his office in the winter, and his face tilted to hers without permission, weak lungs soaking up the clean smell of her. He groaned as she pulled him to sit up at the headboard, right leg burning with ringing pain, trapped between splints to hold it stiff.

"Do you need to relieve yourself?" Lumen asked. "I can call for Gideon."

Face flaming with embarrassment, he shook his head. He did a bit, and Lumen's eyes narrowed as she leaned away.

"After you have some of this then," she said, lifting the soup again.

She pulled a spoonful up as Dominic took in the room. There was frost on the windows, and the bed he was in was lumpy as if it was hastily arranged for use.

"I'm a waste of your time," he said, and then grunted as Lumen took the opportunity of his parted lips to force the spoon in. He swallowed, broth rich and salty and herbed, and it soothed down his ragged throat.

"You're not," she said, not meeting his eyes

"This is Colin's room?"

"No, his is downstairs. Eat, Dominic," she urged, lifting another spoonful.

"Send me somewhere else, Lumen." He tried to shout, but it came out thin and pathetic and Lumen simply fed him another spoonful. "You don't deserve to have to deal with me like this. Send me to the temple."

"No."

He growled, frustrated with her impenetrable calm. "It would've been…been a kind of rightness if I'd died."

Lumen sighed, and the spoon dropped in the bowl with a soft sound. She stared out the window, and Dominic studied her greedily in her distraction. She turned and caught him, straightening her back and squaring her shoulders.

"You told me your life was mine," Lumen said, raising an eyebrow and waiting for his chin to dip in agreement. "Very well. I choose not to see it ended yet. I choose for you to remain here until you are well again. Now, do you want to argue with me?"

He scowled, trapped artfully by his own vow to obey her. Lumen raised a spoonful of soup, and Dominic accepted it when he could think of no argument to answer her.

GIDEON ROLLED GENTLY OFF of Lumen with a last drugging kiss, and he and Finley gathered her between them, legs and arms searching out every available route to hold her. Her breath came in unsteady rushes, body still thrilling from her lovers' attention, a heavy blanket of comfort accompanying the sheets Finley dragged up to cover them.

She waited for sleep to carry her down, but something rose up instead. A reminder, and the image of Dominic's scowling, pale face.

"Do you think he heard us?" Lumen asked, gnawing at the inside of her cheek. She'd spent so many nights watching over Dominic, and now that he was well enough to leave unattended it had been easy to sink into Gideon and Finley's eager embraces. Only after did she consider the mortifying reality of their small house.

"Yes," Gideon said with a shrug.

"If he was awake, which he's likely not," Finley amended. "It doesn't matter. Who cares about him?"

Lumen avoided answering the question for as long as she could, debating the confession over and over again in her mind.

"I do."

Finley sighed. "We know."

"No…" Lumen hesitated. She loved Gideon and Finley. They *were* enough, they were more than that. There were no longer absences in her heart, and yet room seemed to continue to grow. "I mean…I think that I have feelings for Dominic. Outside of any…moral duty to all people."

Gideon rolled to his side and kissed her shoulder. "We know, sweet spirit."

She frowned. She'd only just sorted out her feelings for herself, and was annoyed at the idea that Gideon and Finley seemed ahead of her on the matter. She crossed her arms over her chest and stared at the shadows of the roof beams above.

"You don't think I'm being greedy?" she asked.

They were quiet, and Lumen tensed, looking at Gideon who she found grinning. "You *are* greedy," he said, nearly laughing. "I've got your nails marked on my ass to prove it."

"We know you don't love us less for finding room for Dominic too, is what he means," Finley grumbled, snuggling her closer. "Lune knows the bed is big enough to add him if we must."

It is with the way you sleep in it, Lumen thought fondly as Finley strove to press them close enough to one another to leave nothing between.

"I don't know how far it goes," she said instead. "There are so many ugly memories between us. There are things I don't believe can be forgiven. And then there is everything he's done since I returned…am I only grateful?"

"You can be grateful and desire the same person in separate measures," Gideon said. "Do you admire him as a man or as a person?"

Lumen's chest and core both clenched for entirely different reasons. Dominic was undeniably handsome and even when she'd hated him, she understood his physical appeal. He was not, however, unarguably good. He was prickly, standoffish, prone to arguing rather than listening, and utterly obstinate. He was also determined to his death to see her happy, unerringly loyal, and she knew a playful side of him that she missed especially.

"Both," she said. "I don't want for passion, or happiness, or love in my life, but…"

"You want for him," Gideon finished for her, and Lumen softened. "Then you may have him."

"Provided he makes no attempt to come between us," Finley added. "He's grown a great deal, and if he can make you happy in harmony with Gid and I, I have no objection. If he hurts you, I'll poison him."

"I'm sure he won't argue," Gideon said, laughing.

DOMINIC WOKE ON A SUNNY MORNING, window coated in silver-blue patterns of frost, to find Lumen sitting at the foot of his bed, studying the grain of his blanket.

"Sick of me yet?" he asked, marveling at the slight twitch of her lips.

"On the contrary," she said, looking up at him.

He could think of nothing to say to a response that was so nearly…sweet. Instead, he found himself staring at her like an idiot and wondering why she didn't get up and walk out of the room.

"How are you feeling?" she asked.

"Weak," he said, sighing. "But better. You could send me to the temple now. I'm out of danger, surely."

Lumen hummed and tilted her head, and Dominic wanted to shrink beneath his blankets to hide his own confusion at the warmth of her stare.

"Would you rather Priestess Nemory was tending you?" Lumen asked, just a little tart.

Dominic frowned. "I don't know which one that is."

Lumen huffed a laugh and stood, but when Dominic thought she would leave him, she came to perch on the mattress by his hip. He stiffened as she reached for him, eyes widening as her warm hand framed his jaw.

"You may have to reconcile yourself to my attention, Dominic," Lumen murmured, leaning in.

His hand wrapped around her wrist, the stitches on his side pulling as he struggled to sit up, nearly crashing his face into hers in his panic.

"Lumen! What are you doing?"

Her gaze shone with amusement, nose wrinkling briefly. "I think they call it a kiss."

"You can't!" he said, his heart thumping hard at the word 'kiss,' eyes dropping to her full mouth.

"Can't I?"

He huffed and shook his head, propping himself up on his elbow and swallowing hard as Lumen framed his shoulders, a hand on either side of him, her face hovering over his. "Am I hallucinating?" he croaked. If he was…then he would stop arguing and let her kiss him.

"You're fine, Dominic. Just being difficult, as usual," she said, smiling.

"You're being… Lumen, I forced you into bed with me," he said, relieved when a shadow of sorrow passed over her face. "I was cruel. I hurt you," he said, reaching up and grazing his fingertips over the glitter of her scars. She didn't flinch or look away, and his rapid beating heart stuttered as she nodded.

"I remember, Dominic," she said softly. "Neither of us will forget that. But if I'm judging you on your actions, you have to allow me to admire you *now*. I don't know if people change, or if we are the same as we were when we were born, but making new choices. I only know that you have helped shape the world I find myself so happy in, and now I want you to reside in it with me."

He was breathing like he'd been running for his life, chest heaving, eyes searching her face.

"After everything I've done…"

Lumen's eyes flashed with steel, lips pursing. "Be selfish for a moment, Dominic, please," she snapped.

And so he was. He surged up, just an inch, enough for her to know that he'd relented. Lumen met him there, and he knew his kiss was rough and clumsy, lips chapped, by how smooth and sweet she was against his mouth. He groaned, tongue dragging against her skin desperate for her taste, and Lumen's hands rose to cup his head, fingers snagging in the tangles of his hair as she lowered him back to the pillow.

He had missed her, forgot that her flavor was as sharp as shards of ice, but her mouth was hot and supple against his. Forgot that she would suck and bite on his lip, hum sweetly at the back of her throat. That she had the appetite of a man and the gentleness of a saint.

He gasped for air as she released him and whined as she rose slightly, smiling with wet lips down at him. His neck stretched, greedy for more as his heart beat hard enough to escape his chest entirely. Lumen granted him a second, softer kiss, resting against him as he sucked and licked. He sagged again, exhausted by the effort and the shock.

"There you are," she murmured, nose stroking against his.

Selfish, he thought, cheeks aching as a smile cracked through. He slid his hand up her shoulder, digging fingers into the weave of her braid, and dragged her down for another taste. He could be selfish if that was what she desired. He would claim every greedy moment she gifted him.

"Give up this madness of yours."

The words were murmured so softly, Finley almost didn't hear them. He paused in the upstairs hall of the house, holding his breath as he listened outside of the room where Lumen and Dominic whispered to one another.

"Oh, are we feeling argumentative today?" Lumen asked, brighter. Finley imagined the laughter in her eyes as she teased the bed-bound Dominic.

Dominic sighed her name softly, and there was a telling stretch of quiet.

"You can always turn me down, you know," Lumen said.

Finley scoffed to himself, and Dominic's own huff of disbelief echoed out into the hall. "You know perfectly well I am yours. But you don't owe—"

"Hush," Lumen said.

Finley crept forward slowly, eyeing the pair through the crack of the open door. Dominic's fingers were dark against Lumen's hair as he cupped her head and feasted gently on her mouth. Lumen's head was tilted back, eyes closed, but Dominic's eyes were on her face, gaze openly reverent.

Tension uncoiled in Finley's chest at the sight of them. Dominic was healing, and in healing he was irritable, but Lumen's only complaint on his behavior revolved around his resistance to accepting his place in her heart. Finley had struggled with the idea himself, but Lumen was irresistible and patient. Dominic would give in for good soon.

"You aren't taking anything from me, Dominic. You've offered yourself, and I've accepted," she whispered, their noses touching.

He nodded and swallowed, combing back strands of hair he'd pulled loose in their extended kissing. "That was never really my intention."

Finley rolled his eyes, but Lumen only answered, "I know."

She rose from the bed, and Finley snuck backwards down the hall, pretending he'd only just left their bedroom as she appeared.

"How's the patient?" he asked.

Lumen smiled, pink in her cheeks, and for all his reservations about Dominic, he couldn't begrudge her good mood. "Bored. Probably in need of movement."

Dominic had been bedridden for three weeks, and they'd only just started helping him walk around the upper story of the house. It was about time to start testing the strength and building flexibility again.

"I'll wrestle him while he's feeble," Finley offered, and Lumen just cracked a soft laugh and headed for the stairs.

"Just make sure to leave him as you found him," she teased in return.

Dominic was sitting up in the bed, good leg hanging off the side, while the other remained stretched down the mattress. He sighed in relief as Finley entered the room.

"I think maybe you should've just cut the damn thing off," Dominic said.

Finley's lips twisted in an amused frown. "Not sure that would've helped your chances. Come on, you could use a walk."

Dominic growled. "When you put it that way, it makes me feel like a dog."

Finley grinned and held his arms out for Dominic to hold and drag himself up to standing. "Can you bend your knee?"

Dominic grunted, and the change was slight but it was

enough. Finley ducked under Dominic's right arm and helped support him as he paced the length of the room.

"Gideon's bringing you a pair of crutches today. Mitchell fashioned them for you."

"Any word from the scouts?" Dominic asked.

Finley hummed and glanced at the door. "They'll come here at the new moon when Lumen's at the temple."

"Good," Dominic nodded.

When they reached the end of the room, Finley turned them slowly to head for the hall.

Dominic cleared his throat in the pause. "How do you do it? Accept that she can just...take us back like this?"

"Firstly, I don't think she's taken us *back*," Finley said. "I'm not sure any of us earned our place in her bed until after her return from the convent. And secondly...I don't have the self-restraint not to accept it if she wants me."

"I need you and Gid to make sure I don't fuck this up," Dominic muttered.

"Oh, believe me, we're well aware of that," Finley answered, relieved when Dominic laughed.

THE CRUTCHES WERE a major improvement in Dominic's mood. He mastered the stairs with only a couple life-threatening moments of imbalance, and while he was still trapped in the house with snow a foot high outside the door, he was at least able to move on his own.

The energy of the house was domestic and easy. Lumen read aloud to him or coached Colin through reading, and Dominic listened with avid interest as she planned for the spring planting. She wanted a rooster for chicks and sheep for wool, and as soon as his damned body had fastened itself back together, he'd be on his horse to find her every farm animal and seed she could wish for.

A knock sounded on the door, the morning of the new

moon, as he sat in front of the fire with an empty bowl of porridge, and a snoozing Gideon.

"Who is it?" Dominic pushed himself to standing, balancing on his crutches, and Gideon grunted awake.

He glanced at Dominic wobbling and let out a brief bark of laughter. "Sit down before you fall over."

"It's Harvey, sir," a voice called from outside.

"Go on in, I'll follow you," Finley answered from outside.

The door cracked, and the two men entered with a third, a man named Clarkson from the Oshain soldiers who had arrived to help the battle at the last minute.

"Good to see you up and well, sir," Harvey said with a dip of his head.

"Thank you. I think we might be past the point of calling me 'sir,'" Dominic added, sinking back into his chair gratefully as the men came to join them around the table.

"What's the news from the south?" Dominic asked, eager to know the worst, or perhaps best.

Harvey cleared his throat and nodded. "Stalor built a fort about fifty miles south of here over the summer. They've kept it, but it's a skeleton crew inside from what we can see."

"Oshain has withdrawn from the war, provided there are no further motions from you or Stalor to claim new territory," the unfamiliar man added. "After we came to your aid, more men dropped out of the remaining army. Cannary and his team claim that Oshain is retreating for the sake of its people, which might be true, but they're doing it because their people aren't cooperating."

Dominic scratched at the beard growing over his chin. "Is that really it then?"

Harvey and Clarkson glanced at one another, and it was Harvey who finally spoke. "There are...rumors."

"Of Stalor's plans?" Dominic asked, sitting forward.

Harvey shook his head. "No. Of- of our priestesses. Men from the south are afraid to come up north. They say the New Moon Priestess has the power to take out the sun. To drive the army mad. To be honest sir, our own men help fuel those rumors, and there were a few southern generals on the field that day who would back those rumors up."

Dominic swallowed and frowned, turning to Finley and Gideon. "They're afraid of her, or they think she's a threat?"

"My men say the whispers in the south talk about this place like it's cursed," Harvey said with a shrug. "I can't say for certain that they'll never try and come back, and there's been nothing official said in the south yet, but it seems like they've lost interest in pushing north."

"As far as we can tell, there's almost one hundred miles of no man's land between Oshain and Stalor's official claims. You're almost directly in the middle of it," Clarkson said.

Dominic raised an eyebrow. "That puts the village you hold outside of Oshain?"

He nodded. "I'm sure we'll be absorbed when enough time has passed. That's fine. I never wanted to betray my country, only remind it of its duty to those of us still living in it. What will you do if Stalor changes its mind?"

The very thought left him weary, but Dominic knew the answer immediately. "Fight them back. I have no interest in gaining land, but I'm sick of the pattern of war."

Gideon raised his eyebrows at Dominic, who shrugged in answer. It was true. He used to look forward to battle. Now he looked forward to finding Lumen a pair of sheep and seeing the winter wheat come up in the spring.

Clarkson nodded. "Well, the men and I were impressed with you and your soldiers. You'd have our support if it came to another battle."

Dominic pursed his lips and resisted asking where they were when he and his men fought Stalor. Instead, he gritted out a, "Thanks."

Harvey and Clarkson left a little while later, and together the three men sat in relative silence for a long stretch.

"Do you really think it can be over just like that?" Finley asked.

Dominic's eyebrows shot up. "By just like that, I take it you mean the three decades of war, and all three of us nearly losing our life more than once? Taking on two separate countries and their military? Lumen drawing the moon up to cover the sun at midday?"

Gideon snorted and waved a hand at Dominic whose voice had begun to rise steadily. "Enough," Gideon said. "We get it."

"Stalor will try again someday," Dominic said, groaning as he propped his sore leg up on one of the vacated chairs. "But I hope it's when I'm old and infirm, and there's some young blood around to manage the work instead of me."

GIDEON AND LUMEN walked home in the dark—Colin sleeping at the temple—a small lantern in Lumen's hand making the shadow of trees spin and sway on the path ahead of them. The thin crescent moon was high in the sky, and her devoted silence was over for the day, but she enjoyed Gideon's silent company without needing words to fill the space.

It was mid-winter, and while it was cold and the world looked barren, her own life was rich. They'd had the best harvest she'd known since she was a little girl, she had company at all hours of the day but none that she found too abrasive. She had love in many forms.

She squeezed her fingers around Gideon's warm grip, smiling when he answered her touch.

"There was good news today," Gideon whispered as they neared the house. "We think we are in for a long stretch of peace, sweet spirit."

Lumen's feet stopped on the path, the cold snow sneaking into her boots. She twisted to stare up at Gideon, heart drumming in her chest. He smiled down at her and nodded, dipping his head to press a kiss to her lips before she could speak.

"I'll tell you more in the morning. Oshain has laid down arms, and Stalor has retreated to lick its wounds."

Peace? Her concept of peace growing up was being out of reach of the war. And then when that was no longer the case, she had thought peace was simply a matter of a day that didn't tax her emotions and body too much. To be entirely out of the danger of war was...unfathomable.

They'd done it, and now she was unaware of how to proceed.

Like you always did, but a little less afraid, she thought gently. Yes, that would do to start with.

Gideon tugged her hand, and they finished their walk to the house. The fire was damped down in the hearth, and the floor-boards overhead creaked softly, but the main room was empty. Gideon took her cloak off and hung it on a hook, shucking his boots off by the door and then bending to unlace hers. Lumen combed her fingers through his hair as he attended to her, and he caught her palms when he was done, pressing more kisses to the center of each.

This wonderful man had brought her *peace*. Even during the summer, while battles were thick on the ground, he'd managed to bring her a steadiness in life.

"I love you," she whispered as Gideon stood.

He grinned at her, hands circling her waist and pulling her close. "I love you, you've saved me. Saved all of us," he said. Lumen's eyes widened, and he shook his head. "Don't deny it. We'd be dead or on our way to it by now if it weren't for meeting you."

Lumen sighed as Gideon bundled her close, pressed her face into his throat as he lifted her from the floor and carried her to the stairs.

"How is Dominic?" she whispered.

"A bit wary, but satisfied, I think. Restless without you all day."

Lumen smiled to herself and patted Gideon's shoulder to be set down. Finding her feelings for Dominic hadn't been immedi-ate, or a result of him nearly dying. It was a slow clarity. He belonged to her. He'd said as much, and she hadn't believed it or hadn't wanted to take possession of him, but the reflex was there as she watched him bleeding out over the forest floor.

Dominic Westbrook was not allowed to die without her permission. And maybe if she kept her distance and allowed enough time to pass, he might fall in love with someone new.

She would never be unfulfilled with Gideon and Finley in her life and her bed, and it didn't make her burn with jealousy to think of Dominic moving on. Because he was *hers* and he always would be. No matter how much space she might try to put between them, their lives were tied now.

It helped that he was taking care now to be not just a good man, but a pleasant one. Pleasant for Dominic, at least.

"Are you going to check on him?" Gideon asked.

Lumen blushed and nodded, and Gideon bent his head, pressing his lips to her forehead. He pulled away and moved down the hall to their bedroom, sending her a wink over his shoulder.

Lumen licked her lips and took the shorter trip to Dominic's door, opening it as quietly as she could before sliding inside.

"You're back." He wasn't asleep. He might even have been the one she heard overhead when they'd arrived back.

Lumen clicked the door shut behind her and stared at Dominic. He sat up in the bed, chest bare and brow lined with a slight furrow. When she raised her dress up over her head, his breath caught on a soft gasp.

"Lumen?"

"Can I join you? To sleep."

He grunted, shifting to one edge of the bed, and Lumen tiptoed across cold floorboards to slide in at his left side. Dominic held himself stiff and awkward as she curled up under the blankets, but she didn't even have to speak before he was sighing, sinking down and wrapping his arms around her to pull her tight to his left side. His skin was hot against hers, not the painful burn of a fever but the warmth of a man.

"These narrow beds are always more comfortable when I share them with you," he mused softly.

Lumen smiled against his chest and then rolled to lay halfway across him, her shift the only barrier between their skin. Dominic was ready, face turning to hers, catching her bottom lip with his teeth and nibbling sweetly. Lumen's hands traveled over his chest and shoulders and neck, hips pressed to his side, breath held in her chest. One of his hands cupped the back of her head to hold her for his kiss, while the other stroked her hip over thin fabric.

She wanted more. Wanted to tear her shift away and straddle Dominic's hips. Relearn him with all the knowledge she'd acquired since their ending. And yet, there was a small part of her that enjoyed their slow courting of one another during his recovery, the patience Dominic proved he possessed.

He slowed their kisses, the hand on her hip sliding to her back and holding her tightly enough that she couldn't squirm against him for more friction. His lips pecked softly at hers until Lumen settled drowsily against his shoulder.

"Even if you do take up more than your share of the bed," he added in a low mutter. Lumen pinched the skin of his chest, and Dominic breathed a laugh against the top of her head.

The house was quiet around them, the looming specter of war was retreating, and Lumen lay in the peace, listening to Dominic's heartbeat. In that moment, it wasn't impossible to believe that this serenity might last.

As it turned out, there were new kinds of conflicts, even in the midst of peace.

"Woman, if you don't stop barring me from the door like an *infant*, I will take you over my knee," Dominic snarled down at her.

Lumen, back pressed to the door, raised her chin and narrowed her eyes. "If you would act like a grown man instead of a child, I might not have to watch you like I was your damned *nanny*!"

He growled, stepping forward, leaning heavily on his cane, and Lumen risked her own step forward to help steady him, their chests pressing together.

"Lumen, I am going mad inside. It's been months."

"You were outside yesterday," she said.

"I was on *the back porch*! Please. Let me go out to the fields with the others," he said, eyes growing wide, shoulders slumping.

Winter had offered a temporary crack in its resolve a month after midwinter, and while most of the men of the community would spend the rare warm day out of doors...

"It's all mud and ice, Dominic. You're barely steady as it is. If you lose your footing, you'll undo all the healing of the past two months."

"Do you need me to prove to you exactly how steady I am?" he asked.

Lumen was used to his dark looks and his snarls just as much as she was now used to his gentle lips pulling away when she chased for more. It was infuriating. She had made up her mind about the man, only to be held in a dull middle ground of restrained passion.

"I wish you would," she snapped back.

The cane clattered to the floor, and Lumen gasped as Dominic's arms snatched her around her middle, slamming her back to the surface of the door. Her head bounced against the wood lightly, and then she was crowded, lips claimed and possessed by Dominic's own greedy mouth. His hands held her ass in a tight grip, fingers flexing around her soft flesh as he wedged his hips between hers.

Lumen moaned, the crack in the smooth and impenetrable exterior of the man a relief after so long waiting for him to *move*, damnit. Her hands clutched at his head, holding him to her. Her hips churned against his, both for friction and to ruck her skirt up out of the way. Dominic's tongue thrust between her open lips, a demanding rhythm against her own that she mimicked with her rocking hips and pleading whines. When she sucked on his tongue, Dominic's hips slammed against hers, pinning her to the door, and Lumen let out a brief triumphant cry.

And then the impossible man tore himself away, stumbling back and nearly falling to the ground before Lumen snatched his arm and helped him balance.

"Wait, wait. Shit," he grunted, covering his face with his hand.

"Oh, honestly, Dominic. If you'd really rather be outside in the fields than fucking me, I'll carry you out there myself!"

Dominic's hand dropped, and he stared open-mouthed at Lumen for one long pause, and then his face cracked with a brilliant smile and he released a great laugh. Lumen's irritation took a sudden twist out of the house at the sight of his grin, dark eyes catching on hers with laugh lines creasing the corners.

"What? Gods, no, of course not, you mad creature. I'm trying not to *rush* you," Dominic said, huffing out a sigh. "But it's impossible when this house is full of you, and I can never escape how *badly* I want to be back inside you again. I'm trying not to *ruin* this, Lumen."

Lumen blew a long breath out between her lips, glancing around the empty house, before traveling back to Dominic and squinting. "Why would you think you'd be rushing anything? I've told you over and over how I felt."

Dominic raised his eyebrows and nodded slowly. "Yes, but… Gideon and Finley both said you sort of…took charge when you were ready to be with them."

Lumen blushed and released Dominic's arm, bending to grab his cane for him. *Thanks a lot, Gid.* Not that it was really anyone's fault. She and Dominic had been dancing around the physical end of their relationship as he healed and grew strong again. And it made sense between them for him to be wary of pushing her into sex again.

"Yes, well, I suppose I was looking forward to being seduced for a change." She stood and passed Dominic the cane. "You're right, it's too nice a day to trap you inside."

She made to walk around him but before she could, the end of the cane was pressed against the door, trapping her in place.

Dominic's stare was predatory and dark again, but the fiery temper of minutes ago had bled away. Now he was studying her in his thorough way, warm and focused on every inch of her.

"Have you been waiting on me, Lumen?" he asked, low and quiet. He stepped forward, limping carefully, but holding the cane as a gate she could not pass to go around him.

"Haven't you been waiting for me for a year?" she asked.

"No," he said, eyes holding hers. "I meant it when I said I had no expectation. I still don't, even now that I know you care for me."

"I'm falling in love with you." *You moody bastard,* she added privately.

Dominic's shining smile appeared again, sunlight parting the usual storm clouds of his expression. "Are you telling me I *should* have expectations?"

"Dominic," Lumen said, in a fair imitation of his own growl.

He leaned in, and Lumen found herself pinned between

371

Dominic and the door once more. "I love you," he murmured. He bent, brushing his lips over hers in a featherlight kiss. "I think I'd better take you up to bed."

Lumen tipped her head and pursed her lips at Dominic, reaching between them to brush a curl of black hair out of his eyes. She had been looking forward to the slightly rough and desperate direction they'd been taking earlier, but he *was* still recovering from his injuries.

"I think if you don't, I'll go out to the fields and find someone who will," she said.

Dominic laughed again, and Lumen squeezed out between him and the door, heading for the stairs, listening to the steady thump of his following, the rough beat echoing in her chest. She passed his usual bedroom door in favor of the larger room she shared with Gideon and Finley, and Dominic caught up to her in the doorway. He gripped the waist of her dress and fit himself against her back, lips nuzzling the back of her neck.

"Do you know how many nights I lay awake, listening to the three of you, nearly tearing the sheets trying to hold myself back from joining you?" he rasped against her skin.

"As many as I waited for you to appear in the doorway," Lumen answered with a huff.

Gideon and Finley were organized in how they shared her body between them, and Lumen thrilled as she wondered what difference Dominic would make to their lovemaking.

"Fuck," he muttered, hand circling her waist and sliding up between her ribs, her breasts, to cup her throat. Lumen leaned back and tilted her head, sighing as Dominic sucked a wet mark over her pulse, his hips nudging against her back. "I was so afraid that I might ask for this before you were ready, I'd half convinced myself that I could go without you entirely."

Lumen spun in his arms, arching into him so that the hard length of him nuzzled her sex through her skirts. "Don't you dare," she whispered. "We've survived this war—each other, our separation, all of it—just to reach this point together. Don't deny either of us the joy of being together."

His smile was softer, not the arrogant smirk or the surprised joy, but the man beneath who had craved honest affection from her since the moment he'd clumsily demanded his way into her bed and body. Now she was his as much as he was hers. Lumen recalled the uncertainty and confusion of their first time together and then let the old emotions pass.

"Undress me."

It was a faint echo of the first night, or a rewriting of it, but Dominic allowed Lumen to spin again in his embrace, his fingers gently tugging the ties loose on her dress. This time, it was his hands and not hers that pulled her free of the garment, his mouth warming her skin through her shift, trailing over her shoulders and across her back, up to her neck again to lick and nibble at her muscle. His fingertips mapped her shape, cupping her hips, belly, and then up to her breasts, stroking over her nipples with his thumb until they were pebbled and tight.

Lumen stepped out of the dress and back against Dominic, sighing as he surrounded her. He took her earlobe between his teeth, one hand trailing down between her legs and rubbing the crease of her sex with two fingers. Lumen's own hands traveled behind her back, cupping and stroking him through his trousers until they were rocking against each other's hands. Dominic's breath was harsh on her neck, and he seemed reluctant to pull away from her touch, his own fingers urgent between her thighs, rooting for her opening.

"Dominic!" She moaned as he pressed two fingers inside of her, the friction of her shift shocking and delicious.

He groaned and pulled his hips out of her reach. "Gods, I just realized I'm going to embarrass myself with you this time." He caught her smile and answered it with one of his own. "You don't need to look so pleased."

It was a powerful thing to think of though.

Lumen pushed Dominic's hand aside, even though a part of her wanted to let him continue. She tore the shift off over her head, crossing to the bed, and then found Dominic frozen and staring at her, fully dressed.

"I know I said I didn't have any expectations before...I meant that but...Lumen, I've dreamt of seeing you like this again every day since—" His face tore with a sudden pained frown, and Lumen perched herself at the edge of the bed, legs folded beneath her.

"Don't go there today," she said. She hadn't forgotten either. Neither of them would. They'd only made it this far because Dominic was as haunted by memories of himself as she'd been, but it wouldn't serve them in happiness to linger over the pains.

He sighed and stepped closer until he was within reach, still drinking in the sight of her, even as her hands pulled his shirt loose and tugged it over his head. His scars were healing nicely now, and Lumen traced one with her fingertip, delighted when the powerful man in front of her shuddered at the simple touch. His hands framed her face and Lumen held her breath, hands paused on his waistband, as he bent his head and kissed each of the small starry scars on her face. Tears rose to her eyes, and she tried to think of words to reassure his guilt, but Dominic only turned her face to his and caressed her lips with his own, tongue licking.

She unfastened his pants and reached inside to clasp him in her grip, pumping as his length surged to life, hard and pulsing against her palm. Dominic groaned, and fabric dropped to the floor.

"Don't you dare finish me in that wicked, perfect hand of yours," Dominic rasped, panting like he'd been running to reach her.

Lumen smiled coyly up at him, delighted with his thunderous stare, and then gasped as he grasped the back of her knee in one hand, and held her chin with the other. He pushed her back onto the bed, spreading her open as he rose up to fit between her thighs, and Lumen landed with a soft 'oof.'

"This might seem rushed at first—"

"Dominic, I don't care, I just want you."

"—but I swear to you, I don't intend to let you out of this bed until you're too weak with pleasure to stand on your own."

Lumen laughed at the threat, aware he knew perfectly well how to deliver on it, but her laugh turned into a moan as Dominic lay over her. His mouth wrapped around a nipple, sucking roughly, and then he slid over her. The head of his cock was nestled against her entrance, and Lumen's lips were parted in shock and anticipation. Dominic's gaze hovered over hers, studying, waiting, hand holding a bruising grip on the back of her thigh.

"You're wet," he said.

Lumen nodded. "Dominic, please—"

The rest of her plea was cut off with a cry as Dominic drove in to the hilt with a sudden thrust, filling and stretching her in the sudden crash between their bodies. Lumen arched, body bowing to take him at a deeper angle, chasing the throbbing echo in her cunt. He groaned above her, arm circling her back to hold her in place, the hand on her thigh sliding up until his thumb pressed to her clit.

He dragged out in one slow retreat, thumb circling over her little nub in a quick pace. He smiled down at Lumen, gaze holding hers as his throat bobbed with a rough swallow, and let her catch one deep breath.

"Gods, I missed you."

Then he began a rough urgent pace of deep thrusts that drove Lumen across the mattress and shook her to her core, pleasure pounding in time with his cock. Her pulse drummed in her veins, a flush of heat rising up her throat and making her eyes water with the bittersweet ache.

"Dominic! Gods, yes!"

Her arms wrapped beneath his, clutching at his back, a startled laugh rising from her breathless chest as their skin slapped noisily and Dominic's thumb urged her into a fiery pleasure.

"That's it. I won't last long. Come for me, Lumen."

Lumen whined as Dominic ducked, teeth nipping and dragging down her throat to suck a mark against her skin. She pushed back against his rocking hips, the groan of his voice musical in her ear as stars burst in her vision. He was swelling inside her, panting and gasping, and she realized he'd meant it when he said they would rush. He'd been without her for over a year. Just the thought of him waiting for her, burying his desire while he fought for her on the battlefield, had Lumen clinging tighter to him.

She turned her face to his, demanded his kiss, and tightened herself around his length. The great fullness of him, his desperation to have her clutching on him in her finish, and his ever determined touch on her clit sent Lumen spiraling, a weak cry escaping between their shared kiss as she shuddered beneath him.

Dominic's moan was relieved and shocked, and he shook like an animal who'd suddenly discovered themself caught in a trap, rutting hips roughly between her cradling thighs as he flooded her with heat.

Lumen was still tense, wrapped around him, as the orgasm passed. It had been too brief and sudden, and she already wanted more. Dominic sighed, forehead resting against her, and sucked briefly on her bottom lip.

"There, that's done," he murmured, moving his hands to either side of her shoulders, balancing himself above her and grinning down at her pout. "Oh, look at you. Do you think I'm done with you already? Not likely."

"What are you—Oh!" Lumen whimpered as Dominic pulled out of her, a sticky flood of release following in his wake.

He scooted down, head dropping to kiss her collarbone, licking away a sheen of sweat. "I'm sorry. I was too greedy not to have you right away and too desperate to last. I'll make it up to you," he whispered against her skin.

Lumen huffed, staring down her nose as Dominic littered kisses over her chest, down to her breasts. He cupped one in his hand, gentle and thorough in his exploration of her skin until Lumen found herself smiling and relaxing.

"The taste of you," Dominic whispered, tongue flicking out and licking at the underside of her breast. "Sol, I meant to be patient, but now I have to know."

He twisted on the bed, seating himself between her open legs and hunching his back down, face nuzzling a long path down to where she was slowly leaking the evidence of their activities.

"I think you went a little mad, abstaining for so long," Lumen teased him.

Dominic only grinned and combed his hair back from his face, gazing at her opening with a hunger that *still* left Lumen blushing in response. But as his head dipped again and he took a slow lick around the lips of her sex, that embarrassment faded beneath desire.

"Yesss," she hissed, mouth dropping open as Dominic hummed in agreement against her sensitive flesh.

She couldn't begrudge his impatience now, not when he was so thorough and teasing as he mouthed and kissed and licked her core. Lumen was writhing in the sheets, shifting so he could lay on his belly as he feasted on her, churning her hips up to gently encourage his attentions.

"You taste even better mixed with me like this," Dominic growled, dipping two fingers inside of her and fucking her so slowly, Lumen found herself dragging his face back down to her skin.

"You sound even sweeter with your mouth full," Lumen gasped.

Dominic laughed, and the vibration left Lumen shaking, toes curling in the sheets. He wrapped his lips around her clit—sucking and humming—and Lumen crashed, swallowed under a wave of heat and dizzying sunlight. Dominic's fingers pumped and his lips pulled until she was trying to wiggle away, and then his hands gently turned her onto her belly.

Lumen lay recovering, half tempted to fall to sleep as Dominic kissed her from her toes to the crease of her ass all the way up to the nape of her neck in a lazy rediscovery of her skin. He rolled her again and repeated the path downwards.

"I see your plan now," Lumen hummed, propping herself up on still weak arms to watch Dominic in his worship of her knees.

"I hate to be rushed. Even by my own desire," he said, stroking at her other calf.

His cock was bobbing against his stomach, a little bead of fluid waiting for Lumen's lips.

She sat up and reached for his shoulders, and Dominic looked up, smiling as she pulled him closer. His smile rounded in surprise as she turned them both on the bed, pushing him down to his back and taking his cock in her hand, pumping him till he was bucking into her grip. She caught the drip of arousal off him with her thumb and carried it to her lips as he watched with wide eyes.

"My turn," she said, holding him in place and sinking down on his length. She was swollen and satisfied, but it was still a joy to watch his jaw flex, head dropping back as she surrounded him, low groan rising up from his chest.

"I love you," he gasped.

Lumen laughed, fully seated and rocking gently over his hips. "I love you too. Eyes on mine, Dominic."

His stare was hot, and she knew she only had a little time holding him under her power like this before he would take the reins back from her. That was fine. She liked Dominic's command, his urgency, and his relentless attention.

"Fuck me, Lumen," he growled.

Lumen took a deep breath and began to ride him, squeezing him from tip to base, watching his pulse pound in his throat. This man was hers, completely.

GIDEON LEANED AGAINST THE DOORFRAME, admiring the picture on the bed. Lumen was tangled in the sheets, pressed to Dominic's side, the man's fingers still tangled in her loose braid. It was a bit of a relief to see they'd finally fallen into bed together. Dominic had been growing antsy, and Lumen quietly insecure. Leaving them alone for the day had done the trick. Gideon privately congratulated himself and smirked at the sleeping pair.

Now Lumen would have the best of each of them. Finley's intelligence, Gideon's sweetness, and Dominic's determination. Together, they could make her happy, *happier*.

"What do you want?" Dominic opened one eye and glared at Gideon.

"Harvey and Jennie are downstairs. They want to see Lumen, but you should come too."

Dominic hummed, fingers pulling gently from Lumen's hair to brush up and down her spine. He and Gideon shared a private, fond smile, as Lumen burrowed against Dominic's chest.

"Wake up, sweet spirit," Gideon called.

Lumen's cheeks filled with a smile at the sound of his voice, and Gideon's heart thumped in his chest. *Lucky bastards, all three of us*, he thought.

"Dinner?" Lumen mumbled against Dominic's chest.

"Visitors."

She groaned and started to roll, Dominic following her to kiss her face. Gideon grinned and shook his head.

"I'll be downstairs. Don't get distracted," he warned.

Lumen hummed and waved a hand in agreement as Gideon left them to their private moment. Finley was serving some of Lumen's mint tea downstairs, Colin rattling happily at a patient Harvey, and Jennie raised her eyebrows as Gideon arrived alone.

"Waking up from a nap," he said, and Jennie let out a dubious snort.

If Dominic tried to coax Lumen to linger in bed, he failed, because she came skipping down the stairs in a few minutes, braid redone crisply and wearing a smooth dress. The only evidence of her afternoon with Dominic was the pink mark on the base of her throat, and Gideon figured she hadn't even seen it for herself.

"I didn't realize you were coming to visit," Lumen said, eyes bright and smile wide. "Is everything alright?"

"Everything's fine, Lumen. Harvey has some news for Dominic if he—" Jennie stopped as Dominic's slow steps and thump of his cane sounded down the stairs. "Ah good. Inda sends her love. We went to check on her at the temple before arriving."

Gideon and Finley exchanged a quick glance. Neither had

said anything to Lumen, but they both shared a secret relief that she'd passed her position as New Moon Priestess on to Inda.

"How is she?" Lumen asked, frowning. Gideon lifted one of her hands to keep them from wringing together with worry.

"Peaceful, actually," Jennie said with a smile. "I...I told her I was moving out of the temple, and she was happy for me. She's doing well."

Lumen sighed and smiled as Dominic reached them. "Congratulations then," Lumen said nodding to Harvey. "I'm happy for you both."

"Well I hope you'll be happier to hear we'll be married in the spring," Jennie said, smile stretching as she let out an uncharacteristic bubble of laughter.

"Oh, Jennie," Lumen cried, pulling from Gideon's hold on her hand and wrapping her arms around her friend. She grinned at Harvey. "What a strange bit of magic you've worked over this woman."

"Hush," Jennie growled.

Harvey combed his fingers through his graying beard and looked on his future bride with a heavy and proud stare. "She's taking mercy on my heart is more like it."

"Enough," Jennie groaned, pushing out of Lumen's arms and wearing the brightest smile in the room. "Anyway, you'll have to perform the ceremony of course, and don't argue," she added quickly as Lumen's surprise wiped her face clean.

"I...I won't argue," Lumen said slowly, blushing. "I'm barely a Priestess lately, you know."

"I don't care," Jennie said with an easy shrug. "I want you to do it as my friend, not my Priestess."

"Then yes, of course," Lumen said, dragging Jennie in for another hug.

"I have news as well, though I don't know if you'll want to hug me for it," Harvey said, stepping forward and drawing his satchel down from his shoulder. "Stalor and Oshain made new maps, and the scouts got their hands on a couple."

"Can't think of a better sign of a war being over than new

maps drawn up," Finley mused, stepping aside to offer the table to Harvey.

"That was my thought. They're a bit curious though," Harvey said.

Lumen fit herself between Gideon and Finley's hips as Dominic settled himself in a chair, watching closely as Harvey unrolled one map, vast and open.

"That's Stalor," Gideon said, recognizing the southern deserts and the thin pocket of coastline on the east. The reach of the map extended considerably to what Gideon had seen last. He and Dominic had been using Oshain's map while fighting for the army, and a good third of that land was now applied to the south.

"And here's Oshain," Harvey said, spreading out a second map.

Oshain held the northern coast and the western mountains, but much of its previous farmland was now swallowed and Gideon wrapped his arm around Lumen's shoulder, tugging her closer. Dominic shifted the maps until the shared borders faced one another. After a quiet pause, fingertip outlining the winding curve of a line on Stalor's northern edge, he barked out a laugh.

"I don't know what it means," Colin said, standing close to Dominic's side.

Dominic shifted to let him lean closer. "See this dip here? And the one here?" he asked, pointing to curving edges on either map. "There's a gap there. That's us." He tapped his finger in the empty space between. "Stalor and Oshain are both claiming we're the other country's territory."

"We aren't on a map?" Finley asked as Gideon laughed.

"Does this mean one of them will try to fight us? Or each other?" Lumen asked, frowning.

"If I had to guess, it means they came to a mutual agreement to ignore us," Dominic said, frowning at the paper. "We'll keep our scouts listening for news though, just in case."

Dominic's hand reached back over his shoulder, and Lumen caught it in her own, their fingers squeezing briefly. Jennie caught Gideon's stare, wiggling her brows. Jennie had tried to wager with Gideon on when Lumen and Dominic would end up together, but Gideon wasn't enough of a fool to lose the little coin he had to the woman who had Lumen's ear on matters of men.

"Can I keep these?" Dominic asked.

"Of course," Harvey said. "My guess was the same as yours about them wiping their hands of us. Good riddance to them too, I say."

Lumen tried to coax Jennie and Harvey into staying for dinner, but the couple left before the sun finished sinking. Colin was plating food, and Gideon wrapped his arms around Lumen's waist as she stood at the front door, waving goodbye.

"Do you think we'll get to that place?" Gideon asked Lumen in a low, private tone.

She leaned back in the circle of his arms, tilting her head to look him in the eye. "Jennie and Harvey's? I should think we are in that place," she said.

"And you'd marry me?" Gideon murmured against her ear, his heart hammering in his chest.

"Oh, Gid," Lumen said, gaze softening and body melting. "Of course I would. But what do you think of letting the others catch up first?"

He beamed at Lumen. "I think that's a very wise idea."

Spring never rushed its way north, arriving in small measures one month at a time. Lumen savored the slow thaw, teaching Finley and the Priestesses the order of growth in the woods. Dominic was more or less healed, his gait a little stiffer than it had been, but he was out in the fields with the first group of men when it came time to plan the farming. Gideon continued building, working with Rodney Mitchell to learn the trade and help grow the homes in the village. Colin ran wild in the woods, hunting and playing in a mix of self-fashioned games and work, learning the role of childhood at last.

"I like this dress on you," Gideon said, running his fingertip along the back collar of Lumen's white gown.

Priestess Nemory had offered to let Lumen borrow her own pale robes for Jennie's wedding, but Lumen declined. She wasn't sure what she was now—not Lady of the Manor, not New Moon Priestess—but her place wasn't in the temple. Helping there, yes, but not as a priestess. As High Priestess Wren had said, she would always be one of Lune's daughters, but she craved finding a new rhythm to her life. One with more company and affection and color.

"You're beautiful," Finley said, lifting Lumen's hands to his lips to brush a kiss across her knuckles.

They walked home from Jennie and Harvey's wedding with the sound of the festivities still loud at their backs. Colin was watching the Ramsey children, and they had the evening to themselves. Based on the warm and longing looks her men had been giving her all through the ceremony, Lumen suspected they planned to make the most of the night.

Dominic led the way on the path so they could match his slower pace. There was always work to do now, even with the land in peace, but there never seemed to be a rush.

A chilly breeze carried her loose hair off her shoulders, and Gideon combed her strands back as they blew into her face.

"We can start a fire when we get home," Dominic said, turning his face into the breeze and closing his eyes.

"If you three have planned what I think, we won't need it," Lumen said.

Dominic flashed her a wicked grin over his shoulder.

"You're looking flushed already," Gideon teased, and she bumped her shoulder against his side.

"Are you tired?" Finley asked, gentle and cautious.

"Not in the least," Lumen reassured him, blood warming in anticipation of the night.

The house in the woods waited for them, a small and orderly herb garden started on the western side, Gideon already preparing to expand the second story over Colin's little room. Dominic opened the door and stepped aside to let Lumen enter first.

When she stepped through, he caught her around her waist, tugging her roughly against his chest. He nuzzled at her cheek, kissing the shell of her ear. "You're exquisite. I couldn't take my eyes off you the whole day," he rasped, stepping into the shadow of their home, clutching her in his arms.

"I noticed," Lumen teased, nestling back against him, taking care to rub herself against his crotch.

"Don't start down here," Finley grumbled. "You'll break the table again."

Lumen laughed, and Dominic let her slip free to head for the stairs. Her lovers followed her with quick steps, the sound of their boots on the stairs making her breath catch in her chest. No matter how many nights she spent with them, how many times they made love, even kissed, Lumen marveled at the thrill that ran through her veins. Especially when all four of them shared the bed together.

Gideon caught up to her first, spinning her back to press against his chest, tipping her head to the side to suck along the muscle of her throat. One of his hands fought its way down the front of her dress, grasping a breast and massaging it roughly. Finley was there next, catching Lumen's moan on his tongue, fingers working smoothly down her laces.

There was a thump on the floorboards in front of her and Lumen pulled away from Finley's kiss to find Dominic on his knees, rummaging under her skirts.

"Your knee!"

"I'll be dead before you can stop me from kneeling to worship you, Lumen," Dominic growled.

Finley helped him fist the fabric up out of the way, and then Dominic was leaning in, mimicking Gideon and Finley's kisses against her sex. Lumen sighed and relaxed into the grip of his hands around the globes of her ass. She knew better than to argue with all three of them. One on one and she stood a chance of stealing control in bed, but when they'd set their mind to ruining her with ecstasy, it was better to let them have their way.

"You're grinning," Finley mumbled against her lips. "Are you laughing at us?"

"Not entirely," Lumen teased.

Finley leaned back, thin lips trying to hide his own smile. "Gid. Get her dress off."

Lumen gasped as Gideon tore away from her shoulder, hands managing the work roughly before returning to grasp at her flesh. Dominic pressed harder against her mound, tongue slicking through her lower lips, groaning as she began to grow wet and hot against his mouth. He pulled away, chin shining, and stood in front of Lumen, fully clothed and breathing heavily.

"Put her on the bed. Fin, hold her down."

Lumen laughed as Gideon and Finley rushed to follow orders. In one respect at least, Dominic was still General Westbrook. Secretly, she didn't mind. Gideon lifted Lumen in his arms as Finley stripped out of his own clothes, before climbing onto the bed. Gideon lay Lumen down, mouthing at her breasts, down between her breasts, and over her stomach. His tongue dipped into her belly button, and Lumen squirmed, ready to reach out to him, when Finley's hands clasped around her wrists, pinning them to her sides.

Gideon was nuzzling against her damp core while Dominic joined them on the bed.

"Go ahead," Dominic said to him.

Lumen groaned as Gideon's hot hands spread her thighs apart, rough beard rubbing against her throbbing core as his tongue lapped at her arousal.

"Please," she moaned, hoping that begging early might grant her mercy sooner. She arched and found Finley's cock not far from her lips, his eyes flashing as she studied him. Gideon's tongue thrust against her opening and Lumen stretched, flicking her own against the underside of Finley's cock, catching a brief taste of him before he shifted out of her reach.

"Careful now, my lady," Finley said swallowing as he watched her writhe in his grasp. "You know how they like to hear you crying out."

Lumen whimpered as Gideon pulled away, his wet lips traveling up to her breasts. Beyond his head, Dominic settled between Lumen's thighs, calloused hands running up and down the inside of her legs. He shuffled closer, draping her legs over his, and nestled his iron-hard and scorching hot cock against her sex. Lumen held her breath, Gideon's lips suckling at a nipple, Dominic's cock stroking the outside of her sex to coat himself in her juices, and Finley slowly stroking his thumbs over the pulse in her wrists. Having all three of them at once was often overwhelming, the world going dizzy and hazy around her.

Dominic notched the weeping head of his cock against her entrance, and Lumen wiggled to try and pull him deeper, her core aching to be filled.

"Dom, please," she whispered.

His hands cupped around her hips, fingers digging in once, and then his hips flexed, and he slid in and out again. Lumen shuddered and he repeated the motion.

"Shift closer to her, Fin," Dominic said. "Keep her distracted."

"Oh, and I need something to drive me mad?" Finley asked, but he settled closer, cock tapping softly against Lumen's bottom lip.

She accepted him greedily, humming around the head of his length and blushing as Finley hissed above her. She licked and sucked, moaning as Dominic picked up the pace, sinking deeper with every slow thrust. Finley was bitter and salty on her tongue, but the clench of his fingers around her wrists drove her to try and take him deeper. Her tight arch pressed her breasts closer to Gideon, who lavished attention on them with hands and mouth, patient for his own time at the end of Fin and Dom's games.

"Wanton goddess," Dominic muttered as he sank in to the hilt, grinding himself against her clit.

Lumen blushed at the praise and pulled back to catch her breath, Finley painting her lips with his arousal. She hiccuped a squeak as Dominic fucked her in rough, steady thrusts, deep and grinding with every push in. Gideon leaned back, and Lumen watched as he pulled his shirt off over his head, admiring the size and angles of him all over again. He was getting softer around the edges, and she loved the pressure of him against her and the pillowy comfort of his chest.

"Open," Fin groaned, sliding in deeper between her lips, his rhythm a gentler version of Dominic's.

Distantly, Lumen knew that a year ago, she would've been appalled by the way the three men used her body. Now she felt the generosity and affection in their hunger for her. Even if it didn't satisfy her physically to fill her mouth with the taste of Finley, it satisfied the possessive animal in her heart that wanted to own every inch of him the way he owned her.

"Fuck, she's getting close," Dominic moaned. "Why can I never resist this?"

"She's made for us," Gideon agreed.

Lumen moaned and squeezed around Dominic, and Gideon's hand left her breast to reach between them, toying with her clit until she was fluttering and gasping around Finley and Dominic. Finley retreated, scrambling backward and leaning down to nip at Lumen's lips as she cried out, a flood of stars shooting through her head to toe as she rushed and came on Dominic's cock.

Dominic's rocking faltered, hands gripping tighter as he finished with a handful of uneven, harsh kicks of hips. His head tipped back, releasing his groan up to the ceiling. Lumen rolled against him, grinning as he hissed, and then Finley backed away just enough to drag Lumen out of Dominic's grasp.

"Could've given me a fucking minute, Fin," Dominic laughed.

Lumen scrambled to follow Finley's desperate leading as he spun her on the bed, pulling her legs up to rest over his shoulders, stroking the backs of her legs.

"You still make me mad for you," Finley breathed, leaning down and pressing her knees open until her body ached deliciously. She fucked his mouth with her tongue, retaliating for his cock in her mouth.

Hands soothed over her skin as Finley wrapped his arms around her to cup her head and stroked his cock through her weeping sex. He pressed in with small teasing pumps, gaining ground just an inch at a time, sighing into her kiss as she surrounded him.

"You're sane," Lumen assured him. "Just in love."

Finley beamed at her, all his usual gravity paling under his joy for a moment. "Let me watch you shatter, my lady."

Lumen relaxed in his embrace. Finley had her to himself in this position, folded and pinned open to his taking. Finley pushed her knees wider apart and began to fuck her in long surges, just the deep drumming of his cock inside her. He braced himself up, palms on either side of Lumen's head, Finley's head tipped and his brow furrowed as he watched himself pump in and out of her. It was a sweetly aching sensation, and fresh from her orgasm from Dominic, she was enjoying the aftershocks shivering through her at Finley's encouragement.

"Sore?" Gideon murmured, coming to kneel on the floor at the edge of the bed. His voice was in her ear, his fingers skimming in the gap between her and Finley's chest to brush across her breasts.

Lumen shook her head, tilting her head back and turning it to take Gideon's slow, probing kiss until she was melted on the sheets. Finley shifted, bracing his feet against the bed, and Lumen whined against Gideon's lips as he struck a new angle. Her body shuddered in reflex, and she watched as Dominic appeared behind Finley's back, the two men exchanging one brief look as Finley's rocking slowed. Finley's eyes shut, chest stilling as Dominic's hands mapped his back, and then lower, Finley hissing and bucking against Lumen and then groaning lowly.

"Fuck her," Dominic growled in Finley's ear, tongue licking the outer shell.

The new pleasure was piercing, Lumen tensing as it jarred through her, coiling tight in her muscles.

"Oh gods," she gasped, trying to squirm but held in place by her lovers, forced to take sharp sensation as it rushed through her with every rough plunge of Finley inside her.

"That's it, Lumen," he gasped from above. "Like a vice."

"Finley," she pleaded. Could he make it stop? Or maybe make it even more violent until she broke apart in bliss?

"Close, fuck—I'm close," Finley gasped.

She didn't know where she was, how far from crashing or how close. Not until Gideon shifted from her side as Finley lowered himself to pin her down. His weight stole her breath and his thrusts were frantic, voice growling praises in her ear. His hips ground against hers and his cock stroked in a sudden, urgent race, and Lumen's vision exploded in white. Finley groaned and continued, wild on top of her, the muscles of her legs burning with a stretch that heightened her orgasm into an inferno rush as she squeezed so tight, she thought she might push him out completely.

He came, hips twisting against hers, release bursting inside her and then slipping out of her sex in a sticky rush, her cunt already full. He sagged, pulling her legs gently down to relax, lips kissing her cheek and jaw as they caught their breath together.

When Finley rolled gently off her, Gideon was there at her head, pulling her up by her armpits, and bending to feast on her swollen sex. Gideon licked and hummed, working his way up her belly and between her breasts as Lumen trembled.

"Ready?" he asked, voice thick with gravel.

She nodded, head lolling on her neck, ecstasy running through her veins like a drug. Gideon crowded her back, hands skimming her sides, up her front, rubbing gently over her shoulders and then holding her still in a tight grip. Finley was barely out of her, a flood of wetness making its way between the lips of her sex, when Gideon was there, pushing in.

Lumen groaned, low and ragged. "Yes," she hissed as he pulled her flush against him, cock filling her to the brink. "I want you."

Gideon nuzzled against her cheek, and Lumen mouthed the words 'my beast' for him, their private teasing.

"My sweet spirit," he whispered back.

He kissed her cheek once, and Dominic settled on the bed next to an exhausted Finley to watch. Gideon didn't hold back, wrapping himself around Lumen, bending her forward to brace her hands against the mattress.

There was no hesitation, and very little warning, just a few quick nudges of his hips to find his angle, and then Gideon was rutting, hip bones against her ass and one hand holding her hair. His hand fumbled against her breast, playing with her nipple erratically as Lumen gasped and moaned. It was desperate and raw, and just on the delicious side of painful. Gideon rode her with abandon, the other's release making his movements smooth and slippery. Lumen clutched around his thick cock, the pressure of him inside of her beautifully blinding.

Gideon rumbled at her back, tugging gently on her hair to make her see stars as she shuddered. She praised him in simple terms, sometimes without words at all, and Dominic slid forward to take her mouth in a messy, licking kiss.

"He loves it like this," Dominic said against her mouth. "With you stretched and slick from us."

"*I* love it," Lumen gasped, and then cried out as Gideon pulled her back in a deeper arch, driving in faster.

This time it was Dominic's hands against her pussy, spreading the wetness that leaked out with every one of Gideon's thrusts. Finley crowded in too, kissing her shoulders and forehead, hands gripping at her breasts.

It's like drowning, Lumen thought, chest tight and body floating between the hands and mouths that caressed her like water. Gideon growled and bowed forward, head dropping against her back and hands moving to the front of her hips to hold her steady.

The rising pleasure was slow and thick, syrupy and scalding, and Lumen let it drag her under in its heavy tide, moaning against one man's kiss, clutching another's hand, rolling her hips back to ride Gideon's cock. It consumed her, her eyes falling shut and arms giving out, held up by her lovers as she vibrated and cried out.

Her thighs were coated in their shared fluids, and even more gushed out as she came. Finley and Dominic lowered her gently to the bed as Gideon rode out the last of his own thrusts with a great shout of pleasure and a shocking filling sensation in her core.

"I always forget how well she bares it," Dominic murmured, combing her hair back from her sweaty face.

Gideon grunted, rolling to his side. The bed shifted, and there was a little splash of water in the room before Finley returned, gently cleaning Lumen's tender sex. She released a little whimper, and Dominic and Gideon lifted and arranged her farther up the bed between them.

"Beautiful," Dominic said, kissing her numb lips.

"Exhausted," she managed, warming at the sight of his grin.

"Oh, don't worry. We'll give you a few hours rest."

Finley huffed and climbed in under the sheets at Gideon's side. They would rotate at some point in the night. Likely after Dominic made good on his playful threat.

Lumen stretched and groaned, and Gideon chuckled, kissing her shoulder. "You may have to get more creative on the next round," Lumen mumbled, burrowing her face against Dominic's chest, pinching his skin as he shook with laughter.

MORNING ARRIVED, and Dominic woke somehow feeling as though the night had lasted an eternity, and also that he'd barely blinked before it was time to get up. Of course, he had spent most of the night trying to keep Lumen awake.

She was curled on her side, facing him but staring out the window at the growing light, and the peaceful cool picture of her was so enormously different from the flushed and moaning woman he'd held in his arms the night before. He knew Lumen now, the deeper version of her that Gideon could coax out so easily, but even then he learned her in rare glimpses.

"What are you thinking?" she asked, eyes trailing slowly from the window to his, all her cool dignity in place.

"I...saw something earlier, last night, while we all had a hold of you."

She tipped her head, and Dominic searched her eyes, wondering if he might catch the vision again. "Tell me," she said.

"Your eyes. It was like a wall I didn't know existed was coming down. Ah, see, there. Three more just went up in its place." He waited for a minute as if she might know how to take them down again, and then realized it was futile.

They remained quiet. He thought she might fall back to sleep, but then she pressed closer and rested her chin on his chest in a way he loved but never mentioned.

"What was behind it?" she asked.

Dominic's lips parted, but no words came out. *Your soul*, he thought but grimaced at the idea of voicing. "I don't know," he said finally. "But I knew in that moment, I belonged to you."

Ah! There it was, heat and affection and possession. He pressed his lips together to keep from speaking and scaring it away.

"Maybe it's a bit of the Goddess left in her," Gideon rasped from the edge of the bed, pushing to sit up at the headboard and smile down at them. Finley was pretending to sleep at Lumen's back, his face hiding in her hair, but Dominic could see the fold his frown peeking out.

"I think she's done with me now," Lumen said, relief in her smile.

"Sol is certainly sick of us," Dominic said with a shrug.

Lumen hummed, gaze floating over the ceiling, lips twitching with unspoken words. "Maybe we are their wedding bed. The union where they meet," she said.

Dominic's throat was tight, heart achingly full, but Gideon found words. "Are you making myths now, sweet spirit?"

Lumen blushed, and Finley stirred in her hair. "'S'not a myth if we exist," he mumbled and then, after a stretch of quiet long and thoughtful, he added, "Who's getting out of bed to make breakfast?"

EPILOGUE

PRIVATE KIP GREER, OF STALOR'S THIRTY-THIRD REGIMENT, frowned at the open, rolling scenery around him. Why hadn't anyone put the place on a damn map? It was a long enough journey to come up so far North, but to do it without proper directions seemed like a fool's errand.

Guess I know what that makes me, Kip thought, clucking at his horse to continue along the road. Modestly sized crops grew on either side of him, enough food to support a village and maybe a little trading, but nothing like the great fields on the other side of the Stalor border. Of course, he knew the rumors about the no-man's-land. The temple priestesses ate souls, the men were starved and wild. But someone must've been sane enough to farm, and Kip didn't really believe in stuff like that.

Lieutenant Monroe's stories of the war *were* chilling, though. And Lunars did always give him the shivers.

He swallowed hard and shook his head, scanning the horizon once more, jumping in his saddle as a new figure appeared in the distance.

"Don't be an idiot," Kip hissed to himself, staring at the horse and rider plodding slowly out of the fields and onto the road ahead of him. He raised his arm to signal to the man, but the horse was already holding steady, waiting for his approach.

Kip had plenty of time to study the man as he neared. He was old, late forties, with skin browned from the sun and thick streaks of gray hair leading back from his face, mingling with black. His hair was tied back, and he sat high and straight on his horse, watching Kip with dark narrowed eyes.

Kip expected the suspicion, of course, dressed in Stalor's red and gold colors. What he didn't expect was the slight gleam of a scar running down the man's left cheek. *Could it be...?*

"What brings you this far north, soldier?" the man asked.

Kip had to clear his throat twice. "My army sent me. I'm searching for a man...General Dominic Westbrook. Do you...do you know him?" Kip asked. *Are you him?* he thought, eyeing the man's scar. It matched the description he was given.

The rider stared at Kip for a long stretch, creases at the corner of his eyes growing deeper. Finally, he sucked in a deep breath and smiled.

"No such man in these parts," he said. "Not in a long time."

"Are you...are you sure?" Kip asked.

"Positive," the man said, nodding. He rode closer, hands loose around his old gelding's reins, and Kip resisted the impulse to reach for a weapon. The man was unarmed, and Kip had been given *strict* orders to maintain a peaceful relationship when delivering his message.

"Y-you look like him," Kip said.

The man laughed and reached out a rough and calloused hand. "James Smith," he said. "And I'm afraid I'm a farmer, not a general of any sort. Unless my cows count."

Kip swallowed and shook the man's hand, "Right. Sorry. Um...there's someone else I was sent to speak to. Uh- the- the New Moon Priestess."

James Smith's eyebrows rose, and he blinked at young Kip.

"Do you know...where I might find her?"

"Of course," Smith said, with a shrug. "At the temple. You know the way?"

Kip shook his head and Smith smiled at him, plainly laughing at the soldier's nerves. "You're not far, but it's in the valley so you haven't seen it yet. Follow me."

James Smith rode ahead of Kip farther up the road, and Kip muttered softly to himself on the way. "This is what comes of you volunteering. You're a shit spy. Now you have to go and see...see *her*."

The woman who still haunted Monroe's dreams so thoroughly, Kip woke to his screams echoing through the barracks most nights.

They reached the top of the hill, and suddenly the temple was visible, a monstrous round building that glowed like fire in the setting sun. Another man rode towards them, pulling a small cart of vegetables, a woman walking along the side. She grinned at James Smith, a gap in her toothy smile, and waved.

"Evening Farmer Smith," she greeted, easing a fraction of Kip's suspicion.

"Inda," Smith said with a nod. "Danny."

"Evening Smith," Danny said as they passed.

There was another man in the fields closer to the temple, and he and Smith called to one another by name. Kip caught up to the farmer, who glanced at him out of the corner of his eyes.

"What business do you have with the New Moon Priestess?" Smith asked.

"Mostly to see if she knows the whereabouts of a few men," Kip said. The rest was simply to check and see if she was still living. Which she was. Which Kip found particularly dreadful news.

"Ah," Smith said as they reached the drive to the temple. Smith remained on his horse, staring back at Kip. "Go on. Just straight through the courtyard and down the long hallway to the dark temple. They say she spends most hours there. That or one of the other Priestesses will guide you."

Kip swallowed the lump in his throat and nodded absently. What had he expected? For the farmer to hold his hand? He dismounted and headed for the stairs. Surely he could go back with this much news? Westbrook was gone and the Priestess remained?

But at the idea of going back and being teased for turning tail, Kip gathered his courage and headed for the doors. The temple was eerily quiet and shockingly sterile. A whip of pale light fluttered out of the corner of his eye and Kip turned his head, watching a woman in a shroud of gray round an upper hallway and vanish into a room.

"Fuck," he whispered to himself, forcing himself forward. He followed Smith's directions, but the temple was a dizzying arrangement of rooms and the hallway he found was cold and dark, even in the midst of summer.

Light flickered at the end, candlelight glinting off silver.

Kip's hands were clammy, and he tightened them into fists, heart thumping as he marched down the stone, following the pinpoint of light until it grew into an open doorway.

She was there, inside, a cloud of darkness that seemed to waver and pulse. Kip's breath wheezed in his lungs at the sight of her, pale face barely visible beneath the hood, only a brief glimpse of her lips. Her tongue was blood red, flashing out briefly and Kip swallowed a whimper.

"Can I help you?" the New Moon Priestess hissed.

⸙

FARMER 'SMITH' was still wearing his grin as he walked up to the sprawling house in the woods, voices noisy and bright inside. A little girl with white-blonde curls dashed around the side of the house, hands coated in mud, giggle ringing.

"Papa!"

"Oh, Liza!" he cried, catching her before she could dash away, scooping her up in his arms and kissing both her sticky cheeks.

"I've been gardening," she said, breathless and thrilled.

"Oh dear," he said, and she cackled.

The door opened, and Dominic's heart flipped at the sight of his wife, harried and annoyed, her own blonde hair wild around her pink face. Her hands were braced around her rounded belly, and she scowled at him as he approached.

"This is the last one," she said. "I'll drink the tea every day after this one, or I'll lock the three of you out of the bedroom."

Dominic bent to Lumen's cheek, pressing a soft kiss over the heat of her irritation. "You say that now."

"Careful," she growled, but she stepped aside to let him in. Liza squirmed out of his grasp and went screaming back into the woods. "Leave it," Lumen said to him, sighing. "Finley's out there. Probably napping, but he's out there."

Christopher, two years younger than his questionably sane sister and with glossy dark hair, sat sedately on the floor, flipping through a book he couldn't read and had mostly scribbled over. Which left the twins and Liza as the cause of Lumen's grief. Or the new baby in waiting, perhaps.

"Sit," Dominic said, ushering her to her favorite chair and grumbling as he made his own way down to the floor to take her feet in his lap. He slipped her shoes off, and Lumen watched him from above with a wary acceptance. "The twins?"

"Are in their room plotting my demise, or have broken out of the window by now maybe, I don't know," Lumen muttered.

"And where's Gideon?" Dominic asked, smiling as he started to work the tension from Lumen's feet, and she sighed in relief.

"He'll be back soon with Colin for dinner. They were working on Inda and Danny's addition."

"I saw Inda on the road back," Dominic said, hesitating before adding, "I was with a Stalor soldier."

"Dominic!"

"Shh, it's alright. He was looking for me, but I was James Smith. It went smoothly," he said, working his thumbs over a spot that was sure to make Lumen melt. "I left him with the New Moon Priestess. Who is it now, by the way?"

Lumen huffed a laugh, and a smile broke free. "Ohhh, Priestess McCabe. She's suitably frightening."

"There you have it," Dominic said with a shrug.

The Smiths had been invented within the first year of peace, and implemented when Oshain came sniffing around the territory a few years later while Inda was still holding the New Moon Priestess position. Now she was married, Dominic was a father to a shocking amount of children, and Lumen and Finley shared the role of the local healer and wise woman.

The door opened, and Finley came in with a wriggling Liza tossed over his shoulder. "My love, I think we have a changeling child. Shall I toss her in the lake and see if she floats?" Finley announced.

"Oh, won't you? She could use the bath," Lumen answered.

Liza giggled and went limp. "Is it time for dinner?" she asked.

Lumen sighed and made to stand, but Finley stopped her. "Stay there. I can manage. Even with my cargo."

Dominic squeezed Lumen's feet in his hands. "I'll skip the fields tomorrow and manage the children with Fin. You can spend the day in bed. Or in one of the beds at the temple."

Lumen gasped. "Think of the quiet!"

Dominic grinned and the front door opened again, Gideon and Colin striding in. Christopher raised his arms immediately and was scooped up in Colin's grasp before the young man came and delivered a kiss to Lumen's cheek.

"Where's Neave?" Lumen asked him, and Colin blushed.

"She might come. She was at the temple."

"We got a good look of the tadpole Stalor sent as he rode back south like the Priestesses had set fire to his horse," Gideon said, grinning. "Where are the twins?"

"Banished," Dominic informed him, and Gideon laughed and went to retrieve them.

"Brace yourself, Chrissy," Colin murmured to the little boy in his arms.

Lumen's toes wiggled against Dominic's palms, and he looked up to find her smiling at him, gaze full of warmth and affection and possession. "Get back to work," she said sweetly.

You don't deserve this, a cruel voice whispered. He didn't, not really. But nothing could stop a man like Dominic from holding onto this beautiful life, his wife and his best friends and his children. They were happy now, together. That was something they would never surrender.

FIN

ALSO BY KATHRYN MOON

The Kingdom's Crown

SERIES IN PROGRESS

Sweet Pea Mysteries
The Baker's Guide To Risky Rituals
The Knitter's Guide to Banishing Boyfriends

Tempting Monsters
A Lady of Rooksgrave Manor
The Company of Fiends

ACKNOWLEDGMENTS

First off, thank you to the pit crew on this book who made sure to keep me on track and running smoothly:

Lana and Chloe for brainstorming and for being alpha queens! Not to mention Lana for the gorgeous cover and photoshop advice!

Jami, Desiree, and Ash for betaing this book.

Kathryn Barr, eternal cheerleader and my PA guarding my back!

And Meghan at Bookish Dreams Editing for the work you put in but also the love. You demanded this story be finished and I could never disappoint you!

Next, thank you always to my parents and my family, including Lindsay, Loraine, and both Sara's!

And always always, thank you to the Moongazers for hopping on the bandwagon and keeping me company on this adventure of a lifetime. My words will always be yours!

ABOUT THE AUTHOR

Kathryn Moon is a country mouse who started dictating stories to her mother at an early age. The fascination with building new worlds and discovering the lives of the characters who grew in her head never faltered, and she graduated college with a fiction writing degree. She loves writing women who are strong in their vulnerability, romances that are as affectionate as they are challenging, and worlds that a reader sinks into and never wants to leave. When her hands aren't busy typing they're probably knitting sweaters or crimping pie crust in Ohio. She definitely believes in magic.

You can reach her on Facebook and at ohkathrynmoon@gmail.com or you can sign up for her newsletter!